"Do you know what it would do to my reputation if we were to be seen together? People will think I'm as crazy as you are. Why do you want to buy me breakfast?"

"Because you look like you don't eat much," Audrey replied.

"Why would I want to go anywhere with a crazy person?" Joan asked.

"You think I'm crazy?"

"Everybody thinks you're crazy. Are you, Audrey?"

"Yes."

W9-BHB-507

save me a seat

rhea kohan

Fawcett Crest ● New York

SAVE ME A SEAT

THIS BOOK CONTAINS THE COMPLETE TEXT OF THE
ORIGINAL HARDCOVER EDITION.

Published by Fawcett Crest Books, a unit of CBS Publica-
tions, the Consumer Publishing Division of CBS Inc. by ar-
rangement with Harper & Row, Publishers, Inc.

ISBN: 0-449-24281-1

Printed in the United States of America

First Fawcett Crest Printing: April 1980

10 9 8 7 6 5 4 3 2 1

For my papa,
Max Arnold

save me a seat

Prologue

As soon as the school bus pulled away, Joan made herself an English muffin and spread it with orange marmalade. She poured herself a cup of instant coffee and sat down to read the paper and eat her breakfast. After the last page had been read, she cleared the table and went into her bedroom to make the bed, straighten up, go to the bathroom and dress. After that, she fed the parakeets and cleaned the cage, and then she went back to her bedroom, dropped down on the bed, lit a cigarette and called her friend Audrey. She did this every morning of the school week, and had been doing so for the several years she had known Audrey. The routine rarely varied, except that sometimes she would have strawberry preserves on her muffin, or sometimes she would get dressed before breakfast, or sometimes just as she reached for the phone, it would ring and it would be Audrey calling her.

On weekends, the schedule was different and looser. The kids woke up later, breakfasts took longer, the house was noisier and more unsettled. Plans were discussed, her husband, if he didn't have to go to the office, shared the paper with her and helped her make the beds. Because everyone was home and privacy rather scarce, she would take the telephone into the bathroom with her and call Audrey from there, or if Audrey called first, she would walk into the bathroom with the phone, lock the door, sit down on the toilet and speak and laugh and joke with her friend until her husband or one of the kids banged on the door and demanded her attention.

If Audrey went out of town, the day would seem strange and uncertain, and she would feel quiet and restless and vaguely anxious, and the hours dragged along one after the other like weary old men, just passing, passing, passing.

It was the same for Audrey when Joan was away, for she had told her so. Those glad moments during the day of nothing to do, usually so anticipated, when one would automatically reach for the phone to call the other, or the gleeful putting off of a necessary task in order to chat and have a quick laugh before the intrusion of this responsibility or that, all those beats and pauses and in-between dashes that were so much a part of the life of each day would somehow sink into a thick soup of irritation and inefficiency, leaving a yawning gap and causing a child to whine or a returning husband to ask warily, "What's the matter with you today?"

Joan, although she hated to admit it, found Audrey unique and appealing, deceitful and exasperating. It was not that the relationship was idyllic. They quarreled and fought with each other frequently. They disagreed with and put down and insulted and spat at each other. They occasionally told each other the truth, devastatingly. They mercilessly, viciously, gossiped and laughed, amused, competed, were nasty and forgave. They did each other favors and sometimes their eight-year-old daughters played together.

Joan and Audrey did not see each other every day. Often a week would pass without a face-to-face, without a hug, a pinch. But they spoke on the phone daily, many, many times. Somehow Joan filled in Audrey's empty spaces, and Audrey filled in Joan's.

Neither really knew what the attraction was. Audrey said that Joan was funny and made her laugh better than anyone. "I don't like you," Audrey would giggle. "You know that, don't you?" and Joan would reply, "I *hate* you, Audrey," and Audrey would say, "Fine."

At eight-thirty the phone would ring and when Audrey, always breathless, always husky, fumbled and dropped the receiver and finally coughed out "Hello?" Joan would say, "Hello, rotten," and Audrey would answer, "Hello, cunt," and Joan the rotten, the funny, would say, "Do you know what I like about you, Audrey?"

"What?"

"Nothing!"

"Uh-huh. Well, nobody good likes you. You're too hard. Everybody thinks you're terrible."

"That's because you say bad on me, bitch."

"That's because you *are* bad . . . but not me. I'm writing a book and I'm gonna be a star. I have no talent but it doesn't matter. Do you want to know why it doesn't matter?"

"No."

"I'll tell you why . . . it's because I'm charming and I make everybody love me. I make them think that if they don't help me and love me I'll fall apart and die. I make them think that loving me and holding me up is the most important thing they can do . . . and so they do it. I touch people, cunt. I touch people. I touch them and they can't refuse me. Now, you . . . if you clean yourself up a little, could be terrific . . . if you ever get off your ass and do something besides wiping Naomi's nose, you could be better than your friend Nan or that other one, Marlene."

"Are you crazy? Nan and Marlene are very successful writers."

"They're not that successful. I know all about them and the book business. I have my spies everywhere."

11

"*You* should be so unsuccessful."

"I should have their money. But Marlene has the shittiest image in the publishing business. Nobody likes her. I don't give a damn how good she writes, she's not Joseph Heller and what's worse she's not charming and America doesn't love her. They don't *care* about her, you see."

"And they care about *you?*"

"Not yet, but they will. I'm charming, you stupid ass. Don't you know that yet?"

"I know what's under your good black suit, Audrey. That's what I know."

"Well, don't tell anybody...How's your husband, the animal who only works, eats and fucks?"

"How's your husband, the schmuck who does none of those?"

"Well, he's not too good on the first, but on the other two, he does just fine. Don't worry."

"Why should I worry?"

"I'll bet Eric's on you all the time, right? Isn't he always on you? Guess who woke *me* up at three in the morning all ready with it standing up?"

"A crazy blind person with a stuffed nose and a disease?"

"You're really terrible, Joan. Nobody knows why I like you."

"Because I'm charming. So you had dealings with Melvin last night? Did he do heavy work?"

"Do I know what he did? He was there, that's all I know. Do you like when Eric does that?"

"What?"

"You know."

"What?"

"Heavy work...in the low. Do you like that? I think you like that."

"What *I* like is lasagna! *He* likes that."

"They all like that. Why do they like it so much?"

"They're all retarded. Once Eric gets down there, he can stay a week."

12

"Sally Brayman has a vibrator. You know why? Because her husband never does her."

"I wouldn't know from such problems."

"Well, neither would I."

"Poor Melvin."

"Melvin's just fine. Three o'clock in the morning. Twice he put it."

"The man's demented."

"Oh, shut up. What are you doing today?"

And so it would go, and they would laugh and joke and be outrageous to each other. At times, they would decide to "play" and spend a few foolish, fun hours together, but not that often, because both were now busy. By some combination of chutzpah and magic, Audrey had published a book of letters and poetry and was now making appearances on TV programs and radio and trying to write a novel. And Joan was thinking that she ought to be doing something, too—and wondering what. Both agreed that it was more fun before they got the guilts about being "just housewives," when they could have a brunch together and grab cheese off each other's plate and the middle out of each other's sandwich and talk loud in restaurants and roam the aisles of discount stores. Joan loved buying bargains. Audrey loved stealing them.

One December, when Joan was up in Arrowhead for a week with her family, in a sudden surge of upward mobility Audrey was picked up for shoplifting in Bonwit's.

"Tried to better yourself, did you?" Joan said sarcastically when Audrey called long distance to tell her. "I go out of town for a few days and look what happens to you. What happened to you, dummy?"

"Reuben fixed it." Reuben Stern was Audrey's lawyer. "But I can't steal anymore."

"Ah, Audrey. It's over, isn't it," Joan sighed, making a statement, not asking a question.

"I know, isn't it terrible? We can't do anything good anymore. Nothing's fun anymore . . . and my stomach hurts. I'm going to get another ulcer attack, I just know it. And I have a headache."

"You're falling apart, Audrey."

"I'm better than you, so just hold yourself."

"Your stomach looks like the map of Santa Monica, your legs have blue veins, and your thighs are fat . . . you better hold *your*self, because when Melvin puts his glasses on, it's all over for you."

"Good-bye, Joan."

"Good-bye, Audrey."

"Why are you so mean to me?"

"Because you're dumb, Audrey. How dare you get picked up in Bonwit's?"

"It was terrible. It really was. *God!*"

"Well, it could have been worse."

"How?"

"You could have been picked up at the Akron—how humiliating—or Pic 'n Save!"

"Oh God! Joan, my leg hurts. Why does my leg hurt?"

"I think it's cancer."

"I think so. All right, I have to hang up now. I'll call you later. Good-bye."

"Don't call until after seven."

"I'll call when I want. Good-bye."

Joan hung up smiling. Audrey always made her smile. Even when they acted like adults and spoke to each other like grown people, Audrey left her smiling.

The first time they met, Joan had known without a doubt that she would never, *could* never establish a friendship with an impossible woman like this. Never. And even today, Joan still found it impossible to comprehend how Audrey had managed to become so important to her . . . so dear.

1

For ten years Joan had been a wife, a condition she couldn't wait to get into from the time that being single and the possibility of continuing singleness had first begun to frighten her. Therefore, underlying her love for her husband was a vein of gratitude which in a pensive moment she had verbalized. "Eric," she had said, and when her husband looked up from his magazine, continued, "Eric, thank you for marrying me." He smiled at her, patted her hand and said "You're welcome," and went back to his magazine. She now sometimes told that little story at parties.

Joan loved being married. It was motherhood that lay heavily upon her, and for eight of her ten married years she had been a mother. The Brenners had three children: twin boys aged eight, and Naomi, who was three.

Immediately after the birth of her sons, when for the time in her life she discovered the meaning of real physical torment, she lay in the hospital bed attached to tubes dripping colorless liquid into her arm and marveling at what she had accomplished. She tried to analyze what she was feeling, and aside from enormous excitement and a throbbing pain from her stitches, where, after all, it had all begun, she couldn't quite put her finger on what exactly this elusive feeling was. She remained awake all that night and when at six in the morning a nurse, who looked to her like Ilse Koch, came to catheterize her, she barely had the strength to protest and just managed to mew piteously, "Please, nurse, please stay away from my parts. They've been through enough." Unheeding, the nurse began to pull away the covers, and Joan pleaded, "Couldn't you catheterize me somewhere else?" and when that too received no response other than a withering frown, she again begged hopelessly, "Please don't hurt me." The shock of cold air hit her now exposed pain center and she gathered her waning belligerence and continued weakly, "I swear on my newborn children I'll get up and kick your Nazi ass from here to neurology."

The nurse remained unimpressed, hooked up her tubes and catheterized her patient, and did so painlessly, to Joan's amazement and relief.

Joan's stay in the hospital was a lengthy one for a non-Caesarian birth. She remained there for ten days through three shifts of new mothers, and battled anemia, unsuccessful breast feeding, constipation and the ever-present torture of healing stitches. To Joan, mother, sacrifice became sitting up. Her husband visited her twice every day and brought flowers and books and an antique coin minted in 1746 when the Dauphin of France and his wife also had twins. Joan was awash with love over this perfect gift and never had the slightest feeling of anger toward her husband, despite the fact that her stomach looked like a wrinkled, deflated beach ball and was still, days after delivery, the size of a five-month pregnancy.

Her family came in droves and peered through the nursery window at the two perfect babies, each one well over six pounds at birth, and then came and peered at her, the mother of twins. Her own mother complained that the babies looked terrific, but "You look

16

like hell. You're green as celery." She busied herself straightening the sheets, smoothing Joan's hair and watering the flowers Eric's television associates had sent her. She picked up a five-pound box of chocolates and moved them out of Joan's reach, saying "You don't need these," and then sat down on the bed, took Joan's hand lovingly in hers and mused in wonder, "Twins. Where do twins come to me? And such horses!" Her father kept asking, "Are you sure you're all right, ketzeleh?" and ran back and forth between her room and the nursery, where he buttonholed all the doctors and nurses he could grab and asked them, "Are you sure they're all right? The twins and my little girl, are you sure?"

Her mother-in-law bent down to kiss her and whispered almost in tears, "Thank you, darling," and then flew to the nursery, where she bragged to the other grandmas who had only one baby to look at, "This is my doctor and that one is my lawyer." Her father-in-law cried each time he came to see her and, in a loud emotion-choked voice, directed the most uninterested of visitors—even those who had gotten off at the wrong floor—toward the nursery window and forced them to admire "my son's sons."

All through those ten interminable days in the hospital, and even after she had bade a tearful and semihysterical good-bye to Elfrieda, the baby nurse who had taken over the complete care of the infants for three weeks after she came home, the mysterious feeling eluded her. She knew she was feeling something, she knew it made her uncomfortable and vaguely frightened, but she couldn't define it. To complicate matters and upset her even further, she did not love her babies. That overwhelming rush of mother love that was supposed to wash over newly delivered mothers had not washed over her. She was instead left high and dry, buried in tons of smelly diapers, with her hair full of Desitin and still wearing maternity clothes because she couldn't get into her others. She was exhausted from endless nights of interrupted sleep, when

17

she staggered out of bed to give 2 A.M. feedings to one screaming baby, finally finishing him off only to have to busy herself with another screaming baby. Then she would fall back into bed to be awakened after what seemed like two minutes, because the first one was up again. So it went, through every day and every night. She seemed forever to be holding a wet, warm, wailing piece of humanity. Forever feeding, changing, bathing, dressing, walking, rocking, burping, picking up, putting down, and doing laundry for a baby. She never went out, except to market and to air her children. Once she called her mother and said, "Ma, it would be nice to see you—and I could use some help." Her mother replied, "Darling, *I* had mine, now *you* have yours," and declined the invitation.

Her husband was rarely home now. Not deliberately; he was just very busy writing, on the staff of his first television show. He loved her, he sympathized with her, he commiserated with her, but all over the phone. He was busy. He never got up in the night to give feedings. He had his work, Joan had hers. She thought it was supposed to be that way. One day she walked through the doorway of the bedroom, but it wasn't the doorway. Blood dripping from her nose caused her to realize that what she thought was the doorway was, in actuality, the bedroom wall. She washed her nose, reassured herself that it wasn't broken and called the doctor. "Lester," she said nasally into the phone, "something is wrong with me. I'm walking into walls that look to me like doors." He offered her a prescription for sleeping pills to assure her a good night's rest. She refused. "I don't need a pill to sleep, Lester, I could sleep like Rip Van Winkle if they'd let me. What I need is something to keep me *up!*" He offered her a prescription for Dexedrine to assure that she would function alertly during the day. She accepted.

Joan found she liked Dexedrine. She stopped walking into walls, she lost weight. She didn't mind getting up in the middle of the night because, thanks to the Dexedrine, she already *was* up in the middle of the night. She began to meet other women with new babies in the park and quite enjoyed the attention that pushing a twin carriage brought her. She sat on the bench in Central Park, pushing her carriage back and forth, laughing, talking and comparing maternal notes with others of her ilk.

She began preparing proper meals for her hardworking husband, and they ate together and talked about the twins, whom she had somehow managed to put on a less demanding schedule. She and Eric resumed making love. Dr. Kempler, her obstetrician, had given them the go-ahead after her six weeks, checkup. That had been a while ago, but they had not gone ahead. Joan was always too tired and Eric, ever considerate and pretty tired himself, had not pushed it. "Having twins and caring for them can be quite a strain," they assured each other when they got a chance to talk, and then both of them, drained by the conversation, would fall into bed and drop into sleep like bricks off a cliff.

The twins were now seven months old, and although they ate like loggers and felt as if they weighed eighty-five pounds apiece, they still were not sleeping through the night. She fed them cereal at six, tons of it, and awakened them to drink a bottle at eleven-thirty, but like Pavlov's dogs they responded to some inner alarm and punctually awoke to howl at 2 A.M. One night Joan did not get up. Eric heard them and jiggled her pillow, but Joan did not get up. He propped himself on one elbow and leaned anxiously over his wife. After ascertaining that she was not dead, he turned over and went back to sleep. The babies yowled on, but Joan did not get up. The following night was a repeat of the previous one. By the third night, the neighbor with whom they shared a common wall called to complain and threatened to inform an agency that dealt harshly with child abusers.

On the fourth night the twins slept through without a peep. Nevertheless, at 2 A.M. Joan's eyes snapped open and after trembling in the silence, broken only

19

by an occasional snore from Eric, she ran panicked and barefoot into the babies' room to verify that they were still breathing. It was at some point during that singular night, when the babies slept through and the mother could not, that Joan at last identified the feeling that had eluded her all those months. With a flash of recognition, she finally realized that she was irrevocably imprisoned by a crush of immense responsibility, overwhelming and oppressive, and by a delayed upsurge of love that in the interim had grown so encompassing and so completely consuming that she knew that no matter how long she lived, no matter what she did or how, she would never *ever* be free again. She was a mother.

2

Los Angeles, California, is a sprawling, sun-baked, deceptively lush D.P. camp, filled with lazy, brown, slow-moving, car-loving natives with salty skin and sun-streaked hair. The seasons pass unnoticed and identical until one morning you look into the mirror and realize in a panic that you have grown old. There are restless people here who have moved far away from family and accepted values (now discarded) and who therefore, perhaps, behave outrageously and divorce each other impulsively, because what you wouldn't do by reason of the fact that it would kill your grandmother, you are now free to do since grandma is far away. It is by the same token a guilt-giving city and one that absolves. One becomes guilty because, after all, the sun is shining, it's a gorgeous day, get off your ass and *do* something . . . but how does one work on a beautiful day like today?

If New York is an amphetamine, then L.A. is a tranquilizer.

The Brenners moved to the City of the Angels in 1967 and Naomi, their youngest child, was born there in 1969. It was a move necessitated by Eric's increasing success in the TV field, and L.A. was where it was at. Joan reasoned that even if they had moved to Timbuktoo, her life would remain the same. When one has young children, one does the same things wherever one ends up. They ended up in Beverly Hills—for the schools, of course—and settled in.

The entire era of turmoil and upheaval that was the sixties had passed Joan by completely, so immersed was she in motherhood. She was vaguely aware of the unrest of the young, the riots, the drug culture, the hippies and other afflictions of the times, but thank God her children were not affected, and that was all she was concerned about. The twins were soon enrolled in the Good Beginnings Education Center, nursery division. She hired a Latin housekeeper who fell in love with Naomi and protested strenuously over the diet Joan was feeding the child. She and Eric had a social life composed mainly of going to parties given by Eric's friends in "the business"—as if the television business and those involved in it were the only things in the world that mattered. Well, to those in "the business," they were. Joan was not in "the business." She was only related to it by marriage, and often felt excluded from the conversation, which was exclusively shop talk. She felt that way not because of a low self-image or an inability to hold her own; she felt excluded because she *was* excluded. She was not one of them.

Still, Joan loved going to the parties, and in sheer self-defense—and because she hated sitting alone and because she became enraged when eyes slid over her, recognized a "nothing," and moved on to seek out a "something" connected in an important way with this show or that—she forced herself to develop an arresting line of patter aimed solely at surprising those slippery eyes and establishing some sort of position for herself, even if it was only that of "Eric's funny wife, what's-her-name."

Surprisingly, in this milieu of people who were paid exorbitant sums of money for writing catchy and clever

22

lines, for being amusing and quick, Joan became adept at maintaining their startled attention. They were amazed that they could be made to laugh from such an unexpected quarter as this, and she became what to them was a freaky phenomenon—a funny non-pro. She was even quoted at times. From "Hey, did you hear what Eric's wife just said?" she advanced to "Hey, did you hear what Joan just said?" and from there was promoted to "Joan, tell Bob your line about placentas." It was all very heady, and although at times she pushed too hard and her husband had to poke her, she had at least reserved a small niche for herself in the world of "the business."

She also made a friend of Nan Blake, a writer on the same show as Eric. This was accomplished at the home of Harry Goldblatt, Eric's agent. Agents live a schizophrenic existence. That they are allowed to live at all is a show-biz mystery. They are simultaneously needed and hated, and their clients are doubtful about the needed. The deals they make are never satisfactory. The money they get for their clients is never enough. The 10 percent they receive for their services is never deserved. The words used to describe them are many and varied, but never complimentary: "My schmucky agent did this," or "Did you hear about the deal that asshole made for me?" or "And for doing absolutely nothing I have to give that sonofabitch piece of dreck a percentage for the next thirteen weeks." The kindest accolade they receive is "parasite." Agents give a lot of parties because they sense this lack of affection, because it's a good way to launch a package, and because it's a great tax write-off.

Tonight was again party night at the Goldblatts, and also the climax of a difficult day for Joan. The twins, who by now had graduated to first grade, had been home all day with a stomach virus. Naomi had swallowed a dime and eaten half a crayon. Joan's car wouldn't start, and Raquel, the housekeeper, was sulking because the dishwasher had broken down and she had to do all the dishes by hand. Joan tried to rise above this irritation by mumbling to herself throughout the thirty-hour day: "I am a privileged American. This is not major surgery, it isn't leukemia, it isn't a nuclear war, it isn't Eric fucking a secretary..." But it wasn't fulfillment either, a new concept, lately popular, that a woman was supposed to be, or have, or something.

All Joan knew was that it was difficult to be fulfilled when a sick and irritable child vomits on your hand. She found it ludicrous that Gloria Steinem, an unmarried woman with no children or responsibilities whatsoever, could set herself up as the champion of downtrodden wives and mothers. "What the hell does she know?" Joan demanded of Eric, furious at finding herself in the ranks of those disadvantaged, put-upon masses. "Does *she* have Ralston in her hair? Does *she* wipe shitty asses? Does *she* have stretch marks and a stomach you can play 'Lady of Spain' on?"

Eric listened patiently. "She's jealous," he comforted.

Not in the least convinced, and her hand still faintly redolent of barf, Joan readied herself for the party—nor did it help to discover that she could barely zip up her good pants.

When they arrived, the festivities were well under way. The band was playing. The bar, set up on the patio, was three deep in thirsty revelers, waiters were carefully picking their way through chattering guests offering a variety of hot hors d'oeuvres and, as far as Joan could ascertain, none of the gorgeous girls so ubiquitous at agents' parties looked as if they'd had any trouble at all with the zippers on their tight white pants, which clung, like the skin on a bologna, to their tight, white, rhythmically swaying behinds.

The guests who were not already deep in conversation about the foibles of the industry were meandering through the crowd, drinks in hand, looking to see who was there. The "names" or celebrities were clustered, self-aware and blasé, in small groups or at tables, being *served* drinks rather than waiting in line for

24

them at the bar like the rest of the peasants, and complaining sadly to one another about their shitty material, their shitty ratings, and their shitty lack of privacy. Every now and then one would look up at a greeting or a pat on the shoulder, to wave, shake a hand or smile broadly. Writers talked seriously to writers; producers to producers; like to like grouped together in earnest confab. The wives, too, had their little conglomerate, and as Joan passed by calling to and receiving greetings from those whom she had met at other parties, she heard snatches of familiar chants.

"So I said to the decorator, 'Beau, those chairs were supposed to be delivered six *weeks* ago.'"

"And don't you know, the maid got sick on the very night I was having ten for dinner?"

"I love to be with my kids, but not every minute. I mean, Bernie and I have to get away *alone* once in a while."

"But first you add two tablespoons of kirsch and *then* the beaten egg."

She skirted them adroitly while her eyes roamed the room looking for Nan. She spotted her near a window, talking to her manager. Nan was a liberated woman. She had a husband, two sons the ages of Joan's children, and a fabulous career. Nan was a successful writer, the only female on the staff of the *Helen Curtis Show*. She v ·ked with her partner, Teddy, who was hip and hila₁ious and homosexual. Nan was that rare bird who was able to manage both marriage and a demanding career. This was made possible not by her ability to juggle, but by having had the foresight to marry a man who earned less money than she and who therefore, along with his job, took over the responsibilities of the house and kids. It wasn't so much a liberated marriage as a complete role reversal. Carl hired the maid, drove the car pools, did the marketing, gave the baths and threw it up to Nan whenever the opportunity presented itself. He was, without a doubt, the best possible person with whom to discuss pediatricians, summer camp or your hysterectomy. He was a nice man, a free-lance photographer who depended upon the fates, weddings, bar mitzvahs and June graduations for his livelihood. Also upon Nan. He had beautiful auburn hair, which Nan envied, and a cute upturned Howdy Doody face that somehow inspired a lack of confidence on the part of his clients, who expected a darker type behind the camera. Carl was thirty-nine years old, looked about fourteen, and had a deep, resonant announcer voice that was disconcerting, coming as it did from behind all those freckles.

Joan liked him and adored Nan. She was not jealous. She sincerely wished her friend every success, but lately she had begun to feel that it would be nice to have a little of her own.

"Jo-nie," Nan said, walking slowly toward her. "Hi."

Nan was a heavy, very slow-moving, slow-speaking girl. She wasn't pretty; maybe she could be if she lost the weight, but she didn't really have to be. Nan was funny and talented and successful. Nan had it all and Joan was glad they were friends.

They discussed their respective children, the novel Nan was working on, and Good Beginnings, where, since Joan was sending Naomi, Nan had decided to enroll her son Brian.

"So, Jo-nie, it's a good school?" asked Nan slowly.

"Would I send the female fruit of Eric's loins to a juvenile detention center? Of course it's a good school. My boys went there and they managed to survive to throw up on my hand today," said Joan.

"Will Brian like it?"

"I sincerely hope so, Nannie."

"Well, what if he doesn't?"

"Tell him that you'll drown him if he complains more than five times and I'm sure he'll think it over and adjust."

"He's so little. You know Brian, he's tiny."

"So give him vitamins. How's your diet?" Joan asked, patting Nan's stomach.

"I'm losing, but very, very slowly."

"Why is that?"

"Well," Nan said, defending herself, "I work at Teddy's house and he always deliberately has this bag of pretzels around and they look at me..." Nan helped herself to a stuffed mushroom from the tray of a passing waiter. "Mushrooms aren't fattening, right?" she asked, with her mouth full.

"Right," said Joan. "How's the book?"

"Coming along, but very, very slowly."

"Nan, do you remember when we took the kids to play in the park and we had to cross Olympic Boulevard and the light changed four times before you made it to the other side?"

Nan laughed.

"The point I'm getting at is that you do *everything* slowly. Watching you climb a flight of stairs is an experience... but you always manage to get where you're going. When can I read it?"

"Probably by the weekend, Joanie, I think *maybe* it's good."

"What's good?" asked Teddy, drifting over.

"We were talking about Nan's book," answered Joan, giving Teddy her cheek, which he pecked.

"Oh, that," said Teddy offhandedly, dismissing the book with a languid wave. "Tell me, my precious," he purred at Joan, "what do you think of *me?*"

"Not much," answered Joan, smiling.

"I'm crushed," said Teddy. "I've *always* thought highly of you, bitch. Oh hi, Warren." He waved to someone across the room and sauntered off.

"Could it be that he resents your book?" asked Joan.

"Of course he does," said Nan. "He feels very threatened by it. The irony of the whole thing is that I started this novel because of him. He didn't want to do any more television. He thought he was too *good* to write for TV. What does he care? *He* has plenty of money, but *I* have to work. I have a family to support."

A friend of Nan's whom Joan did not know approached, and without acknowledging her presence, stepped between them and started a conversation with Nan. Nan, embarrassed, took Joan's hand and made

27

as if to introduce her, but Joan shook her head, disengaged her hand and walked off to look for Eric. This type of rudeness was not unusual at gatherings of this sort. It happened all the time to a nobody—to a nonentity, someone not in "the business" or indeed any other business.

Joan suddenly realized that in her present frame of mind she was reduced to snubbing herself. "Honest work is good work," went the old ethic. So why was she feeling so ashamed, so embarrassed, so invisible?

"I work," she thought to herself. "I work at home. If I weren't doing what I'm doing, Eric couldn't do what *he's* doing—not with any peace of mind, he couldn't." But she was not comforted. She felt lousy. Scarlett O'Hara would have said, "I'll think about it tomorrow." All Joan Brenner said was, "Ah, shit!"

Eric, a glass of white wine in hand, stood talking to a producer friend. He had spotted Joan in the corner when she was talking to Nan Blake. Joan was laughing and animated. He loved her. He loved the fact that he could bring her to a party and she could function on her own, unlike some other wives who clung like burs to their husbands' sides, with fixed smiles and glassy eyes, and who stood forlornly alone when their husbands went to the bathroom, waiting nervously outside the door to grab on to them once again when they emerged. He loved Joan's independence.

Eric still could not believe he was in California. He flourished in the sunshine, he smiled at the palm trees. His idea of perfect bliss was lying on the patio beside the pool with his face up, kissing and being kissed by the sun. It was a never-ending source of amazement to him that he was making more money in one month than his father had made in a year. He liked writing, he enjoyed turning a vague notion into an hour-long show—millions of people listening to his words, famous stars, whose names were household legends, dependent upon *him,* a boy from the Bronx, to make *them* sound good.

Eric was a happy man. His career was going well,

he was respected in the industry, his marriage was alive and well in a sea of dead and dying and ever-changing alliances. His only responsibility was to make a living, kiss his wife and kids and trim his beard. He looked around for a piece of wood to knock on, and breathed a silent little prayer of thanks for all his blessings and hoped that whatever beneficent power was smiling on his head would forever smile on.

He looked again at Joan, who was beginning to maneuver her way through the crowd toward him. She looked tired and a bit depressed now, and it saddened him that he was unable to help her with whatever was causing this unrest, this discontent that he knew had been plaguing her lately.

"Hi, puss," he said, kissing her forehead. "Having fun? Did you make any points?"

"Hi, honey," she said, linking her arm in his and taking a sip of his wine. "Nan's terrific and Teddy is aggravated about her book. Would you like it if I wrote a book?" she asked, smiling up at him.

"Sure I would. Why don't you?" he asked. "Why don't you take a shot at it?"

She shrugged. "I don't know, I can't write a book. I'm super at getting bubble gum out of hair. I'm a whiz at playing 'Go Fish,' but a book—I can't write a book."

"What's all this? I won't have a husband and wife playing kissyface with each other. Whaddaya wanna do, ruin my party?" Harry Goldblatt, smiling broadly, capped front teeth aglitter, strode over and clapped Eric on the shoulder.

"How's it going? Having a good time? Have you talked to Joe about the Bob White special yet?"

"Not yet, Harry," answered Eric. "That's *your* job. Do you think I'm giving you ten percent of my hard-earned money to make parties? *You* talk to Joe."

"Joan," Harry said, "how do you live with that guy? What do you think of my new house? Nice, huh?"

Joan looked at the beautifully decorated room, the brick patio, the Olympic-size pool, the hanging plants and lush carpeting.

"It's gorgeous, Harry," she said. "Nicer than mine, I'll tell you. Where's the part *our* ten percent built?"

"Don't you like your house?" he asked, ignoring the rest of the remark.

"Well, I guess it'll do, Harry. Let me put it this way—mine is the kind of house I'd go out with, but I wouldn't wanna marry it."

Harry laughed. "Now I know who writes all your material, Eric." He kissed Joan on the cheek and went off to mingle with his other guests.

"Scored again," Eric said with a smile. "You're charming, fucking charming."

"Do you love me, Eric?" asked Joan.

"You're the best, puss. I adore you." He kissed her again and led her toward the dining room where the buffet dinner was now being served. "C'mon," he said fondly, "let's eat."

3

Joan Brenner took her daughter by the hand and
they walked together past the yard filled with swings
and slides and sandboxes, past the water play area,
around the corner and in through the door of the nursery school. She spoke softly to the child, telling her of
all the joys and surprises she would encounter in this
big wonderful building filled with happy children and
their sounds. The little girl held tightly to her mother's
hand, thinking thoughts three-year-olds think and
looking straight ahead. Not once did she glance at the
children who were enjoying the facilities, except occasionally when a loud laugh or a shrill squeal startled
her. She would gaze up into her mother's face from
time to time and stare intently until Joan's smile made
her look quickly away. Except for a momentary tight-
ening of her grip on her mother's hand, she seemed
oblivious of the many children who were weeping and
sobbing and clinging to their mothers' legs or skirts or
hands or jean-encased thighs, terrified of what lay
ahead on their first day of nursery school—this first
rite of passage.

Joan was proud that her daughter did not cry. Her

31

sons had not cried either. She felt secretly that the reason for her children's composure was the strong sense of security she had instilled in them—or the equally strong attraction of the ice cream cone and Play-Doh she had bribed them with to behave themselves.

She glanced at the other women trying to soothe their children, smiled at them, shrugged a shoulder in sympathy and said reassuringly to one harried mother, almost in tears herself, "Don't be upset. They *all* cry." When the woman looked questioningly at Joan's daughter, she added, "Except mine. Mine know that *anything* is better than being at home with me."

They continued down the hall, pushing through the throng of mothers and children, looking at the signs above the doors. "Carol's Room," Joan read aloud, "Beth's Room." All the classrooms were equipped with one-way mirrors so that the parents could observe their children at play without their being aware of it. Already there were parents in front of the windows, noses pressed to the glass, anxious eyes fixed on their offspring whom they had left only moments before. Finally, Joan and her daughter arrived at their destination. Above the door was a sign identifying it as "Jeri's Room."

The teacher was standing at the door of the classroom, face asmile, eyes alight. She looked dedicated, earnest, child-oriented. Joan and Naomi had met her the week before and, while Naomi had amused herself coloring, Joan amused herself by counting all the psychological phraseology that fell so comfortably from Jeri's lips. It seemed to Joan that, in essence, Jeri was assuring her that all the emotional damage she had done while ineptly raising her child would be corrected here by her.

"Hello, Mrs. Brenner," the teacher said. She squatted down so that her eyes were level with the child's and greeted her softly. "Hello, Naomi. Do you remember me? My name is Jeri and I am your teacher. I'm

32

so glad to see you today. Would you like to come into the room? There are many toys and games and other good things that children like. You may play with anything you wish, and if you need to see your mommy, she will be in that room right over there all morning until it's time to go home. Okay?"

The child nodded, taking in the scene and already irresistibly drawn to the array of color and activities within. The room was filled with noise and with children playing, children running, children wailing, children sucking their thumbs. Jeri had four young aides, Early Childhood Ed majors who were directing children toward the many play centers and wondering why none of their Ed books ever explained how to handle a three-year-old who picked his nose and wiped it on your leg, and other occupational hazards. They were still smiling, but wanly.

Sitting in the back of the room on chairs so low that they could rest their chins on their knees, sat a row of mommies so embarrassed, so chagrined, so resigned, so disappointed that their despair was palpable. These were the mothers of the children who, when Jeri had asked, "Would you like to come into the room?" had yowled "No!" and shrieked so deafeningly and clung so tenaciously that mother was forced to remain, console, and in some cases change the pants of her frantic child.

Naomi looked upon all this, realized it was good, and spotted a plate of Oreos on a table near the door. She withdrew her hand from her mother's and without a backward glance walked into the room, snatched a cookie and began to eat and play. The teacher straightened up. "She'll be fine," she said to Joan. "She didn't exhibit any separation anxiety. Still, we prefer the mother to remain at school, at least for the first week, in case the anxiety manifests itself later on."

Joan glared at the teacher. "Look, Jeri," she said, "you screwed me already by telling Naomi that I'd be across the hall. So *today* I'll be across the hall. But just today. My idea of heaven is having all my kids in school. It does not include my joining them there."

"But, Mrs. Brenner, what if Naomi becomes anxious and needs to see her mommy?"

"She won't," replied Joan. "Naomi doesn't get anxious; *I* get anxious. Getting anxious is *my* hobby. All Naomi gets is hungry and tonsillitis. And call me Joan."

Before Jeri could protest further, Joan turned and hurried toward the parents' lounge, almost colliding with a woman who was down on one knee in the middle of the crowded corridor, tying her child's shoelace, while the little boy held on to her hair with one hand and clutched his penis with the other. "Seth," Joan heard her wail as she circled around them, "why didn't you tell me you had to sissy. Just look what you did to Mommy's pants. You sissied all over Mommy's pants," and, her voice rising, wailed, "Get your sticky hands out of my hair."

Joan sank gratefully onto the yellow Naugahyde couch, put her feet up on the coffee table, lit a cigarette and looked around her. With the exception of the scholarship and day-care children, the Good Beginnings Educational Center catered to a varied clientele who had in common their ability to afford the exorbitant tuition. The parents who enrolled their children in Good Beginnings were generally professional people, people in the entertainment field and those who were successful in business. The women, Joan recalled from experience, fell into five overlapping groups. There were those with frizzy hair who suckled their infants in public and were serious about ecology and not eating sweets, who wore no makeup and had husbands with vasectomies. And those who wept when their nails broke, wore designer pantyhose, got their names in the columns and had maids who either spoke English or stayed with them for over six years before quitting.

Then there were those who had a foot in each of these camps but didn't really belong in either. These were the women who were usually college graduates,

34

were vaguely dissatisfied and guilty about it, were Jewish, had happily or unhappily stayed married to the same man, were devoted mothers who read every book on child development ever printed, wanted an important career someday, were irritated at their housekeepers but unable to be really firm with them, knew how to spell, pronounce, and at a moment's notice prepare bouillabaisse or boeuf bourgignon, had Vuitton handbags, favorite charities and husbands who were born poor.

The fourth group was composed of women who (a) had successful careers (like Nan) and (b) divorced women who were forced to work and had their kids in Good Beginnings day care. Those belonging to group four were rarely if ever seen in the parents' lounge. Being good friends with someone in (a) was a plus; being good friends with someone in (b) was dumb.

Group five were those ladies who could not be characterized: they were oddballs. Oddballs were either (a) accepted by all the other groups, or (b) rejected by them. This year there were destined to be two oddballs: Joan Brenner and Audrey Miller. Joan was destined to belong to the (a) subgroup; Audrey to the (b).

Joan remembered all this from the time her sons had attended Good Beginnings when Good Beginnings first began. She looked hopefully around the lounge seeking a familiar face and encountered one or two that seemed vaguely familiar from five years before. The groups had not yet formed, although there were already intuitive separations. However, all was still tentative—the only known common denominator being that the mothers here all had three-year-olds whose separation anxiety was not acute and who were able to be in class without their mothers. All voiced smug compassion for those women who obviously had children with an immaturity syndrome.

"Have you a cigarette to spare, please?" asked a soft voice next to Joan. "I've stopped smoking, but today I need one."

"Sure," answered Joan, and proffered her pack. "Whose class is your kid in?"

"Jeri's," replied her seatmate, lighting up gratefully. "She's the best."

"Oh," said Joan, "my daughter has Jeri, too. How do you know she's the best?"

"Well, she's the oldest. She has the most experience. I can just tell by the way she handles the children."

"Hmm," said Joan, eyeing her. "Well, I hope you're right. Do you have a boy or a girl?"

"A boy," answered the woman, a pretty young blonde with "Made in France" emblazoned across her well-filled T-shirt. "His name is Brett. I'm Zoe Newman."

"Hi. I'm Joan Brenner."

They looked up as a newcomer entered the room. Joan recognized her as the girl whose son had sissied on her pants. She was still dabbing at her pantleg with a damp paper towel.

"Bobbie," Zoe called out. "Come over here and sit down."

Bobbie, a very tall girl with inexpertly applied false eyelashes, stepped over to the coffee table, knocking over someone's purse, and flopped down next to Zoe.

"Hi, Zoe," she said wearily. "I hope Seth adjusts well to nursery school."

"You'd do better to hope that pee doesn't stain gabardine," Joan said, smiling at her. Bobbie crossed one long leg over the other and grinned at Joan.

"You noticed?" she asked.

"I did indeed," answered Joan. "Seth is a pisser, all right."

"Well," said Bobbie, one eyelash flapping, "my husband's a psychiatrist."

"That explains it," said Joan.

"What?" asked Zoe.

"Seth peed on my leg," replied Bobbie.

"Oh," said Zoe, and took a puff on her cigarette. "I wonder what that means?"

"Ask your husband," Joan suggested to Bobbie.

"He'll only tell me that to Seth, I must symbolize a toilet."

"You *were* pretty rigid when you trained him," Zoe said. "Maybe he's still angry at you, and in stressful situations he exhibits his anger by regressing."

"Yeah," said Bobbie, closing her eyes. "Rigid." She leaned back and seemed to sleep. Joan leaned across Zoe and nudged Bobbie.

"Bobbie," she whispered, "this is America. It doesn't matter what Seth does as long as he's tall. Don't worry."

"Tall," said Bobbie, grinning, eyes still closed. "What's your name?"

"Joan Brenner."

"Joan," mumbled Bobbie, loosening her grip on the paper towel to extend a hand. Joan straightened up. The lounge was now crowded and noisy with conversation. Mothers were introducing themselves to one another.

"Hi. I'm Stacy's mother. Are you Kimmy's mother?"

Suddenly a loud, husky voice was heard over the din.

"Why the fuck do we have to sit around this hole for? Why can't these smart-ass teachers deal with anxious? Hello, hello, everybody. I'm Audrey Miller."

All eyes turned toward the door. Standing there, framed in the doorway and smiling broadly, stood a woman somewhat older than the rest, dressed completely in black. On her largish mouth was the thickest, reddest, greasiest lipstick Joan had ever seen, and one of her two front teeth was also smeared with it. Her blue eyes were ringed with coal-black pencil, smudged, and on her ancient black wool sweater was a big wet stain. For a fleeting moment Joan wondered if Seth had claimed another victim.

The woman wore a vintage black cape thrown back over her shoulders, and covering her dyed black hair was a dirty, frayed black scarf, bound so tightly that, along with her very white, slackening skin and high cheekbones, it gave her head a skull-like, almost fright-

37

ening appearance. Her black slacks were also stained and very tight, and the hem of one leg was coming down, almost covering her black suede wedgies. She looked to be in her mid-forties.

The room was completely silent now. All stared in shock at Audrey Miller.

"Oh God," whispered Zoe. "I saw her during interview week. She's crazy!"

"At these prices," continued the apparition loudly, "the least those bastards could do is provide some coffee. Is there any coffee? And, by the way," she said, skewering Zoe, "I heard that remark."

She advanced into the room, picking her way through the furniture and stepping on hastily pulled-back feet. "There aren't even enough fucking chairs here. Sydelle," she bellowed in the direction of the doorway, "we need some more chairs in here."

Sydelle Keller, the principal of the nursery division, poked her head into the room. "What do you want, Audrey?" she asked.

"I want to get the fuck out of here," replied Audrey, "but I'll settle for a chair."

One was hastily provided and Audrey sat herself down, her busy blue, black-encircled eyes darting around, touching on everyone, missing nothing.

"Does anyone have a cigarette?" she demanded. "Who has a cigarette? Someone give me a cigarette!" She shot the words out of her mouth so quickly, one question following another so rapidly, that there was no room for reply.

"Ah," she cawed triumphantly, spotting Joan's pack on the table. "There's some cigarettes. Whose are they? Can I have one?" While speaking, she was clumsily prying one out of the pack, her eyes questioning the group of possible owners.

"Mine," answered Joan, and waiting until Audrey lit up, said, "No, you can't have one."

"Hah," laughed Audrey, exhaling in Joan's face. "That was cute. I like you, you have blue eyes." She
38

stubbed out the cigarette after two puffs and asked the room at large, "Does anybody live near Rexford? I need a lift to Rexford. Can you give me a lift to Rexford?"

She directed this last question to a slim, perfectly coiffed woman with a five-carat diamond ring named Carol Lighter, who, when she realized she was being addressed by Audrey, looked ready to faint. She managed to whisper a pained "Uh, no. I don't think so."

Zoe stood up abruptly. "I'm going to observe my son in class," she announced, and relieved by this inspiration, half the room rose and hurried out after her.

"Ha," sneered Audrey at the departing women. "Why do you want to look at them for? Don't you see enough of them at home? Where's a damn phone? I have to get a lift to Rexford." She too stood up and, teetering on her four-inch wedgies, danced out of the room. At the doorway she stopped, turned around and barked at the languid Bobbie, "You, the big one." Bobbie slowly turned and looked at her. "Your eyelash is falling off and anyway it's too long for your face. *And* the wrong color. If there's one thing I know about, it's makeup."

Suddenly Joan laughed. "We can tell," she said, "by the interesting way you apply yours."

"Well," Audrey said, pausing, "I was in a hurry this morning." She looked at Joan appraisingly and left the room, her voice drifting back from the hallway. "Sydelle, where the hell is a phone around here? Give me a dime."

The remaining women sat silently for a moment. "What on earth was that?" asked Carol Lighter wonderingly. "She looks like a madwoman."

"She is," said a girl named Myrna over by the window. "She's really crazy."

"I wonder what her kid is like," mused Joan, lighting another cigarette, and suddenly all the women were talking and laughing, united in a warm camaraderie, guessing at the emotional disturbances afflicting the child of this bizarre woman.

"Whatever else she is," said Joan, "she's a terrific ice breaker," and she leaned back, joining the flow of conversation, realizing in surprise that she was enjoying herself. "Crazy Audrey," she thought, smiling. "What a banana!"

4

There were some mornings, terrible mornings, when, after the boys were picked up for school and Naomi dropped at Good Beginnings, Joan didn't know what to do with herself. She had no desire to go back home, she didn't need to market, there were no clothes to pick up at the cleaners. The mail wasn't delivered until nearly noon, and nothing important ever came for her anyway. She had nothing to do. Sometimes free time, like great beauty or hope, is more of a curse than a blessing.

It was on mornings like these that she hung around the nursery school looking for someone to talk to, to breakfast with, to do nothing with. And it was on mornings like this that everyone she saw looked purposeful and intent, in a hurry and busy, busy, busy.

Today was that kind of morning. Joan took herself over to the viewing window and watched Naomi play for a while. When she spied Sydelle walking into her office, she wandered in after her and, grateful for someone to talk to, pulled out a chair and plopped down. They talked about Joan's boys and how they were

41

doing. They talked about Naomi and about Sydelle's kids. Then, for some reason, Joan asked, "Sydelle, who's this crazy Audrey Miller?"

"Crazy Audrey Miller is not as crazy as everyone thinks she is," answered Sydelle.

"How can you say that?" Joan asked. "The woman's a nut cake. Every time she walks into the lounge, the room clears out like someone farted or yelled 'Fire.'"

Sydelle replied, "Well, it's hard to explain. *She's* hard to explain. She's very conspicuous, very flamboyant, but not really a nut. It's hard to know why—but I find her sort of interesting. She's different."

"Do you like her?" asked Joan.

"Do I like her? Yes. I think I do."

"What's her kid like? Is the kid normal? *Can* a kid be normal with a mother who's a weirdo?"

"Denise is fine. She's really doing fine."

"Hmm," said Joan, and as if on cue, the phone on Sydelle's desk rang shrilly and at the same time a commotion was heard in the hall. Sydelle picked up the phone and Joan poked her head out the door. There was crazy Audrey Miller, in the black outfit she never seemed to take off, delivering a child, whom Joan assumed to be Denise, to her class. Late, of course.

"We're late, I know, I know," said Audrey to the teacher, and to Denise, "Come here, dreck, we're late, but it's okay. I love you, good-bye." With that she kissed her daughter, pushed her into the room, and waved to the teacher. As she turned to leave, she spotted Joan and walked over.

"Hello, hello. Do I know you? What's your name? Hello, Sydelle, my friend," and totally ignoring the fact that Sydelle was on the phone, continued, "How come you're having a conference without me?"

Sydelle dismissed her with a hurried "Not now, Audrey," and went back to her conversation.

"Well," said Audrey loudly. "It's obvious we're not wanted here. C'mon." With that, she took Joan by the arm and pulled her out of the office and into the lounge.

The lounge was empty. Most of the children were

42

now free of their anxieties and mothers were no longer required to remain. At about 11:15 it would begin to fill up once more with mommies who had come early to find a good parking space and enjoy time for gossip and conversation before the noon dismissal.

Joan and Audrey sat on opposite sides of the room and looked at each other. Audrey saw a small woman in her early thirties, slim, with long brown hair, blue eyes, no makeup. A woman who was carelessly dressed in this town of clothes-coordinated females, who smoked a lot and had big feet and unpainted toenails.

"Why did you schlepp me in here?" asked Joan. "Do you know what it would do to my reputation if we were to be seen together?"

"I don't want to fuck you," said Audrey. "I just want someone to have breakfast with."

"People will think I'm as crazy as you are," said Joan. "Why do I have to have that?"

"I'll pay for the breakfast," said Audrey. "Have whatever you want, I'll pay for it."

"You don't even know my name," said Joan. "Why do you want to buy me breakfast?"

"Because you look like you don't eat much," replied Audrey, "and I do too know your name."

"What is it?" asked Joan.

"I forget," said Audrey. "What's your name, cunt?"

"Wrong," said Joan.

"What is it?"

"Would you believe Golda Meir?"

"I'll believe anything. What is it?"

"Joan."

"Let's go to Farmers Market. I liked Golda better."

"Why do you call your kid 'dreck'? That means shit. Why do you call her that?"

"Because I call her that. What do you care what I call her? Let's go to Farmers Market."

"No."

"Not no, but yes," insisted Audrey.

"Why would I want to go anywhere with a crazy person?" asked Joan.

"You think I'm crazy?"

"Everybody thinks you're crazy. Are you?"

"Yes," said Audrey.

"Sydelle is the only one. She says you're not crazy."

"Well, Sydelle is a crazy person. Where's your car?"

"Stop asking personal questions," said Joan. "Where's *your* car?"

"I don't drive," said Audrey.

"How the hell do you live in Los Angeles without driving?"

"I have people who take me wherever I have to go, don't worry. My friends love me."

"Why?"

"Because I'm fun," said Audrey. "Come on."

"You have lipstick on your teeth."

"I always have lipstick on my teeth. I have lipstick everywhere. I have lipstick on my ass."

"Yours, I hope—unless you're a dyke. Are you a dyke, Audrey?"

Audrey laughed. She crossed her legs and wiped her front teeth with a much-used and shredded tissue she had unearthed from one of her pockets. She did not have a handbag.

"No, schmuck, I am not a dyke. No one who gets done as much as I do can be a dyke."

"Who does you? Do you have a husband?"

"Of course I have a husband. We're separated at the moment, but I have one. Do you?" she asked.

"Yes," said Joan.

"Living with you in your house?"

"Yes."

"How boring," said Audrey.

Joan stood up. She wasn't hungry, but she had decided to have breakfast with Audrey anyway. There was no one else around. She had nothing else to do.

"You're paying?" asked Joan.

"Naturally," replied Audrey, getting to her feet. "You're going to be my new friend, Golda. You know that, don't you?"

"One breakfast does not a friend make."

44

"You'll see," said Audrey, linking her arm in Joan's. "You'll fall so madly in love with me you'll want me every minute. You'll see."

"You *are* a dyke," cried an alarmed Joan, quickly disengaging her arm from Audrey's. "Get away from me."

"I am not," laughed Audrey. "You are *so* stupid. Come on."

"All right," said a still suspicious Joan, "but just don't start with me. I do not dine with dykes, and leave my arm alone," she said hastily as Audrey tried again to take it.

They walked out of the lounge and through the glass doors to the street. Joan's station wagon was parked a block from the school, and they headed toward it.

"How come you don't have a Mercedes?" asked Audrey, climbing into the car. "Everybody good has a Mercedes. I don't like Fords," she said.

"So get out," retorted Joan. "Who needs you?"

"You do, dummy," said Audrey. "Now listen, Golda, I'm paying for breakfast, but do you have money with you in case I don't have enough?"

"Oh God," muttered Joan, glancing sideways at Audrey. "What have I got myself into here?"

Five years later Joan would say on the phone to Audrey, "You bought me for a breakfast, for a lousy breakfast with cold eggs and spilled coffee." But at this moment, Joan wouldn't have believed in a million years that she'd ever have anything more to do with crazy Audrey Miller, not ever again . . . not even for five *minutes,* not even for breakfast at the Beverly Hills Hotel.

5

The lounge was abuzz with excitement. It was fund-raising time again and Sydelle had asked the parents to put on a show in order to raise money for the school. Joan was selected to write it, not because she was a writer but because her husband was. Women were volunteering their services as performers, musicians, and dancers. There were also to be booths selling the creative efforts of those who had no performing talent or no desire to be in the show. There would be booths selling needlepoint pictures, bargello pillows, felt puppets, hastily put together recipe books, plants, outgrown clothes in good condition. You name it, and someone could make it, get it, or already had it. Committees were formed. Dates had to be set, tickets printed, invitations composed.

Carol Lighter, the lady with the big diamond who was also the very chic wife of Beverly Hills' busiest gynecologist, was in charge of publicity. Zoe handled the booth assignments. Bobbie said she would make eighty-seven pillows. Wives of well-known performers, like Gloria and Sharon, vowed to supply their husbands. Nan Blake, whose novel had just been published and seemed already to be a best-seller, had promised Joan that she would be there to personally autograph and sell her book.

"But keep that Audrey Miller away from me," Nan warned. "Whatever possessed you to take up with her?"

"She's taken up with *me*," Joan corrected. "She waits for me in the lounge, she brings me cigarettes, she gets me coffee."

"Why does she do that?" asked Nan.

"I don't know."

"Why do you let her?"

"I don't know that either . . . I have a good time with her."

"Well," Nan repeated, "just please keep her away from me."

Audrey, who claimed to have been an actress who appeared on Broadway and in films before motherhood and had abruptly ended her career on what she said was "the brink of enormous success," stated loudly that she wouldn't dream of involving herself in any way whatsoever with any "stupid, amateur, piss-ant show," or lift even a finger for this "fucking overpriced school."

"That's wonderful," said Joan. "Nobody wanted you anyway."

Privately she complained to Nan that it was all too much for her. "I can't write a show, Nannie," she whined over the phone. "What the hell did I let myself in for? Eric's the writer, not me. You don't learn to write a show through osmosis, for Christ sake!"

"Joan, you're always saying you have nothing to do. Try it. I wouldn't be surprised if you found you really *can* write," said Nan.

"Do I say I have nothing to do?" asked Joan.

"All the time."

"Nan, I have *everything* to do," said Joan defensively. "The kids take up all my time. I'm always busy with them, or the house, or other related activities. My free times comes in spurts, like arterial blood."

"Listen, Joanie," Nan said, laughing, "I'll help you."

"I have a better idea. *You* write it. You're a writer

47

and you have a kid in the school. I can't write shows. It's ridiculous—but *you* can. What do you say?"

"Uh-uh."

"Why not?" asked Joan.

"I'm so busy working and publicizing the book that I don't even have time to plan Brian's birthday party. Did Naomi get the invitation?"

"Not yet," said Joan.

"Damn. I bet Carl forgot to mail them." Nan sighed. "It's too much," she said.

"What's the matter, Nannie?"

"I'm tired, I'm just tired."

After she hung up the phone, Nan lay down on the bed and picked up her writing pad. She was a very disciplined writer and knew herself to be, like Caesar, also ambitious. There was a knock on the bedroom door and Carl looked in.

"Nan, can you get off the phone long enough to say good-night to your sons? Oh, you're off. Sorry. Boys, come in and say good-night to your busy mother."

Nan sat up, annoyed and angry at her husband. "Carl," she began heatedly, but he vanished as her pajama-clad sons entered the room. She opened her arms and held each tightly as she kissed them good-night. Nan adored her children. She often felt guilty about not spending more time with them. In all the years of her marriage she had never made a bed, never even bathed her children. Fortunately, she had Carl to handle all domestic matters. It was the least he could do. His salary was negligible compared to hers, and it was she who provided the support for the family. If Nan could have two wishes they would be, in order of preference: (1) to be thin, and (2) to have a successful husband.

Nan knew it always annoyed Joan when she complained about Carl's inability to make money.

"What do you need him to make money for?" Joan would ask impatiently. "You make enough, more than enough, for the both of you."

"I know," Nan would reply. "But if he earned more,

I wouldn't have to take jobs I don't want to take. I could relax a little and not have all this responsibility."

"Nan, that's crap," Joan would retort. "You'd work just as much as you do now, and you know it. Besides, if Carl were more successful, he couldn't do what he does with the kids, which is what enables you to work in the first place. So hold yourself and be grateful that you have him around."

Joan was fond of Carl and always defended him, at least in this situation—and she was right, of course. Still, Nan couldn't help it. It was hard for her to respect a man like Carl. To her, a child of the fifties, masculinity and respect were directly related to earning power, and in that department Carl batted zero.

"Nan," bellowed Carl from downstairs, interrupting her thoughts, "this is the first night you've been home in a week. If we try, I'm sure we can find something to talk about."

"I'm coming," Nan bellowed back, and started downstairs.

"Stop yelling," said a voice from her older son's room.

"Okay," said Nan to his door. "Go to sleep."

She went down to the den and found Carl in front of the television set. "Carl," she said curtly, "Joan never got an invitation to Brian's party. You *did* remember to mail them out, I hope?"

"Yes, Nan, I remembered," said Carl. "They went out this morning."

"This morning?" she said angrily. "The party is Saturday afternoon. Today is Tuesday. Why didn't you wait until Friday?"

"Look, Nan," Carl said, tight-lipped, "if you don't like the way I do things, then do them yourself. I'm getting sick and tired of being criticized."

"Okay, to whom did you send them?"

"To everyone on the class list. Wasn't I supposed to do that?"

"I told you not to send one to Audrey Miller's kid or Carol Lighter's kid," said Nan, enraged. "They're obnoxious, like their mothers!"

"How the hell do you send invitations to fifteen kids and leave out two? Just because you can't stand their *mothers?*"

"Yes," screamed Nan.

"Well, tough shit. I forgot. I sent them all and you'll just have to make the best of it," Carl screamed back. "Jesus Christ, Nan, do we even have to fight over invitations to a kid's birthday party?"

Nan stared at him, seething. "I'm going upstairs to work," she said coldly. *"Someone* around here has to make a living." She turned abruptly and left the room. Carl sank down into his chair. He passed his hand across his face and turned back to the detective story on the television screen.

Nan entered her room and closed the door. She picked up her pad from the bedside table and sat down on the bed. Leaning back against the headboard, she wrote in big black letters: WISH NUMBER 3: TO BE IN LOVE. She read what she had written and added LIKE JOAN. Then she closed her eyes, the white pad covering her stomach like a sabbath cloth, the pencil still held in her fingers. Two tears slipped from her eyes and down the sides of her face. "Why aren't I happy?" she sobbed. Her blessings ran across her mind like subtitles on a movie screen. Married, kids, career—everything. So why?

Once she had asked Joan why an educated woman like herself did not look for more out of life than being a wife and mother.

"More?" Joan had asked, and then after a short silence said, "Nan, I have someone I love, who loves me. I have healthy, normal children. None of us is in pain. If God never gives me more than that, if indeed there *is* more than that, if all I have now is all I ever get, dayenu, I'm already ahead of the game."

"Dayenu?" Nan asked softly.

"Dayenu is a Hebrew word that we sing at Passover. *You* remember. It means 'it is enough.'" Again a short silence.

50

"Joan," said Nan gently, "you're actually happy, aren't you?"

"Yes, I think I'm . . . I'm *almost* happy. I allow myself the luxury of complaining, at times I get depressed, but on the bottom, in my liver, I'm almost easy . . . I'm almost happy."

"You're very lucky, Joanie."

"I know I am, Nannie. I've known from birth what is important and what isn't," and she knocked the wood of her chair leg seven times.

With a sigh, Nan sat up, rested the pad against her knees and wrote dayenu. Then she crossed it out. She was not yet ready for dayenu, but she had other options. She flipped over the pages of her pad and began to work on an article she had agreed to do for *Cosmopolitan* magazine. In two days it was completed. By the end of the month, she had lost eleven pounds.

6

Carol Lighter was annoyed. She had worked her tail off doing all the school's fund-raising publicity and then, out of the blue, that tacky Joan had crapped out and refused to write the show. They had to make do with the booths and a mini-amusement park idea that Joan had come up with to atone for reneging on her assignment. Naturally, it all added up to more work for Carol. They had reached their goal, but Carol would never forgive Joan for causing her such grief and aggravation. Even now, three months after the fact and two weeks before Good Beginnings closed for the summer, Carol was still seething.

"I hate people like that," Carol said to Zoe one morning in the lounge. "I hate it when everything is decided and then, because *one* person can't hack it, everyone else has to suffer."

"No one had to suffer, Carol," Zoe said mildly. "Joan told us she wouldn't write it in plenty of time to set up the amusement park."

"For *me* to set up the amusement park, you mean," Carol answered heatedly. "It all fell on *me*."

52

"Well," said Zoe, "you did a beautiful job."

"I hope so," Carol said, somewhat mollified. "But let me tell you, it took everything out of me."

She took a lipstick from her purse and, without benefit of mirror, expertly drew a line of color on her lips. Zoe watched her admiringly. Carol was all Zoe yearned to be. Carol was perfect—her hair, her clothes, her accessories. Zoe had never, not once during the entire school year, seen her in the same outfit twice. She had managed, by shameful ass-kissing and abject flattery, to become Carol's friend and faithful servant. She had even changed gynecologists and, deserting the doctor who had delivered her son and cured her vaginitis, switched to Carol's husband, Dr. Lighter.

Carol was aware of Zoe's adoration. She was bored by most females, and considered herself a man's woman, but still, one sometimes needs an alter ego. Of course, Carol's *best* friend was Sharon Silver, whose husband was *the* Artie Silver, one of moviedom's hottest box office draws. The two women met right here at Good Beginnings and had taken to one another immediately. Zoe, Carol knew, was insanely jealous of her friendship with Sharon but was content with the crumbs she tossed her—lucky to be even noticed by her. Zoe was a nobody—her husband owned, of all things, a hosiery store. And she would pay, Carol thought vindictively, for even that mild and, come to think of it, surprising defense of that tacky Joan Brenner.

For some reason, one that Carol couldn't fathom, Joan was well liked by the group. Even Sharon liked her, and once the three of them had had lunch together. Carol was embarrassed walking in with Joan because her clothes were all wrong. And that was another thing. Joan certainly had enough money, her husband was a big something-or-other in TV, and yet she always looked tacky. The Brenners went to some good parties, with Joan looking as though she'd come off the racks of a May Company budget store. Carol was mystified by the whole thing and avoided Joan whenever she

53

could, especially now that she had taken up with that insane Audrey Miller. Well, thought Carol, birds of a feather, after all.

"Zoe," Carol said, "if you're going for a coffee, bring one for me." Zoe, who had no desire for anything to drink, jumped to her feet. "Of course I will," she said, happy to be of service. "I was just going to get one. You must have read my mind."

At that moment Joan and Audrey entered the room, followed closely by Bobbie, Myrna, Gloria and Sharon.

"Oh, and Zoe," said Carol, seeing her opportunity for revenge, "bring back a cup for each of the girls, unless of course Joan and Audrey don't want any."

"We want it, Zoe," croaked Audrey. "Whatever you're getting, we want it."

"Well, darling," Carol said to Sharon, "where have you been and why?" and to Zoe, "Well, go on. Eight coffees, can't you count?" Zoe left on her errand.

"We were at Saks," Sharon said, sitting down next to Carol.

"Getting a gift certificate for Sydelle," Joan continued, "and one for each teacher."

"Oh," said Carol.

"We are the end-of-term-gift committee," laughed Gloria.

"Oh," said Carol, "you weren't on that committee, were you, Sharon?"

"No," answered Joan, "but she was in Saks, buying out the fifth floor. When she started on sportswear, we dragged her back with us."

Carol was relieved. She would have been extremely distressed had Sharon voluntarily sought out that company. Bobbie, Gloria and Myrna were all right, but certainly not crazy Audrey and tacky Joan.

"Don't worry, Carol, Sharon still loves you the best," Audrey said gleefully. "Although why that is I can't imagine." Carol ignored the remark and turned to Sharon, but before she could speak Audrey continued, "Since I for one think you're shit!"

"Shut up, Audrey," Joan admonished, while the oth-

54

ers, including Carol and Sharon, looked stunned. Carol rose haughtily to her feet.

"Are you coming, Sharon? The air in here is suddenly vile." Sharon stood with her friend, as did Gloria and Myrna—the last two throwing an apologetic look at Joan as they left. Bobbie, as usual, seemed to be asleep.

"Why did you *do* that?" Joan asked Audrey in exasperation. "Having her for an enemy is like having Martin Bormann."

"I'd *rather* have Martin Bormann. I can't *stand* that bitch. Did you see her face?" Audrey chortled. At that moment the faithful Zoe, carrying a tray with eight Styrofoam cups of coffee, entered the room and looked about her, bewildered. "Where *is* everybody?" she asked.

"Off to find the wizard," replied Joan, reaching for a cup.

"Where *are* they?" Zoe asked again.

"Everybody good is right here, asshole," said Audrey, also taking a cup. "Sit down and drink your coffee."

"There's six cups of coffee left," said Zoe abjectly.

"Then you'd better start drinking *now,* honey," laughed Joan.

Even the lanky, dozing Bobbie seemed to smile. "Asshole," she murmured dreamily.

7

Audrey would not leave her alone. It got so that Joan was loath to answer the phone, although normally she welcomed calls, so apprehensive was she that the caller was Audrey. Audrey pestered her to the tune of twenty calls a day. And always at the most inconvenient times. Half the time Joan would just hang up on her, but Audrey remained unperturbed and undeterred, and five minutes later the phone would ring and there she'd be again.

Rudeness, coldness, even direct threats and desperate pleas had no effect on Audrey Miller, who never seemed to take offense at even the most blatant insults or snubs.

"What it is," Joan said to Eric at dinner, "is a courtship. That crazy woman is trying to woo me." She would have put it more succinctly, but they always ate with the children. The time would come when she would allow herself to say "fuck" or "bitch" or "shit" in front of them, or even *to* them, but that time was not now.

It was obvious that Audrey wanted to be her friend. But "friend" to Audrey meant a complete takeover. It meant total subservience of one's needs to Audrey's. It meant being at the mercy of her dictatorship, constantly on call, ever ready to listen, to lend, to chauffeur around, to baby-sit, to applaud. Audrey demanded a fidelity of the sort dedicated priests give to the church, of the sort good and faithful wives give to their husbands. She was also intensely jealous.

"Oh, really?" she would say, terribly offhand. "You had lunch with Nan instead of me? Okay, Joan. That's all right. I'll remember that when you want theater tickets."

And Audrey could, Lord only knows how, get tickets to anything. She could get house seats to the biggest, sold-out hit of the season ten minutes before show time, in row B, center, at half price, during a convention of theater lovers on a Saturday night, with the President of the United States flying in just to see *that* show—and get his autograph for her son, and an invite to the White House. How she did it would remain an irritating mystery to Joan.

"How do you *do* it, Audrey?" she would ask, exasperated, and Audrey would reply, "Oh, I have friends, lots of friends. Good friends. Not like you, bitch." And then, despite furious and continued nagging, say no more.

"And she lies," Joan would complain to a bored Eric. "She lies about everything. Her age, her kids, her veins, *everything*."

Despite all this, despite Joan's resistance, Audrey managed to work her way into Joan's bloodstream. They began to market, shop and have breakfast together. Their daughters started to play and fight with each other. Mostly fight. They enrolled Naomi and Denise at the same dancing school, which meant that they came and went together. Audrey was ever optimistic, good-humored and brash. Joan grew sullen.

She met some of Audrey's "good friends"—"slaves" was more like it—and vowed fervently *never* to become one of what Audrey smugly called "my people." Joan was very curious about these people of Audrey's. The

57

only one she had become friendly with was a sweet quiet woman named Dolores Levy. Dolores was relatively "new," having been with Audrey for only about a year and a half. Audrey had picked her up in the playground by demanding first a cigarette, then insisting that Dolores remove her daughter Melissa from the swing because Denise felt like swinging and, finally, graciously permitting Dolores to go out of her way and drive her and Denise home.

Dolores was having marital problems. Audrey advised her constantly as to the proper course of action to take with her difficult husband. As far as Joan could surmise, Audrey's imparted wisdom boiled down to "Look, Dolores, if he gets nasty, just kick the bastard in the balls!" Once Joan asked Dolores why she listened to Audrey, why she was so obedient to her demands and suggestions.

"Why do you let her walk all over you? And why are you such a puppet?"

Dolores thought for a minute. "Because," she said slowly, "Audrey is a good friend."

"Good friends don't take advantage of you."

"Oh," said Dolores, "I know she takes advantage of me."

"So why do you allow that?"

"I allow that," said Dolores quietly, "because when you're Audrey's friend, no matter what you do and even if you're wrong, when you're in trouble, she's *always* on your side."

What bothered Joan exceedingly was Audrey's irritating habit of boasting about the lengths to which her "people" would go to please her, of her uncanny ability to manipulate them in any direction she wished, or to bully them into acquiescence. "My people will do anything for me," she would say complacently. "Don't ask me why, because I don't *know* why. It's just always been like that."

Joan did not want that to happen to her. She refused to acknowledge the unthinkable possibility of becoming one of them. Therefore she rarely called Audrey.

One day, after they had known each other for about a year, Audrey called Joan for the fifteenth time that day and she was peeved.

"Why don't you ever call me?" she whined. "Why am I always the one to call?"

"Because," Joan answered with great satisfaction, "I don't need you, I have other people to talk to. You're not the only one with friends. I also have friends, *normal* friends. What do I want with you?"

"Who's your friend, that Nan, the big writer? You call her a friend? My enemies should have such friends!"

"Now, now, Audrey. Stop acting like a jealous wife."

"Uh-uh, honey, I'm not jealous. Who could be jealous of you? But at least I don't say bad on you."

"Like hell you don't."

"Well, I don't *like* you—but Nan's supposed to be your *friend,* right?"

"Not supposed to be—*is.*"

"Well, then, I won't hurt you by telling you what she said."

"Hurt me. I won't believe it anyhow."

"Do you remember at her kid's birthday party?"

"Do I remember *what?* The color of the jelly beans?"

"I was talking to her."

"Wonderful. Now I know you're lying. She can't stand you. She wouldn't talk to you to ask you to save her kid's life if she were pinned down under a heavy beam and you were the only one around during an 8.7 earthquake."

"Well, she talked to me *then,* I'll tell you."

"So tell me already!"

"I was talking to her about you, that you are the funniest lady in the world and have more talent in your ass than she or I or Joan Rivers has altogether."

"So?"

"So, you know what your good friend, Nan, the big writer, said to me?"

"What?"

"Nothing!"

"Huh?"

"She said nothing!"

"Audrey, what the hell are you talking about?"

"She just stood there and looked at me."

"That's because you're weird-looking."

"Uh-uh, honey. That's because she didn't want to say anything good about you. She could have *agreed* with me, but she didn't. All she said was, 'Really?' and I said, 'Yes, really,' and she said, 'Well, she hasn't written anything, so how do you know?'"

"Go on."

"And so I said, 'How do I know? Because I'm her friend, that's how I know.' So you see, cunt, that's your friend, Nan Blake!"

Joan was silent for a while, and then she said, "I can't, Audrey, I just can't," and hung up.

But if Audrey liked constant applause, Joan was not immune to it either. She didn't have the same need for it as Audrey, but still, appreciation, like an overdue paycheck, is eagerly awaited and happily received. To give Audrey her due, she gave as good as she got and, in Joan's case, she gave even more. The one pleasant aspect of speaking with Audrey on the phone was that she was a marvelous listener. Even the most banal of Joan's utterances were greeted with gales of gasping laughter from Audrey. She laughed so hard that she could barely speak, so hard that she peed in her pants— or so she said. Joan didn't care. It was nice.

"Oh, oh," Audrey would laugh, losing her breath. "I can't ... stop ... I'm having pee-pees. God, Joan, you are the funniest ... no one makes me laugh like you ..." and off she would go again.

Gradually, so gradually that Joan was unaware of it, she began to look forward to Audrey's calls. She still often hung up on her, or cut her off abruptly, but her annoyance at Audrey's intrusions was lessening.

Audrey was right about one thing, Joan thought to herself; she *was* fun and never boring. Outrageous, exasperating, manipulative, untruthful, flamboyant, noisy, appealing, good-natured, generous, disorganized and totally unembarrassable; but never dull. She had more chutzpah, more sheer gall, than even the crassest of opportunists. Audrey Miller could make Sammy run. She could have cowed Mike Todd. She could, she would modestly aver, "charm the paper off the walls and make a pregnant bear dance."

She lived on the wrong side of the tracks, south of Wilshire, "in the poor." They had fallen on hard times, Audrey explained on Joan's first visit. When Joan entered the apartment, the front door of which was always unlocked, she saw what Audrey meant. The apartment was as Audrey had described it—a sewer. The kitchen sink was piled high with unwashed dishes. Her husband used to wash them when he got disgusted enough, Audrey said, but since their separation no one was around to do them. She never got disgusted. If she needed a plate for something, she would simply pluck one from the pile in the sink, rinse it off and use it. On the dirty, encrusted stove were pots half-filled with congealed messes. Some lay on their sides, dripping their unmentionable contents into the burners. The refrigerator too was horrendous, with salami, chocolate cake, uncapped soda bottles, some of them empty, and cheese with a bite taken out of it. Moldy lemons and the remains of a half-cooked chicken spiced the interior. From time to time Audrey would find a Carmen or a Lupe or an Esperanza to clean up the place. They earned their money, those poor ladies, and often had to wait weeks for it.

The rest of the apartment was equally squalid—unmade beds, newspapers and cookies on the floors, magazines and three years' worth of mail on the table, an opened loaf of bread on the TV set, candy wrappers all over the once-handsome velvet couch, an unfinished glass of orange juice decorating the arm.

"I'm not into cleaning," Audrey told Joan. "I don't do that. I have a friend, Sally Brayman, who has the cleanest floors in Beverly Hills. No germ could live in her house for more than five seconds. The bedrooms are perfect and with wallpaper. But you know what?

61

All her kids get D's and her husband doesn't fuck her. My house is on the condemned list, my kids are super and my husband, that demented animal, is always on me, even though we're separated. I must be doing something right!"

It was the kind of house where you examined each chair before sitting on it and where you never, except in the direst emergency, went to the bathroom. Joan, who was not exactly enthusiastic about housework herself, was appalled. "Toilet paper, Audrey, is a symbol of the civilized world. Remind me," she said, deciding to keep her legs crossed rather than risk going, "*never* to shake your hand. I don't wonder that your husband left. I'm only amazed he stayed *this* long. Shame on you."

Audrey's relationship with her husband, Scott, was a strange one. She had been married to him for fifteen years, after a murky history, Joan gathered, of one or two previous adventures in wedlock. He worked sporadically at something in insurance—Joan never was sure what—and although he was not living with Audrey, seemed always to be around. He talked about returning for good, Audrey informed Joan, in honor of the upcoming bar mitzvah of Marc, known as Mendy, their son. Joan had met Scott Miller a few times at nursery school, liked him, wondered at his staying power, and called him Melvin ever after. He was a nice man who was prone to violent headaches. As to the reason for his headaches, Joan wondered not at all.

Audrey boasted continually about her children, especially Mendy and his academic achievements. She was not at all afraid of being goosed by the spiteful and ironic fingers of those avenging fates that so often plague bragging Jewish mothers. Audrey had none of the superstitious certainties that kept Joan quiet—that if you said it aloud, or even let yourself think with any frequency that things were good, they would get bad. That if you mentioned the perfect health of your child, pneumonia or worse would then afflict him. That if you beamingly exhibited your son's straight-A report card, he would proceed to fail math.

"Shh," Joan would caution her in horror when she ran on about the amazing Mendy. "Shh. Don't talk about it." But Audrey laughed and scoffed, defied the gods and got off scot-free. Mendy continued to win awards and never sneezed, not even once. Even those vengeful spirits who pricked the perfect bubbles of mortals who prospered and proudly proclaimed it— they too were Audrey's people.

Audrey had aging parents to whom she was very attached, especially her father. He had suffered several strokes and as a result had become rambling and forgetful. She was worried about him and was annoyed when her mother, Sadie, complained that he was smelling up the house. "Keep him here with you," Joan suggested. "*Your* house smells *already*."

But it was Sadie, whom Audrey expected would go on forever, who became ill. "She's in the hospital," Audrey wailed tearfully to Joan. "I hate her. Why is she doing this to me?"

Sadie had developed a benign tumor in her abdomen which had grown so large that she gave the appearance of a tiny, wizened seventy-six-year-old pregnant troll. She needed surgery, and after Audrey had researched and alienated every doctor in America, she settled on a young surgeon named Jeffrey Applebaum.

"His credentials are terrific," Audrey confided to Joan. "He's Jewish, and I know I can get a prescription for diet pills out of him."

Since Joan's initial experience with Dexedrine, she had been relatively "clean." This was not a result of fear about the harmful effects of such pills on the system. Rather it was an inability to find a doctor in Los Angeles who would prescribe for her. But Audrey could get anything and usually she did. They both were constantly alert to the possibilities of encountering sympathetic M.D.'s and never let an opportunity go by. Of course, Audrey was the more successful of the two.

"You're gonna kiss my ass," she would exclaim gleefully. "Guess what I got?"

"Gonorrhea?" Joan would ask, her heart soaring, knowing that Audrey had scored.

"No, putz—a prescription for thirty. What do you say to that?"

"Audrey, you're a genius. How many are mine?"

"Why should I give you? You never get *me* anything."

"I want fifteen—I'll pay."

"I've got people all over town who want diet pills— they beg me to let them pay."

"Okay, good-bye."

"Fine, it's all over."

"Right. I wouldn't take them now even if you promised to tell me how old you are."

"I can't give you fifteen. I'll give you ten."

"Fifteen."

"Okay. When are you coming?"

"I'm there already. Good-bye."

Now they sat in the hospital waiting room, Audrey strained and for once quiet. The operation had been under way for over an hour. Audrey stood up and approached the volunteer worker at the desk.

"Are there any progress reports or anything from the operating room? It's Dr. Applebaum."

"Who's the patient, dear?"

"Mrs. Sadie Gittelman."

The volunteer sifted through her papers. "No, dear. Nothing. She's only been in there for an hour."

"I know, I know. I'm her daughter, I know how long she's been in."

Audrey returned to the couch and sat down again next to Joan. The waiting room was full of people, families talking quietly together, a young man sitting alone staring down at the pot of African violets he held in his lap. There were people pacing back and forth, back and forth, tracing and retracing their footsteps, and doctors and nurses, in earnest conversation or laughing, going on a break. The vending machines were doing a brisk business in candy bars, crackers, cigarettes, soda pop, even chicken soup.

"What if she dies?" Audrey said loudly, incapable of whispering even here. The young man with the African violets looked up, his eyes blank.

"Shush," whispered Joan sternly. "She won't die. It's not such a serious condition."

"When you're seventy-four, a splinter is serious."

"She's not seventy-four, she's seventy-six. Even about *her* age you lie."

"Joan, what if the rotten egg dies?"

"She won't, Audrey. She'll live to buy you quilts for many years yet."

"Are you sure?"

"I'm sure. Come on, let's get out of here and take a walk."

"What if they call me?"

"They won't call you. Come on."

They went downstairs and walked out the large glass doors into the sun. Walking was not a habitual pastime for Joan in this city on wheels, and she stretched her legs gratefully, happy to be away from the tense bustle of the waiting room. They walked down the street, making little conversation, occasionally commenting nastily on the young long-haired, firm-bodied, bare-legged California girls who paraded by.

The city was full of girls like these. It was one of the things Eric enjoyed most about L.A. He ogled and leered and encouraged the twins to do the same.

"For God's sake, Eric," Joan angrily admonished him one day when he had almost driven the car onto the sidewalk. "Keep your eyes on the road, will you?"

"But there aren't any cute young things on the road," he explained to Joan, maneuvering the car back into its lane.

"You'll leer your way right into intensive care," Joan said indignantly.

"Just be happy that all I do is look," he said, disregarding her dire prediction. "Look, boys, look at that one across the street." As the three men in her life turned to gape, Joan settled back and sighed. She was very happy indeed that all Eric did was look.

"Let's go in," Joan suggested to Audrey as they passed a shoe store. Audrey could always forget her troubles in shoes. They spent an hour there, trying on boots and five-inch platform sandals, joking around and adding greatly to the probability of the salesman's having a nervous breakdown.

"Audrey," Joan asked, "why are you so into shoes when you have the ugliest, veiniest, fattest legs I've ever seen?"

"Oh? Well, let me tell you, bitch, even with these legs, men like me."

"Blind men."

"Uh-uh. They like them."

"Audrey, your legs are an emetic."

"What emetic?"

"They're to throw up from."

"Shut up. Even with these legs I do better than you."

They left the store and turned back in the direction of the hospital. They toyed with the idea of eating lunch, but since both had swallowed diet pills, they weren't hungry. They returned to the waiting room. The boy with the violets was gone.

The volunteer, still at her desk, informed Audrey that there was no word as yet.

"Do you know who that guy with the flowerpot was waiting for?" asked Joan.

"His wife just got out of surgery," answered the volunteer, a pleasant woman in her fifties.

"What was she in for?" asked Audrey.

"I'm not supposed to tell anyone," said the volunteer, lowering her voice, "but it was cancer. Mastectomy."

Joan and Audrey went back to the couch, ashen.

"Jesus," Joan muttered.

"Joan, what if my mother has cancer?"

"Shut up, Audrey."

Joan fished for change in the bottom of her bag and bought a pack of cigarettes from a friendly machine. They sat smoking and waiting.

Suddenly Audrey stood up. "That's him!" she said urgently to Joan, grabbing her arm. Joan looked up and saw a glimpse of green way down the corridor. A doctor, still in his surgical gown, was coming toward them.

"Dr. Applebaum," bellowed Audrey, "is my mother all right?"

The doctor continued toward them, nodding and smiling.

"She's okay," Joan said in relief. "Look, he's smiling."

"Dr. Applebaum, I love you," Audrey yelled and, as all eyes swiveled toward her and unbelieving mouths hung open in shock, she continued, "Tell me my mother's all right and I swear on the lives of my children I'll go down on you, right here!"

That night as they were preparing for bed, Joan recounted the day's events to Eric, shuddering in recollection.

"I finally understand what it means to want to disappear into the woodwork. I thought I would die," she said, turning down the bedclothes.

"She's a pistol, all right," Eric said, getting under the covers.

"And when she had him there, helpless, in the grip of an embarrassment so acute that he was unable to move, she hit on him for a prescription of Dexamil!"

"That was very poetic, honey, but I don't want you taking any of that shit."

"Don't worry."

"If she gives you any of that crap, I'll break her neck."

"Okay, I won't."

"Yeah, I'll bet."

"Isn't that something, though? God!"

"Are you going to spend all night talking about Audrey?"

"Do you want to talk about something else?"

"I don't want to talk at all."

"No?"

"No! Did you take a bath?"

"If you *really* loved me, it wouldn't matter."

"Shut off the light. Come here. Now...show me what Audrey said to Dr. Applebaum."

8

The Beverly Hills Unified School System is said to be one of the best in the country. Comprising the district were four elementary schools and one high school, Beverly Hills High—which, from a distance, resembled the Concord Hotel and had services and grounds which, at the very least, equaled it. The published test scores of the various grades in all five schools were high enough to place the system among the top ten nationwide. Ninety-nine percent of the children graduating after twelve years of Beverly Hills schooling went on to college. The citizens of the city attributed this to the high quality of the teaching. Joan attributed it to the fact that the majority of the kids were Jewish.

It was therefore upsetting that her children, all three of them now in elementary school, were only doing what she considered to be average work. Joan, who could never remember which day of the week it was or what she had had for dinner the night before, managed to recall vividly that she knew more in fourth grade than her sons did in sixth.

"How have we, two superior people, managed to

spawn such dummies?" she would ask, perplexed and depressed, of an annoyed Eric.

"It's not from *my* side of the family, *that* I know," Eric would reply. "Every one of the kids in *my* family is gifted."

Generally Eric refused to be goaded into conversations of this sort. He much preferred to read the trades and sip his white wine. He much preferred believing that his children were not dummies.

"Why aren't our children academically motivated?" she would ask the back of his head. "Is it my fault? Am I doing something wrong? Should we take them out of here and put them in private school? Do you think they might possibly need therapy? *Eric!* I'm *talking* to you!!"

"What? No, they'll be fine."

"Shit!" she would say, and march off in disgust.

Naturally, Audrey's children took to schooling like moths to flame, like bees to honey, like Beverly Hills matrons to eighty-dollar jeans. They loved homework, they adored assignments, they thrived on projects. Whereas her kids couldn't wait for school to begin, Joan's couldn't wait for it to end. This even extended to the piano lessons their daughters were now taking. Denise refused to stop practicing. Naomi wouldn't go near the piano, and wanted only to quit her lessons and watch television. Every time Audrey called her, Joan could hear Denise practicing in the background. To add insult to inquiry, Audrey would ask, "How are you kids doing in school? Mendy won the French award and Denise, that little dreck, likes reading better than *Happy Days.*"

The best a down-hearted Joan could come up with was "Fuck off, Audrey," and slam the receiver down. She vented her frustration on the teachers, the system, her children, the smog. But to no avail. Audrey's kids kept excelling. Hers kept squeaking through. She discovered at subsequent parent-teacher conferences that her son Jason had perceptual problems; her son Michael talked back to his teachers; her daughter, Naomi,

70

refused to follow directions. A bad report from school or an argument with her kids was enough to plunge her into a depression which hung over her head like a London fog.

She moped around, teary and exhausted, completely forgetting how "almost happy" she was, too enervated even to prepare dinner. She discovered the truth of her mother's words spoken to her when she was agonizing over Michael's bout with croup when he was two. "Joan," her mother had said, after Michael had choked up his entire dinner on the front of Joan's dress, "it's not from nothing you get the name 'mother.'"

And, of course, she could not speak to Audrey. The "my kids are better than your kids" tenor of her conversation was just too painful and just too possibly true.

"Why don't you *do* something?" Eric would prod helpfully. "Get involved in something and it'll take your mind off the kids."

"Nan," she would moan into the telephone, "I'm going crazy." But even Nan could say little to comfort her. *She* had kids who loved Hebrew school and ordered fish in restaurants.

Joan tried to follow Eric's advice, tried to involve herself in something. She called Gloria Chase, still her friend from nursery school days. "Come to our consciousness-raising group," Gloria suggested. But all Joan wanted raised were her children's grades, and she declined with thanks. Apparently she had no room for secondary involvements, so involved was she with her children. She sank so low as to call Carol Lighter, who informed her coldly that she had no time to speak with her since she had an important appointment with her hairdresser. Strangely, it was that brief conversation that lifted Joan's spirits. Compared to Carol Lighter, Lizzie Borden came off looking good; so, too, did even a Jewish mother whose children were underachieving.

At eleven that morning, Joan was still dragging around the house. She was feeling a bit better lately, but was not yet of sufficient cheer to face Safeway.

71

When the phone rang she ran to get it, hoping it was Eric, who had taken to phoning at odd times in order to check on her emotional barometer and perhaps give her a laugh. But it wasn't Eric, it was a desperate, subdued Audrey.

"You've got to get over here right away," Audrey said urgently into the phone. "Dolores is here and I'm afraid she's going to kill herself. Hurry!"

"Come off it, Audrey. Don't pull that actress shit on me. All you probably want is a lift to the bakery. Call one of your many slaves, not me." She hung up. A moment later the phone rang again. Curious to hear Audrey's comeback, Joan lifted the receiver.

"What!"

"Joan, I'm serious. Listen." Audrey must have carried the phone closer to Dolores, for in the background, instead of Denise practicing, Joan heard a sobbing so desperate that the agony was audible even over the phone.

"Now do you believe me? I can*not* be alone with her. Hurry up and get your ass over here."

Joan scurried around getting dressed. She was genuinely fond of Dolores, a gentle girl who was one of the world's victims. Dolores was now being divorced by one of the world's bastards, Stu Levy, and he was giving her a very hard time. She was under psychiatric care and well tranquilized, but it didn't seem to be helping. Stu was being unnecessarily nasty about money, about everything, and their children were reacting terribly to the whole scene. Poor fragile Dolores, just barely functioning, was reeling under this enormous shattering of her ego. With the children so difficult, there seemed to be nothing at all in her life to provide a soothing balm for her wounded and weeping spirit. Joan ached for her.

Joan scrambled out of her car in front of Audrey's apartment. She raced up the short flight of stairs to the door, through which could be heard Audrey's imploring voice attempting to comfort a grieving Dolores.

She pushed open the unlocked door and stepped quietly inside. Dolores was seated on the couch, eyes shut, crying and moaning, rocking back and forth, all the while ripping out clumps of hair with her desperate, clawing hands. She kept up a jerky, robotlike rhythm: rock forward, pull hair, rock backward, release hair, over and over, trancelike and possessed.

Audrey paced in front of her, wringing her hands and chewing her lips, begging "Stop, stop," cursing Stu Levy. Joan ran to the couch, knelt in front of Dolores and grabbed both thin wrists with her own shaking hands, pushing Dolores' limp, unresisting body down until her head lay on the arm of the couch. She pressed her dry, flushed cheek to Dolores' wet one and lay half on top of her, hands gripping hands, until the trembling form beneath her was finally still.

After a while Joan sat up, removed the tufts of hair which Dolores still clutched in her hands and threw them on the floor. She looked up at Audrey, standing immobile in front of them, and they stared at each other wide-eyed and horrified. Without a word, Audrey dragged over a chair and sat down. She smoothed Dolores' matted hair back from her forehead and she and Joan sat quietly regarding their friend until she opened her eyes.

"I'm sorry," she whispered.

Joan drew a ragged breath and fumbled for her cigarettes. She gave one to Audrey and lit the two in her own mouth, handing one of them to Dolores. They smoked in silence, exhaling huge puffs of smoke. The voices of playing children drifted in through the open windows from the schoolyard across the street.

"I'm so sorry," Dolores repeated, attempting to sit up, and, still exhausted, falling back.

"Are you feeling better?" Joan asked.

"Yes."

"Do you want some coffee?"

"No."

"Do you want us to call your doctor?"

"No."

"I'm gonna get that fucking Stu Levy for this," Audrey said angrily. "How dare he, how dare he do this to you?" She took Dolores' smoked-down butt and crushed it viciously in the ashtray. "I'll make that bastard sorry he was born."

Joan stood up and looked down at Dolores. "I think you should see your doctor," she said. "Come on, I'll drive you over."

"No," said Dolores, sitting up. "I'm all right now, really. I'd better get home."

"You'll leave when I say so," said Audrey.

"She's right. You shouldn't be alone. Is anyone at your house?"

"The maid."

Joan nodded. "I still think you should call your doctor, Dolores. He's got to be informed about this little episode. Maybe he can give you something. What if we're not around and you wack out again?"

"I won't wack out again."

"You'd better not," said Audrey. "It's bad for my stomach."

Dolores smiled. "I promise," she said.

"What brought this on?" asked Joan. "What set you off?"

"I spoke to Stu this morning. He wants me to sell the house. He told me to get a job if I need money."

"That prick," muttered Audrey.

"I haven't worked in thirteen years. What am I going to do? What kind of a job can I get? He said he won't pay my charge account bills."

"Let your lawyer deal with that," said Joan. "That's what he's there for. You shouldn't even say *one* word to that sonofabitch . . . who, by the way, you're well rid of. He's not good enough to wipe your ass, that bastard."

"He's not even good enough to wipe *my* ass," said Audrey.

Joan smiled. "Nobody's *that* bad, Audrey, not even Stu Levy."

Dolores laughed. "Thank you both," she said. "It's

74

good to have friends." She looked at them and tears welled in her eyes.

"Well," said Joan hastily, attempting to lighten the atmosphere, "any time you want to have a nervous breakdown, just let us know."

"Yeah," said Audrey. "I'll get some potato chips and make a dip, we'll have music and guacamole. But if you wouldn't mind, could you let us know the day before? I don't want to be at the market and miss it all."

"Okay. I promise to notify you in advance."

Dolores stood up and got her handbag. She was very thin and very sad. Her eyes were red and on either side of her head just over her ears were two uneven bald patches of scalp. It was the first time in her life that Joan did not envy a thin person.

They walked Dolores to the door and watched as she got into her car. "Call when you get home," Audrey hollered, and they saw Dolores smile and nod. As soon as the car turned the corner, they went back into the house.

"Poor thing," said Audrey, putting on some water to boil. "Poor thing."

"How does this happen?" asked Joan. "Why does something that starts so hopefully have to end so miserably?"

"Because she's stupid, that's why. Stu Levy could never have done that to me, I'll tell you. If he lived five minutes with me, he'd grab Dolores back so fast that Tuesday would come before Monday."

"Oh, come on, Audrey, it's easy to talk when it isn't happening to you."

"It *wouldn't* happen to me. I wouldn't *let* it happen. I'm too rotten and mean. I'd never allow myself that kind of injury. I'd kill him first."

"Yeah, yeah. You're wonderful. I remember when Melvin went out of town for three days, you couldn't get from here to the bathroom. Stu Levy is gonna be out of town *forever* for poor Dolores. You're full of shit, Audrey."

"You want a coffee or a tea?"

"Coffee—but let me check the cup first."

"It's clean, it's clean. Melvin was here yesterday. He washed everything."

"And that's when you're separated?"

"He's decided to move back in."

"Why?"

"He's not a well man. Here's your coffee."

"Aud?"

"What?"

"Why did Stu leave her?"

"She made him crazy. She's very dependent. Can't make any decisions, and handles everything wrong. He's moved in with a shiksa with four kids."

"Poor Dolores."

"She'll survive if she doesn't kill herself."

"That's logical."

"No, I mean it. She was put away once already."

"In a sanitarium? A loony bin?"

"Yup."

Joan sipped her coffee, lost in thought.

"Aud?"

"What?"

"Will you do me a favor?"

"Depends."

"Will you or won't you?"

"I will, what is it?"

"I want you to promise me that if you ever in this lifetime hear me say 'I'm depressed,' you'll kick my ass from here to Calabasas!"

"Delighted."

Joan put down her half-finished cup of coffee and stood up.

"Good-bye, dreck. I'm going home."

"Good-bye, cunt. I'm glad you came."

They walked together to Joan's car, and even after the car was out of sight, Audrey continued to stand there. She missed Joan already. She missed her intactness and the limits she imposed upon her. She needed the stability, the reality that Joan exuded. Audrey was well aware of her effect on people—and was almost grateful to Joan for liking her anyway. The first time they had gone to the Akron together, Joan almost fainted when Audrey appropriated a goatskin wine carrier and two perfume bottles made in Taiwan.

"You're really crazy, Audrey," Joan gasped when they got back to the car. "Why do you do things like that?"

"Like what?" asked Audrey, giving her one of the Taiwanese perfume bottles.

"Like stealing," said Joan, examining the bottle.

"I don't know. I wanted it."

"So why didn't you *buy* it?"

"I wouldn't spend the money I don't have on crap like that."

Joan stared at her. "I'm not going with you anymore."

"Yes, you will."

"There's something wrong with you, Audrey," Joan said, putting the perfume bottle into her purse.

"But you're here, aren't you?"

"Maybe there's something wrong with me too. Do you do all this for effect? Is it deliberate? Do you really want people to think you're certifiable?"

"Do you think that?"

"I think you're mad."

"But you're here, aren't you?"

Joan started the car and switched on the radio. Audrey immediately turned it off. For a moment they sat and stared at each other.

"You're like Scott," Audrey said calmly. "You see all the shit but you stay."

Joan drove out of the lot and turned onto Sunset.

"I see *beneath* all that shit," said Joan.

"What do you see?"

"More shit."

Audrey laughed and gently smoothed Joan's hair. "But you stay," she said.

In spite of everything, she stayed.

Faintly smiling at the memory, Audrey continued to stand on the curb staring at the empty street until the ringing of her telephone forced her back inside.

9

"Now you are all clouds," said Miss Pamela. "Soft, fluffy, graceful clouds."

Eleven little girls began tiptoeing about the studio, small bodies bending, arms flailing the air, heads moving from side to side, some eyes closed, others open and unseeing, turned inward, lost in a blue sky. They twirled and ran, twirled again, each in her own rhythm, her own interpretation of a cloud.

There were some slim, quick clouds, some stubby, chubby clouds, some awkward and ungainly clouds falling on the floor, dizzy from spinning. Miss Pamela nodded happily, foot tapping, signaling to the accompanist to speed up the tempo. She looked around the room, paused, and advanced on Naomi, who instead of spinning and floating gracefully was stamping and thumping around the room, her hands high over her head, fingers curled, a frown on her intent little face.

"Naomi," she said, smiling kindly, "Miss Pamela told you to be a cloud." Naomi stopped in mid-thump, lowered her hands and looked angrily at the dancing teacher.

"I *am* being a cloud," she said, annoyed and embarrassed at the interruption.

"You weren't floating, darling," crooned the teacher. "Clouds float."

"Well, I don't care. I'm not that kind of cloud."

"What kind of cloud are you, dear?"

"I'm a storm cloud, a black storm cloud, with rain in it."

"Very good, Naomi. Please continue."

But Naomi would not. Mortified at being singled out, she ran over to the bench which ran along one wall and crept under it, turning her back on the class and sticking her thumb in her mouth.

Miss Pamela glanced over at the group of mothers watching the class and gazed meaningfully at Joan. Joan frowned at the teacher and looked at her unhappy child sitting under the bench, thumb in mouth, head lowered. All the other children were still floating and spinning, being perfect clouds, while hers was sitting under a bench.

Myrna patted Joan's hand in silent sympathy, her eyes glued to Cecily, her daughter, now swaying from side to side in cloudlike concentration.

"Aren't you going to go to her?" asked Audrey, who had missed nothing.

"No."

"I would."

"I'm not you, thank God."

"Why won't you?"

"It'll just embarrass her even more. Naomi doesn't like to be singled out, except for glory."

"Why is she so strange?" Audrey asked, smiling at Denise, now being a leaf.

"Shut up, Audrey."

Joan glanced at the ten other women absorbed in watching the recital. Most pretended not to have noticed. Carol Lighter, feeling Joan's eye on her, looked up and gave her a malicious smile.

"Bitch," Joan thought, "you have a very homely, klutzy daughter. In a few years you won't be smiling."

80

Immediately ashamed of herself, she turned away.

Miss Pamela's school of classic interpretive dance was *the* dancing school in Beverly Hills. Everybody who had a daughter sent her there to dance out her fantasy, learn grace, and prepare for Miss Pamela's more advanced class in Junior Ballet I. There was a waiting list a mile long, and mothers began registering their daughters years in advance to assure them a definite place, and a firm, disciplined body. Miss Pamela was a living example of the benefits of a lifetime of exercise and dance. She was fifty-two years old and looked better than Joan—bodywise, that is. "Start your daughters in the classic discipline of the dance at an early age," advised the brochure. "Have you ever seen a dedicated dancer whose body has disintegrated into flabby obesity?"

The mothers of Beverly Hills were passionate in their desire to raise beautiful, tight-assed daughters. They reacted with horror to the possibility of condemning their female children to a lifetime of flabby obesity and flocked in droves to Miss Pamela, who assured them absolutely that only she, of all the dance instructors in Beverly Hills and surrounding communities, had the skill and training to avert the catastrophe. Miss Pamela had a versatile establishment. She offered classes in interpretive dance, ballet, jazz, tap and exercise. She had made a fortune and was expanding to form a class in adult dance and mother-daughter fitness. If the demand were sufficiently great, she would even add professional voice and drama instructors to her already large staff. Miss Pamela had struck gold in gold-struck Beverly Hills.

Joan stared at her child, wasting a five-dollar lesson under the bench. Why the hell couldn't she at least sit *on* the bench? As she watched, Miss Pamela approached Naomi and, bending gracefully from the waist, whispered something in her ear. Immediately the child removed her thumb from her mouth and followed Miss Pamela back onto the floor. Soon she was an east wind, wafting with the others. Joan sighed in relief. She

81

hoped Naomi would cooperate enough to continue through the lifetime course offered at Miss Pamela's and never have to agonize over her inner thighs.

Joan herself had never been to a dancing school. Her mother had never given a passing thought to the possibility that she might someday weep over sagging buttocks. She desired only that Joan eat her dinner and marry a professional man—Jewish, of course. She expected Joan to finish college, marry immediately after graduation and give her some grandchildren, who "I hope don't aggravate you the way you aggravated me." This was in direct contradiction to the threats she had heaped on Joan's head when she was disobedient. So important is marriage and motherhood to Jewish families that even curses glorified it. "May you grow up and get married and have children who do to you what you are doing to me," she would shriek at a tiny Joan. "Now finish your vegetables." Never would she wish on her these dreadful children without first mentioning the "grow up and get married" part.

When Joan was little, all mothers were definite about the proper order of things. Unlike Joan, so often unsure, they always seemed to be certain of what was right and what was wrong, what was good, what was bad, and what was what. Joan's mother believed that only food prepared at home was safe to eat and, as a result, Joan never tasted the joys of a sidewalk-stand hamburger (God only knows what they put into it, or if they wash their hands), or ate in anything other than a Chinese restaurant, and that only twice, and at great risk.

Her mother knew for a fact that if you wanted things done right, you did them yourself, and they therefore rarely had household help. To this day Joan paled at the sight of a dusty venetian blind. Her mother informed her that high heels ruined one's arches, lipstick worn too early made the lips turn white, makeup and Hershey bars caused pimples, and girls who were fresh to their parents died young. She said a messy room indicated a messy mind, and warned Joan never to eat
82

standing up or she'd get piano legs, and to wipe herself from front to back, twice, with neatly folded toilet paper, preferably white.

Joan never saw a movie until she was eight because of the unsupervised children there who sneezed in people's faces and spread germs. When she went to summer camp, her mother wept and cautioned her not to drown or anything foolish like that. She alerted her to the dangers of strange men, fighting with boys or with girls who weren't Jewish, getting lost in department stores, not brushing her teeth, getting a draft, disobeying a teacher, swallowing cherry pits, and later on, reading *Forever Amber* or *The Amboy Dukes*. Those last two, she informed her, "will make you old before your time." Not getting a good night's sleep would do likewise. She watched Joan like a hawk to ensure that she was standing up straight and advised her continually to "modulate your voice." She praised her for being an avid reader and then, grabbing away the book, would order her to "go outside and get fresh air."

When Joan graduated from college and informed her mother that she was off to graduate school, her mother told her to "marry a rich doctor and let *him* send you to graduate school." But she also kissed her and told her she was proud. "Just don't read so much. You don't have a face for glasses." Despite the fact that she didn't want to, Joan had believed everything her mother said. Even now, she couldn't rid herself of the notion that the reason she needed glasses was because, despite her mother's repeated warnings, she had continued to read so much. And in poor light yet.

Today Joan mocked the admonishments of her mother, but ached for the confidence with which they were delivered. Of course, she disciplined her children, but often doubted the validity of her stand. And she frequently allowed them to answer back, a crime of the first water, something her parents had never permitted *her* to do. Was her permissiveness based on conviction, or on cowardice? She didn't know. Despite her smug contempt for the methods her mother employed while raising her, Joan found herself repeating her mother's dictums to her children. The day she heard herself tell her sons that "every time you say a dirty word, God writes it down in his big black book" was the day she conceded defeat.

She tried to be very careful of how she spoke to her children, knowing that it would stay with them forever, as it had with her—certain that her words would echo down the centuries and into the ears of her children's children and her children's children's children as centuries of words had echoed into hers. There would be mothers along the way who would make valiant attempts to erase this self-perpetuating, timeless tape, but they would be as unsuccessful as she to alter the basic text. Joan realized more and more that this was the sticking stuff, the vital adhesive which binds child to parent, parent to child. She sighed. It was a heavy, very heavy business.

Miss Pamela's class of six-year-old interpretive dancers was ready to perform the finale. The piano played a cheery march and the children formed a lopsided circle around one little girl. There in the middle stood the righteous Naomi, trying hard not to smile. Joan beamed proudly as the dance began. She realized what the all-knowing Miss Pamela had whispered into her daughter's ear. She had selected Naomi for glory. She had made her a star. Joan heaped silent blessings on the head of Miss Pamela as she watched her daughter interpret whatever it was that the music inspired in her rhythmic little soul.

After about three minutes, Audrey stirred. She was not content. "Denise," she blurted out, "you get into the middle too, with Naomi."

Denise, the carbon-copy kindred spirit and exhibitionist alter ego of her mother, equally noisy and demanding, who managed to stay just this side of obnoxious, but barely, scurried to obey. But it was not to be— Miss Pamela intercepted the rush and returned a protesting Denise to her original position. Naomi spun and dipped, twirled and swayed. If a six-year-old is capable of orgasm, then Naomi was fast approaching *le moment critique*. She was in Lollipop Land, and so was Joan.

"Joan," hissed Audrey.

"Shush. If you're going to tell me Miss Pamela sucks, forget it. I intend to put that dear lady in my will."

"Am I in your will?"

"No, you're in my way. Now be quiet. I want to watch this."

Audrey subsided and sulked until class ended. She collected an equally morose Denise and put on her shoes in uncharacteristic silence. She waited while Joan gushed her thanks into the ear of a gracious Miss Pamela.

Joan said a pleasant good-bye to Gloria and Myrna—and even extended herself to include the bitchy Carol Lighter, who was preparing her daughter, Stacey, and Sharon's daughter, Kim, for departure. Even Carol's nasty remark about Naomi's performance could not upset Joan.

"Your Nancy is quite a pain, isn't she?"

"No, Carol dear. Getting stuck in the eye with a pointy stick is quite a pain."

"And so is talking to you," interjected Audrey. "Come on, Joan. Let's take the girls to Baskin-Robbins."

"Okay. Good-bye, Carol. And my daughter's name is Naomi, by the way. Not Nancy. Of course, I can see how you might forget—you've only known her three years. Oh, and please say hello to Sharon for me."

Carol gave a slight confused nod and turned away. Audrey grabbed Joan's arm, and with the girls walking and bickering noisily behind them, they left the studio. They piled the children into the back of Joan's wagon and set off for Baskin-Robbins. Conversation was difficult because the girls were making so much noise.

"You two better shut up," threatened Audrey, "or you won't get ice cream."

Joan stopped her car in front of 31 Flavors, directly under a NO STOPPING AT ANY TIME sign, and Audrey and the girls got out.

"Hurry up," said Joan. "I'll circle the block and pick you up—and you better be ready."

"Why can't you wait here?" asked Audrey.

"Do you see that sign?"

"Oh, fuck the sign."

"Just get the damn ice cream and be out here when I come around. Hurry."

Miraculously, Joan only had to circle once. Naomi and Denise, clutching double-scoop cones, climbed into the car. Audrey, carrying two cups, handed one to Joan through the open window and then got in herself.

"What's this?"

"Seltzer. It's good for you."

"How am I supposed to drive holding a cup of seltzer?" Joan asked, maneuvering the car back into the traffic with one hand.

"Can you stop at Safeway a minute?"

"No."

"Joan, there's no food in my house."

"Is that my problem too?"

"Why are you so mean?"

"Because I don't like you. I *never* liked you."

The girls had stopped their quibbling and were licking their cones and listening to their mothers with delight.

"You *love* me, bitch."

"Uh-uh. I love chopped liver. I *hate* you."

"So, why am I here?"

"Because I'm a retarded person."

"Joan, I'll only take one minute, I swear to you."

"No, I'm late as it is. The only thing that takes you one minute is having sex with Melvin."

Audrey turned and threw a quick glance at the girls. They were still licking, still enrapt.

"Joan, I must get to Safeway."

"I'll drop you off."

"Then who'll take me home?"

"You'll walk."

"With a thousand bags of groceries and Denise?"

"Leave Denise."

86

"Joan, you must."

"Audrey, leave me alone."

"I would do it for you."

"That possibility will never arise. It's an easy promise."

"Joan—"

"Audrey, leave me alone or I swear I'll spill this seltzer on your head."

"You wouldn't dare."

"Don't push me, Audrey."

Naomi poked her mother. "Do it, Mommy," she said.

"Do it," echoed Denise.

"Thank you, Denise," said Audrey sarcastically. "What time is it?"

"Five-thirty."

"Fine. Drop me at Dolores'."

"Why? Did she suddenly open a supermarket?"

"Hah, very funny. I'll get her to take me to Safeway."

"Oh, Audrey, you're really rotten, you know?"

"Not as rotten as you."

"How can you put her out like that? You know she works all day."

"Well, she's home by now. You won't take me, so I have to get her to do it."

"That's wonderful, that's beautiful—now *I'm* the villain."

"Among other things."

Joan glared at her. "You're really a bitch, Audrey."

"No, I'm not. She loves me, and she loves to schlepp me."

"Yeah, like she loves acne."

"So *you* take me."

"No, Audrey. And don't ask me again."

"Are you going to take me to Safeway or not?"

"Not."

"Fine. Don't take me. I'll get Dolores."

Joan looked out the window. Traffic was very heavy. Rush hour was upon them. She was hot, she was tired, she hated seltzer.

"Audrey, you will not bother Dolores."

"I'll bother whom I please."

"I'm warning you, Audrey."

"You can stand on your head for all I care. Drop me at Dolores'."

Joan turned and dumped her practically full seven-ounce cup of seltzer on Audrey's head. She took her eyes off the road long enough to enjoy the sight of Audrey, drenched and amazed, blinking seltzer out of her eyes. Naomi and Denise exploded with gleeful shrieks.

Recovering immediately, Audrey returned the favor, flinging seltzer in Joan's grinning face. From the back of the car came a renewed explosion of delighted laughter.

"Idiot," sputtered Joan. "Can't you see I'm driving?"

"I can't see anything. I've got seltzer in my eyes."

Joan pulled over as soon as traffic allowed. She and Audrey, hair sopping, wet shirts and pants plastered to their bodies, eyelashes beaded with seltzer, stared silently at each other. Slowly they began to smile.

"We're bigger babies than those drecks back there," Joan said, indicating the convulsed children. "How can two grown women act like this?"

"Do it again, do it again!" roared the drecks.

"Joan," said Audrey softly, "you really are my friend, aren't you?"

"I don't understand how the hell it happened, but I suppose I am."

They stared at each other again, still smiling, and after a moment Joan turned and started the car.

"But not," she interrupted, as Audrey began to speak, " a good enough friend to schlepp you to Safeway."

"Bitch," laughed Audrey.

"Cunt," whispered Joan.

"I think I love you, you rotten shit," said Audrey. Joan was silent. "Do you love me?" asked Audrey.

"No."

"You don't?"

"No, I hate you."

"The world should hate me the way you do, shtunk," Audrey said, laughing.

Joan turned and grinned at her.

"Keep your eyes on the road, stupid," snapped Audrey. "Here's my house."

Joan pulled over, her motor running. "Get out," she said. "I'm wasting gas."

Audrey dragged Denise from the car. "Good-bye, Joan."

"Good-bye, Audrey."

"I'll call you."

"Call me what?"

Audrey turned, Denise in tow, and walked up the stairs and into her house.

"Mommy," said Naomi, as they pulled away from the curb, "do you really hate Audrey?"

"No, cutie."

"Do you like her?"

"I believe I do. For some strange, unfathomable, mysterious reason, I do."

"Mommy?"

"What?"

"Is Audrey your friend?"

"Yes, sweetie. Audrey's my friend."

10

By now Eric considered Audrey a dangerous woman. There were times, after Joan hung up the phone after an hour's conversation with Audrey, when she would turn on him and accuse him angrily of not being home enough, not taking any responsibility for the children, of having phony and unfair priorities. "Audrey knows many people in the business," she would shrill, "big people, big writers and producers, and they all seem to make time for their families. They have weekends together, vacations. None of them work seven days and seven nights a week like you do. The boys are twelve years old and you've never once taken them for a haircut."

That would enrage Eric and he, normally the most gentle and generous of spirits, would yell in a fury, "Fuck Audrey! I don't want you to speak to that dangerous, jealous, destructive bitch ever again. I mean it, Joan!"

And for the moment he did. Generally, however, he was aware that Audrey was very important to Joan. She bolstered and flattered her, amused and confounded her. They had fun together. Somehow Audrey made Joan feel like something of value. She gave her a sense of personhood, of validity. Among all her friends, it was only when she spoke to Audrey that Joan did not feel the need to censor herself. She could say anything she damn pleased and Audrey would still like her. And it was for all that that Eric tolerated Audrey Miller. Joan's involvement with Audrey, Nan, Dolores and various new names that cropped up periodically mostly pleased him. Eric became uncomfortable when Joan laid her unrest on his head, and these friends helped dissipate and diffuse her difficulties. The time she spent discussing vague discontents with them meant fewer distractions for him.

It was also a fact that the problems of her friends seemed to minimize her own. She would listen and advise and cluck sympathetically—and then hang up and count her blessings. She would keep Eric up to date on the soap-opera lives of her friends and amuse him with anecdotal accounts of their founderings. Nan, he learned, was, despite her success, so disillusioned with her marriage that she was seeking counseling. Dolores had a job—not a good job, but a job. Audrey, of course, was Audrey. She needed money, owed money, borrowed money and cried "Why don't I have money? I want to live at the beach. For that I need money."

There was a new friend now—Pauline somebody, who had all the money Audrey would have wished. Pauline had enough money to buy thirty-six beach houses. She was a Cinderella story, this Pauline, a little girl from Queens, New York, whose father never earned more than a hundred dollars a week. Somehow, she had contrived to marry a wealthy Middle Eastern type and lived in a house the size of Radio City Music Hall. She had a son the age of Joan's boys, about whom

91

she complained incessantly. She also had a daughter a little older than Naomi. She also could hardly speak the English language.

"It's funny," Joan said to Eric. "Life's ironies are absolute proof positive that God watches television."

"Hmm," said Eric.

"Pauline has all this money and can't even speak properly."

"What has that got to do with it?"

"Well, it just strikes me funny. Do you know what she said the other day?"

"What?"

"She told me that Rosamanda had trouble cutting her six-year molders."

"Molders?"

"Yeah, molders. On her wall hangs a 'pitcher,' and she likes to 'axe' questions. She does things on the 'spare of the minute,' and her uncle died of a 'blood clock.'"

Eric smiled. "I love it," he said.

"So do I. She's a perfect character. A darling, innocent, appealing, sweetheart of a girl. We were sitting in her living room, which is the size of a football field. The entire house is filled with treasures. There are rugs on the floors that are indescribably beautiful. I mean, you walk on hundreds of thousands of dollars every time you take a step. She has magnificent vases, Sèvres vases. You know what she calls them?"

"What?"

"Her Serves. 'These are my Serves,' she says. Pauline can also make any drink in the world. Ask her for a dead yellow elephant fizz and she'll make it for you. In her blender yet, with crushed ice. I adore her."

"So?"

"So we were in her living room, drinking—I've become a drinker since I met her—and all of a sudden she says, 'I know you must think we're very rich, right?' And she flings out her arm to indicate the room. 'Yeah,'

I say, 'I did sort of get that impression.' 'Well, we're really not,' she says to me. 'I mean Maurice'—that's her husband—'Maurice can make a deal and get, oh, about six, seven hundred thousand on it, but then that's it. He might not make another deal for three, four months.' Eric, it was so perfect, I can't tell you. Isn't that something? Imagine, they actually have to make do with six, seven hundred thousand for three, four months. I treasure that line, I really do. I treasure *her*."

Eric nodded, smiling. "There's a whole world out there, m'darlin'. A strange and wonderful world."

"Do you know what else?"

"What?"

"Another day, another drink, and she was telling me about a lawsuit Maurice is involved in. 'I hope he doesn't settle for only six million,' she says to me. 'Why not?' I ask her. 'What's wrong with six million?' 'Well,' she says, 'six million—do you know how fast that goes?' Fifty dollars I'm acquainted with—even a bit more. But Pauline, who maybe has heard the name Harry Truman but can't tell you for sure who he was—*she* knows how fast six million goes. It's amazing."

Eric rose and kissed her cheek. "I've got to go, my love."

"Oh, shit. When will you be home?"

"I don't know, hon. I'll call you."

"Don't you want to hear about Myrna's aunt who's been driving for twenty-six years and has never made a left turn?"

"I just did," he said, kissing the top of her head and walking to the door. "See you later."

Joan began clearing the table. She did it very methodically, very irritably. It was at times like this that she regretted having fired her live-in maid. As she explained to Nan, "I couldn't stand it anymore. My happiest days were those when the maid was *off*." Nan, who couldn't do without her Serena, was curious.

"Then who does everything?" she asked.

"I do," Joan replied. "My mother would throw up, but I don't care. No, I *do* care, but not enough to have anyone sleeping in. Their very presence annoys me. I would take my irritation with the maid out on the kids. You're never home, so it doesn't bother you. I'm *always* home and it makes me crazy."

Joan stacked the dishwasher, wiped the tile counter and went off to fight with her daughter about going to bed. The boys were doing their homework to the deafening strains of their favorite rock group. "Shut that thing off," she screamed. "How the hell can you concentrate with all that noise?"

They looked at her blankly. "It's all right, Mom. We like it."

"Do you also like getting a 'C' in social studies? Shut it off. Naomi has to go to sleep now anyway. And don't say, 'Oh, shit.' Just do it."

"You say shit," they retorted. "You say lots of things. You say the 'F' word. Why can't we?"

"I also pee sitting down. When are you going to realize that you boys cannot do everything I do? Huh? When?"

"Where's Dad?"

"Daddy's working."

"Shit."

After the children were put away for the night, Joan lay down on top of her bedspread, clicked the remote to start the TV and lit a cigarette. She picked up a book and began to read. When the phone rang, she answered it before it could ring twice.

"Hi, Joanie. How are you?"

"Okay, Nannie. How are you?"

"Lousy."

"What's the matter?"

"You know."

"Nan, stop it. You're successful, you've lost forty-eight pounds, you have kids who love to do compositions, so just stop it."

94

"I want Richard to love me."

"Nan, this is dangerous. Forget crazy Richard, you're a married person."

"Oh, Joan. I love him. I can't help it."

"This business with Richard...an affair is one thing, getting emotionally involved is another. Why are you doing this?"

Joan heard Nan's other phone ringing in the background. "Joan, can I call you back?"

"Sure."

Joan hung up and leaned against her raised pillow. Ever since Nan had written a best-seller, lost all that weight, styled her hair and met Richard Brown, she had been living her life on the edge of her seat. Richard was all the men who had previously been out of Nan's league. He was bright and funny and very handsome. He was the kind of guy Nan had wanted to bring to her senior prom. The kind of man who would never look at a fat, funny, not pretty Jewish girl. The kind of guy who had wrecked her adolescence by not being a part of it. Nan had always wanted to marry. She had dreaded receiving her college diploma in a hand that had no engagement ring on it. When Carl Blake came into her life and seemed interested in remaining there, she grabbed on to his offer of marriage the way a starving man grabs a hamburger, with overwhelming relief and salivating gratitude. They were married the first Saturday after graduation, in the fanciest temple on Long Island, with a sumptuous reception and a dinner menu that offered a choice of three main courses. She married Carl for two reasons: one was that her girl friend said he was cute, and the other because she feared no one else would ever ask her. She began married life with the sinking suspicion that she had embarked upon the turbulent seas of matrimony without any Dramamine.

She had always yearned for popularity, for men to call her in September to ask if she was busy on New

95

Year's Eve. She wanted passionate love, frenzied kisses, filled-up date books. Now she wanted to do it all over again...right. Success and money and being thin had altered her perceptions and raised her timid expectations. She wanted what she had never had or ever hoped to have, a Richard Brown. And she was, at last, able to interest a Richard Brown. Nan couldn't stop talking about him and continually sang his praises to a disapproving Joan.

"Oh, Joan, he has everything. He's handsome, he's bright, he's funny—"

"He's Catholic," Joan interrupted.

"He has such *style*, Joan."

"He has no money, Nan."

"I love him."

"Be careful," said Joan. "You're a married person."

Richard gave Nan the rush and knocked her on her ass. She arose gasping and grasping. When she went to New York on business, they dated and laughed and loved and teased. Back in California, she sat with shining eyes and hovered over the telephone. He flew in to see her, and Nan discovered what it felt like to walk on air and not give a damn about scripts or deadlines, which put Teddy in a snit. Carl was totally unaware that this handsome, Catholic southerner was destined not only to screw his wife, but also screw up his life. Richard had never kept a job for more than two years— either leaving on his own or being asked to. At present, aside from doing an occasional free-lance article for whatever publication would hire him, he was unemployed. He and Nan had met at a cocktail party.

"So you're the famous Nan Blake," he said.

"Yes," she replied, looking up at his face and feeling faint. "Do you only talk to famous people?"

"Famous and beautiful," he corrected.

"Darn," she said. "I guess that's that."

"Why?"

"You left out sexy."

Richard smiled and Nan felt her stomach jump. "Do

you want to do it in my car?" he asked.

"What kind of car do you have?"

"A rented one."

"Okay," she said. "Call my secretary."

Richard signaled to a waiter, who brought over two glasses of champagne. He handed one to Nan, who took a long sip and tried to calm down. Richard offered her a cigarette.

"No, thanks," she said. "I never smoke with strangers."

"Will you have dinner with me?"

"Will you tell me your name?"

"Richard Brown."

"What kind of a name is that?"

"A rented one."

Nan smiled. "Are you married, Richard?"

"No," he said. "Are you?"

"Very."

"Good," said Richard Brown. "Do you like Chinese?"

What Nan, in her first flush of overdue realization, had forgotten was that even popular girls, even girls who date every Saturday night, can get their hearts broken. She was realizing it now and taking Valium instead of vitamins.

Joan went into the bathroom and began to fill the tub. She poured some dishwashing detergent in to make bubbles and began to undress. Before getting into her bath, she returned to the bedroom, got her book and the telephone and carried them back with her to the bathroom. Everywhere Joan had lived, she always ordered a twenty-five-foot cord for the telephone nearest the bathroom. Talking on the phone while sitting on the toilet or in the tub was a pastime she enjoyed in equal proportion to the frustration she experienced when she heard the ringing of an unreachable phone. Even when she had her own apartment, before she married Eric, she had a telephone with a cord long enough to reach the john.

She put the phone down on the floor where it was

easily reachable from the tub and placed her book beside it. She climbed in and leaned back into the bubbles with a sigh of pure contentment. She closed her eyes and, with her feet, stuffed a washcloth against the overflow drain. Joan liked high, white water. She picked up her book and read while the bubbles around her slowly burst and disappeared. As a child, she used to ask her mother where the bubbles went. She still sometimes wondered. By the time the phone rang, the bath water was patchy. Joan put her book down and reached out a dripping hand for the receiver.

"Joan?"

"Yes, Nannie?"

"No, it's Myrna."

"Myrna, how are you?"

"Fine, fine. Listen, Joan, I'm giving a little party for Gloria. Can you and Eric come?"

"*I* can, I'm always free, but I'm never sure about Eric. What's the occasion?"

"We're celebrating Gloria's divorce."

"You're kidding!" Joan sat straight up, almost dropping the receiver into the tub. "When did it happen? I knew they were rocky, but I didn't realize it had gone that far." She paused. "I'm really sorry to hear it."

"Don't be sorry. Gloria's very happy. She's looking for a house and she's seeing a nice guy, so don't be sorry. She's cool."

"When is the party?"

"You'll receive an invitation in the mail. It's got all the information. I just wanted to let you know. Try to come."

"Yeah. Thanks, Myrna. Oh, Myrna?

"Yeah?"

"Does one bring a divorce gift? Is it like a shower? Do you have a cake with a jagged split through the middle?"

"Very funny. See you then."

No sooner had she replaced the receiver than the phone rang again.

"Joanie, it's Nan."

"Hi, Nannie. Do you remember Myrna Roth from nursery school?"

"Vaguely. Why?"

"She just called to tell me that Gloria and Jerry are getting divorced."

"Well, I'm not surprised."

"She's going with someone else already."

"Another actor?"

"Who knows? How are you? Feeling better?"

"Worse. I just had a terrible fight with Carl."

"Oh, Nannie."

"I have nothing to say to him. He complains that I'm never home."

"Well, you're not."

"I hate to come home. He just irritates me, so I deliberately stay out longer than I have to, in order to avoid being with him."

Joan sighed, troubled. "What does your marriage counselor say?"

"I don't know. He says we need more communication. Carl is just so—so dull. I don't enjoy being with him."

"Especially with Richard in the picture."

"I guess so—but *he's* driving me crazy, too."

"Nan, what do you want?"

"Richard."

"That's not exactly the proper attitude for saving your marriage."

"Maybe it's not worth saving."

"Nan, you need Carl. The kids need him. What the hell are you doing?" She sat up, splashing water on the blue bathroom carpet. "Look, Richard's giving you a hard time. You'll end up with nothing. What are you doing?"

"Joanie, I have to go."

"Carl just came in?"

"Yes. Talk to you later. Bye."

Joan hung up the phone and shivered. The water was now cold, the bubbles completely gone. She stood

99

up, wrapped herself in a towel and stepped out of the tub. She dried herself quickly, slathered moisturizer on her face, ran into the bedroom and slid swiftly into bed. With a curious mixture of dejection and excitement, she clicked on the news and waited impatiently for Eric, dear Eric, *her* Eric, to come home.

11

The following day, while speaking to Audrey on the phone, Joan began to muse about her disconnected life.

"I lead," she said, "an ambiguous existence. Last night I'm at a glamorous Hollywood party, rubbing elbows with famous stars, being served by butlers with white gloves, in fabulous homes that would sell for over a million smackatoons in today's market—and today, this morning, I'm up to those same elbows, cleaning out a toilet bowl, or separating white wash from colored, or comparing the prices on two cans of tuna fish. It's really weird."

"How come you never take me to those parties?" Audrey demanded.

"And do you know what I once did?" asked Joan, ignoring the question. "My dryer broke down and I hung all my wash around the pool. I kept that wash out there even after it was dry because it struck me as being so ludicrous. It amused me for days. I managed to turn some of the highest-priced real estate in the world into a crummy Brooklyn neighborhood with one load of wet wash."

"I take you everywhere, but not once did you ever take me to a big party. I hate you."

"I have dinner with some of the best-known performers in the world, and I'm wearing underpants that cost three for a dollar."

"I got house seats for *Chorus Line* for you and your drecks. Do you know how impossible that was? And do I get to go to your fancy parties? Thank you, Joan. I'll remember that."

"What do you want from me, Audrey? How can I get you to a party like that? We are invited because of Eric. Be realistic."

"It's that rotten Eric. He's the one. Why doesn't he want to take me?"

"Well, you're not exactly inconspicuous, Audrey. You do tend to be an embarrassment."

"I embarrass Eric?"

"Well, the possibility exists."

"What does he know? P-yew to him."

"P-yew to him. I love that."

"All he knows to do is work and fuck."

"He knows to eat an artichoke."

"Wonderful."

"So?"

"So nothing. I'm hanging you up now."

"Why? Where are you going?"

"I'm going to the bathroom to take a thousand aspirins. I have a headache and my leg hurts."

"You're a mess, Audrey."

"You think I'm dying?"

"I do."

"So do I."

"Okay, have a good time."

"I have something to tell you."

"So tell."

"I started writing something."

"Go on."

"While Melvin and I were separated, I would get up and eat chocolate cake."

"That's nice."

102

"One night I got up and instead of eating chocolate cake, I wrote letters to my children, to Mendy."

"How come?"

"There wasn't any cake. Anyway, I now have twenty-seven letters."

"But no stamps?"

"I read some to Dolores and to Roger and a few other people. They think I should publish them."

"How come you didn't read any to me?"

"Because you're so rotten you would probably laugh."

"I'd love to hear them, Aud. Seriously."

"You would? Really?"

"Why not? Call me tonight after I put away my kids and you'll read to me."

"Why shouldn't I have a book? Maybe that book will get me a beach house."

"Maybe so. Everybody else is writing books."

"I'll call you later, bitch. *You* should write something too. You're getting fat from doing nothing."

"I really needed to hear that. Thank you."

Joan hung up the phone and made herself a cup of coffee. She sat down to drink it and read the newspaper. After a while, disgusted by her aimlessness, feeling worthless and unproductive, bored by the quiet and oppressive sameness of her kitchen and the meaningless sloth of her empty days, no longer excused because of chores imposed by pre-school children, alone doing nothing while all around her people were producing, she hastily folded the half-read paper and began to pace, cup in hand, around the house.

When she got to the bedroom, she realized she was crying. She opened her closet door, on the inside of which hung a full-length mirror. She put down her coffee cup, took off her bathrobe and stood naked before the mirror, looking at herself. She did this in trepidation, fully aware that she would see herself not as the reality, but as colored by her own feelings and unhappy—she hoped momentary—self-image. For ten minutes, through her tears, she examined a thirty-six-year-old ruin seen in a spotted, smudged, slightly

103

chipped reflecter of subjective truth. She ran her hands over breasts once perky and proud, now lying there on her chest, lethargic and drained, drooping melons withered on the vine. Her stomach, once so flat and hard and concave, jiggled and quivered, flaunting its stretchmarks with every ragged breath, threatening to spill over onto her white, pudgy, cellulite-creased thighs.

Slowly, she turned her sluggish body, now twenty pounds overweight, and strained for a glimpse of her flat, fat behind, noting almost clinically the folds of flesh rolling and bulging along her rib cage. Then she looked up and met her wet, red, pain-filled eyes in the mirror. Her uncombed hair hung split-ended and limp, one strand pointing spitefully at the groove between her shaggy, unplucked eyebrows. This unfortunate shape, this result of years of indolent neglect, was now the flaccid and crumbling temple of what used to be a graceful, butterfly soul.

Numbly she pushed the closet door shut and, still weeping and fumbling, threw on her bathrobe inside out. She sat on her bed and lit a cigarette with clumsy hands, mumbling disjointed words of comfort to her shaken ego, filled with a frantic need to deny the picture she had painted with her eyes on that treacherous, and surely false, piece of glass.

Recalling how bravely she had resolved never again to sink into the unworthiness of depression, she wiped her cheeks with the back of her hands and smiled ruefully at her bout with self-pity—neither winner nor loser in this hopeless race in which the prize is paralyzing self-delusion.

She splashed cold water on her face, furious with herself. Why, she wondered, if she was reduced to self-delusion, must it be such *negative* self-delusion? Why couldn't she have given herself a slightly overweight but still *attractive* self-portrait? "I must really be extraordinarily disappointed with myself," she said aloud, stepping into a pair of admittedly tight, but still size twelve pants.

She combed her hair and dabbed on some lipstick. She took a deep breath and began to brush her hair. She was appalled at the extent of her dissatisfaction. "Dayenu," she scolded herself. "Dayenu, you stupid horse's ass." She put down her hairbrush and left the bathroom. She ran through her litany of bummer-dispelling charms and was suddenly struck by the realization that she probably wouldn't be able to feel this awful if everything else weren't so good.

She was a housewife, just a housewife. Not a doctor, not an architect—a housewife. So what? So Audrey was trying to get a book together! Audrey. Even Audrey. Audrey was just a housewife, trying to write a book. Joan was just a housewife—trying not to mind.

The night before, at the party, she had been talking with a record producer who laughed at every line.

"What do you do?" he asked.

"I'm a housewife."

"Oh, come on," he replied, "you're not just a housewife. What do you really do? I know—I bet you're a comedy writer. You're a comedy writer, right?"

"No, I'm a comedy housewife. See ya," and she walked away before he threw his next sentence, which was sure to be, "Well, you really ought to write. You're very funny."

Nan introduced her to the wife of one of her colleagues. "She just submitted a *Rhoda* script. Why don't you talk to her?"

Joan did. They talked about *Rhoda*, and after Joan snapped in answer to the woman's question, "Yes, of course I work. I'm a housewife," they didn't talk much longer. The bitch was too full of herself.

On the way home Eric had asked her why she was so quiet.

"Everybody thinks being just a housewife is shit."

"So why don't you do something? Why don't you write?"

She had never been tempted to hit Eric before, but she was then. Instead, she scrunched down in the car seat and looked out the window at the lights on the

105

Sunset Strip, squinting her eyes to make them blur, feeling the wrinkles pop out on her lowly housewife brow.

12

It was now ten-thirty and Audrey's line had been busy since eight forty-five. Joan lifted the receiver and dialed.

"Operator, I need to make an emergency breakthrough—224-1906—Joan Brenner...She won't accept? Operator, ask her again, please. Tell her the baby is coming and I'm all alone with no hot water. Yes. I'll wait, but hurry, honey...Audrey? What's the matter with you, putz? Who have you been on with for two hours?"

"I'm on a toll call to El Monte. There's a printer there who doesn't want to do my book—but he will."

"Audrey, you need more than twenty-seven letters for a book."

"I know. I'm writing more, don't worry. Where are the letters you wrote your boys in camp? I need them."

"I'll look. Listen, you want to go to a party tonight?"

"Maybe."

"You want to date me?"

"What party?"

"Myrna Roth from nursery school is throwing a dinner divorce party for Gloria Chase. Eric is working, and he wouldn't go anyway."

"You asked that rotten Eric first—before you asked me?"

"I realize I've been behaving strangely lately."

"You like him better than *me?*"

"Much. Look, do you want to go or not?

"My foot hurts and I'm having bad doodies."

"Good-bye, Audrey. You always complain that I never take you to any parties. So now I want to take you and you give me excretory excuses. Would you believe I don't give a shit about your doodies?"

"What time is the party? You know it takes me a week to pull myself together."

"Seven-thirty."

"What are you wearing? Your usual horribleness? Look, Joan, if you wear your red with the birds, I'm not going."

"I'll wear what I want—I don't know yet and it's none of your fucking business."

"You'd better be nice to me, bitch. I'm having a book and I'm gonna be a star."

"Yeah, fine. I'll pick you up at seven-fifteen."

Joan scurried through her day. She marketed, picked up some pants for the boys, sorted the wash for her evidently color-blind cleaning lady, dealt with huge decisions like whether to buy the blouse now or wait until it was marked down, took the kids to their various lessons after school, prepared a hurried dinner, quickly cleared and cleaned the kitchen, ran down the list of bedtime instructions for Eric, who was working at home tonight, applied new nail polish over her old, did a quick pressing job on her birds outfit (fuck Audrey), put her hair in electric rollers and finally sank gratefully into her bath.

From time to time one or all of the kids came to pound on the locked bathroom door, either to retrieve something of urgent importance they thought might be in there or to inform her that they just remembered they needed to bring such-and-such to school tomorrow,

108

would she please get out of the tub and buy it for them *now*.

She howled at them to go away and leave her alone. "Tell Daddy!" she yelled. "Tell Daddy how a twelve-year-old boy who knew two weeks ago that he needed to bring a compass to school tomorrow suddenly just remembered. Get away from me."

No sooner was he gone than Naomi came sobbing to the door, lay down on the floor and peered through the crack under the door. "Mommy," she wailed, injustice in every sob, "all the kids are allowed to stay up for *Kotter*. Why am I the only one? Why?"

"Naomi," Joan said quietly, menacingly, "Naomi, get away from that door, because if I have to get out of this tub," and her voice rose to a shriek, "I promise you such a kinock that they'll find pieces of you in Westwood. Go to Daddy."

"Mommy," Naomi wept on, fearless, "Daddy said ask you. Please, Mommy. Oh, please."

"Leave me alone. We'll see. Can't I ever take a bath in peace? Get away now."

Joan tried to relax. She leaned back, consciously attempting to rid herself of tension. She and Eric were fond of joking that the only reason they stayed together was because neither one of them wanted custody. Through the walls she heard the blast of her sons' stereo, heard Eric urging Naomi to get into her nightgown, "and then when you're all ready for bed, we'll discuss *Kotter*." She couldn't wait to leave for the party. She willed the minutes to pass quickly, the way she had willed them many times before—all the while aware that she was willing her life away, foolishly pressing her impatient spurs into the flanks of time. In everything she did, she found herself unaccountably holding close with one hand and pushing away with the other.

"Oh, shit," she moaned, re-rolling the two bottom rollers on her head which she had managed to get soaking wet in the tub. "Shit."

She heard Naomi trying to pick the lock on the bathroom door. "Mommy," she said, walking in, "wait, don't holler. I have to brush my teeth."

"Naomi, there are five bathrooms in this house. Why do you have to brush your teeth in this one?"

"Because I also have to make a sissy."

"Oh, and why do you have to make it here?"

"I like it here. This is my favorite bathroom."

"Mom," called Jason.

"Don't come in," yelled Joan, frantically covering herself. "I'm in the tub. Don't you dare come in."

"Mom," he continued, thumping on the door, "you forgot to give me my allowance. Can I have it?"

"Now?" she cried. "Now? I'm in the *bathtub!* Do you want me to turn water into money? What's the matter with you?"

"What's the matter with *you?*" And a moment later, "Can I take it from your handbag?"

"Jason, please. I'll give it to you later. Go away now. Finish your homework."

"I finished my homework. Can you check it?"

"Not at this point in time, Jason. Have I mentioned that I'm in the tub?"

"Mom?"

"What?"

"Are you going out?"

"If I live long enough."

"Are you?"

"Yes."

"Good!"

"Jason?"

What?"

"You're my only blue-eyed child, Jason."

"So?"

"So, I just thought you ought to know."

"Mom?"

"What, Jason?"

"Can I go with you?"

"No."

"Why?"

"Because you're ugly."

110

"I know. I look like you."

Joan laughed. "Good," she said. "That was funny. I think you got a future, kid."

"Mom?"

"What?"

"Will you be home late?"

"I hope so, son. Jason?"

"What?"

"I love you."

"I love you too."

"Good."

She heard him gallop away. Naomi finished brushing her teeth and carefully rinsed her toothbrush.

"Mommy?"

"What?"

"Can you turn water into money?"

"Of course. I'm a mother."

"Then why aren't we rich?"

"We *are* rich."

"We don't have a tennis court, we don't have a beach house."

"We have underwear."

"Everybody has underwear."

"How do you know? Are you peeking where you shouldn't peek?"

"Oh, Mommy."

"Oh, Naomi."

Joan pulled the plug and stood up to towel herself dry. She watched her daughter examining her body.

"Mommy?"

"What?"

"Do you think you're pretty?"

"Yes. Do you?"

"I better not say."

"Why not?"

"I don't want to hurt your feelings."

"Thank you."

"Sometimes you're pretty."

"Thank you."

"No—you're always pretty."

111

"Thank you."

"Mommy?"

"Naomi?"

"Do you like the boys better then me?"

"Yes."

"You *do?*"

"No."

"Then you like me better than the boys?"

"No."

"Then who do you like better?"

"Nobody. I don't like any of you."

"Really?"

"No, you goose. I adore all of you."

"If a robber came and said who should I kill, you or your daughter, who would you say?"

"I would say, 'Oh, robber, kill me instead of my little girl.'"

"You would?"

"I would—but that will never happen. There will be no bad robbers here. I won't allow it."

"How do you know?"

"A mother knows."

"But what if there is?"

"I will take my big foot and kick him right in his pants."

"Oh, Mommy . . . Mommy?"

"What? What? What?"

"The towel is in the water. Shit."

"Naomi, don't say shit."

"You say it, why can't I?"

"Because people will think I'm a bad mother. They'll think I didn't bring you up right. Besides, right now that's *my* line."

She wrung out the towel and hung it over the rack to dry. Walking to the counter, she looked through the array of beauty aids, some of them older than Naomi, picked up a plastic bottle of colorless liquid, tilted her head back and squeezed some Visine into her eyes.

"Mommy?"

"Now what?"

112

"Does that hurt?"

"Not as much as a punch in the nose."

"Why are you putting that in your eyes?"

"To get the red out."

"Mommy?"

"Naomi, will you get out of here already? You'll miss *Kotter*."

"Are you trying to get rid of me?"

"Yes."

"Why?"

"So I can put on my makeup in peace."

"*Kotter* isn't on yet."

"Go talk to Daddy."

"No."

"Not no, but yes."

"Not yes, but no."

"Naomi," she said threateningly, "go!"

Joan picked up a bottle of makeup base and shook it vigorously. She stood close to the mirror and tried to spread the makeup evenly over her face. In the mirror she caught sight of her daughter, watching her intently.

"I thought I told you to go."

"You *did* tell me to go."

"So why are you still here?"

Naomi shrugged and began playing with Joan's assortment of lipsticks.

"Naomi, I'm losing my patience."

"Don't worry, I'll help you find it."

Joan turned and smiled. "That was good," she said. "That was a very funny reply. You have a terrific sense of humor, cutie."

"You think *I* have a future?"

"The best. I think you have a wonderful future. Now, get out of here. I love you."

They smiled at each other and hugged. Naomi laid her head against her mother's bare stomach, closed her eyes and began to suck her thumb. Joan took her by the shoulders and pushed her gently away. She leaned down and kissed her. "Go on," she said, turning her

113

toward the door. "Scram." She gave her a light pat on the behind and sent her off.

"Naomi?"

From the little hallway just outside the bathroom door, the child turned and looked questioningly at her mother.

"I love you, Naomi. I love you an enormous amount."

The child nodded. "I know," she said. "I love you too."

Joan finished putting on her base and, wrapped in an old pink terrycloth robe, walked into the bedroom and took a bra and a pair of underpants out of her dresser. Two down, one to go. She returned to the bathroom, locked the door, and put on her underwear and the rest of her makeup. She heard Michael bellowing for her, and hastily re-donned her robe. She was unwinding her rollers when he finally found her.

"Mom," he called, banging on the door, "open up." She opened the door and returned to the mirror.

"Mom," he squawked, "that asshole Jason took out all of my records and left them lying on the floor. I'm gonna kill him. I hate that stupid horse."

"Hello, Michael."

"Mom, aren't you gonna do anything?"

She turned and looked at this son of hers, born four minutes after Jason—in birth weight, her smallest baby. Already at twelve, he was beginning to enter adolescence and was so proud of his sparse, newly acquired pubic hairs that he showed them to her before every shower, lest he lose one in the process. Neither of her sons displayed any modesty whatsoever, although they displayed everything else. They paraded around nude right in front of her, without the slightest self-consciousness.

One evening, she remembered, as they both stood by her bed where she was attempting to read, she asked them about it.

"As you know," she said, "I have many friends with sons your age. None of them, not one that I know of, has seen her son naked since he was seven. You two

114

drecks present your parts for admiration every time you think of it. My question is: how come?"

Michael, jockey shorts lowered to insure her an unobstructed view, looked up from the object of his pride and smiled delightedly. "Maybe your friends' sons have nothing worth showing," he said gleefully. "Isn't humungus getting big?" He looked at her expectantly, and she smiled back.

"Humungus," she said, "is super. Gorgeous. If I weren't holding a book, I'd applaud."

"I know," said Michael. "Isn't it big?"

"Compared to what?"

"Compared to other twelve-year-old humungi?"

"It's big even compared to thirteen-year-old humungi. It's perfect. It's elegant. It looks great on you. Now go give it a shower."

Jason, who was not as physically mature, looked sadly at his "Fritz." "Mom," he asked, "when is Fritz gonna get big?"

"Never," yelled Michael from the bathroom.

"When, Mom?" Jason persisted, ignoring his brother.

"Well, I'll tell you. You take after your daddy. Daddy didn't begin to mature until he was past fourteen. Have patience, my love. You and your part are gonna live happily ever after. You'll do lots of fun things together, I promise you."

"Will I be as big as Daddy?"

"Maybe even bigger."

"How come Michael's is bigger than mine?" he whispered, not wanting his brother to overhear.

"His is bigger now," she whispered back. "That doesn't mean it's *always* going to be that way. When you mature and reach your full growth, yours will be big too."

"Are you sure?"

"I'm positive. It runs in our family."

"Daddy's isn't so big."

"I beg your pardon. Take it from one who knows, it's plenty big when it has to be."

"It is?"

115

"Absolutely. You and your brother and your sister are living proof that all is as it should be in that department. You have nothing to worry about, son. I promise you that."

"Should I take a shower?"

"Should a midget wear heels?"

"What midget?"

"Yes, tati, take a nice shower."

"Mom?"

"What?"

"Tell that stupid faggot to pick up my records."

"Michael, pick up the records."

"Very funny."

"Michael, if you keep calling your brother names, I will be forced to knock your face off. I'm serious. Just stop it."

"He always pisses me off."

"I know. I'll tell him about the records. Just quit being so insulting."

"When *he* quits pissing me off."

"Michael. Enough."

"Mom?"

"What?"

"Do you and Dad have oral sex?"

"That's none of your business, Michael."

"Come on."

"I do not discuss my sex life with twelve-year-olds."

"Where are you going?"

"To a party."

"With Audrey?"

"Yes. Michael, stop that."

She rescued her long thin plastic tube of mascara, the tip of which he was using to clean out his ear.

"Go tell Daddy to ask Jason to pick up your records," she said, wiping the end of the mascara with a piece of toilet paper. "Go on. Git!"

"Mom?"

"What?"

"Will there be pot at the party?"

"God, I hope so."

Michael grinned up at her. "If there is, will you bring some home for me?"

"Uh-uh."

"Why not?"

"Gonna smoke it all myself, that's why."

"Would you really?"

"No, dummy. Would you?"

"Maybe. Danny smokes it, so does Bobby Kline. What would you do if you found out I was smoking pot?"

"Well, after I wake up in the coronary unit of intensive care from that bit of news, I suppose I'll think of something. Unless of course I get a stroke."

"In which case, *I'll* have to think of something."

"Right. Michael?"

"What?"

"Do you still want to be a doctor?"

"I don't know. I think I'd like to be a rock star—lead guitar."

"Tell me, tattele, have you ever heard of more than one forty-year-old rock star?"

He thought for a while. "Elvis."

"I said *more* than one."

"No."

"What are you gonna do when you're forty?"

"Retire."

"Okay. We'll go to Israel together. Me and my forty-year-old retired rock star son."

"I guess I'll be a doctor."

"You can do both, honey. Be a rock star *and* a doctor."

"Yeah. Mom?"

"What?"

"Are you shaving your legs?"

"Well, my foot is up on the sink, I'm holding a razor in my hand, and I've just drawn it through the lather up to my knee. I guess you could say I'm shaving my legs."

They grinned at each other and Joan finished one

leg and started on the other.

"Mom, have a good time at the party."

"Thank you, darling. Oh, and Michael," she said as he turned to leave. "It might be a good idea not to get too friendly with Danny and that Bobby Kline. Should I tell you why?"

"I know why."

"Why?"

"Because everybody will think *I* smoke too."

"Right. How did a retardo like me ever get such a smart son like you?"

"Just lucky, I guess."

"I guess. I love you, rotten."

"Love you too."

He left the room and started fighting with Jason about the records. A few minutes later Eric began to make peace. Joan finished her legs and got her birds off the hanger. It was a two-piece pants outfit—printed blue, green, yellow and black birds on a bright red background. The top was loose-fitting and long-sleeved. The pants had an elasticized waist and wide legs. Joan bought it when the price went from $50 to $13.90. It was comfortable and loose enough to disguise where *she* was loose enough. She slipped it on and combed her hair, sprayed on some Estée Lauder she had gotten as a bonus gift, put blue pencil on the inside of her lower lids, and was ready.

"Eric," she called, grabbing her purse and making sure her glasses were inside, "I'm leaving now."

"What time do the boys go to bed?"

"I told you—nine o'clock lights out."

She went into the boys' room. "Now remember, Daddy is working at home as a special favor to me, so I can go to the party. Don't bother him, or next time I'll have to get a baby-sitter. Bye, boys. Bye, Naomi," she called in the direction of her daughter's room. "Be a good girl."

She walked over to Eric, who was sitting at his typewriter.

"Going?"

"Yes. Bye, honey. I'll see you later."

"Drive carefully."

"Eric, how do I look?"

"Fine," he said, eyes glued to the page he was typing.

"You didn't even look at me, putz."

"I saw you before. Lookin' good."

"Oh. Are my eyes all right?"

"Fine."

She sighed. "Eric?"

"Hm?"

"Like my birds?"

"Love your birds. Go already."

When she arrived at Audrey's, she parked and honked for her friend. Audrey appeared at the window and motioned for her to come in. Her kids and Melvin were eating in front of the television set. The place was in unbelievable disorder. The desk Audrey worked at was littered with scraps of paper illegibly scrawled on in red ink.

"Is this your stuff?"

"Yup."

"Audrey, it's impossible to read," Joan said, scanning one of the scrawled sheets. "I can't make out a word."

"Who cares about you? Mary can read it, and that's all that matters."

"Who's Mary?"

"A typist. Melvin found her. She's a blond shiksa with high boots who can fix everything and read my writing."

"Maybe she's fixing Melvin."

"I hope so. Poor man deserves something."

"Melvin," Joan called to his unhearing profile. "Are you having dealings with Mary in her boots?"

"Mary, Mary," he said, eyes still on the TV. "Lovely girl. Oh my God, yes."

Joan glanced over at him. Once when Scott Miller had come to the nursery school to pick up Denise, Joan

119

took him into the lounge, got him a cup of coffee, and in an attempt to unravel the mystique of Audrey, began to question him.

"Are you a saint, Melvin?" she asked. "Are you 'Saint Melvin the Civilized'?"

"Oh my God, yes," Melvin replied.

"Do saints take sugar?" Joan asked, holding up a packet.

"Saints don't take anything. That's why they're saints."

Joan smiled. "Melvin," she said, "can I ask you something?"

"Certainly."

"If it's none of my business, tell me it's none of my business. Okay?

"Melvin, what is a fine gentleman like you doing sitting on dirty chairs and washing dirty dishes?"

"What?"

"I think I'm asking what keeps you. Why are you still there?"

"You mean with Audrey? Why am I still with Audrey?"

"Yes."

"Why are *you?*"

"That's what's at the bottom of my question, Melvin."

"Why do I stay with Audrey." He thought for a moment, sipping his coffee.

"I met her," he said slowly, looking off toward the door, eyes looking inward, seeing a memory, "seventeen years ago. I was in a restaurant with a date. The waiter was taking an order from the people at the next table and the girl at that table looked at my plate and said, 'What is that? It looks good.' And then this complete stranger leaned over and with her fingers picked some food off my plate and ate it. 'I like,' she said to the waiter. 'This gentleman will give you my order,' and she pointed to me."

He looked at Joan and smiled.

"That was Audrey?"

120

"Oh my God, yes. That was Audrey."

"What did you do?"

"I gave the order."

"And then?"

"And then I looked at her and fell in love with her face. She was very beautiful."

"And then?"

"The rest is history."

"But Melvin! Why even when you're separated are you together? What *is* it about her?"

Melvin thought for a minute. "What is it about a person for whom it's normal behavior to do things that anyone else in the world would never dream of doing? Would you have done what she did in that restaurant?"

Joan shook her head. "No," she said softly.

"Well, to Audrey that was normal. She didn't know what to order, mine looked good, and she decided to sample it first to make sure. So she did. The fact that in order to do it she had to stick her fingers into the plate of a person she never saw before in her life didn't make one bit of difference."

He put down his cup and, taking a pack of cigarettes from his jacket pocket, offered one to Joan. They lit up, and Melvin leaned back.

"What it is," he said, "is this. Being with her is like being in the middle of an Errol Flynn movie. When you're just an ordinary man, it's not often that you get the chance to live in the middle of an adventure. She's not like other people. Do you see?"

Joan stared at him. Then she nodded. "Yes," she said, "I see. But Melvin, is it worth dishpan hands?"

Scott Miller smiled. "I left something out," he said.

"What?"

"That amazing person needs what I am."

"Yes," said Joan.

"And one more thing. I love her. She's murder to live with, but I love her . . . Don't you?"

"Certainly not."

"Well," said Melvin, "just you wait."

The dismissal bell sounded and the children began

running out of the classrooms. Joan threw her cigarette into what remained of her coffee and stood up.

"You know something?" she said, looking down at Scott Miller. "You're not such an ordinary man as you think you are."

Now Audrey took Joan by the arm and pulled her into the bedroom. She stood her in a clear space and circled around her, moaning.

"What is that on you?" she said. "Why are you wearing that? It's the ugliest thing I've ever seen. I hate birds. You look in that like a big red duck. How can I go with you in such an outfit?"

"I don't recall asking your opinion, so hold yourself. Compared to you, I'm Cleopatra."

"Are you crazy?" Audrey asked, indicating her own getup. "This blouse cost sixty dollars. It's nine dollars even to clean. And the pants, feel these pants. That's real velvet, lined, not that shit they sell in Ohrbach's."

Audrey was dressed in a long-sleeved, mandarin-collared white overblouse belted over tight black velvet pants. Over it she had thrown a matching black velvet cape. The high collar of her blouse was already rimmed with makeup, and one cuff was missing a button. Audrey dressed only in black, white and red.

"When I walk into a room," she said to Joan, "people know someone arrived. Then I find my light and I stand in it. Are you kidding? My clothes are the best. What is this shit?" she asked, grabbing a handful of Joan's pant leg. "Polyester?"

"Stop it," Joan said, pushing Audrey's hand away. "Stop pulling on my clothes and let's get out of here."

"You don't like it here?"

"There are many other places I'd much rather be. I didn't take a bubble bath to stand in a dirty bedroom and argue with you."

"How can I go anywhere with you dressed like that? Wait—I know." Audrey went over to her walk-in closet and opened the door. Inside was an old white French Provincial bureau with one drawer half-open and a

122

scarf hanging out of it. The floor was piled high with clothing, heaps of it.

On the two closet walls were racks filled with clothes—hers and Denise's—all hanging askew on bent wire hangers, threatening momentarily to slide off and join the pile on the floor. Some were shoved in so hastily that one corner of the hanger stuck out and up like a crooked elbow.

Audrey waded over the huge mound of clothing and began rummaging through the racks, finally unearthing the object of her search from a dark recess in the back of the closet.

"Here," she said, pushing a long red velvet cape into Joan's protesting arms. Joan held it up and away from her. The cape was at least twenty years old and, although of excellent quality, had obviously, like Audrey, seen better days. Like most of Audrey's things, it had a stiff mandarin collar which closed at the neck with two braided satin figure-eight frogs.

"What the hell is that?"

"*That* is a Jean Lousi, that's what that is. Dick Bell bought it for me, I forget for what. It cost him six hundred dollars, *then*. It's too good for you, cunt, but wear it anyway. You ruin that cape and I'll knock you across the room in green." She took it from Joan's arms and draped it across her shoulders. She turned her around and propelled her into the bathroom, facing the mirror. Without even looking, Joan removed the cape and handed it back to Audrey.

"Thanks, but no thanks. That thing is older than I am and it's dirty. I know it was once gorgeous, but it definitely passed away ten years ago. It smells from musty and old perfume and it's the wrong red."

"Listen, anything I give you is better than those facockteh birds you're wearing. Wait, I have another cape that'll hide them better even than this one. It's white." She started back toward the bedroom.

"Audrey, I don't want anything from that closet. That closet looks like a shmattah cemetery. I wouldn't

123

be surprised if you had a body under that pile of crap. Please, I'm going dressed this way and leave me alone." She walked back into the living room, followed by a resigned Audrey.

"Okay. Do what you want. *I'll* look terrific and *you'll* look like shit, but that's fine because you're a stupid ass."

Audrey began to undo her own black velvet cape. "What do you want? Do you want mine? Here, take it."

Joan waved her away and patted Melvin on the head in passing. "Good-bye, Melvin. St. Melvin," she called as she walked to the door and started down the stairs to her car.

Audrey's face appeared at the kitchen window, which fronted on the street. "Wait a minute," she hollered out the window. "I'm coming."

"Well, you'd better move yourself, because I'm leaving. If you happen to be in the car when I *do*, fine. If you're not, also fine."

Joan started the car and turned on the lights. She glanced up at the sound of a slamming door and in a moment Audrey was beside her reeking of Intimate and ready to take on the world.

"Well," she said, smiling at Joan, "what are you waiting for?"

13

Myrna Roth lived high in the hills above Coldwater Canyon. Her husband was in the liquor business. He supplied booze to bars and restaurants and owned about half the liquor stores in L.A. Joan pulled up before the large white modern house and turned the car over to one of the valet parkers. Myrna was really going all-out tonight. The door was opened by a uniformed maid who greeted them with a smile and took Audrey's cape. "Be careful with that, honey," Audrey said to her. "You lose that cape and death will come to you."

Myrna came up to them and happily kissed the air beside their proffered cheeks.

"Eric couldn't make it?" she said.

"This *is* Eric," Joan said, indicating Audrey. "He's gone Hollywood."

Myrna smiled. "Hi, Audrey. Glad you could come. Go on in and have a drink. Gloria's over there." She pointed vaguely toward somebody in the crowded living room.

They stepped down the two marble steps into the room. Through the large floor-to-ceiling sliding-glass doors they could see the pool, lit for the occasion, surrounded by round, cloth-covered tables with flowery centerpieces. Beyond the pool, spread out endlessly, were the lights of Los Angeles winking and glimmering below them. Most of the women were accompanied by their husbands. Many of them were old nursery school faces that Joan hadn't seen for a while. Joan and Audrey headed toward the bar, greeting and being greeted by old friends, all the women looking very different from the way they used to look in the lounge at Good Beginnings.

The bar was packed. "We'll be waiting a year to get a drink," Joan said disgustedly, eyeing it.

"Are you kidding? You know I never stand in lines. Wait here." Audrey pushed through the thirsty mob and elbowed her way to the front of the bar. Interrupting Zoe's husband, Ralph, who was in the middle of giving his drink order, she leaned over the ice-filled glasses and pinched the cheek of the young, busy and obviously gay bartender, whom she had never seen before in her life. "Hello, darling," she said, patting the reddened cheek. "How's your mother? Listen, I need two vodka tonics immediately—put in a nice piece of lime, but rub it around the rim first, thank you very much. This gentleman doesn't mind," she assured him, putting her hand on the arm of a speechless Ralph Newman. "Do you? Of course you don't. By the way, I'm Audrey Miller. I'm a friend of your wife's. Which one is she?" Leaning close to him, she whispered, "Will you do me a favor and tell the fegelah to give me my drinks before I faint? Please."

Ralph turned to the bartender, who was rooted to the spot, rubbing his cheek, and gave him a dazed nod. The bartender, galvanized into action, started pouring vodka. Audrey picked up a napkin from the bar and began rubbing the sleeve of Ralph's faun-colored suede sports jacket. "I think I got some lipstick on your

126

jacket," she said, smiling sweetly into his glazed eyes. "But don't worry, if it doesn't come off, go to my cleaners. If they can clean *my* filth they can clean anything. What is that? Suede? It's gorgeous. Oh, thank you very much, young man," she said to the bartender, who was holding out her drinks. "Just a minute. Here, rotten," she said to Ralph Newman. "Hold this a second." She handed him the crumpled napkin with which she had managed to wipe off a minute portion of the lipstick, but a goodly amount of suede. She took her drinks from the bartender, who was staring at her and shaking his head from side to side. "Be sure to leave your card, honey," she told him. "I give lots of parties." And with a friendly nod, holding the drinks at arm's length so that if they spilled, it wouldn't be on *her,* she walked quickly away, leaving a paralyzed group of drinkless barflies staring after her.

"Don't ever say I never do anything for you," Audrey said to Joan, handing her a drink.

"That was fast," said Joan, again eyeing the crowded bar. "How did you get them so fast? Never mind," she added hastily. "I can just imagine how."

They made their way through the drinking, munching, chattering crowd toward Gloria, who was standing near the huge white grand piano surrounded, as a guest of honor should be, by an excited group of women anxious to hear the details of her impending divorce. Her almost ex-husband, Jerry, was beside her.

"Joan," Gloria shrieked, hugging her. "How *are* you? Come say hello to Jerry." She pulled Joan over to her husband, who immediately wrapped his arms around Joan and planted a wet one on her cheek.

"Hello, my darling," he breathed dramatically. Joan was fond of Jerry Chase, who was an excellent performer and had appeared on many of Eric's shows, and she hugged him back.

"You all remember Audrey Miller, don't you?" Joan asked. Audrey nodded to them, sipping her drink and smiling. "I couldn't drag Eric away from the typewriter,

127

so I'm dating Audrey instead."

"Oh?" said Jerry, raising his eyebrows and pulling her off to one side. "So that's how it is, is it?"

"It doesn't have to stay that way, Jerry, especially now that you're an almost divorced man. Wanna straighten me out?" She smiled at him gently and patted his cheek. "How ya doin', tattele? You okay?"

"We'll see how much she hits me for, then I can tell you how okay I am. How's Eric?"

"Fine. Working, always working."

"Well, that's good. Don't knock it."

"Where are you living now?"

"I took a place at the beach. Trancas."

"Nice. Jerry?"

"Yes, baby?"

"This divorce. Is it for the best?"

"I hope so."

"And the kids?"

He shrugged and they walked back to the group. Jerry put his arm around Gloria's shoulders. She looked up at him, smiling.

"Gloria, Joan wants to know if our divorce is for the best."

Gloria laughed. "It better be," she said. "We just sold the house."

"Well," said Joan with a wry grin, "at the very least it got you a great party." She touched Gloria's cheek and sighed.

"Anybody want a drink?" asked Jerry. "I'm going over to the bar. So many women around me all at once makes me thirsty."

"If that's all it makes you, I can understand why Gloria's getting out," snorted Audrey, handing him her empty glass.

"Oh God, there goes that idiot Audrey again," said a disgusted voice.

"Hello, Carol," Audrey sneered. "What's new? Getting all ready for Halloween? Got your broom waxed? Hello, girls." She nodded at Zoe Newman, Sharon Sil-

128

ver and Big Bobbie, standing near Carol. Big Bobbie tittered and immediately clapped a hand over her mouth. Joan noticed she was still having difficulty with her false eyelashes. Zoe threw a quick glance at Carol. Sharon rolled her eyes and began to twirl her half-finished drink, clicking the ice cubes on the sides of the glass. Carol walked over and stood in front of Audrey. The other women looked on silently, wide-eyed and breathing rapidly.

Joan wondered what would happen if Carol actually attacked Audrey. Under that sleek, expensive exterior, Joan knew, beat the heart of a vicious street fighter. Carol Lighter was entirely capable of lifting her smooth, tanned, perfectly manicured hand, making a fist and gouging Audrey's eye out with her sparkling blue-white five-carat diamond ring. That elegant veneer was as thin and phony as a counterfeit dime.

Joan picked up her handbag from the piano and moved closer to Audrey. Carol, pale under her tan, her nostrils flaring, lifted her arm and stabbed Audrey in the chest with the tapering red nail of her index finger. Punctuating each word with a painful poke—in rhythm with Sharon's clicking ice cubes—she said in a whispery voice so filled with malice that Joan's toes curled, "You are without a doubt a disgusting [poke], ugly [poke], stupid [poke] slut [poke]. If you just dare to insult me one more time [poke, poke, poke] ..."

Audrey made a quick recovery and slapped off the jabbing finger. In a voice trained at the Neighborhood Playhouse, to project to the farthest balcony of the largest theater, and with diction precise enough to please Lee Strasberg, she thundered, "Take your miserable hands off me, you odious toad, and don't you *ever* touch me again."

The words reverberated through the large room and transformed a noisy celebration into a roomful of people so quiet that the only sounds were those of rapid breathing and the clink-clink-clink of ice cubes on glass.

129

Embarrassed and beside herself with rage and shame, Carol exploded, reared back, and smacked Audrey across the face. Audrey staggered, her hand to her cheek. She turned to face the aghast gathering, "You all saw it—that dirty cunt hit me first," she gasped, and with a movement so swift that Joan almost missed it, spun around and smacked Carol back. Carol careened into Sharon, who dropped her glass onto the thick gold carpet, where it lay spreading melting ice cubes and pale amber liquid over the lush pile.

Carol and Audrey, cheeks aflame, stood immobile, staring at each other, tears glinting in eyes, not knowing what to do next. Then Herb Lighter emerged from his horrified trance and grabbed his wife in an effort to forestall further retaliation. He led her away and Sharon went with them, leaving her glass on the floor. Zoe and Bobbie looked at each other, turned and melted into the crowd, eager to find their husbands.

The silence broke in an excited buzz of conversation, stimulated by the unexpected show that had livened up what would otherwise have been just another Hollywood party. A number of people went to retrieve their wraps, convinced that the best part of the evening now lay behind them.

"I think," Joan said, taking Audrey's arm, "that unless you want to wait for dinner, this might be a good time to go home and clean your closet."

"Did she do anything to my face?" asked Audrey anxiously. "Not even Melvin would touch my face, not my face..." Gingerly she touched fingertips to her cheek, on which was clearly outlined the complete handprint of Carol Lighter.

In her salad days, Audrey had been quite lovely. Joan had seen many professional photographs attesting to this: big blue eyes, high cheekbones, elegant nose, pale beautiful skin. Audrey seemed unaware that although time had not changed the basic structure, considerable erosion had occurred. Whenever she looked in the mirror she saw the face of twenty-five years ago,

130

somewhat changed, of course, but to her eyes negligibly. How lucky. Joan envied her her blindness.

"Come on," she said. "Let's go home."

"I will not," Audrey replied heatedly. "No stupid fucking bitch—may she rot—is gonna make me miss my dinner." She walked over to a chair and sat down. Joan's eyes circled the room, meeting nervous glances thrown their way. It seemed that Audrey had once again found her light. There was a stir at the door. Sharon Silver and the Lighters were leaving and Myrna stood holding both Carol's hands in hers and talking earnestly.

"They're going home," Joan said to Audrey.

"They should better drop dead."

The buffet dinner was now laid out and tempting. People were carrying plates around the table, being served by the uniformed catering crew. Joan spotted Big Bobbie waiting in line with her husband, deep in conversation, eating a carrot stick and occasionally gesturing in their direction.

"Everybody's talking about you," said Joan.

"So let them," said Audrey. "Is my cheek still red? She left a welt on my face, that stinking turd."

"You gave it back pretty good yourself, Rocky. I wouldn't be surprised if she also has a welt."

I hope so. Should we get in line? God, I hate lines."

Joan nodded and they got up and walked toward the deliciously laden table. As they reached for their plates, Myrna approached and drew them aside. "Put down your plates," she said. "I want to talk to you." They sighed and followed her into the family room, a large, wood-paneled, gamesy place adjacent to the living room. There was a huge television screen flush against one wall and a billiard table in the center of the floor. Myrna led them to a voluptuously pillowed, rust suede couch and they all sat down, sinking into the cushions.

"You know, of course," said Myrna, turning to Audrey, "that you absolutely *ruined* my party."

"Myrna," said Joan, putting a hand on her arm, "she

131

didn't *ruin* your party; she *made* it. The whole town will be talking about Myrna Roth's little do forever. You're gonna be famous, putz."

"What do you mean, *I* ruined it?" demanded Audrey. "That insane Nazi bitch attacked *me*. I didn't lay a hand on her until she absolutely *lunged* at me. Look, everybody saw it. I don't have to defend myself, Myrna."

"You started with her, Audrey. She said you insulted her, that you insult her constantly."

"I don't care *what* I do to her, and I really do *not* wish to discuss it further. If you don't mind, Myrna, we'd like to eat."

"Well, I do mind. Carol was my *invited* guest who was forced to leave because of you. Half of the party left because of you." She turned to Joan. "I'm only sorry that you have to be the innocent victim of all this, Joan, but you brought her."

"And now you want me to take her home?"

"I just feel terrible about the whole thing, Joan."

"I feel worse than that, Myrna, I feel hungry." She paused. "Are you throwing us out?"

"Yeah," said Audrey, struggling to sit up and finding it impossible to slide across the suede. "Are you throwing us out?"

"Well, Joan can stay if she wants."

By putting both hands behind her and pushing mightily, Audrey managed to propel herself to the edge of the couch and get up. Velvet pants on suede pillows are like tight skirts on fat ladies: hard to get over. Without a word or a backward glance, she left the room.

"Shame on you, Myrna." And Joan left too.

She found Audrey at the sweets table filling up a large cloth napkin with an assortment of goodies for Mendy and Denise. Joan also took a napkin and filled it with as much as it would hold. She too had children. She waited while Audrey retrieved her cape and they both left, but not before Audrey announced to the room at large, in stentorian tones, that Myrna had kicked

132

her out "for defending myself against a demented maniac. I'd like you to know," she roared, "that your hostess has no manners and even less of a sense of humor, because what happened here tonight was, if you think about it, really rather funny. Good-bye, everybody."

On the way home, Audrey said that her only regret was not having killed Carol Lighter.

"My only regret," said Joan, "was not having tasted the beef Wellington."

14

Richard Brown was a bewildered soul. Throughout his life the only commitment he had ever adhered to was that of indecision. Although he was very bright and very good-looking, he was dogged by an amazing ability to make wrong choices. At the age of thirty-seven he was still unsure of what he was going to be when he grew up. His rueful smile and wistful air attracted women the way horses do flies, and he found them just as persistent. He himself had never been married, but innocently managed to break up the affiliations of three women who were. For these and equally destructive romantic disasters, including two threatened suicides by thwarted and despairing anglers unable to hook him, he suffered agonies of guilt and began to entertain notions of joining the priesthood. But even the Catholic Church couldn't elicit a definite commitment from Richard Brown. They couldn't hook him either.

Naturally Nan Blake, unwise in the ways of sad-eyed and beautiful men, and a-yearn to live happily ever after with the hero of her adolescent daydreams, fell for him like Napoleon at Waterloo. Since Nan preferred her men successful, she got him introduced to the right people, got him invited to the ritziest parties—and for all this got herself only aggravation and misery and tears. Their sexual relationship, which had flourished wildly when *she* was pursued, languished and became at best sporadic now that the hunter and quarry had reversed positions. Nan was in love with Richard Brown and he wasn't loving her back, at least not in the way he was supposed to: not according to the fairy-tale equation that love equals marriage and bliss and riding off together into the sunset of eternal harmony.

What Nan wanted was total reciprocal possession. What Richard wanted was for them to be good friends who fucked once in a while—or never. In the evening when Carl was reading or watching television, or late at night when he was asleep, Nan would call Joan and weep. She told her that she was unable to function, to work, to do anything. Her life had about as much promise as an empty gum wrapper.

"I don't know what happened, Joan. What did I do wrong?"

"Everything, Nannie. You let him know that you were available."

"But I *told* him I was married."

"That's why he got involved. You were safe."

"I can't even work. I can hardly get up in the morning. He told me he loved me. What happened?"

"You loved him back."

"What am I going to do?"

"Break off with him."

"I can't."

"Pray."

"I do."

"Push him in front of a train."

"Los Angeles has no trains." She began to cry.

"Nan, please darling, take it easy."

"I'm going to take a Valium," Nan sobbed.

"Does it help?"

"It tries."

Nan began to live on Valium, and with the forlorn hope that perhaps a miracle would occur in Hollywood—that perhaps Richard would perceive in her a flower bed for his wandering hummingbird heart. She prayed desperately for him to love her and want her. She asked Joan to concentrate and send out good vibrations so he would feel about her the way he used to, the way he did in her foggy and cherished memories, when he had promised to love her forever—when forever really meant forever.

Joan listened and sighed. She concentrated energetically. She aimed her vibrations, as if they were daggers, at the heart of the unworthy Richard Brown. She needed to have Nan net this man. She needed to know that it was indeed possible for *someone* to have her cake and eat it too.

Carl too, it seemed, was increasingly difficult. He was restless and discontented. He wanted Nan home more and involved in the domestic side of their lives. He was tired of being responsible for the kids' dental appointments and haircuts. He no longer wanted to be the only adult in the family who knew Brian's shoe size and the price of chopped sirloin. He no longer wanted to be a wife.

Nan made valiant attempts to involve herself in her work. She wrote desperately. She enrolled for est classes. She spent sixty-five dollars at the Transcendental Meditation Institute for a personal mantra. To Carl's astonishment, she even offered to drive the car pool one morning. He delightedly handed her the car keys. This, however, was a mistake. She forgot to pick up two kids on the route and the entire gesture merely supplied him with added justification for mocking her pathetic attempts to master motherhood. Even her kids were annoyed with her. She began to suspect that Carl was preparing his farewell address and grew terrified.

Her partner, Teddy, became smug and righteous. "You made your bed," he kept repeating, "now lie in it." He also told her she was writing shit.

136

The more Nan wept and demanded and declared her love and despair, the further Richard retreated and fended her off. He didn't want to hear. He had warned her in great detail of his past romantic history. The possibility of her becoming divorced and therefore available sent him into such spasms of guilt and horror that he turned silly. He would sit in the dark for days, or fly off to Hawaii, or bite his nails until they bled. She said it was all his fault for leading her on and saying he loved her. He said it was all her fault for believing him in light of what he had told her about his transient character.

Joan said they were both masochistic nuts. "Forget that bastard, break it off, let go," she begged. "Make it good again with Carl."

"I can't," whispered Nan. "Richard has ruined my life and I love him."

"Then divorce Carl and get your shit together."

"I can't be alone."

"You can't have it all."

"Why not?"

"I don't know."

"Oh, Joanie, what am I going to do?"

"Deal with one thing at a time. First decide what you want to do about Carl. Then do it. The rest will follow."

"I'm so unhappy. Will you concentrate?"

"I love you, Nannie. I'll do whatever you want."

"Make Richard love me."

"Sure—after I make the world safe for democracy. I hate him, you know. How can you love someone who only gives you grief?"

"Will he ever love me?"

"Nannie, take a pill and go to sleep now."

"You're the best, Joan."

"*You're* the best. Don't forget that. Too good for that bastard, that baby. You're both crazy. Go to sleep. I'll talk to you tomorrow."

For some strange reason, unhappiness looks good on some people. Their eyes seem to deepen and look inward, noses thin out, lips become full and trembly, cheekbones more sharply defined. Inexplicably, even the skin appears tighter, lines fade away, pimples pop and recede, to be replaced by an interesting pallor. For whatever reason, Nan never looked better in her life. In an effort to steady herself, she began sending out "It's possible that I might be interested" signals, but found no one worthy of reception. Carl was angrier than ever. Richard, like the moon, had his cycles, his interest in her waxing and waning. He made her happy for two days and miserable for three. He seemed to become frightened after the good times, frightened that she would misinterpret and begin to expect more. He put Nan, or she put herself, on an emotional seesaw—up one moment, down the next.

Carl was unaware of Nan's relationship with Richard. He attributed her depression to work pressure. They had very little communication, avoiding the confrontation that would erupt if they faced each other.

Joan cautioned her against confiding in too many people. "Nan," she warned, "you must not allow this business with Richard to leak out. What if Carl finds out?"

"Who's going to tell him?"

"Are you kidding?"

"He won't find out."

"I hope you're right. Carl has enough to put up with as it is. He can*not* be asked to deal with your achievements or lack of them in strange Catholic bedrooms."

"What has he got to put up with?"

"Do you have an hour?"

"Yes. Go on."

"Well, your success, for one. The fact that all your friends consider him a joke, for two."

"Why do you say that?"

"At your last dinner party, Teddy asked him to clear the table—and he did. And you allowed Teddy to do it."

"But why did Carl?"

"It would have been even more obvious had he protested. *You* should have."

"Go on. What's number three?"

"Your affair with Richard."

"He doesn't know about that."

"It *must* be affecting your sex life." When Nan didn't answer, Joan went on. "Well, isn't it?"

"Not really."

"What do you mean, 'not really'?" Again Nan was silent. "Are you embarrassed?" asked Joan.

"I still have sex with Carl. I have more sex with him than I do with Richard," she said bitterly.

Carl, unlike Richard, whose emotional indicator resided in his cock, was always able to get it up. The fact that his marriage was disintegrating seemed not to affect the battery that powered his parts. It was like Carl, ever ready to do what it had to do. Nan attributed their continuing sex life to Carl's continuing interest. Joan felt that Carl wanted to get fucked and Nan was better than a bagel. Carl liked any situation in which he was the aggressor. Despite the warning signals he was emitting, Nan still believed that she was basically in control of her marriage, and of Carl's restless feet. She was wrong. She did not realize how much Carl cried for respect and traditional husbandhood. She did not realize the extent of his desire to be the center of someone's life. He was angry and tired of living in the suburbs of Nan's affections.

One evening he walked into the bedroom where Nan was trying to work and told her he was leaving. A week later he found an apartment. Nan became catatonic. She called Richard and was generally incoherent, but he got the gist. The next day when she called him again, his service informed her that Mr. Brown was in Hawaii for an indefinite period of time.

When Joan could not reach her by phone, she drove to Nan's house. Serena, the housekeeper, opened the door and told her hysterically that Señora Blake had not eaten or left her bedroom in two days. The señora would not permit her to enter the room. Each time she made an attempt, Señora Blake would tell her to go away. *"Yo soy muy nerviosa,"* she told Joan. "I very

139

worry. Is not good with the señora. The childrens," she went on, "are with the mister. I all alone here. She tell me, no call. *No*-body." Serena wrung her hands.

"Okay, Serena," said Joan. "I'll take care of her. You make me a coffee, all right?"

Joan raced up the stairs and plunged into Nan's bedroom. It stank. Nan was in bed, red-eyed and unmoving, surrounded by a mess of empty pretzel bags, orange peels and cans of diet soda. Her hair was hanging in strings and her face was pale and puffy. Joan wrinkled her nose and looked in anguish at her friend. Nan lifted a limp wrist and dropped it again heavily. It fell onto an empty pretzel bag, which crackled loudly in the quiet of the room. She closed her eyes and began to cry. Joan opened all the windows and started collecting the garbage from the bed. "Get up, Nan. Get into the bathroom and take a shower."

"I can't," she wept.

"I said, get up!" and Joan swiftly pulled the bed covers down. Nan lay there, her nightgown bunched around her waist, her thin legs pathetic against the flowered sheet. Beside her lay a half-empty bag of Snickers bars, crumpled wrappers obscuring the daisies and littering the field.

"Get up!" Joan commanded. "Or I'll be forced to call your mother."

This was a powerful threat. Nan had worked hard to make her parents proud of her. Her mother was pleased with her success but still felt that a woman's place was under her husband. She criticized Nan's way of life and sided with Carl about the little time she spent with the children. "You'll be sorry later," she would scold, "when they are all grown up and you realize what you missed." Nan knew that if her mother were to see her like this, she would move in immediately and blame her for everything. She would rearrange her silverware drawer as well as her life. Nan did not protest as Joan hauled her to a sitting position and helped her into the bathroom.

"Take a shower," Joan ordered. "And leave the door

open." Joan stripped the bed and threw the soiled linen over the banister to the hall below. "Wash these, Serena, and bring up fresh sheets. Leave them outside the door." When Serena did so, Joan began making the bed.

"What the hell is everyone making out of *me?*" she raged over the noise of the shower. "Am I a fucking Florence Nightingale? First Dolores Levy and now you, you horse's ass. Was I born to deal in nervous breakdowns? With every one of my friends cracking up, who's gonna be left to take care of me when it's *my* turn? Audrey Miller? God forbid."

What was happening to everybody? Was this becoming a trend? "Serena," Joan yelled down the stairs, "is my coffee ready?" Nan emerged from the bathroom, freshly nightgowned and smelling of Neutrogena. "I made your bed, you stupid idiot," Joan told her angrily. "Now lie in it!"

15

When Joan was little, her grandmother used to sing an old Jewish song which included the words "Every beginning is hard." For the men and women caught in the confusion of having grown up in the forties and fifties and hurled unprepared into the changing values of the sixties and seventies, these words were especially true. No one quite knew what to do. Joan found that the women closest to her tended to depend upon one another for the support for which most women formerly depended upon their husbands. Either their husbands were rarely around, as in Joan's and Audrey's situation, or they had moved out, as with Dolores and Nan. Eric, working continuously, was not there for the minor traumas or the big decisions of everyday life, and what she would once have discussed with him, Joan now discussed with her friends. Where previously she would have gone to dinner or a movie with Eric, it was with her girl friends that Joan now spent her nights out. These were few and far between, of course. Joan, being the guilt-ridden and nervous idiot that she was about her children, couldn't bring herself to leave them alone or with a sitter merely for her own pleasure. The only times she got out were when Eric was able to work at home, and that was about as often as a chicken baked a pie.

Most evenings, when the children were finally in bed, she spent reading and on the phone with Audrey or Nan or Dolores, because none of them had husbands at home either. Those of her friends whose husbands were at home at night, where a husband *should* be, Joan talked to during the day. She and Eric had been over his nonstop work schedule many times. He felt it was important to work while work was available. She felt she had two choices. One was to make Eric's life miserable—the other was not to. Now that Audrey had almost completed her book, Joan found herself often disgusted and bored enough to consider filling in the lonely hours of the night with a bit of writing herself. Writing, she reasoned, was a good occupation for housebound people. Not that she was qualified to write, but it beat being a salesgirl in a department store. And wasn't everybody always telling her she should write?

I am a college graduate, Joan thought to herself, I am well read, with a respectable IQ, and I couldn't get a job as easily as all those girls I used to feel superior to. All those girls who took a commercial course in high school, all those girls who managed to get through life without ever having done the Sunday *New York Times* crossword puzzle in ink. She was everywhere bombarded with volleys of the new philosophy that a woman must make a life apart from her husband and children, a life geared to her own personal fulfillment—a life which totally contradicted every ground rule Joan had been brought up to obey. It seemed that if a woman didn't move out of the suffocating environment of home and children, she was not a complete person, or worthy of the respect of her liberated peers. She was a schmuck—a housewife.

Not ten minutes ago, Joan had been asked to drive a contingent of boy scouts to an outing at the planetarium. "Why is it always me?" she railed at Arline, the scout leader. "Why can't some of the other mothers do it? I'm not the only one with a station wagon, for Christ sake."

"Because a lot of them work," Arline replied.

"Well, what do you call what I'm doing?"

"You don't work."

"Like hell I don't. Can't you call Libby Bass?"

"Look," Arline said, *"you* call her."

So Joan did. Libby proudly informed her that she was now an interior decorator.

"I'm doing this enormous house," said Libby. "I'd love to help you out, but I'm working now."

"Do you work every day?" asked Joan.

"Yes. I have no time at all for anything."

"Tell me, Libby, which do you love most, your kids or interior decorating?"

"What do you mean?"

"It's not that hard a question, Libby."

"Well, my kids, of course."

"In that case, how do you justify spending the greater amount of time with what you love less and the lesser amount of time with what you love more?"

"What are you *talking* about?"

"Think about it, Libby," said Joan, and hung up in disgust.

She took a deep breath and went into the kitchen to defrost something for dinner. "I have nothing to be ashamed of," she said to the rock-hard lamb chops. But it was shame she was feeling. Almost in tears, she acknowledged her total surrender to the propaganda that had turned her chosen housewife existence into mashed potatoes. She had done what her mother had told her to do. She had been a good girl and gotten married and had children. She had successfully battled "ring around the collar" and won. But she had lost the war against the braless advocates of total independence. She had succumbed to the ever-present pressures flying like bullets around her feet, making her dance to a new tune, making her realize, with every beat and every step, that what she had strived for all

144

her life, and attained, was now considered nothing but duck shit.

"We live in a small, rarefied world of creative people," she said to Eric the next morning.

"That's nice."

"Practically all our friends are involved in some way in a creative area."

"That's true."

"Not *all* our friends, but most."

"Ya."

"Naturally, then, if I were to think of working at anything, I would tend to try something creative, because that's all I see."

"Hm."

"But the problem is, I'm not particularly creative."

"It's a problem, all right."

"And we don't have live-in help. Even if I *tried* something creative, it's hard to concentrate when there's no more clean underwear."

"So get live-in help."

"But it's even harder when there's an alien presence continually around."

"So buy new underwear."

"If we're both out working, Eric, our lives will undergo a drastic change. It's going to be an upheaval."

"So?"

"So *I'll* be the one who'll have to shoulder the entire responsibility of reorganizing our lives. It will be difficult for the children, and *you'll* have to share that part of it with me. There'll be adjustments for you too."

"That's okay."

"Eric, you're leaving me with no excuses."

"Right."

"Nan has Serena and Carl—he deals with the kids even though he's out of the house."

"Good for him."

"You do nothing."

"Good for me."

"I always said I'd begin to do something when Naomi got to first grade. She's almost in second."

145

"Time flies when you're having fun."

"You're a putz."

"Thank you."

"Having a career isn't the answer. Nan is super-successful, but she's unhappy. She'd give it all up in a minute for some heart's peace."

"Don't bet on it."

"Audrey is writing and busy. She has no live-in help either, but Melvin does everything."

"I'll try to help you."

"Eric, I'm afraid."

"The whole world's afraid. Look, hon, nobody's forcing you to work."

"So why do I feel forced? You're wrong. Everything and everyone are forcing me. Forces are forcing me."

"You do what you want."

"Yeah."

"Don't worry about it."

"If I get too successful, when you dump me it'll be that much harder to take you for everything you've got."

"We'll worry about that then. In the meantime, you're not doing anything."

"I'm gonna try to write something."

"So do it already."

"It's my only option. There's nothing else I can do, and I don't even know if I can do *that*."

"I have to go, puss. I'll see you later. Stop worrying."

"Eric, tomorrow is your birthday."

"Don't remind me."

"You age beautifully. You look better now than you did when I married you. You're handsome now."

"I wasn't handsome then?"

"Nope. You were homely then."

"Homely?"

"Very."

"Thanks a lot."

"Marriage did a lot for you. You look terrific now. I look like shit."

"Whose fault is that?"

146

"You think I look like shit?"

"No, you're fine."

"I feel as if you're Dorian Gray and I'm the portrait."

"Stop it. I have no time. I think you're fine."

"I could lose a little weight."

"So lose it."

"You think I'm fat?"

"Joan, I've got to go. I'm up to here in work. Everybody's after me."

"Will you be home for dinner?"

"I'll call you."

"Bye."

"Bye, puss."

She began to straighten up the house. She called Audrey. She read the paper. Finally, when she could no longer procrastinate, she sharpened some pencils, opened the new notebook she had bought for the occasion and looked at the blank page. After a few minutes she got up and made herself a cup of coffee and carried it to the table. She sat and drank it while she stared at the blank page. Then, slowly, she began to write Eric's birthday poem.

TO ERIC

Today is your birthday and you are very quiet—
But I want to tell you something . . .
    you know—
I have loved you for a long, long time
Through worlds created and destroyed
Through simple, single-cell entwinings
Through infinite complex equations
And I am far from single-minded
And hardly anything I do sustains
And I forget things
And I lose things
And I like to be alone
But I have loved you as a constant
Without questions
Without answers

Like a show without commercials
Just occasional interruptions
Just the merest hint of static
From beyond familiar places
Where we hardly ever go.
And every day while I am living
While I am looking
While I am choosing
I stop my life for just a moment
And I smile and wonder what you're doing.
And love comes on me from my inside
From deep within, right near the section
Where all the tears and fears are growing
And I know *without instruction*
That I love you.
Not because of
Not in spite of
I just love you
And have done so
For a long, long time.

After she finished, Joan read and reread her poem until she knew it by heart. She was teary because it was either so beautiful or so embarrassing—she was not sure which. She called Audrey and with great pride announced that she had written a poem.

Audrey was unimpressed. "So you wrote a poem. So what? I have a whole book full of poems and I'm gonna get them published if I have to publish them myself. Then I'll be a star and what will I need *you* for?"

"Good-bye, Audrey."

"So read it to me already."

"No."

"Come on, I want to hear it."

"No. You'll only hate me."

"No, I won't. Read it."

"Uh-uh. It's so much better than anything *you've* ever done that it would be cruel."

"Read it."

"No, I can't."

148

"Why?"

"Because I can't—I feel shy. Maybe later," and she hung up.

Joan called Nan, not to read the poem, just to tell her, but Nan was out. So she read it to herself aloud, and cried again.

She wrote for the rest of the morning, a two-page story about a housewife who wrote a television show and was instantly successful and surprised everyone. She thought about starting a play and wrote ACT I on top of the paper. When Bobbie called to ask if she wanted to go to lunch with her, Joan replied, "I can't, hon, I'm writing."

That evening, before Eric left again for the office, Joan said, "You know, all my friends feel that if I were to go and get myself a decent haircut and went regularly to the hairdresser and spent more time and money on some good clothes, I could really look fabulous."

"So go."

"That's not the point. The real truth is that no matter how often I were to get a facial or whatever, there wouldn't be that discernible a difference. Perhaps it's better not to go and let them keep believing that I could be great-looking than it would be to get myself fixed up and have them realize that they were wrong."

"I lost you somewhere."

"What I'm saying is that a lot of people, including you, feel that I can write. Everyone tells me to do comedy scripts. If I ever write one and it stinks, I would be in a more compromising position than if I wrote nothing and left them still believing in my promising ability. Do you know what I mean? Like this, they think I *can*. If I do it, and it's *bad*, I'm not even left with a possibility."

"With that attitude, you'll never accomplish anything."

"With that attitude I'm preserving the little I *have* accomplished."

"You're a coward."

"I know."

After he left, Joan rewrote the poem on good, unlined paper, in ink. She put it carefully away to present to him in the morning. She felt unreal, as if she had been manipulated into a decision not her own. She was nervous and excited. She was scared. She felt she had taken the first step toward allowing herself to be judged by strangers with dispassionate eyes. She had permitted them to make her feel ashamed of herself—and she was ashamed of herself for being ashamed of herself. Joan was aware, cerebrally aware, that she was very fortunate. She had managed somehow to achieve what most people struggled all their lives for. She was loved. She was almost happy. Why did she permit those strangers to influence her into feeling that it wasn't enough? Why wasn't she intact enough to withstand them? Why was she so easily undermined and spurred to self-doubt when she knew very well that, for her, depression and self-pity were a self-indulgent luxury. She felt guilty, even sinful, when she lapsed into discontent. How dare she when she had no right?

"I haven't even begun to get my shit together," she said aloud. It was clear that unless the gap between her thinking self and her feeling self were bridged and joined and wed and welded—unless she matured sufficiently so that her needs and wants were one, unless she was finally capable of connecting her head to her liver—she'd be mired in a limbo of free-floating yearnings, waiting for the nonexistent blue fairy and wishing on stars and doubting her own worth until the day she died, disappointed and wondering. "So," she said, gazing in awe at her newly born revelation, "how do I *do* that?"

16

Audrey sat at her desk writing furiously. She was finishing an essay entitled "On Getting Slapped in the Face by a Bitch Named Carol." All her life Audrey had been able to disguise her disappointments and rejections and pain by simply retelling them and turning them into triumphs. It was infinitely more pleasant to believe her own revised account of a difficult situation than to live with the reality. Joan called her a pathological liar, although she realized on some level that it was not lying at all, it was necessary self-insulation, without which Audrey could not surive. Audrey needed the people she loved to stick around and prove to her that she was wonderful. Well, thought Joan, who doesn't? Nothing upset or enraged Audrey more than when Joan discovered a discrepancy between the fact of the matter and the fiction Audrey had devised to camouflage it, and called her on it. "How *dare* you dig out things about me that I don't want you to know?" she would scream.

Now, as Joan sat in Audrey's apartment reading the completed pages of the essay, she marveled at her friend's ability to see life only as she wished to see it, as she would have preferred it to happen.

"Audrey," she snapped, "this is *not* the way it was at all. Carol is not five foot eleven and one hundred eighty pounds. She did not threaten you with her shoe, and your 'people' did not rush to defend you and slap her around when she attacked. Why don't you write what *really* happened?"

"Why don't you mind your business? This is *my* piece for *my* book and I'll write what I want."

"Okay, fine. You write what you want, but this *still* never happened."

"So why is that so important? It sounds better this way, doesn't it?"

"No, it's soppy."

"Well, Mary will fix it."

"Then it's no longer yours, it's hers."

"Bullshit. It's *my* concept, it's *my* story—she just edits it."

"Do what you want. How soon do you think you'll be done with the whole book?"

Audrey stood up and stretched. "Very soon," she said. "I need only about eight more pieces."

Audrey also possessed the ability to take someone else's story and make it her own. Sometimes, only days after recounting an adventure of hers, Joan would hear the exact same anecdote—embellished, of course—only in *this* telling, Audrey was the one it had happened to. It got so that Joan never fully believed anything Audrey told her and she was very careful of anything she told Audrey.

Once she had described an incident that occurred when she and Eric went up to the Concord Hotel in New York with the star of Eric's first show. "That night," she said to Audrey, "I got all dressed up in a new white skirt and paraded around the lobby of the hotel like I was really something. After all, wasn't I with a star? Well, then we went up to the room of another celebrity to a party, me with my nose in the
152

air, swishing around like the Duchess of Windsor, and I sat down with a drink. Suddenly Eric looked at me and gasped. There, stapled to the bottom of my new skirt, was a huge white card which, in big black letters, announced 'Every Day a Sale Day at Alexander's.'"

Two days later Joan heard the same story, only this time it had happened to Audrey. "Damn it, Audrey. *I* told you that two days ago. That happened to *me!*"

"Oh," Audrey said, "was that you? I thought it was me."

Audrey had several friends, "old people," whom she had known for something like twenty years—friends like Dick Bell, Roger Fingerhut and Roberta Licht. Joan had by now met all of them and, according to Audrey, none of them liked her.

"They are very protective of me," said Audrey. "They would kill for me. If anyone were mean to me, my friends would kick that person to another country."

"So what has that to do with me? Why don't they like me?"

"They think you're too hard."

"Audrey, they don't even *know* me. How can they think *anything?*"

"I don't know. I can't help what they think."

"The only things they could possibly know about me are things that *you* tell them. What the hell have you been saying?"

"None of them are interested in you. They are *my* friends."

"You're saying bad about me, Audrey."

"There's nothing else to say about you, Joan."

It was only after she had established a friendship of her own with Dick Bell that Joan understood Audrey's motivations. In discussing her life with Joan, Audrey had invented happy endings for sad stories. She changed events and people around so that they bore no resemblance to the ones who figured in her history. It was very important to Audrey to keep the old friends separate from the new, so that the image she presented to the new friends would remain intact. She could not risk the possibility that one of her old people might let something slip that would contradict a fiction she had confided to a new person. In talking to Dick, Joan finally began to understand the unique character that Audrey was. "She was a spoiled-rotten Jewish brat," Dick said. "Her father promised her a rose garden and she never, ever got it. Her first and only success was Mendy. She managed to squeeze out a baby boy—and that was *it*."

"What about her daughter?"

"That little cunt? I hope she gets kidnapped."

It was necessary for Audrey to keep her various friends apart, and what better way than to create an enmity between them? Lord knows what she said to do it, but Joan could just imagine. Of all Audrey's old people, Dick Bell was the only one who ever spoke to her.

Joan began to realize that as close as she was to Audrey, she wasn't close at all. There were parts of Audrey so clouded and covered over by layers of fabrication, that they could never be unraveled—even by Dick Bell, who had lived through much of them *with* Audrey.

In one of their big fights, Audrey had accused Joan of attempting to force her way into her private life and asking personal questions which caused her only pain—and of talking to Dick Bell.

"You are trying," said Audrey, "to get into my pee-pee. I may have a big mouth, but underneath I'm a very private person. I don't *want* you in my pee-pee. I don't want *anyone* there. My own *husband* doesn't ask the questions you ask. Why do you *do* that? Why do you want to cause me pain? My other friends don't treat me like that. I've known them much longer than I've known you, and they wouldn't *dare* try to get into me like you do. They wouldn't even *think* of it."

"I don't know what you're talking about. How am I supposed to know which of my questions cause you pain? Am I a mind reader?"

"Look, when you see my face start to sweat, you should know to stop."

"When I see your face start to sweat, I figure you're feeling *hot,* not pain. If I ask you something and you don't wish to answer, simply say so. Don't expect me to know what is impossible for me to know. After all, I'm *not* in your pee-pee."

"You just push too hard—you want to know *everything.*"

"That's not unusual. Friends generally are curious about one another. What *is* unusual is a person who purports to be a friend and who refuses to give *anything* of herself."

"I give you plenty."

"Headaches you give me—plenty of headaches."

"None of my friends treat me like you do."

"Oh? How do they treat you?"

"Perfect, not like you. Roberta calls every day to ask can she do anything for me. Dick would kiss my doodies. Roger lends me money and wouldn't *think* of asking me to pay him back."

"A nice lot of schmucks you've surrounded yourself with. And Roger notwithstanding, you owe me a hundred bucks—you've owed it to me for six months and *I* want it back."

"When I sell my book, you'll get it back. I wouldn't keep your money even if you told me to."

"Don't worry, I'll never tell you to. You know, Audrey, I'm really a bit bothered by your concept of friendship. I don't bombard you. The questions arise naturally out of our conversation. What other basis have we got? We met when we were old and wary—you, anyway—without the benefit of shared experience. We did not grow up together. It's normal to be curious about the life of someone you care for. Especially since every time you describe some incident in your life that was 'painless,' it's totally different from the previous description. Look, you lie anyway, so what the hell difference does it make?"

"It does to me. Look, I *can't* tell you everything. I

155

need you to love me without having to tell you everything. Why is it so important to you? Why are you like this?"

"I am what I am."

"When someone hurts me, I walk away."

"We accept each other as we are, Audrey, or not at all. I'm going home now."

"Stop peeling me, Joan. I'm not an orange."

"Start sharing, Audrey. An unpeeled orange hardly fulfills its function."

They said their good-byes and Joan left. They did not speak for a day and a half. When Audrey finally called, they talked to each other as usual and neither ever mentioned the argument again. Neither one wanted to lose the other. Neither exactly knew why.

Audrey finished *Letters to Mendy* about a month later and began to send it off to publishers. Joan had read a Xeroxed copy of the manuscript and thought it uninspired. With the exception of a turn of phrase here and there, she found little in it that would immortalize Audrey and make her the star she desperately needed to be. She dreaded the day Audrey would ask for her opinion of the work. It was always difficult to express an unflattering opinion, especially to people with fragile and easy-to-topple egos. Audrey was not one of those, but she had worked hard, and Joan thought it a major miracle that she had even gotten this far. Joan doubted the book would ever be published. How was she going to tell Audrey what she thought of it and still maintain the friendship?

Joan recalled an incident that had happened about ten years ago in the Hamptons, where she and Eric and the twins had gone to get away from the hot New York summer. So far, that had been the best summer of her life. She had met many people, some of whom she still kept up with. Among them was Iris Lakin. Iris was married to an attorney and had just finished a book. She was considered somewhat eccentric and very bright, and knew all the beautiful people. Joan was in awe of all of them and, although she bravely denied it and was sick of herself for feeling so and said things like, "So what if he has a hit show, he gets cramps from eating bad fish just like the rest of us," she still could not rid herself of the feeling of inferiority when she was with people like this. Nothing she could ever say would interest a "beautiful person." It didn't shut her up, of course, but why was she always in the position of a little girl who spends her life looking up at every adult she speaks to, never quite able to leave her level and get on theirs?

Iris lived down the beach from her, entertained frequently, and was a weekend wife. During the week, when Iris's husband, Grant, was in the city, Iris would come and visit with Joan and the twins. She drank a lot, talked a lot, cried a lot and introduced Joan to marijuana. They became good friends and still saw each other whenever Iris made a trip to California. Iris was nervous and hyper about everything. She kept thinking that if she didn't get Grant's favorite white pants from the laundry before the weekend, he would divorce her. She worried herself into many real and imagined illnesses, and even into sterility. After the Brenners moved to L.A., she and Grant had adopted a child, although not one of the many doctors Iris consulted ever found anything wrong. As soon as she woke up, Iris would fix herself a drink and forget to eat breakfast or dress. She often went to town in her baby dolls, totally oblivious of the stares she attracted from natives and summer people.

Iris had just received the galley proofs of her novel and brought them over for Joan to read. She wanted Joan's opinion of her book. Joan was terrified at the possibility that she wouldn't like it. Iris was not the sort who could accept a negative reaction calmly.

"I'll read it tonight," she promised, carefully placing it out of reach of her curious boys. "I know I'll just love it."

"I think you will too," said Iris, and Joan's mouth went dry. "It's your kind of book."

Iris put her drink down and rolled a joint. "We'll

157

finish this and then go into town. I need a new bikini."

Joan's mouth went drier. Iris was built in a rather unfortunate way. Her body was put together strangely. Her behind was low-slung and receded so that her swimsuit bottoms creased and bunched because they weren't filled; her breasts under her baby dolls were droopy like empty mittens; her arms and legs were thin and knobby. But her stomach and hips were, surprisingly and somewhat obscenely, rounded like a beach ball, with no indentation whatsoever where other people normally have a waistline. She looked like a bumblebee. So unaware was Iris of her grotesque physique that she wore only bikini bathing suits, much to the dismay of her husband and friends, and she had generously offered to do a nude layout for *Playboy* in exchange for serializing her book. She was indignant at being turned down. Joan earnestly wished not to be in the shop when Iris stepped out of the dressing room and cheerfully asked, "How do I look?"

"I can't, Iris," said Joan. "What'll I do with the kids?"

"You can leave them with my Clovelle, she loves children. She has six."

"I will *not* go into town with you in your baby doll pajamas. Go without me ... Clovelle has six children and she still loves kids?"

"Come on, Joan. I'll change when we drop the kids off. Please?"

When they got to the village, Joan told Iris that she needed to do some marketing. "You buy your suit. I'll get my groceries, and we'll meet later."

But Iris would not be put off, and dragged Joan into the shop. The salesgirls were all young and good-looking. They had a way about them that curdled Joan's stomach. It was as though they did you a favor by waiting on you. Iris was used to supercilious salespeople. She only shopped in stores that had them. Now, recognizing a customer who cared not a whit for lifted eyebrows, they loaded Iris's arms with bikinis and ushered her into a fitting room. Joan, ignored and fidgety, sat down to wait.

158

After a few minutes, Iris emerged. Turning slowly around in front of Joan, she asked, "Well, how do I look?" Joan stared at Iris, half-naked and almost deformed in the wispy suit. Iris gazed back expectantly. The salesgirl, who had not previously seemed to notice Joan, now smiled maliciously at her. She too was waiting.

"Well?" said Iris. "What do you think?"

Unable to lie under the nasty gaze of the salesgirl, and equally unable to tell the truth, Joan stalled for time and fumbled for a cigarette. She lit up and exhaled slowly. She coughed and looked up at Iris.

"Uh, Iris—you have lots of bikinis, right?"

"Yes. So?"

"So why do you want another one?"

"I don't know," said Iris, adjusting a strap. "I just feel like another one. What do you say, Joan? How do I look?"

"Iris," said Joan cautiously, "do you like the way you look in your other bikinis?"

"Of course," said Iris, eyeing herself in the mirror.

"Well, you look the same in this one," said Joan, disguising a sigh of relief in a puff of smoke. The salesgirl turned away, looking amused. Iris happily bought the suit. Joan felt gleeful. She couldn't have done better. She had carried it off like a diplomat.

Thinking about that incident now, Joan smiled. She only hoped she would be able to be as smooth with Audrey. And Audrey was becoming impatient.

"You've had the fucking Xerox for three days already. *Naomi* could have finished it by now!"

"Audrey, when I'm done I'll tell you. What do you care what I think anyway? I'm not an expert on this sort of thing."

"Well, you read a lot. You should know by now what's good and what isn't."

"Only when it comes to eating. Only when I eat do I know what's good and what isn't—for example, your chicken with raisins."

"What about it?"

"It isn't."

"Joan," she snapped, *"Letters to Mendy* is not chicken with raisins. I need to know what you think."

"Okay, I'll finish it," she lied. She had finished reading it the day Audrey gave it to her.

"But *hurry.*"

Joan could put it off no longer. The next day when Audrey called to check on her progress, Joan told her she had finished the book.

"Well?" said Audrey.

"Well, I don't know if it's good because I so much want it to be, or because it really is."

"I *knew* you'd like it," said Audrey. *"I* think it's terrific, don't you?"

"What a terrific accomplishment, Audrey. You've written a book. You're an author."

"It's just a *little* book, only eighty-five pages, but it's a *book.*"

"It certainly is."

"So why aren't you jumping up and down? Why don't you get excited?"

"That's what Eric keeps asking me. Is anything happening with a publisher?"

"Not yet, but don't worry. So far they love it."

"Enough to publish it?"

"You know, Joan, you always spoil everything. Let *me* deal with publishing."

"Fine."

"Who published your friend Nan's book, or the other one, what's her name?"

"Iris? Marlene?"

"Yeah."

"I'll ask."

"So why aren't you jumping?"

"I don't jump, Audrey. I hardly even move. After I empty an *ashtray,* I have to lie down."

"Maybe now some money will come to me."

"I hope so. I want my hundred back."

"Now you bring that up? Joan, I have a *book.* Even *you* like it, and you never like anything."

160

"Ain't that a kick in the head?"

"I'm a genius, a fucking genius."

"Good-bye, Audrey. If you don't stop patting yourself on the back, you'll dislocate your arm."

"Will you buy me lunch? *In good?*"

"As soon as it's published."

"Not before?"

"I can't afford it before—I'm out a hundred bucks. Pay me back so I can buy you a lunch. In good."

"Bitch. By the way, what have you got against my chicken with raisins? Everybody else *loves* it—that and my egg salad. My friends die for it."

"For it or from it?"

"Fuck you. I have a book. It doesn't matter about my cooking. Stay home and cook, Joan. Nobody knows your name."

"The people who need to know it, know it. Stop carrying on. Just get published and pay me back so I can got rid of you."

"But I'm a star! Why do you want to get rid of me *now?*"

"I have enough stars. You'd think you just wrote *Macbeth* the way you take on."

"To me this *is Macbeth.*"

"I hate to burst your bubble, Audrey, but you're not Shakespeare."

"I thought you *liked* it."

"Audrey, you may *not* compare your work to Shakespeare."

"What about Sylvia Plath?"

"Sylvia Plath was a genius!"

"And I'm not?"

"Only at being a pest."

"I don't see *you* doing anything."

"We are not discussing me. And I'm sick of discussing you. Make a book out of your Xerox and I promise to jump."

"Emily Dickinson?"

"Oh God. Good-bye, Audrey."

Joan hung up the phone and reread her poem. Eric

161

had said he loved it, that he would treasure it, and Joan felt that he meant what he said, that he *would* treasure it—but not, she knew, putting her copy tenderly away at the bottom of her underwear drawer, not nearly as much as she.

17

Joan was amazed at her friends' ability to survive the type of situation that would have sent *her* to Bellevue or Camarillo State for life. In the early years of her marriage, she used to have a recurring nightmare. In the dream she would find herself helpless before Eric's indifference. Eric wanted out of the marriage, not for any particular reason, not because he had found someone else, simply because he had lost interest and didn't want *her* anymore. She was powerless to dissuade him, despite her desperate pleas and promises. He just didn't care, was offhand, with faraway eyes. He had already removed himself from her life and erased her meaning and presence from whatever inner part of him she had previously occupied. He was completely unconcerned and unmoved, even bored, by her grief.

She would awaken terrified and filled with dread, cling to her sleeping husband and, for the rest of the day, be enveloped in the suffocating and miserable atmosphere created by the dream—numb, frightened, paralyzed, bereft. There is no defense against indifference. It is an insult, a deadly affront. Joan was lucky.

For her the nightmare remained only a nightmare. For Nan and Dolores it had become a reality. Dolores suffered most, on all levels: functionally, emotionally, financially, socially. For thirteen or so years she had been sheltered, protected, supported and loved. Stu Levy's departure had undermined the entire foundation of her life. For three years she had wandered into a vistaless purgatory—fighting with her children, fighting with Stu, fighting with herself—directionless and very lonely. Dolores was, but for the grace of God, Joan herself. She was living out Joan's nightmare and wearing Joan's weighted cloak of mourning. How had her mother known to name her Dolores? Forced by Stu Levy's vindictiveness to find work, Dolores took a job as secretary to a real estate agent, unearthed her meager typing talent and learned to deal with leases and escrows. The work was boring and so was the ridiculously small salary, but at least she was struggling through the days with her hair combed.

She was in great pain over her inability to give her children what she wanted them to have. Her youngest, Melissa, six years old at the time of the divorce, had to be placed in a day-care center. Her other two, aged eleven and eight, came home from school to an empty, uncared-for house and waited for her to return from work. Gone were the lessons, the outings, the special treats, the loving attention, the always present and gentle mother. Dolores agonized over the calamity that had befallen her children.

She would come home exhausted and make dinner and separate her angry youngsters, who fought with her and with one another, and who hated every meal she prepared for them and pushed their plates away, petulant and whiny. She had not made these children alone, but she had to raise them that way. She cried and cursed her empty bed and empty life. She railed against her cruel and undeserved punishment.

As time passed, the effects of stumbling through the threatening black emptiness of her existence took its toll. She was lost, and no matter how she strained her

164

eyes, she could see no saving light at the end of the winding and tortuous tunnel. Always very thin, she became gaunt. Always unaggressive, she became robotlike and passive. Always quiet, she became mute. She no longer dreamed of happy family days at the beach, of smiling, bright, achieving children, of chiffon dresses and Cinderella balls. There was no strength left for wishes.

When Joan asked her what she wanted, all Dolores could manage to summon up from her vast store of deprivation was, "Well, it would be nice . . . You know what would be nice?"

"What, honey?"

"I think it would be nice to go out to dinner . . . with someone nice, to a nice restaurant, and, you know . . . talk and eat . . ." and her voice faded away like the wistful moan of a sad-songed cello, leaving only an echo where once there was sound. "But," whispered Dolores, "I don't think . . . I really don't know anybody . . . It's so hard to meet . . ." and again, the sound was gone.

Joan looked at this girl, who, like the last of the just, had taken on Joan's mantle of living nightmare, who had awakened from Joan's dream to discover, in horror, that she hadn't been dreaming at all; and Joan held her close.

"Dolores," she said in a voice so filled with compassion that Dolores moved away, "if that's what you want, if that's *all* you want, say hello to your fairy godmother." From that day on, Joan went to parties for two reasons only, one, to make points, and two, to find for Dolores someone nice who would take her to dinner. It was a difficult quest, not only to find a nice man, but also to find a nice man who would trust Joan enough to believe that she wasn't sticking him with a dog. It was difficult to find a nice man who was unmarried and heterosexual and hungry. It was also difficult to make points and make contact with possible escorts at the same time. Once in a while this latter effort would take precedence over the other and Joan was in danger of becoming a pest.

Still, she persevered, despite the well-known fact that L.A. is a rough town for single women, even when they're young and pretty and unencumbered by children. For someone like Dolores, forty-one years old, unused to making herself noticed, living with three divorce-shocked kids, past the age when men crane their necks and walk into lampposts, poor, unsure and insecure, *every* town is a rough town.

The day after one party at which Joan had resorted to nagging and had been told to "cut it out and get lost," she morosely took her coupons from the drawer and set out for the supermarket to bury her failure in gourmet foods. Ordinarily, she marketed hurriedly, hating every minute of it, impatiently kicking the wheel of her cart on the long check-out line, glumly thinking ahead to lugging in and unpacking and storing away the overloaded bags of groceries—one of which was always destined to rip apart and spill its contents over the kitchen floor. She detested washing fruit and vainly searching for room in a refrigerator that never seemed to have any. But today she welcomed the anonymity of the market. She was relieved at her invisibility, and marched slowly and purposefully up and down the aisles, selecting carefully, placing items into her cart as though they were giving awards for neatness.

The only thing Dolores wanted was a nice man to dine with, and right now the only thing Joan wanted was for her to have it. She did not realize, until she arrived home and tried to shove a box of Tide into the refrigerator, how angry she was. She grabbed the Malibu phone book out of the pile under the counter, some of which dated back to 1971, and began turning pages furiously, in her haste leaving a long ragged rip through the miles of Birnbaums. She ran her finger down the list of names and stopped at Gomberg, Milt. Quickly she dialed, counting the rings while her unpacked quart of burgundy cherry ice cream slowly liquefied.

"Milt, this is Joan Brenner ... Yes, the same one you

told to get lost last night. Listen, you old putz, I'm trying to do you a favor, how stupid of you not to realize that ... *You* wait a minute. You are forty-eight years old and wasting your time fucking eighteen-year-old girls who are only doing it because you're successful ... Don't you dare hang up on me, Milton Gomberg ... Did you think they were going down on you for love? What do you do after the last hurrah? Help them with their math? No, I am not crazy, you are ... or maybe you're just afraid to date a grown woman, in which case I don't want you for my friend. Go back to your babies, Roman Polanski—you don't deserve my charity ... Yes. Her name is Dolores Levy and she's too good for you. Pretty? Compared to you, she's Miss Universe. Yes, divorced ... well, so are you, lumphead ... No, three kids. She's terrific, thin with good hair ... 562-8177 ... How do *I* know her exact height? Listen, Milton, you don't have to make her your beneficiary, just take her out to dinner ... I didn't say 'shmuck' I said 'old putz,' but shmuck suits you too ... You will? Good. It's the only smart decision you've made since 1968. Take her out nice ... Okay, okay—don't get excited. At your age you have to be careful about blood pressure. She lives in Beverly Hills. When you call, you'll get directions. Yes, 562-8177. When will you call? When? Uh-uh, Milton, tonight! Why not? You are? You must be paying them plenty, Milt. Call her tonight and make a date for soon. Good. Of course I'm hostile—I resent being told to get lost when I'm trying to do something nice for someone ... I'm a what? Oh, yeah? Well, you're an old fart ... Don't worry, Milton. I don't like you, but I wouldn't stick you with a dog, trust me. Yes, Eric and the kids are fine. Now remember, call *tonight*. And Milt, after your first date I'll expect flowers and a thank-you note—oh, and a quart of burgundy cherry ice cream. I'll explain why another day. You're gonna owe me, Milton. Good-bye."

Joan hung up and stood gazing at the phone, smiling and smiling. She felt wonderful, she felt that she had just added a piece of pavement to her precarious pathway to paradise. Still smiling, she unpacked the rest of the groceries and put them away. The melted ice cream went into the freezer and she washed the fruit without cursing it. After she was done and everything was stowed away, she called Dolores and told her to expect a call that night from someone named Milt Gomberg. Then she called Eric and Audrey and told them what a super person Joan Brenner was. "Now," she said aloud, sitting down with a freshly washed apple and a cup of coffee, "now we'll see about Nan."

Joan didn't worry about Nan the way she did about Dolores. Nan was strong and determined. She hadn't gotten to where she was by weeping into lace hankies. If she had to bet between Nan and Carl as to who would be the more successful survivor, she'd put it all on Nan. She wasn't minimizing the enormous blow that had befallen Nan, nor her uncharacteristic reaction to it, but she felt that Nan would arise from the ashes of her burnt-out marriage and her trash-strewn bed and go on to make her altered situation work for her. Fortunately she had no financial worries, had many friends and was in an excellent position to meet someone new. The trouble was, she didn't want someone new, she wanted Richard Brown. And had wanted Carl to stay with her until Richard obliged. Unfortunately, neither Carl nor Richard shared her aspirations.

Nan had begun working again, and word of her separation got around. She was a very funny lady and could be dazzling when she chose. She chose a lot, and men began to call and ask her out. For all her success, Nan was basically a homebody. She needed the security of a stable situation. She wanted to be part of a happy family. To her, the desired outcome of love was marriage and a permanent commitment. She could not flit easily from man to man or bed to bed. She enjoyed dating, but not unless it was with a man she would consider seriously. Nan was an old-fashioned lady thrown into a newfangled world. She realized that Richard was immature in his attachments and unstable emotionally. She knew all his fears and all his faults. She loved him anyway, and clung fiercely to the thin, frayed line he threw her.

Except in traffic, Nan refused to yield. She never gave up—not with anything. She even held tightly to worn-out feelings that no longer applied. She truly believed that Richard was the love of her life and that she would never find another. Despite this, she hated losing Carl. She was confused and emotionally disrupted. She was a single body with a married head, who wanted to be secure in a comfortably furnished nest, where she would live happily ever after—preferably with Richard Brown, if she could get him. And she was determined to get him. And if it was at all possible for *someone* to get him, that someone was Nan Blake.

"I wouldn't be at all surprised," Joan lectured her, "if once you *had* Richard, you no longer wanted him. You would realize that he is incapable of fulfilling your needs. Right now your eyes are so fogged by the sweat of the chase that you can't see anything clearly. Once you wash your face, you'll be able to focus again on reality. Richard is opposite to you in every way, Nan. He won't make half the father to your kids that Carl is. You are steady, Richard is flighty. You are ambitious, Richard is erratic. You're used to being catered to, Richard is used to splitting at the first indication of need. You are used to permanence, he to transience. You are strong, Richard is weak. What the hell is it about him that you love? Are you so childish that you want him simply because you can't have him? What *is* it?"

Joan realized she was asking an impossible question. Not a woman alive understands the mysterious and tremendous attraction that draws her to Mister Wrong. Nan wanted Richard. Joan felt that everybody, especially those she cared about, should have whatever they wanted. It would be a better world. Well, maybe. It was unfortunate that there was no guarantee or warranty attached to the realization of one's desires. It was really too bad that no one could ever be sure of anything. A person could develop a cold.

Nan told Joan she was right. She knew she was being illogical, that her feelings didn't make sense. But her need was so great that she intended to make use of every weapon known to woman to capture the wriggly Richard Brown. He was no match, that little boy, for her extraordinary and single-minded relentlessness. Joan was betting on her, not to show, not to place, but to win.

"I'm gonna have a party," Nan told her. "I'll invite every guy I know who has shown any interest in me—and, of course, Richard."

"It would be politic to have a few girls there too, Nannie."

Nan smiled. "Good idea."

"What about a couple of couples? Maybe Richard will begin to realize that married people exist."

"Of course there'll be couples. Half the guys who've called to ask me out are married."

"Was Eric one of them?"

"The first. That's why I'm inviting you."

"And when everybody is there, then what?"

"I'll serve them drinks."

"And then?"

"Hors d'oeuvres."

"And then?"

"Then I'll spend time with everyone but Richard."

"What if Richard gets lonely and decides to spend a little time with everyone but you?"

"He won't."

"Why not?"

"Because *you'll* be with him."

Joan stared at her. She thought for a moment. "On one condition."

"Name it."

"Invite Milt Gomberg—and tell him to bring Dolores Levy."

"Joan, *I* can't tell Milt Gomberg whom to bring."

"In that case, *I* can't guard Richard Brown."

"In that case, I'll do it."

"In that case, so will I."

Joan wished she were able to throw a party with the same assurance that Nan displayed. Nan never worried, the way Joan did, about whether or not her guests would have a good time. She always assumed they would. Joan always *hoped* they would, but was constantly assailed with the possibility that her party would be a flop. She had discovered that she was an uncomfortable hostess. Fortunately Eric was not what her friends would call a "social person" either. On the rare occasions that he found time to relax at home, all he wanted to do was relax at home. He wanted to look after his *own* comfort, not that of his guests. He was a quiet man who hated crowded and noisy rooms—especially his own. The only entertaining the Brenners did was on Jewish holidays, and then only family was invited. Eric was less than thrilled on those occasions too.

He was a wonderful host when he had to be, but the opportunity rarely arose. They had not given a party in over three years. From time to time Joan would protest their unsociability. "It's embarrassing," she would say. "We owe everybody in town. Let's have a party and at least repay our obligations." Naturally, if she had had the slightest indication that Eric would agree, she would have kept her mouth shut. It was merely a gesture on her part. She didn't want to have a party either, but it was less upsetting and much easier to blame Eric for it. "We rarely entertain," she would say to people, throwing her hands up in defeat. "Eric just doesn't enjoy it. He's the sort of man who prefers to be alone with his family, although he will occasionally attend affairs given by *other* people."

However, "other people" were catching on and their social life was becoming limited. Most of the parties they were invited to were given by associates of Eric's for business purposes. They, as a couple, were not close to other couples, and could boast of very few strong attachments based on true friendship with both husband and wife. They were loners, Joan and Eric, and each had separate friends, but they did not socialize with any of these. It boiled down to Joan's friends and Eric's friends, but rarely to the Brenners' friends. It also boiled down to many evenings at home alone, just Joan and Eric and the kids—and now that Eric was working every night, just Joan and the kids.

On hearing of parties to which they had not been invited, Joan would say, "It's because we never invite anyone *here*. Why else would a fun couple like us be overlooked when the invitations are being addressed?" And when Eric didn't answer, she would continue, "Unless, of course, we are not a fun couple. Maybe we're a *dull* couple. Maybe we're the B-movie of couples." Then she would add, "Come on, Eric, let's have a party," and when Eric would say, "No, Joan," she would sigh in relief. So, by Beverly Hills standards, they were considered to lead a quiet, almost reclusive life. Joan, however, could count on Nan to invite her to everything she threw. Nan was one of the few friends she and Eric shared in common, though still mainly Joan's friend, and if Eric were unable to attend Nan's party, Joan would go alone.

As it turned out, Eric could neither go to the party nor work at home that night. Naomi and Michael had colds and Joan felt uneasy about leaving them with a sitter, so she spent the evening of the party moping and picking up used tissues from the floor of every room in the house.

Dolores had had a wonderful time and Milt asked her out to his Malibu pad, with the kids, for the following Sunday. Richard had been jealous of the attention Nan was being paid—even without Joan there to guard him. He looked put out and asked Nan if she wished him to stay after her guests had gone. Nan told him she'd let him know *then,* and when *then* came, informed him, with a yawn, that she was exhausted and would like a raincheck. When Nan reported in the next day, Joan marveled at her friend's strength of will.

"You are absolutely amazing, Nan. I doubt that I would have been as strong."

"What could I do? He needs a challenge. If playing hard to get doesn't work, I'll try something else."

"It's wonderful—you're young again."

"I know. I'm finally living out my adolescence. I'm doing all those things I should have done twenty years ago but never had the opportunity to do. I was *the* most unpopular. Lots of girl friends, but never a date for the prom. I gave my mother many a headache, and she kept sending me to weight-reducing summer camps—first as a camper, and then as a counselor. Naturally I gained eleven pounds by September. One night I ate two complete bunches of celery and twenty-seven carrots. Some nights even more."

"Can you gain that much weight on only vegetables?"

"If you eat them with onion dip, you can."

"And you did?"

"Two full packets of Lipton Onion Soup and two pints of sour cream—every night for two months. Plus an occasional pizza that someone would manage to sneak in. You don't how what real misery is unless you weigh one hundred eighty-five pounds in high school. I had a larger dress size than my mother. And my brother, of course, was a stick. I had the distinction of being the fattest girl in the senior class of Elizabeth Gatt High School. My thigh measurement was larger than Cheryl Amsterdam's waist."

"Who was Cheryl Amsterdam?"

"The girl I wanted to be."

"Where is she now?"

"I don't know. She liked me, girls always did, but I couldn't really be friendly with her."

"Because she was pretty and thin?"

"No, because I couldn't bear standing or walking next to her. The contrast was too much for me."

"'Well, baby, look at you now,'" Joan sang. "Cheryl

Amsterdam has probably become what you used to be—and you, you gorgeous thing, look better now than ever before."

"I'm peaking. I hope it lasts awhile, at least long enough to see me through my campaign."

"You sound good, better than you did that last time. Has Serena recovered yet from your nervous breakdown?"

"Oh, Serena...I can't believe what happened to me."

"Why did it?"

"I don't know. I suppose I needed a change. When I think about it, which I do a lot, I realize that a trip to Paris might have been more fun."

"Nah."

"I finally took a few days off...and spent it regressing. I overdosed on pretzels. Now that I don't need it, I find I have enough material to write a 'How I Spent My Vacation' composition. Nothing like this would happen to Cheryl Amsterdam. One look at her high school yearbook picture would be enough to cheer her up."

"Only if she's better *now*. It can be just as devastating to peak early and fall apart at twenty-five. You spend the rest of your life on a down escalator."

"At Lane Bryant...Richard called twice today."

"I don't care about Richard."

"I wish I could say the same. He's ruined my life."

"Stop feeling morose. You'll take to your bed again."

"Never."

"How do you know?"

"I got rid of every pretzel in the house—I'm unprepared for collapse."

"Nothing left to feed your habit."

"Exactly. It's hard to go crazy on bean sprouts and unflavored yogurt. That was the second craziness in my life."

"What was the first?"

"Wearing a dress with horizontal stripes to my sweet sixteen party."

174

Joan laughed. "What did Cheryl Amsterdam wear?"

"A sheath, yellow, with shoes to match. My mother took one look at her and decided to trade. She pulled me over next to a plant and said, 'Nan, good things come in small packages.'"

"Aah," Joan said sympathetically. "What did you do?"

"Nothing. I looked at this woman who was supposed to love me. I realized she was only trying to cliché me into dropping sixty pounds. She had tried everything else and even resorted to taking me to the movies on Saturday nights just so that I could tell my girl friends I had gone out. She wanted me to reduce—and I did. I reduced her to hurting what she loved best in the world. Me! I tried to comfort her. I assured her that someday I too would turn into a small package. Now," Nan laughed, "she tells me that I would really look healthier if I put on a few pounds."

"Well, at least *we're* not the only mothers who make mistakes. Do you know what *my* mother said when I told her I was pregnant with twins?"

"What?"

"First she denied it. 'No, you're not,' she said. 'Twins do not run in our family.' When I assured her that despite that fact I was indeed full of twins, she said, 'You know something, Joan? You always did overdo.'"

"I love it. Joan, do you think Richard will ever love me?"

"He loves you now. He *must*. This is his only relationship that's ever lasted any length of time. It's over a year now."

"I know. I've just got to keep hanging in, especially now that I'm a small package. We have a date for Friday. He became hyper when I told him I was going out tonight with Milt Gomberg."

"Tell him to calm down, because you can't go out with Milt Gomberg—he's for Dolores. Find someone else. Nan, it would be a sin. Find someone else."

"Are you serious?"

"Very. You've got to break the date."

"What will I say?"

"Think of something, you're a writer."

Nan paused for a moment. "I really don't think I want to go out with Milt anyway. For some strange reason I didn't realize that until just this minute."

"You're the best, Nannie. The best. I'm gonna tell you something else that my mother, in a rare burst of pride, once told me. 'Joan,' she said, 'there are times when you reek class.' But, Nannie, *you* are the classiest reeker of us all."

18

Audrey, despite the fact that her leg hurt, that her head hurt, that Melvin, the animal, was always on her, that the pain from her ulcer was so tremendous that her stomach was on the street, said she had at last found a publisher and was very busy talking to printers and being a star.

"Who's the publisher?" asked Joan.

But Audrey wasn't answering. Why should she? She had written a book that was going to be published. "And, of all my friends, only *you* didn't help me!" she said, patting her manuscript. "Only *you* gave me bad letters, you gave me letters your rotten *kids* wrote!"

"That's because they were better than *mine*. I still think

> Dear Mom,
> Last night our cabin had a farting contest.
> Lenny Gold won. I am having a good time.
> I lost my night brace. I have a girl friend
> named Melanie. She has big ones.
>
> Love, Jason
>
> P.S. I hate my counselor. He is a fag. Love
> again, Jason

would have given your book an interesting tone."

"You have terrible children. Mendy would never think of writing something like that to me. Never!"

"Is that so? Well, Mendy reminds me of Jason's counselor."

"Mendy? You're crazy. He's just like his father—an animal. Well, what do you say, cunt? I have a book. It's going to be published—so start jumping."

"Have you gotten an advance?"

"Stop doing this. I *said* I'd pay you back when I can. I owe plenty of money to much bigger people than you."

As it turned out, Audrey had indeed found a publisher—her husband, Melvin. Miller Publishing Company was set up in their bedroom, and *Letters to Mendy: A Mother's Odes to Her Children* had been printed in paperback out in El Monte somewhere. Audrey had marched herself into every bookstore in Los Angeles and somehow managed to get a good number of them to place orders for her tome, along with solemn promises to display *Letters* prominently on the counter next to the cash register. She knew a good many people in the industry from the days of her professed former glory and began pushing for radio and TV interviews to publicize the book.

Roger Fingerhut, one of her "old people," was a theatrical attorney, and used his contacts in the business to aid her. Audrey was moving right along and, from what she told Joan, was doing "just great . . . perfect." She actually had been a guest on some local radio shows and was written up in the *Beverly Hills Banner* to the tune of a paragraph and a half. She was invited to give a reading from *Letters to Mendy* before the ladies of her temple sisterhood.

Joan was numb with astonishment at what Audrey was able to do. She didn't believe half of what Audrey claimed to have accomplished, but she had never imagined she'd even go as far as she had. To celebrate, Joan took her friend for lunch "in good," after which she bought three copies of *Letters to Mendy* in various bookstores around town. She listened loyally to whatever local show Audrey was on, and called Nan to ask her for hints as to the proper procedure for pushing a book. Nan, who could take Audrey only in very small doses, told Joan to leave her to her own devices. That her book (which Nan thought was a piece of crap) was even in a bookstore could be considered in itself a major miracle.

Among the items in her book was something Audrey had written about Joan. It was called "Joan," and Audrey felt that Joan should be properly grateful. "You should kiss my ass, cunt. I've made you immortal."

"Kiss your ass! What I should do is *kick* your ass. My enemies have said nicer things about me than that."

"Are you serious? Everybody says it's terrific. One of my best!"

"Only the subject matter is terrific. You have an unusual way of complimenting a person. By the way, Carol Lighter is gonna kill you."

"Fuck her."

Audrey had also immortalized Carol:

On Getting Slapped in the Face by a Bitch Named Carol

> *B—is for Bad*
> *I—is for Ice Cold*
> *T—is for Tough and Terrible*
> *C—is for Compassion, of which she has none*
> *H—is for Horrible, of which she is very*
>
> *Put that all together, it spells Carol, a worm*
> *I know and wish I didn't.*

"Carol is lucky I didn't write worse. But *yours* is excellent!"

JOAN

> *I have a friend named Joan*
> *I really don't like her*
> *I wonder why I have her?*
> *She is hard*

She is mean
She is insulting
Or is she honest?
I really don't know . . . honesty is
    abrasive, like Joan
What I do know is she makes me
    laugh
And maybe that is more important
    than patting my cheek.
If it isn't I've made a mistake
She tells me to get out of her life
And out of her car
What if she means it?
If I got out of her life
What would happen to my life?
Maybe it would get better.
With no one to put me down.
I was fine before I met her
And I know I could be fine without her.
But it wouldn't be as much fun.
And what's fine about that?
I guess I'll keep her
I'll buy a pair of ear plugs and keep
    her . . . you see I need her.
I think.

"I really think there's something wrong with you, Joan. That is a wonderful piece. It's the only way you're ever gonna be a star. I put you in a book, stupid, and you should kiss my ass."

"Will 'Thank you, I appreciate it' do?"

"Not really, but I'll take it. How could you not like 'Joan'?"

"Foolish me, I guess I must have just been kidding around. But Carol Lighter's gonna kill you. She'll sue you."

"Fuck her."

"How come you called your book *Letters to Mendy* and you include all this other stuff?"

"It's my book, I can include anything I want in it. And for this type of book, not a big novel, it's selling very well."

"So where's my hundred?"

"Oh, shut up. First I have to pay the big ones, then you'll get your hundred and I'll be able to get rid of you forever. That was nice of you, bitch, to fix Dolores up with Milt Gomberg. He's terrible, though. I know him."

"Don't give her any of your opinions. He takes her out and she needs that."

"I wouldn't tell *her,* but he's shit."

"So you fix her up with better. In the meantime keep your mouth shut. You called me mean, hard, insulting and abrasive. For that you want me to be grateful."

"I also said you were fun."

"Four bads and only one good."

"I couldn't think of any more goods."

"Bitch."

"Leave me alone, I don't feel good."

"Now what?"

"Everything hurts."

"Everything *always* hurts."

"I have a lump on my behind."

"Leave it to you to get cancer of the ass."

"I think so. And my head hurts."

"Have you ever heard of doctors?"

"I owe all of them money."

"For a doctor I'll lend you."

"I hate doctors."

"Audrey, you're driving me crazy. Have you become a Christian Scientist? Go to a new one, who hasn't heard about you . . . and get some diet pills."

"Am I your pusher?"

"Yes."

"I have a headache and my veins are lumpy. Maybe I'm dying."

"Maybe."

"So you think I'm dying?"

"Sounds like it."

"I'll outlive you, cunt."

"Probably."

"But what if I don't? What if I die first?"

"I'll give a donation."

Audrey laughed. "Will you come to my funeral?"

"Can I wear my birds?"

"Joan?"

"What?"

"What will you do if I die before you?"

"What will I do? I'll ask you to save me a seat—up front, on the aisle. I'll say, 'Save me a seat, cunt—a good one, so I can get an unobstructed view of the show.' That's what I'll do."

"And you know I always get the best seats."

"Okay, it's settled. When are you dying?"

"I can't die yet, I have to go to New York."

"For what?"

"For a publisher to put me in hardcover."

"When are you going?"

"Tuesday. I'm in packing."

"Good luck."

"Can I borrow your luggage?"

"No. Get luggage from Roberta Licht."

"I will—it's better than yours anyway."

When Joan hung up the phone, she wondered how she could have joked with Audrey about death and dying when the very idea of it made her clammy with terror. Joking about dying, she realized, was probably the only way she could handle it without subjecting herself to cardiac arrhythmia. Even now, just thinking about it caused her to grin in panic, eyes wide and unblinking, wiping suddenly sweaty palms on the sides of her jeans. She had always been afraid of one thing or another, but of death she was especially afraid. That focused fear came upon her early, she seemed to recall, and lingered, intruded, moved into her middle and settled down, never ever to leave again.

Joan had been a solitary, broody, dreaming pudge of a child, slow to fathom and quick to cry, and had heard of death of course, but it wasn't until she was about eight or so that she somehow became aware that no matter what she did or where she hid, "it" was going to get her. She realized, with awful certainty, that even if she were very, very good, which she rarely ever was, it was still going to get her. And all the prayers were useless and all the promises were futile, and Mommy, who could always warm her, and her papa, who was the buffer between her and any conceivable danger, could neither keep her from dying nor death from her.

Joan met dread when she was eight years old and now, although it was unthinkable to call it a friend, it had been with her for a long, long time. It was indeed so familiar that sometimes she could fool it with lesser, shorter-term fears. But dread is tenacious and Joan was not, and it was much more cunning than she. She was afraid of death, of it seizing her quickly, or creeping in slyly. She was terrified of death getting her children, because it has a million ways. What did *she* have with which to guard them? Mother love? But not even mother love provides powerful enough protection, merely padding for falling on hard places. Mother love was not invincible. What about God? Joan was a convinced deist. She believed in God, but often suspected He spent a lot of time singing songs to spheres and suns while death was knocking them dead in cities close-by.

She was always afraid. She was afraid of random horrors, of rule-defying evils, of "it" *not* happening to somebody else, of exotic diseases and cureless curses and of growing old and of not growing old. To this day, she denied the inevitability of her death, even as she had done when she was a child, but denials didn't help the way they used to.

She stood up abruptly and went to the drawer where she hid her cigarettes from her scornful children who, in their zeal to protect her from stupid self-abuse, would surely destroy the pack if they found it, and nervously lit up. She inhaled eagerly, as though her life depended upon it, and sat down again, pulling an ashtray into her lap.

"I'm doomed," she thought wonderingly. "I'm doomed to the human condition...but at least I'll never be lonely, my fear is far from original. Scared and silly souls seeking warm laps to burrow into, and soothing, stroking hands and reassuring voices saying, 'There, there...' and sleep, the kind that one wakes up from, and those schools that teach that death is quite delightful." Joan sat still for a moment, bemused by her insights. She took a last puff and crushed her cigarette in the ashtray. "I'm going to write that down," she said aloud, "before I forget it."

She raced into the bedroom, grabbed up the pad on which she had written Eric's poem and pushed aside the clutter on her night table until she unearthed a ballpoint pen. She wrote for several moments, and then stopped. She had forgotten what followed mother love. All that remained was her trepidation and the ambiguous comfort of knowing that whatever fortunes or afflictions the future held, it remained pretty much out of her hands. Her only recourse seemed to be to worry about it. Along with all her other fears, Joan was also afraid to be optimistic, afraid of the impish energies that were so adept at turning hopeful expectation into sour disappointment, and gay anticipation into gray reality. But it was foolish to fear death. If she allowed her bleak attitude to dominate her, it meant that she already *was* dead—even if not dead enough to bury.

"I will not dwell on it. I will not allow it to take over. *I will not,*" she said aloud, putting down the pen. Instead she would write a short story or read a book or call a friend or do a wash or buy a bright blue dress or ask Eric why he loved her or kiss her children or become Scarlett O'Hara. She was alive, still alive, and so were the people she loved. And she had always managed to function, hadn't she? This was all she knew, but it was enough for now. Admittedly Audrey and Nan didn't torment themselves the way she did, or worry that the school bus would crash or that the tires on a car-pool station wagon were dangerously worn. To them, the beach and ocean were places of pleasure, not

184

the death traps that Joan envisioned. They saw their children splashing and laughing while Joan saw hers screaming and drowning as she stood helpless on the shore. They trusted that the baby-sitters they hired would not abuse their children. Joan had no peace unless her kids were under her face, thereby shackling herself to constant anxiety.

Now that Audrey was pushing successful authorship, she no longer had the patience to hear out Joan's litany of impending catastrophes threatening her dear ones. Audrey wanted to talk about her book sales, not about the fact that Joan's son had promised to call at three and here it was three-fifteen and he hadn't called yet.

"What's the matter with you?" Audrey would demand. "Why do you imagine that everything ends up tragedy?"

"I don't know," Joan would moan.

"When you think bad things, they happen," Audrey warned her. "It's the thinking that's tragic. Why are you such an unhappy woman?"

"I'm not unhappy."

"You certainly are. You try to cover it with a joke, but underneath you're a very unhappy, unfulfilled person."

"Not true."

"Yes, true."

"Well, if I'm overly concerned, it's because Eric and the kids are my whole life."

"Well, they shouldn't be. Other things are important too."

"Like what?"

"Like having something for yourself. Like writing a book."

"Tell me, Audrey, try to tell me that writing a book or painting a picture or being an executive vice-president of something is important. Tell me that and I'll tell *you* if one of your kids sneezed or ran a 103-degree fever or, God forbid, had a dreadful illness, tell me *then* that having something all for yourself is important.

185

You would relinquish all that in one second to have your child not cough through the night. Having a career or something is *nice*. But important?"

Audrey thought for a minute. Joan could hear her breathing on the other end of the phone.

"Okay," Audrey said finally. "You're right. You're absolutely right, but you're wrong."

"I know," said Joan. "I realize that I'm desperately defending myself and my way of life. Can a person be right and wrong simultaneously? My entire existence depends on four people. All my eggs are in one basket and I expend all my energies hovering anxiously over that basket. It's wrong. It's wrong because it's overpowering me, it's killing me. I'm a nervous wreck. Maybe I need another basket, just for relief—but what will I put in that other basket?"

"I don't know, but you better put it quick. You're boring already."

"Of course, the answer may not be another basket at all. It may simply be altering my attitude toward the one basket I've got."

"Oh, shut up with your baskets already. I'm going to New York and I have no good luggage, no clean underpants and no boots. My head hurts, my veins hurt, I have lousy legs and my hair dryer broke. But guess what I'll have in my pocket when I come back?"

"What?"

"Guess."

"Wet hair."

"No, stupid. A publisher."

"Who?"

"I don't know yet. I'll see when I get there. You know I have a blue fairy ... she's on me now. You'll see. I'm gonna have a real book, not just this little one."

"A real book of what?"

"Of letters, poems, essays, whatever. Do you think I've been sitting around cocking with baskets? I've been writing, bitch. Every night, all night. I have enough shit to make one real book."

"How can you write all night? When do you sleep?"

186

"I don't."

"Audrey, you got more pills."

"And now I have shots too."

"Give me."

"I can't. I need for New York."

"Audrey, just a few."

"Why should I?"

"Do you want a friend in half-sizes? Do you want a friend who can't cross her legs and has chafed thighs? Do you want a friend who wears only caftans? Do you want a friend who looks like a tank? Audrey, do you want a friend?"

"No."

"Do you want to borrow a hair dryer?"

"I'll give you five, but that is *it*."

"Done."

"And when the book is published, I'll get on Johnny Carson and Mike Douglas and Merv Griffin. Then I'll write a novel and *then* I'll be able to get what I *really* want."

"A face lift?"

"No. My own television show and a beach house."

Joan sighed. "Oh, Audrey."

"I'd do terrific on my own show, you know it. I can charm the world. Then off to Malibu to sit in the sun with my feet up."

"Dream on."

"Look, bitch, you never thought I'd get this far. I am very aware that you think my book is shit."

"Come on, Audrey, do you think you're Joseph Heller?"

"It doesn't matter what I think. I'm not a writer and I know it . . . but I touch people. That little crappy book is *selling*. I'm a fucking phenomenon."

"There I agree."

"I know you think I'm a talentless dummy. Well, I have no talent, but I'm far from dumb. In fact, I may be the smartest woman in the world." Audrey paused and when Joan remained silent, continued, "Do you know why I'm the smartest woman in the world?"

"Why?"

"Because I always, always, get what I want."

"In my opinion that's a bettter talent than writing."

"You better believe it."

"I don't think you're dumb, Audrey. I never did."

"You don't think I can write."

"Well . . . neither do you."

"So why is my book selling?"

"Because this is America. Put a pretty ribbon on a bag of garbage and someone will buy it."

"My book is garbage? I was the hit of the ABA convention."

"*You* were the hit, not your book."

"So what's wrong with that?"

"Nothing is wrong with that. You are a brilliant salesman—*that* is your talent. You could sell contraceptives to ninety-year-old nuns. And you would be super with your own TV show."

"I really would—and I'll put you on with me, cunt. So you better be nice to me."

"If you put me on, it's because I'll be an asset to your show, not because you're the Salvation Army. Don't give me any 'out of the goodness of my heart' crap. You have no heart."

"Something I have . . . yes, indeed. I'll put you on my show and you'll be mean to me and everybody will hate you and love me."

"I figured as much. I know better than to think you'd do anything that wouldn't benefit you."

"Why else would I want you? You're nobody. Who's gonna tune in to see you?"

"My mother."

"She hates you too."

"Good-bye, Audrey."

"Melvin is out buying me aspirin and support hose."

"He's a saint."

"He's crazy. I hate him, but I need him."

"You use people, Audrey Miller. You're a user and a taker."

"I admit it, but I must give something too. Why else

is he still around? Why are *all* my people still around? Why are *you* still around?"

"I'm as crazy as Melvin. We are not well people."

"I'm getting another chance. Do you know that? It's my time again. I feel it."

"Just don't fuck up."

"I never fuck up."

"You fuck up everybody around you and come up smelling like a rose. You are a dangerous woman, Audrey Miller."

"I'm a pussycat."

"You're dangerous because you have the ability to make people forgive you. No matter what you do, they forgive you."

"So why is that dangerous?"

"Because you know you can get away with murder. So you murder."

"I couldn't hurt a fly. I'm a sweetheart."

"Where's my hundred, sweetheart?"

"Please, I can't think about that now. I have a headache. Where the hell is Melvin with my aspirin?"

"Where are you with my diet pills?"

"Where's the hair dryer?"

"Where's my son? It's three forty-five."

"Maybe he's with Melvin."

"Maybe something happened to him."

"Maybe you should shut up. Your son is fine. Better find out what happened to *you.*"

Joan peered over her shoulder at the kitchen clock. It was ten to four. She began to chew her hair.

"I'm hanging you, Audrey. I have to find my boy." She had just hung up when her son ambled in, eating an ice cream sandwich.

"Oh, Michael," she said as she lit a cigarette in relief. "Why didn't you call me?"

"I did," he answered, "but the line was busy."

19

It was the occasion of Seth's eighth birthday, and Big Bobbie, bemused and relieved that she and Seth had survived eight years together, decided to throw a huge bash in celebration. She invited every child with whom Seth had gone to school—with exceptions, of course—and also their mothers. One of the exceptions was Denise and Audrey.

Audrey was enraged when she learned of the snub. She had returned from New York with a publisher in her pocket, a deal for a hardcover version of *Letters to Mendy* and an option for another book, a novel this time. She was jubilant and full of herself and confident that there was stardom and a beach house in her future. Only two negatives spoiled her homecoming. One was that her legs were badly swollen with painful, ugly, bulging blue veins, and two, that she and Denise had not been invited to Big Bobbie's do.

"I don't give a shit about *me*," she raged to Joan, "but poor Denise is inconsolable. How can she do this to a child?"

"She has nothing against you, Audrey. She just felt

that you and Carol Lighter in the same place at the same time would invite disaster. To her, you're the thirteenth fairy."

"But she invited Carol Lighter and her ugly brat."

"Well, she's friendlier with Carol than she is with you."

"She could at least have invited Denise. I wouldn't think of going anyway. I *hate* children's birthday parties. I hate giving them and I hate going to them. The only things I hate worse than kids' birthday parties are Carol Lighter and constipation."

"You hate constipation?"

"Terrible. I haven't done good doodies since before New York."

"I guess you could say you're full of shit."

"Terrible. My stomach is hard as a rock."

"Ha, you wish."

"My legs are falling off and the pain is so bad that I want to send them to Peru. Dr. Lederer will not even talk to me on the phone. He hates me. He says that I don't listen and that's why my legs are so bad. He refuses to treat me."

"Maybe he'd change his mind if you paid your bill."

"I paid him, I paid him. I paid him the minute the first vein looked at me."

"So go to another doctor."

"Lederer is the best. Don't worry, he'll see me—you know I can wrap anybody up. He *hates* me, but he loves me. I could kill Big Bobbie for doing this to my daughter. If I could walk I'd knock her across the room in green. I'll call her later and ask her to have Denise."

"She won't. The party is for kids and their mothers. She's not having one without the other. I already asked her about Denise and she said no. Nan's and Dolores' kids aren't invited either," Joan added, "because they're both working and Bobbie doesn't want kids without the mothers. Forget about it. Buy your daughter a doll and stay home with your legs. Start your novel."

"How could she invite you and not me?"

"We aren't Siamese twins, Audrey. She's right, anyway. You and Carol Lighter would be the worst combination since fat ladies and pants suits."

"Come over and look at my legs."

"No way. I'm not *that* big a masochist."

"Will you be at the hospital with me?"

"Sure, unless of course something important comes up, like reading the new *Redbook* or flossing my teeth."

"Good-bye, Joan. Dr. Lederer says I'm ruining his medical reputation. He will not treat patients who are stupid and don't listen to him. He says he no longer wants the responsibility of handling my case...he doesn't want the aggravation."

"It serves you right. You're an idiot. Even Richard Nixon had the sense to put his feet up."

"Maybe I'll call *his* doctor."

"Do that. Good-bye. I have to get Naomi a dress for Seth's party."

"How can you go without me? What about loyalty?"

"What about it? Now you can add 'disloyal' to 'hard, mean, rotten, abrasive and horrible.'"

"I hate you. Good-bye."

When Joan was a little girl, birthday parties were simple things. She would invite six other little girls, who arrived on the big day starched, beribboned, patent-leather Mary Janes agleam. White socks were folded down just so, and carefully held in both hands was the inexpensive present, usually Parcheesi or bingo or a card of barettes or a Nancy Drew mystery. She would greet her guests, thank them and put the presents on her bed, along with the coats. Then she would lead them to the kitchen and seat them at the gay paper-clothed table. In front of each child was a paper plate on which was placed a small, fluted paper cup of candies. Next to the plate, on the napkin, were a party hat and a paper blower with a feather on the end. The birthday cake stood, candles unlit, in the center of the table. It was usually decorated with one pink or yellow or blue rose in the center and edged with icing of the same color. "Happy Birthday" was written in red glaze above the rose and the child's name, also

192

in red glaze, below it. The tiny candles circled the rose, one for each year and one extra for good luck.

After the guests were seated, they donned the hats, blew their blowers, admired the cake and ate every piece of candy in their baskets. Then each child in turn would stand up and entertain—recite a poem or sing a song, tell a joke or riddle. Dancing was frowned upon by most mothers, concerned with scuff marks and their neighbors in the apartment below. After everyone had done her thing, the candles were lit, "Happy Birthday" was sung, ice cream was scooped onto each plate from a bulk pack of vanilla and, when all was consumed, one game of pin-the-tail-on-the-donkey was played. The best friend of the birthday girl generally won, received a balloon as a prize, and the party was over. The whole affair lasted perhaps an hour, and cost about six dollars.

In Beverly Hills, however, a birthday party, like everything else, was an elaborate production. The plans for it were as meticulously laid as those of the D-day invasion. Carefully selected invitations were mailed two weeks before the date, and the clown acts or magicians or puppeteers were screened and hired to entertain the children. For Rosamanda's birthday, Joan's friend Pauline had once hired a trained dog act which cost $125 and lasted twenty minutes. Along with the regular entertainment, there would often be a pony and trainer in the driveway and as each guest arrived, he or she was given a little ride around the begonias.

Unless it was specifivally stated in the invitation, parents did not remain at the party, and often long lines of Caddies, Rollses, Jags, and Mercedes' queued up along the curb, each in turn stopping, waiting until its small passenger put his or her present down, slowly opened the door, stepped out, reached back for the present and kicked the door shut with a sturdy foot. No one ever had difficulty locating the home in which the party took place, since invariably a huge bouquet of colorful balloons had been affixed to the mailbox.

The birthday cake would be designed to display some

facet of the personality or hobby or interest of the birthday child. There were cakes in the shape of football fields (complete with plastic teams), baseball diamonds, ballerinas, Raggedy Anns, jungles and open books. At one party Naomi attended, the cake was shaped like a huge mocha money pouch, with a green dollar sign between the "Happy" and the "Birthday" to signify the child's interest in the root of all evil. He wanted to be a banker like his daddy, and gold-foil-covered chocolate coins were heaped beside each plate. At the conclusion of the party, each guest was given a crisp new two-dollar bill as a remembrance. Some of the little angels even managed to run around back, reenter the house, get back in line and receive a second crisp new two-dollar bill.

Refreshments were generously doled out, the children being permitted to request the ice cream flavor of their choice, and they could opt for soda, punch, Kool-Aid, apple juice, milk (white or chocolate) or grape drink with which to wet their little whistles. In addition to the candy, also beside the plates were blowers, hats, confetti, balloons, party poppers and streamers. Maids or housekeepers were on duty to refill cups, pass out cake, clean up spills and clear away the mess when the party was over.

These affairs generally lasted two and a half hours at least, and if you got by for under $250 you were considered lucky—or cheap. And these were parties for the younger set. With ten-, eleven- and twelve-year-olds, the procedure was somewhat different. On one memorable evening, Joan's sons were picked up by a chauffeur-driven limousine, taken to dinner and Disneyland, and returned to their door at 10:30 P.M. in the same chauffeur-driven limousine, each boy clutching a Kiss album, distributed to each guest in honor of the occasion.

There were swimming parties, luncheon parties, dinner parties, bowling parties, miniature golf parties and combinations of all of them . . . you name it. The entire population of Pakistan could be sustained for one week on the food that was thrown out, and the Angolan army could be adequately clothed and armed by the money spent. God bless America and especially Beverly Hills.

Big Bobbie's party for Seth carried on the tradition; in fact, went one better because all the mothers were invited to stay. The kids were whisked away by cheery clowns and the mommies directed to the patio for eating, drinking and dishing. Bobbie's was not a showbiz-only affair. It was a mixed bag which included wives of doctors, lawyers, businessmen, writers, producers, performers, reporters, bankers, insurance executives, etc. There wasn't a daddy in sight, with the exception of Bobbie's psychiatrist husband, Sandy. Sandy Leventhal was six feet five inches tall, had a beard, smoked a pipe, slouched and asked Joan, "How are *you* today?" Being the concerned doctor that he was, he even waited for a reply.

On the long buffet table on the patio was a huge punch bowl filled with a potent sangrialike concoction in which floated succulent slices of assorted fruits and ice cubes, and into which had been dumped, along with soda and a gallon of wine, something like three quarts of vodka. Behind the punch bowl stood Bobbie's housekeeper, Maria, generously ladling punch into the cutglass cups the women eagerly held out to her. The rest of the table was covered with trays of petits fours, assorted hors d'oeuvres, Barton's dietetic candies and cocktail napkins on which was printed "Hooray for Seth Leventhal." Within twenty minutes the ladies had begun to giggle, make inappropriate remarks, stroke Sandy Leventhal's beard and totally forget that they were the mothers of the forty or so kids being entertained by Señor Clown on the side lawn of the house.

Joan, semi-bombed, sat with Pauline and Sharon, smoking and laughing and not minding at all that Carol Lighter was weaving her way to their table. She sipped her brew and extravagantly admired Pauline's two-hundred-dollar French silk blouse that Maurice Benani had bestowed upon his wife just like that. Carol sank gracefully into the chair across from Joan, having first carefully wiped off the seat. She was wearing perfectly fitted white sharkskin Bill Blass slacks and a Ralph Lauren shirt, the polo pony emblem prominent on the cuff. She arranged herself next to Sharon, removed a pale green cigarette from her solid-gold case, lit it with her solid-gold lighter and blew a puff of smoke into Joan's face. She did not even acknowledge her presence. She smiled at Pauline, however, inquired as to her health, and glanced appraisingly at her blouse and the enormous black-opal-and-diamond ring she wore.

Zoe Newman arrived bearing two cups of punch, and carefully placed one in front of Carol. She sat down next to her idol and smiled a hello at the table at large. Her big brown eyes were already slightly out of focus and her T-shirt, which proclaimed "Try It, You'll Like It," was half out of the waistband of her pants. Pauline, who despite her husband's vast wealth could never feel comfortable with the Beverly Hills set, nervously twisted her ring and asked Joan if her hair was all right. She had once bestowed upon Joan the dubious compliment that, of all the women in town, only with Joan did she feel at ease. "Why is that?" Joan had asked, vaguely displeased. "You don't make me feel like a dummy," Pauline had replied. "You're simple like me."

"I would like, just once, to be a threat to somebody," Joan had confided to Eric after Pauline's vote of confidence. She recalled a friend of hers from New York named Betty Rogers, who had lived in their apartment building. Betty was gamely clinging to a rapidly deteriorating marriage with her short, brilliant and neurotic husband, Bruce, and was insanely jealous of any woman who so much as looked at him. Even a waitress in a restaurant who asked for Bruce's order came under suspicion. One afternoon Joan had bumped into Bruce on Fifty-ninth Street and they had gone to lunch together. "Betty will kill me," she said to him over the

196

chef's salad, and she had called Betty immediately upon her return home.

"Betty," she admitted nervously, "I ran into Bruce downtown and we had lunch together."

Betty inhaled on her cigarette and replied nonchalantly, "That's nice."

"Well," Joan said in surprise, "doesn't that bother you? You know how jealous you are."

"Yeah, but it's different with you," Betty told her. "I don't worry about you."

"Oh," Joan answered dully. "I see."

She wondered what it was about her that caused even women like Betty and Pauline to consider her harmless. She realized she wasn't gorgeous and sexy, but she wasn't a total disaster either. Why didn't she excite envy and consternation in the breasts of those women who had a shit fit if their husbands spoke for five minutes with some other female?

"You don't send out covetous signals," Eric explained, smiling and kissing her clenched hand. "You don't make them feel you're after anything they've got."

"But still," Joan had replied sadly, "still . . ."

"Your hair is fine," she now assured the fidgety Pauline. "Relax."

"I had it done yesterday at Vidal Sassoon and they told me to get a body wave. Do you think I need vitamins? My hair is so thin and it never grows."

"It's fine. Drink your punch."

Pauline obediently took a sip. "My Uncle Thomas, the one from Syosset, has stomach cancer," she solemnly informed Joan, "and it's really funny. Not funny where you laugh," she added hastily, "but funny that he should get it in the stomach . . . because my Aunt Carmella, she never gave him no frozen vegetables or nothing like that for dinner. She always gave him fresh . . ."

"Pauline," Joan said with a sigh, "take another drink."

"Hello, girls," said Myrna and Gloria, walking over and sitting down.

"Just like old times, isn't it? I see you're alone," Myrna said to Joan. "Where's your weird friend?"

"Whoever do you mean? Now that *you've* arrived, all my weird friends are right here," Joan said, smiling. "Recovered from your party yet?"

"Finally. You still mad at me?"

"One more glass of punch and I'll love you madly," Joan replied. "I'll want to marry you, I'll love you so much." She drained her cup of punch and felt the vodka spreading its cheer through her system. "Bobbie," she called to the hostess, who was chatting with her guests at the next table. "Great party, Bobbie. Even your eyelashes are on right."

Bobbie grinned and gingerly touched her troublesome lashes. "I had them permanently attached," she said. "They're supposed to stay on for a week if you don't wash your face." Then she went off to check on the kids.

Joan turned back and met Carol Lighter's eyes across the table. She nodded and Carol looked away. "Carol doesn't like me," she said loudly to Sharon. "Why doesn't she like me?" Joan took another cup of punch off the tray that Maria was now carrying around from table to table, aware that many of the women were at this point unable to steadily navigate the distance to the punch bowl. Emboldened by another sip, Joan continued, "Why don't you like me?" she asked Carol directly. "I'm not poor, I'm not black, I'm not better-looking than you, so why don't you like me?"

"Joan," whispered Gloria, "don't start."

"I'm not starting," Joan said. "I really want to know."

"Carol likes you," said a surprised Pauline. "How could anybody not like you? You're the cream of the earth. You like Joan, don't you, Carol?"

Carol looked up at Pauline, whose house could sell on today's market for a million five, and offered her a cigarette. "No, thank you," said Pauline. "I get nau-
198

seous from smoking. I can drink, but I never could tolerate smoking. I don't mind if other people smoke, it don't bother me or nothing, but it ain't good for *me*. No offense intended."

Carol withdrew her cigarette case and replaced it in her bag. "You're absolutely right not to smoke," she said.

"*I* don't smoke," said Zoe, hungry for Carol's approval. "It's very rare that I take a cigarette."

"Well, I *do*," answered Carol, lighting up, and Zoe subsided, stung.

"My mother smokes, God bless her," Pauline went on, all her feelings of inferiority drowned in punch, "and her teeth don't get stained or nothin'. She says if you brush with Pearl Drops, your teeth stay white. Your teeth are nice and white, Carol. Can I axe you somethin'? Do you brush with Pearl Drops?"

Carol smiled. "You're very sweet," she said. Pauline, flushed with punch and pleasure at being part of the group, pulled off her awesome opal and handed it to Carol. "See that ring?" she asked. "My husband bought it for me off of an Arab. It cost thirty-two thousand dollars, but what's money for if you can't buy a ring? I heard that black opals are bad luck, but my husband says it ain't true. He says that nothin' that costs thirty-two thousand dollars could be bad luck. He says that bad luck don't cost nothin' . . . it's free. Do you confer with that? Do you think I'll get bad luck if I wear it?"

"You'll never have bad luck," Joan said fondly. "You are one of the world's innocents. Wear it and enjoy it and insure it."

"Oh, Maurice takes care of all that," she said, retrieving the ring and returning it to her finger. "Everything we got is insured. Ever since Maurice inquired his extreme wealth, he started to insure everything. See this watch?" she asked, indicating a diamond-faced Piaget. "It's insured. I notice you got a Piaget also" (she pronounced it "Piagette"), she said, pointing to Carol's wrist. "Is it insured?"

"Are you for real?" Carol asked in amazement.

"Everything I got is real," Pauline explained seriously. "I break out from base metals."

Joan laughed delightedly. "How lucky. You're a princess. Don't ever sleep with a pea under your mattress."

"A pea?"

"A green pea."

"Oh, like in the fairy tale?"

"You *are* a fairy tale. Never change, because I love you."

"I love you too," said Pauline, "and so does Carol. Right?"

Carol stared at Pauline, whose home she eagerly wished to examine and whose jewelry she wished to own.

"No," she said defiantly. "I don't."

"Why not?" Pauline asked ingenuously. "You're both Jewish, ain't you?"

"That," Joan told her gently, "is about the only thing we have in common—thank goodness. Carol Lighter and I are very, very diametrically opposed. We are totally opposite and for that blessing I am thankful also."

Carol glared at Joan and placed both hands on the table. "One of the things I'm happiest about," she said between clenched, perfect teeth, "is that I'm nothing at all like you."

"For once we agree. Didn't I just say that?"

"I'd kill myself if we were in any way alike."

"If I could count on that, I'd search forever for a similarity."

"Look," said Myrna, "stop this at once. I cannot go through another scene. It's a fucking déjà vu, and it's Seth's birthday and cut it out."

"Right," added Sharon.

Pauline, who had paled at hearing Myrna's profanity, hurriedly crossed herself and looked in bewilderment at Joan and Carol, her hazel eyes going first to one face, then to another.

"Is something wrong?" she asked Zoe.

"I'd rather not go into it," replied Zoe coolly, recognizing someone whom even *she* could lord it over.

From the other side of the house came the sound of the children's voices raised in a stirring rendition of "Happy Birthday," and a flushed and smiling Bobbie soon approached the table, wiping buttercream icing on her pants. Her husband followed, pulling from his Polaroid a snapshot of Seth blowing out his birthday candles. "Okay, ladies," he said, holding the camera in front of him, "let's get a shot of this table." He arranged the women on one side of the table, telling those who could still manage to stand up to get behind those who couldn't.

Joan smiled into the camera, hoping that for once in her life she'd take a decent picture, and looked down onto the top of Carol Lighter's streaked, perfectly arranged head. She blew slightly and noted that Carol's hair did not even move. Audrey, she knew, if given this opportunity, would already have dribbled a mouthful of punch onto Carol's gleaming part. But Audrey wasn't here and Joan was a civilized coward. She blew again, this time more strongly, and felt Myrna poke her in the ribs. "Okay," she whispered, and went back to her chair, wrinkling her nose at the missed opportunity.

"Maria," called Bobbie, checking her lashes, "bring some more punch, *por favor*."

Carol now had her compact out and was applying lipgloss. The punch was having its effect and her unsteady hands left a gleaming smear on the side of her cheek.

Maria arrived and set a glass of punch before each of the women. Bobbie raised her glass. "To Seth, who promised to stop wetting his bed when he turned eight," she said, and all the ladies drank.

"To the mothers of all those overprivileged brats on the side lawn, and to Seth keeping his promise," said Joan, and they all drank again.

"To Bobbie's eyelashes," said Gloria, and they finished the punch.

"To Carol and Joan making up," said Pauline, waving her empty cup.

"Maria!" yelled Bobbie. "More punch, *for pavor*," and Maria quickly refilled the glasses.

The children were now in the pool, swimming and splashing and shrieking. Bobbie had hired the swimming instructor from the local "Y" as a lifeguard, and for once Joan, thanks in part to her vodka-induced condition, was not afraid that her daughter would drown. Still, she kept a bleary blue eye on the pool.

All the women, with the exception of Pauline, who was Gentile and therefore presumably capable of holding her liquor, were sloshed. Even Carol Lighter was loaded and enunciating her words carefully, the streak of lipgloss still on her cheek. Joan, who could get high on one drink and had already had three, looked at her fourth and hoped she wouldn't throw up. She was queasily aware that the gaily striped canopy under which they sat seemed to be spinning and whirling around her. Pauline, only slightly high and full of vodka and confidence, was still lifting her half-filled glass in a toast.

"To Carol and Joan letting bygones be bygones," she sang out, and took a healthy swig.

"I'll think to drat," slurred Bobbie, and put her glass where she thought her mouth was. Half the punch dripped down onto her blouse and white, icing-stained pants. "Shit," she said angrily, and slammed her glass down on the table so hard that the punch splashed up into her face. "Shit," she said again and, forgetting her $7.50 eyelash job, rubbed her knuckles into her punch-filled eyes, smearing her mascara and coming away with half the painstakingly applied lashes glued to her fist.

Carol looked up at Bobbie and pursed her lips. "You are a mess," she said disapprovingly. "You have mascara all over your face."

Bobbie closed her ruined eyes and leaned back in her chair. "Oh, shit," she muttered wearily.

"You can't afford to talk," Joan said to Carol. "You have lipgloss all over your faces."

"You mean 'face,'" corrected Sharon.

202

"Uh-uh, I mean *faces*—she has *two*, you know."

Gloria laughed and leaned across Zoe. "Did you hear that, Carol? Joan called you two-faced."

Sharon, feeling Carol stiffen, began to twirl her drink. She smiled.

"Did you just call me two-faced?" demanded Carol.

"Yup," said Joan.

"You'd give your eye teeth to be lucky enough to have my face, you ugly bitch."

"Yup. I'd love to have either one of your faces, or even both."

"You don't need her faces," Pauline assured her friend loyally. "You have a very nice face of your own."

"Thank you," Joan said, patting Pauline's thigh. "But I would still love to have Carol's two faces. One of them I'd step on, and the other one I'd walk on." She hiccuped gently.

"Girls, girls," said Sharon, putting her hand on Carol's arm. "Let's not get nasty."

"Carol can't help it," said Joan. "She was born that way. Right, Carol?"

Shaking off Sharon's hand, Carol rose unsteadily to her feet. "Drop dead," she said viciously, and sat down again.

Pauline gasped and crossed herself once more. "Jesus, Mary and Joseph," she breathed to Joan. "Are you gonna take that?" Her Sicilian loyalties were aroused in defense of the one woman in town she felt comfortable with.

"Yup. She's too stupid to knoweth what she sayeth."

"Carol is not stupid," said Zoe. "She's the smartest woman I know and the best dressed," and she nodded righteously.

Bobbie opened one mascara-smeared eye and snorted, "You're all stupid," she said, "especially me. My lashes are ruined, ruined." She closed her eye and grimaced in self-disgust.

Myrna pushed her chair back and nudged Gloria. "Here we go again," she said. She took a slug of punch and clinked her glass to Gloria's. "Here's to brotherhood . . . no, to sisterhood," she toasted.

"I'll drink to that," said Pauline.

"Here's to Audrey Miller," Joan said, swaying to her feet, "who would have annihilated two-faced Carol Lighter much better than I ever could." She took a tiny sip and looked over at the pool. Naomi's head, she noted, was still above water, while hers was alarmingly light.

"Audrey Miller should drop dead with you," muttered Carol.

"Run your own errands, fool," retorted Joan. "For all your two faces, there's only half a brain."

"Drop dead."

"You said that already. Tell me, Carol, why don't you like me? Maybe you do, maybe this is only an act. Do you really like me, Carol?" She leaned over and put her nose two inches from Carol's. The two women stared into each other's face. Then Joan straightened up. "She wears contact lenses," she solemnly informed the group.

Sandy Leventhal approached the table, grinning and waving the Polaroid picture at the women. "Every one of you came out beautiful. What's the matter with her?" he asked, nodding at his semiconscious wife.

"She tried to drink punch with her eye," Joan said, taking the picture and trying to focus on it. "You call this beautiful?" She stared at herself in the photograph, hoping fervently that she didn't appear in life the way she did in this picture. Carol Lighter, naturally, looked perfect, marred only by the two donkey-ear fingers Joan was holding up behind her head. The thing that came out best was Pauline's ring, the color of the opal brilliant and the diamonds surrounding it clearly defined.

"Cheekbones," Joan thought to herself, "if I only had cheekbones." She handed the picture to Pauline to be passed around the table, and jumped as the lifeguard's whistle startled her. "All out of the pool," he called. "Everybody out."

Joan jumped again as Maria tapped her on the shoulder. "No more punch for me, Maria," she said. "I have had it."

"No, missus," said the maid. "There is telephone for you." She pointed to the outdoor phone and Joan walked carefully, slightly unsteady, toward it. "It's the boys," she thought. "What the hell do they want?"

The women began putting themselves together and repairing the damage done by too much spiked punch and childish behavior. Only Pauline remained placid, drinking the last of her brew. She sipped contentedly, idly watching Joan speaking on the phone. She realized that Joan was more affected by the liquor than she had appeared. Leaning dazedly against the stucco wall of the house, one hand over her mouth, her eyes wide and staring, Joan looked ready to pass out.

"She's gonna vomit all over the patio," Pauline thought, and stood up to help Joan to the bathroom. She remained standing while Joan tried to hang up, missing the cradle and leaving the receiver tilting against the side of the phone, half on and half off. Pauline imagined she could hear the dial tone and then the shrill, monotonous signal of a receiver off the hook. Joan stood rigid for a moment and then slowly and stiffly made her way back to the table. She bumped heavily into a huge pot of Ficus directly in her path, and as if it weren't there, attempted to continue walking, eyes glazed, staring and unfocused. Pauline went over, took Joan's arm and led her around the plant and back toward the table. Joan seemed completely unaware of her presence. "Don't worry," Pauline whispered. "I'll drive you home and we can pick up your wagon later on."

They reached the table and Joan remained standing, trancelike, until Pauline gently pushed her into a chair.

"What the hell's the matter with her?" asked Carol Lighter, looking up from her mirror.

"Nothin'," replied Pauline. "She just ain't usta drinkin'. Joan," she said softly, shaking her friend, "snap out of it."

"She looks catatonic," said Carol. "It disgusts me to see a woman who can't hold her liquor," and she turned back to her mirror, drawing a shaky line of black eyeliner above her lashes.

The children were now out of the pool and drying off. Several mothers were vigorously toweling the hair of their offspring, aware of what the combination of open car windows and wet heads could bring on. The children headed toward the pool house to change into dry clothing and await the surprises contained in the party bags Maria was now placing on the cleared-off buffet table.

"Joan," said Pauline, a note of concern creeping into her voice. "Come on, Joan, snap out of it." She shook her again, but Joan remained stony and unseeing.

"I think something's wrong with her," said Sharon, leaning across the table and looking into Joan's eyes. "She's not even blinking."

Myrna giggled nervously and looked at Gloria, who said, "Maybe she needs another drink." Zoe glanced over and then went back to her intent study of Carol Lighter's dazzling display of makeup magic. Big Bobbie, finally aroused, was gazing at Joan with interest, her eyes tearing and winking in an effort to rid themselves of the false eyelashes decorating her eyeball instead of her eyelid.

"Joan," repeated Pauline, snapping her fingers under Joan's nose. "Come on, Joan," and she lightly tapped her friend's cold cheek.

"Liquor does that to some people," Gloria noted sagely.

"I don't think it's the liquor," said Pauline. "It was that phone call. Joan, who was it called you? What happened?"

Suddenly Carol put down her makeup mirror, rose to her feet and leaned over the table. She peered into Joan's face and narrowed her glossed lips into a thin line. She drew back her hand and smartly slapped Joan across the face, first one cheek, then the other. Joan's

206

head snapped back and her eyes began to focus. She stared up at Carol Lighter.

"That was Scott Miller... Melvin," she said huskily, her eyes never leaving Carol's face, her voice a raspy monotone. "He called my house and the boys gave him this number..." She paused, eyes still glued to Carol's, then droned on like a recording. "Audrey is dead. She died at 3:45 P.M. in Cedars Sinai Hospital of a blood clot on the brain. Audrey is dead. My friend Audrey Miller...she died today...at 3:45 P.M...." Her voice trailed off. Carol stared at her, her mouth open, and sank heavily back into her seat. The other women sat motionless, except for Sharon twirling her empty glass.

"Jesus," said Pauline, her voice breaking. "Holy Mary Mother of God." She pointed a shaking finger at Carol Lighter. "You done it," she cried shrilly. "You wished it on her, I seen you do it."

"Don't be an idiot," Carol snapped, her face pale. "That's the stupidest thing I ever heard."

"You done it," Pauline repeated, and for the third time that afternoon, she crossed herself.

"She didn't suffer," Joan went on dully. "She went into a coma and died at 3:45 P.M. in Cedars Sinai Hospital, without ever waking up. She didn't have time to be afraid, she never knew what hit her. A fucking blood clot went up her leg and killed her... and that's that. Audrey...crazy Audrey Miller...She's going to be published in hardcover, you know, and maybe even be on Johnny Carson...maybe this fall...She's beginning a novel about this actress..."

The children were now lined up in front of the buffet, receiving their party bags. They squealed in delight or disappointment, and threw the hastily ripped wrapping paper onto the lush grass surrounding the pool. Bright paper bows sprung like flowers around their feet. At a signal from Sandy Leventhal, the lifeguard blew his whistle and the children quieted and looked up. Joan turned and dimly perceived her daughter attempting to exchange her jacks for Stacey Lighter's jump rope.

"Okay, kids," shouted Sandy. "You all had a good time . . . but now the party's over."

Joan sat absolutely still. Then she slowly closed her eyes, put both her hands over her suddenly crumpling face, and with an shudder of painfully dawning grief, quietly began to cry.

20

Carol Lighter drove the three blocks to her home with great caution. Although now quite sober, there was still a goodly amount of alcohol in her system, and she wished neither to be stopped by the Beverly Hills police nor do any damage to her new Mercedes. Her daughter, Stacey, sat quietly in the back seat, having been told to shut her stupid mouth. Stacey was unwilling to risk the smack across the face, or any other part of her body, that was forthcoming if she disobeyed. She had learned the hard way that her pretty mama was totally unpredictable and could slide from smiles to enraged slaps, from bored acceptance to complete rejection in the wink of an eye. Now, her mother sat gripping the wheel with whitened knuckles, upset and distracted, absolutely uninterested in hearing about Stacey's good time at the party, ready to erupt in fury if Stacey so much as breathed a word.

The child clutched her plastic pack of jacks, holding them close so that her mother would not become upset at the jingle, and looked out the window. She was a heavy, thick-featured child. She had inherited none of her mother's sleekness and was aware that her mother was disappointed and irate at having produced a daughter so unappealing as Stacey. There were times when she stopped her play, made uncomfortable by her mother's scrutiny. Carol would examine her closely, turning her around and around, then click her tongue, mutter "It's hopeless," and push her away. Sometimes she would say, "I can't stand to look at you," and then look at her, her mouth grim.

Stacey became stoic and plodding, and very adept at staying out of her mother's way. She recognized every danger signal and realized that this time was a bad time, and that she had better escape to her room immediately upon their return home if she knew what was good for her.

Carol pulled into the driveway and shut off the motor. She sat in the car for a few minutes, preoccupied, oblivious of her daughter's rapid and clumsy exit from the car. Carol had been discomfited by Pauline's idiotic accusation. If her wishes could affect events, then Audrey would have been dead long ago. Still, the whole scene disturbed her. She was shaken by the fact that even dead, Audrey could still unsettle her, and resentful that she should be made to feel this way. Even when Joan broke the news, it was directly to her, as if out of all the women at the table, only she and Joan were involved. Well, she didn't give a shit about Audrey, could never stomach the woman. Death was horrible, but it was much worse to be getting and looking and feeling old. Audrey had been her enemy, and Carol despised her, but her death had pointed up Carol's dissatisfaction with her own life. She realized that now. Life was too short to remain in a rut. She had to make a move, and the events of the day had given her the prod she needed.

Carol got out of the car and walked up the curving driveway and into the house, determined to make a change in her life before it was too late. She had never had an affair, but many of her friends had and still were having. She needed to do something interesting
210

with her life before her face and body fell apart. The fact that death could come at any moment had just been flung in her face, and she wanted to live a little before it came to her. She smiled, realizing that by dying, Audrey had done her a favor. She had helped her make an important decision.

Carol put down her handbag and went to the phone. It was risky to call Phillip at home on a Saturday evening, but it was a chance she had to take.

After five minutes or so, Joan had calmed down sufficiently to assure everyone that she was capable of driving herself home. She was never one to cry comfortably in public, and now was a bit mortified at her display. She told Pauline that it was nice of her to want to follow her home, but unnecessary. She collected her daughter, put her and her jump rope into the station wagon, and started off. Naomi kept up a continuous chatter that Joan found paradoxically both comforting and irritating. She was glad to be away from the women and their awkward attempts to comfort her.

Pauline had hovered over her, almost in tears herself, although she hardly knew Audrey. "If you liked her, she musta been a lovely person, God rest her soul," she comforted, patting Joan's bent head. "She went nice and peaceful, and there wasn't nothin' to be done for her. God took her easy. Where she is now, there ain't no blood clocks. Please stop cryin'."

Carol left almost immediately, and Joan realized the extent of her upset—probably from Pauline's words—because she forgot to take her makeup mirror. Zoe, spotting the oversight, grabbed it up reverently and raced after Carol, hoping to receive a smile for her trouble. Myrna, Gloria and Sharon mumbled the usual words and also went off. Bobbie said nothing at all. She simply put her large hands, with their bitten nails, over Joan's clenched and sweaty ones, pressed tightly, and was gone.

Joan drove slowly, methodically, occasionally nodding or saying "uh-huh" in response to Naomi's never-

211

ending spiel. Her daughter had had a wonderful time, gorged herself with candy and cake and ice cream, and successfully negotiated the trade with Stacey Lighter. She had not noticed Joan's red-rimmed eyes behind the oversized sunglasses, and Joan was relieved to defer the difficult explanation. She was worried about how best to break the news of Audrey's death to the children, who were wary but fond of her late friend. Joan was amazed at her calm. After the initial shock, she found that her feelings were under control and she was now in the throes of a strange, inappropriate, almost self-important excitement. She couldn't wait to get home and tell Eric. She was eager to phone Nan and Dolores to inform them of the tragedy.

She imagined Melvin was occupied with funeral arrangements, doubtless having already taken Mendy and Denise to stay with his parents. Audrey's folks were too old and infirm, and surely too grief-stricken, to care for those poor children. How very, very sad for those old parents to have outlived their daughter. One of the greatest tragedies conceivable was to bury one's child. She shuddered at the thought.

Joan supposed that the funeral would be held on Monday, consistent with Jewish law to bury the dead quickly. She made a mental note to check with the temple Sunday morning. She pulled into her driveway and jumped out of the car before Naomi had a chance to undo her seat belt. She raced inside and greeted her sons briefly. "Where's Daddy?" she asked, and almost ran out to the patio, where Eric, in a rare moment of leisure, was lying on a chaise reading *Playboy*.

She kissed the top of his head and sat down beside him. "Something awful happened," she said, and to her horror, felt a smile spread over her face.

Eric looked up and smiled back. "Can't be that bad," he said.

"Oh, but it is," said Joan, making a valiant effort to erase her appalling grin. "It's awful. Audrey died," and to her everlasting shame, was forced to stifle a giggle.

"What did you say?" asked Eric, sitting up and dropping his magazine. He stared at her, and the more he did, the harder it became to suppress her horrible, unbelievable laughter.

"Audrey Miller?" he asked incredulously.

"Yes," she replied, managing to compress her lips and straighten out her treacherous face.

"Oh my God," he said, leaning back in shock. "That poor baby." They were silent for a while, Eric gazing, stunned, at the leaves floating on the surface of the pool. Joan followed his gaze, concentrating on the water in an intense effort to control her god-awful mirth.

"What happened?" he asked quietly.

"A blood clot. Her legs were always bad," she answered, her voice shaking with suppressed laughter.

Eric stared at her. "Do you find that amusing?" he inquired, looking in amazement and disgust at her contorted face. "What's the matter with you? Your best friend just died and you're laughing about it?"

"I can't *help* it," she quavered, "I just can't help it," and started for the door.

"Joan." She stopped and looked back. "Come here," he said, and patted the chaise beside him. Joan returned and hunched down, cupping her chin in her hand.

"What kind of monster am I," she asked softly, "to have such an incongruous reaction to such a sad and terrible thing?" She paused. "Why?" she asked, looking up at her husband. "Why did I do that?"

"It happens to a lot of people," Eric said, gently taking her hand. "I'm sorry I hollered. You had an awful shock and you reacted inappropriately—I suppose in an effort to block out the reality."

Joan nodded. "I suppose," she said, and looked away.

"How did it happen?" he asked.

"I don't know. I imagine she passed out and they rushed her to the hospital. Scott said she died in Cedars Sinai at 3:45 P.M. She never came out of her coma. I can't believe it. I always thought she'd go on forever like Old Man River. I used to tell her she'd bury us all. I can't believe it. I don't even know what I was doing

213

at 3:45 . . . probably swilling another cup of punch and trading shots with Carol Lighter. I was crapping around at a pissy kids' birthday party while Audrey was dying in Cedars Sinai. You know what bothers me?" she asked, looking up.

"What, puss?"

"I never felt the passing. I always imagined I'd get some sort of psychic signal when someone dear to me was in danger . . . or dying. But I felt nothing. I felt absolutely nothing—no sign, no feeling of unease, no urgent need to get to her . . . nothing."

"When is the funeral?"

"Monday, I suppose. I'll check in the morning."

"Can I do anything for you, puss?"

She shook her head.

"Sorry I hollered."

"I know. It's okay." She stood up.

"Where are you going?"

"I've got to call people—Nan, Dolores, Dick Bell. She has a lot of friends."

"Had."

Joan nodded. "Had."

She opened the screen door and went into the house. She took the telephone off the night table and lay down on her bed, one hand still on the phone, on that so very important link to the outside world. How often had she been here, just so, her hand on the telephone, impatient to make contact with her friend Audrey? She couldn't count the times. She lifted the receiver and began to dial Nan's number, wondering vaguely why she wasn't weeping or grief-stricken or something. But she wasn't. She wasn't feeling anything at all, except eagerness to spread the word about what had happened to Audrey . . . and to her.

Nan lay back in her reclining chair, eyes closed, feet up, a Diet Pepsi in her hand, the phone close within reach. She was attempting to meditate her hunger for Richard and marriage and security out of her system. She wondered if the power of the mantra wasn't dissipated by the mundane presence of the two modern

214

miracles so close-by—the diet drink and the phone. Her whole body ached with the effort, and her heart felt drained of all hope. Nan imagined that her heart was some sort of reservoir in which was contained her lifetime supply of tears. Every time she wept, and it seemed to her that she was forever weeping, she lowered her heart's level. When all her tears were gone, it would be left sere and arid, a Sahara heart, shriveled and incapable of functioning. She was trapped, her head in 1976, her heart twenty years behind. She thought wryly of all those successful and wealthy people who accepted her as one of them, admired and looked up to and envied her.

"They should only know," she had said to Joan. "They see me as very together and dealing perfectly with single life. Ha."

"Why *do* you need a man?" Joan had asked. "You already have children and you're perfectly capable of supporting yourself."

Nan had walked over to the refrigerator, peered inside and closed it again. "Do you know what I miss?" she asked. "I miss having someone around to check the windows and lock up at night. I miss holding hands when I take a walk. Carl and I used to have a favorite song. We'd look at each other whenever we'd hear it."

"What was it?"

Nan smiled. "'True Love,'" she said. "Isn't that a laugh?"

21

Dolores stared at herself in the mirror. She examined the long, thin face, the arched nose, the large green eyes. She searched in vain for the black cloud that she knew hung over her head and rained on her constantly. She lifted her hand and held it above her head, amazed when she lowered it to find it still dry. She cursed silently at her stubborn penchant for doing the right things all wrong, for always being in the wrong places at the wrong times, for making poor decisions, when indeed she made one at all. Today she had managed to accomplish all three idiocies with her usual incompetence and had been thoroughly drenched for her good intentions.

The children were with Stu this weekend, which was unusual because he ordinarily refused to take all three of them together. She had hurried through her work, and by four o'clock had managed to draw up the required number of leases and escrows and was free to leave. She stopped at the market to pick up some wine and crackers and smoked oysters for herself and Milt before they went out to dinner. On the way home she decided she had enough time to drop in at Audrey's for a companionable sip and smoke. She knew Audrey was miffed at not having been invited to Bobbie's party and would welcome her company, she hoped. One could never be sure about Audrey's reaction to even the kindliest intentions. Once Dolores had offered to take Denise so that Audrey could speak at a "Women and Books" luncheon, and Audrey had yelled at her for even suggesting such a thing when Dolores' daughter had a cold and Denise might catch it.

"What are you trying to do to me?" she had asked indignantly. "You *know* I'm leaving for New York soon, and I *cannot* have my daughter sick. How can you even *think* such a thing?" And Dolores had left bewildered, wondering for the umpteenth time why these things kept happening to her.

Dolores pushed open Audrey's never-locked door, holding a bottle of Wente White and gaily calling "Audrey, where are you?" as she walked into the kitchen to search for a corkscrew. "I have a treat for you." When she neither received a reply nor found the corkscrew, she wandered into the bedroom, still holding the wine. There she found Scott, or Melvin as Joan called him, sitting on the bed with Mendy and Denise beside him. The television set was on and blasting, and they were staring at it, mesmerized, like statues.

"Where's Audrey?" asked Dolores above the volume. "I thought we'd have a little wine. Isn't she home?"

Three faces turned slowly toward her and three pairs of eyes regarded her fixedly. Then they all turned back to the set. She stood in the doorway, confused, and noticed that the phone was off the hook. "What's the matter with all of you?" she asked. "Why is your phone off the hook?"

Scott Miller shrugged, but didn't reply.

"Is Audrey out?" Dolores asked, feeling uncomfortable, as though she had barged in on a private moment. When again he made no reply, she continued hesitantly, "I brought some wine," and she held up the bottle. "It's the kind she likes."

As if in slow motion, Scott Miller's head again turned in her direction. "Haven't you heard?" he asked expressionlessly.

"Heard what?"

"She's not here," answered Mendy, almost rudely. "My mother is dead."

Dolores, startled, stared at him. "I don't think that's very funny, Mendy," she said.

"Neither do I," he answered, and turned away. His child's face looked pinched and old.

"She's never coming home again," piped up Denise, solemnly shaking her head. "Because she's dead."

Dolores stood still, rooted in the doorway, not quite knowing how to react, wondering why even little children treated her so disrespectfully. Her eyes met Melvin's, and very slowly he nodded.

"You mean it's true?" she asked, disbelievingly. "She's . . . Audrey is . . . *dead?*" and her whispering voice cracked at the end and came out like the desperate shrill peep of a fallen baby bird. Again Melvin nodded.

"She died earlier today in Cedars Sinai Hospital of a blood clot. It was painless. I thought you would already have heard," he said quietly. It was then that she noticed his reddened eyes.

"Are you sure?" she asked stupidly. "I mean—" She stopped abruptly because she had no idea what she meant. Mendy glared at her witheringly.

"We're waiting for my Grandma Miller," Denise explained. "Me and Mendy are sleeping there tonight."

"That's nice," replied Dolores, and almost kicked herself.

"Melvin . . . Scott, I'm sorry. Nobody told me. You see, I was working today, so I wasn't home . . ." Her voice trailed off. Melvin stood up and went into the bathroom, closing the door behind him with a little click. Dolores stared at the door and then at the two children, sitting so very still in front of the television set. She felt dizzy and weighted, as though the wine bottle in her hand were dragging her down. She took a few tentative steps into the room, wanting to touch

218

the two small heads, but then turned, put the wine bottle down on the dresser, and fled.

She found herself at home without the slightest recollection of the drive there. Methodically she put the food away and the remaining wine bottles into the refrigerator for chilling. She carefully folded the grocery bags along their original creases and then dropped them on the floor. Her heart was pounding so violently that her body seemed to shake with every beat. She reached for a cigarette, but was trembling so badly that she couldn't light it. Again she tried, holding the lighter in both hands, and managed finally to connect flame and cigarette tip. She inhaled deeply, and began a one-handed search into the recesses of her handbag for the bottle of Valium. Knowing that her legs would never get her to the sink, she swallowed two five-milligram tablets, gagging slightly as the dry pills made their difficult way down her dry throat. Almost clinically she watched her hands calm down. After a while, she had no idea how long, she felt that her legs would again support her body, and she stood up. She swayed against the table, steadied herself, and walked to the phone.

Lighting another cigarette, she dialed Joan Brenner's number. She needed badly to talk to her, to someone, and slumped at hearing a busy signal. She listened for some time, and then hung up. Like a blind person, hands reaching out for walls, she made her careful way to the bedroom to get ready for Milt.

Now, staring at herself in the mirror, she was amazed that her face bore no mark of the staggering blow she had just sustained. The Valium was doing its job and keeping her emotions at a distance, so that they couldn't strangle her. The ash on her cigarette grew long, and she watched it fall to the floor, lying on top of the shag carpet, balanced on a slender thread of nylon, until she slowly crushed it and blended it into the rug with her bare foot.

She showered and dressed and made up automatically. When she was done, she rang Joan again, but

219

the line was still busy. She toyed with the idea of making an emergency breakthrough, but lacked the courage to deal with a skeptical operator. After a moment she went into the living room and sat down to wait for Milt.

The house was unnaturally quiet with the children gone. The room seemed dim and shadowed. Sitting in it, she felt drowsy and out of touch. The phone rang five times before she heard it. She put out a limp hand.

"Hello," she whispered.

"Dolores?"

"Yes."

"Are you all right? I can hardly hear you."

"Hello, Joan," she said, raising her voice. "I'm as all right as I can be, I guess." There was a pause and ‾lores could hear Joan breathing.

"I gather that you've heard."

"I heard," Dolores sighed. "I heard in the worst way a person could hear. Leave it to me to screw up even that."

"What do you mean? And Dolores, speak into the phone, I can't hear you."

"I went over there," said Dolores, speaking obediently into the mouthpiece. "I went over there with a bottle of wine to have a drink with Audrey ... but she wasn't home, she was dead and couldn't make it."

"My God. What a lousy experience. How awful for you. Was Melvin there? And the kids?"

"Sort of, not really. I can't tell you. I can never describe how very bad it was."

"I can imagine. Do you want to come over? You shouldn't be alone."

"You always seem to be saying that to me. Aren't you bored?" Dolores smiled into the phone. "Milt is coming over. But thanks anyway."

"That's good. Okay, then ... Dolores?"

"Still here."

"How do you feel?"

"Full of Valium. How are you?"

"Empty. Full of nothing. I don't think it's hit me yet,

220

and I'd like to be in another country when it does."

"So would I."

"Yes... well, I guess there's nothing to say. Do you have anything to say?"

"I don't know."

"How were Melvin and the kids?"

"Awful."

"Yes... well, naturally."

"Mendy seemed angry."

"I don't blame him. He has plenty to be angry about."

"Melvin seemed dazed, like far away. His eyes were red. Denise hasn't absorbed it yet."

"Poor thing." They sat quietly, each on her end of the phone, listening to each other's silence. The doorbell rang loudly.

"Joan?"

"I heard. That must be Milt. Listen, Dolores, life goes on, try to salvage the evening. I'm glad he'll be there with you." The doorbell rang again. "Go ahead," said Joan. "Let him in. I'll talk to you tomorrow."

Dolores walked to the door and opened it. She stood and looked at Milt Gomberg outlined against the dusky sky.

"Aren't you going to let me in?" he asked, smiling.

"Oh," she said. "Of course," and she stood aside so he could enter.

"Why is it so dark in here?" he asked, turning on the lamps. "Dark rooms are depressing. Where are the kids? It's as quiet as a tomb in here." And he stood solid as a rock, surprised but steady when she fell weeping into his arms.

She quieted quickly and explained to him the reason for her tears. Milt held her and stroked her hair. She seemed to him to be weightless and fragile, like a little bird. Her vulnerability and defenselessness touched him. He realized how very dear she had become to him, how strong he felt in comparison. She was too thin, her kids were difficult, her needs inordinate. Milt looked down at her bent head and felt a rush of tenderness and love that was more intense than even the hatred

221

he had long harbored for his ex-wife, the greedy bitch.

"Dolores," he said softly. "Honey, I want you to think about something." She looked up questioningly, the tip of her nose a bright red. "We've been going out for several months now, and in a few days I'm going to ask you to marry me. For now, I'm asking you to think about your answer—and don't go calling Joan or Audrey . . . I mean Joan, for advice, okay?"

Dolores stiffened. She stared at him incredulously. She had long dreamed and prayed for someone to take care of her and had cried wretchedly because she well knew that for people like her, there were no happy endings. Wishes never came true and prayers were ignored. All her life she had made a career out of trying to please, and all her life she had somehow managed just the opposite. For a moment she entertained the notion that Audrey had interceded for her, had wrapped up God and gotten him to do her friend Dolores, a favor. She looked at Milt Gomberg, and the hope he held out to her, the gift he had just given her, the security and comfort he promised. She didn't think at all about whether or not she loved him. Dolores had painfully accepted the fact that love was dangerous and not to be relied on.

She kissed him, a timid kiss of gratitude, and nodded her head. She couldn't speak. Milt was not the man of her dreams, the shining knight of her lonely fantasies—but he *was* the solution to her problems. She could quit her boring job, get back to her kids, be part of a couple again. "Thank you, Audrey," she said to herself. "That was nice of you."

22

On the Monday morning of Audrey's funeral, Joan awoke at six-thirty and padded out to the kitchen to prepare breakfast for the children. She had argued with Eric the night before about whether or not the kids should go to the funeral. Joan wanted to take them. She believed in saying a proper good-bye, and felt that her children should have the opportunity of doing the same. Eric had refused adamantly. "Let them go to school," he insisted. "They don't belong at a funeral. Why should they be exposed to such a depressing and morbid scene?"

"Because it's a fact of life," she said heatedly. "Death and burial is the natural outcome of living. The kids were fond of Audrey. She was part of my life. They should be allowed to see her off. Besides," she went on, "seeing her laid to rest will help them to better accept her death."

Eric looked at her—a long look. "They already have accepted her death. Audrey played only on the periphery of their lives. It's *your* acceptance I'm concerned about. Send them to school." Eric remained firm, and Joan had finally acquiesced.

Now she filled the kettle with water for her coffee and Eric's herbal tea, and went out to get the paper. It was a beautiful morning, sunny and cool. Her pantyhose wouldn't stick and drive her crazy on a morning like this. She picked up the paper from the driveway and scanned the headlines. The world had not taken notice of Audrey's death. She had not made the front page. Nothing had changed at all, life was going on the way it always did. How sad this was, how wise, how unimportant. Only a very few people would never again be the same. Joan looked up at the sky, childlike, wondering if Audrey was up there on a cloud or behind the bright California sun.

She brought the paper inside and poured Eric's tea. He was leaving early this morning, to make up the work he would miss by attending the funeral. She heard her sons waking up and going to the bathroom. Eric entered the kitchen, looking unfamiliar in his rarely worn dark suit.

"So you'll pick me up at the office?" he asked, taking a sip of his herbal brew.

"At ten," Joan replied. They talked for a few minutes about driving arrangements, and Eric finished his tea and left.

She got the boys and Naomi fed and onto the school bus, and did her morning chores. She started for the bathroom to shower and dress, but stopped in the hall, turned back to the kitchen and made two turkey sandwiches. She made them carefully, with Russian dressing and lettuce, wrapped them in foil and put them in the refrigerator. She filled a jar with ice cubes and put it in the freezer.

When she got to the bedroom, she opened her closet door and stood staring at the array of clothing. She flipped her eyes over the blouses, pants, and dresses crowded into the small space, disorganized, blouses mixed in with pants, dresses amid the jackets, shoes on their sides on the floor, black with brown, with blue and red and white—mates far apart, straps entwined with mismatched strangers. Joan was not a clothes

224

person. She bought indiscriminately, with no thought to style. The closet was packed, yet she never seemed to have anything appropriate for whatever the occasion demanded. Her friends clucked disapprovingly over what they considered to be her total lack of taste or fashion. She never knew until five minutes before, what she was going to wear—and when she finally decided, the garment invariably needed a pressing, making her even more hassled and adding to the confusion which going out always created.

Eric would rush her and ask why she was so unprepared when she had known for a week that they were going out. She never had enough time to apply her makeup properly. But the lack of time rarely bothered her because she never had mastered the art of makeup anyway. She might be nonchalant about clothing, but not knowing how to paint her face effectively bothered her. Joan was one of those women who yearned to be selected as a magazine make-over and go from frumpy housewife to gorgeous. She wanted some genius to take her undistinguished face, partly oily, partly dry, partly sagging and totally wrong, and powder and mascara it into a masterpiece that would cause men to gasp and plunge women into despair.

Her hair, too, seemed an insurmountable challenge. She had the Mount Everest of hair, impossible to conquer or subdue. It was disobedient, like a bratty child, refusing to heed curlers or comb. She generally ended up brushing it back and keeping it there with one of Naomi's hairbands. Joan did not know why getting herself together was so difficult for her and so easy for other women. She therefore conceded defeat, did the best she could and defended her ineptitude by convincing herself and others that vanity had never been on her list of sins, that looking perfectly turned out was not her bag.

And now she stood before her open closet and wondered what to wear. She had nothing appropriate for a funeral, for a dignified, solemn, well-pressed occasion. She rarely wore dresses at all and had very few, and
225

those she did own were too summery, too bright, too unsuitable and probably too tight. To the bar mitzvah of Dolores' son, she had worn a print dress that made Audrey speechless and caused Melvin to beg her to buy an outfit and charge it to him. Since he didn't trust her ability to select something decent herself, he even offered to do it for her. She smiled at the recollection. Audrey had never let her forget it. "You looked like my grandmother," she had berated her afterward. "Only my grandmother looked better than you when she was eighty. She wouldn't have flicked a chicken in that horrendousness you wore. She would have been ashamed for the chicken, and worried for the soup."

Joan finally pulled out a dark green pants suit and looked at it critically. The blouse could use a pressing, but it would do. She hung it on the closet door, checked for missing buttons and, satisfied, went in to take a shower and do what she could with herself.

When she was all ready, she stood at the mirror and stared at her face. Her eyebrows needed plucking. She picked up the tweezers and then put them down. No one would notice. Once Audrey had asked her why she insisted on looking like John L. Lewis. But today no one would notice her eyebrows. Not even Audrey.

23

Carol Lighter did not even remember until she heard Herb and the children leave the house that Audrey Miller was being buried that day. Then she stretched, did her morning exercises and promptly forgot. Too many other things, important things, were happening in her life today to dwell on something that affected her existence as little as that. She had lots to do and hardly any time in which to do them. Carol did one last stretch and bend, and got busy.

In an hour, everything was ready—her bags all packed and hidden in the cedar closet, her tennis lesson canceled and the note to Herb all written and taped to the ice bucket where he was sure to find it when he returned from the office. All was ready, and Carol noted with satisfaction as she looked once more around the beautifully decorated living room that Herb's business manager, A. Hitler, had had a coronary over that she even had time for another cup of coffee before Phillip arrived to pick her up and take her away from all this Beverly Hills business manager shit, which she had had up to here.

She pushed open the swinging doors to her modern

227

brick and copper and microwaved kitchen—the floor alone had cost $4,600—spooned some instant coffee into a cup and waited for the water to boil. "Soon," she said to herself, anticipation making her smile, "soon, we'll be on the road, soon we'll be at the airport, soon we'll be in Hawaii, soon we'll be having some fun—finally."

The shrill whistle of the kettle brought her back. She sat down at the breakfast room table with her coffee, pushing aside the dirty breakfast dishes. For a moment she entertained the thought of clearing the table and stacking the dishwasher, but decided against it. Blanca would do it when she returned from her day off. In fact, she should be walking in any minute, and it wouldn't do for Blanca to walk into a clean kitchen. If there was one thing Carol knew about, it was maids, or "housekeepers" as they were called here in Beverly Hills. Lord knows she'd been through enough of them—seventeen, to be exact—until she found Blanca. Once they walked into a clean kitchen, they expected it to be that way all the time. Give the best of them a finger and they grab the whole hand. Give 'em an inch and they take a mile.

Carol sipped her coffee and absent-mindedly looked out through the sliding glass doors, enjoying the view of her brick patio, the hanging plants, the delicious sunshine, the wicker furniture, the flowers. She frowned as she caught sight of Robbie's new bike left lying on its side by the pool and reflected, annoyed, that her kids never took care of anything, had no sense of responsibility whatsoever. Well, Blanca would pick it up and put it in the garage (where Robbie *knew* it belonged, the little shit) when she came in.

Carol lit a cigarette and thought of the two weeks ahead with Phillip. Of course she'd have to fuck him when they got to Hawaii; there was no getting around that, but he was attractive and clean, and anyway it was worth it to be getting away from Herb and the kids. She would even fuck the Japanese gardener to get away from Herb and the kids . . . and Phillip wouldn't be so bad, but she'd refuse to do really *big* work on him.
228

He'd have to come up with more than two weeks in Maui for really *big* work. Uh-uh, if Phillip expected wild abandon, he was going to be disappointed. Hell, she hardly even did that with Herb—maybe on birthdays and anniversaries—but never on just an ordinary Tuesday. Once she had yawned while Herb was making love to her—well, it was twelve-thirty, what did he expect?—and he had looked at her and said, "Try and stay awake, Carol. This will only take a minute."

Herb could really get sarcastic sometimes. Well, now he'd have something to get sarcastic about. But, Carol assured herself, she'd always been able to handle Herb, and she would handle him this time. If he was difficult and refused to understand her running off with Phillip, she was positive she could get him to eventually accept and adjust to it. Herb was a doctor after all, a gynecologist. She would explain to him that this whole two-week thing was just a pre-pre-menstrual flurry, a temporary hormonal insanity, an "I-don't-know-what-got-into-me, desperate-before-I-lose-my-looks last fling." Herb was a scientist. He would nod his head, and if he didn't immediately forget, she was sure he would in time forgive. Of course, he would insist that it never happen again, and, of course, she would promise.

Last March, Carol remembered, Lisa Beckwith had an affair with her pool man—they used to do it in her cabana—and her husband, Peter, walked in on them when he came home early and went to get his bathing suit. It was just awful for Lisa, getting walked in on like that, and Peter was ridiculously stubborn and showed absolutely zero understanding, and moved out. They were still separated, and it was really a mess over at the Beckwiths'. Fortunately, Carol told herself, the one good thing about Herb was that he wouldn't make waves. Carol was positive that, unlike the Beckwiths, they would soon settle back in and simply resume their lives as though nothing had happened. And, *really,* what was the big deal anyway? She certainly was not in love with Phillip.

Carol glanced at the lapis face of the Piaget watch Herb had given her on their sixteenth anniversary. On the back he had had engraved: "My time is your time. Love, Herb." Well, she really loved the watch. It was beautiful, it was expensive, it was the only gift he ever gave her that she didn't have to return . . . and it said 9:15.

Carol stood up and walked to the glass doors that opened from the breakfast room onto the brick patio which ran the length of the house. In exactly one hour and fifteen minutes, Phillip would pick her up and carry her off for an exciting, fun-filled adulterous adventure, the first real adventure of her married life, and in Carol's opinion, long overdue. He would come in and kiss her, but she would put him off—no good to get too involved *here,* since he would be getting reward enough *there*—and he would put her Vuitton bags in the trunk of his white, sun-roof Continental, say something cute, like "Let me take you away from all this," and off they would go. She was excited and impatient and ready to be taken away from all this. Away for two weeks from all her mother's dreams for her come true. Carol smiled as she recalled her mother's first visit from New York to see this new house her daughter had moved into. Mother had gone through the entire house, inside and out, and after having thoroughly inspected down to the last crystal ashtray and Boston fern had turned to her and said, "Carol, my dreams for you have all come true. You're sitting with your ass in a butter tub."

Well, Carol mused, her mother was right. For some strange reason, in an unusual spurt of obedience, she listened to her parents and married the short doctor instead of the tall corrugated-box salesman, and here she was, her thirty-eight-year-old ass (still high) encased in sixty-three-dollar jeans and the whole business submerged in a Beverly Hills butter tub. Her mother was satisfied, her sister was jealous, and she . . . well, she had done just fine. Without a doubt she was the envy of all her former friends back in Brooklyn, none of whom had half of what she had. Sometimes, even after fourteen years of living in California, Carol had to pinch herself to make sure it was all true. She loved the line from the cigarette ad, "You've come a long way, baby," and said it often to herself as she walked through her home, or had dinner with various celebrity patients of Herb's, or gave orders to Blanca. "You've come a long way, baby," she would congratulate herself, "a long, long, *long* way."

She went to her purse, also Vuitton, and took out a gold pillbox and extracted a diet pill, which she swallowed with the last of her coffee. At thirty-eight years of age, she needed a bit of help to keep her weight where she wanted it—down—and her energy level where she needed it—up. Carol admitted that she depended on her pills as much as she did on Ronay, her hairdresser—more, even—and the only time Herb really scared her was when he threatened to stop giving her any more prescriptions. But she could always make him come around, and she now had an adequate supply in case he became spiteful about her going off with Phillip.

"I got ready too early," she fretted. "What am I going to do until ten-thirty?" She walked quickly out of the kitchen through the dining room, den and family room into the bedroom wing, passing Robbie's room, Stacey's room, their playroom, and on into the master suite. The room gave her great pleasure, even though it was a mess, with the bed unmade and her clothing in a heap on the chair. The room itself was enormous and fantastic. She and the decorator, a friend of Ronay's named Brock, had worked on it for nine months, and Brock was fond of saying that they had between them given birth to a magnificent, opulent, sweet baby of a room worthy of a Marie Antoinette, a Madame de Pompadour, a Carol Lighter. It was a dream room with a white Flokati rug, crushed-velvet hangings, a huge brass bed on a raised platform and a mirrored ceiling— a veritable movie set. Sometimes, on dull afternoons, Carol would stand in front of the closet and push the button which caused the clothes rack to revolve. When she saw an outfit she wanted, she removed her foot

231

from the button and the rack would come to a stop with the slacks or dress or blazer of her choice an arm's length away. She had another one for her shoes and handbags. Sometimes she could stand like that for ten minutes, just watching the racks go around and hugging herself. Herb's closet had a revolving rack too. Their closets took up an entire forty-foot wall—all mirrored, all built-in, all chock-full of the latest fashions. Carol had shown it to her friends, throwing open the doors and trilling. "Welcome to Carol's boutique," and they all stood there in awe and envy, watching the racks revolve. Many had tried to copy it, but none had a bedroom like hers, not even Sharon. You've come a long way, baby.

Carol kicked her slippers out of the way and sat down at her built-in vanity in her dressing room—bath combination. She and Herb had separate bathrooms, a luxury—no, a necessity—which greatly gratified them both. She smiled at herself in the mirror, forgetting for a moment her impatience, and remembering instead the four-room, one-bath apartment she had shared with her parents and sister back in Brooklyn. For the life of her she couldn't understand how she ever managed to survive for nineteen years in four rooms and only one bathroom. When they first moved in, she had called her sister, Elaine, on Long Island and described the entire house to her, not forgetting the revolving clothes racks. Elaine had said, "It sounds very nice, Carol." "Very nice," indeed! She'd give her eye teeth for it. The following day Robbie had broken his finger in football practice, and Carol knew positively that Elaine, instead of being happy for her, had sent out bad vibrations. Of course, it was only natural. All Elaine managed to get was a small house in Far Rockaway and a husband in the rug business.

She flicked a switch under the vanity and the light bulbs surrounding the mirror went on. They were on a special switch so that they could be brightened or dimmed according to the type of makeup the occasion demanded. She generally was merciless and turned the lights up to full brightness, figuring that since she would never subject herself to this type of lighting anywhere else, *ever*, she would always look better out than she did in her mirror ... and if she looked terrific in her mirror, she would look spectacular out. Carol knew she was good-looking. She had always been popular, and was once a runner-up in the "Miss Lakeside in the Hills" beauty contest at the singles resort where she had met Herb eighteen years ago. When she paused to think about life and how short it was and how you only get one chance at it (although she derived some comfort from reincarnationists), she realized that she did not want to go to her grave after her one time around (maybe there *was* something to reincarnation, but maybe not), she adamantly did not want to die knowing that she had not lived her life in the thinnest, best-looking way she could. It was a sin to waste herself and not make the effort to look her best, of this she was sure. Once she had stated this philosophy to her best friend, Sharon, over lunch, and Sharon had agreed with her, but Joan, who was also lunching with them, seemed astonished and said, "But you must be joking."

"No," Carol had replied. "Why should I joke about it?"

Joan looked at her for a beat and said, "Wait a minute. Let me get this straight. Did you just say that you don't want to die without having been the thinnest and best-looking you could possibly be?"

"Yes," answered Carol, bewildered. "What's so funny about that?"

Joan was quiet for a while, and then said a strange thing. "What about," she had asked softly, "being the best *person* you can be, or finding the cure for cancer? I can't believe you're serious. I don't *want* to believe it."

"So don't believe it," Carol retorted angrily.

That had been the last time she met Joan for lunch, although she had spoken to her on the phone a few times and had run into her and her husband at a party or two. Now, thinking it over, Carol realized that the

233

whole thing was just a sour grapes reaction on Joan's part. Of course Carol wanted to be a good person. She *was* a good person. Didn't she do volunteer work at Herb's hospital? Didn't she give one afternoon a week to retarded children? Didn't she and Herb contribute generously and regularly to many charities? Carol shrugged. Joan was just the sort of woman Carol couldn't stand, the type who had to argue about everything, combined with a superiority complex, and what Joan had to be superior about, Carol couldn't imagine. Her clothes were horrendous, she hardly ever had her hair done, and she bit her cuticles—and that certainly spelled insecurity. She was also a friend of the late and hated Audrey Miller, and that spelled insanity.

Carol leaned forward to apply another coat of mascara, and looked at herself with satisfaction. Her hair was perfect—Ronay had finally gotten the exact color she wanted for her streaks, and the effect was very natural. Her nose had always been super and, unlike Sharon's, was the original one she had been born with. She worked hard keeping her body in shape with tennis and exercise class and diet and, except for a few stretch marks on her stomach—thank you, Robbie and Stacey—it was almost as good as when she was practically named Miss Lakeside in the Hills.

Once at a swimming party and barbeque at Sharon's a man she had just met told her, behind the pool house where she had gone to get a towel, that she had beautiful breasts—and then reached out and tweaked her nipples. Well, that man was Phillip, and she had just stood there, her mouth open in shock. He continued to play with her nipples while looking her straight in the eye and talking, and then, taking advantage of her inability to move, lowered one side of her bikini top, bent his head down and kissed and tongued the nipple of her left breast. Finally, after what seemed like days, she managed to push him away and, adjusting her suit, slapped his hand indignantly and spat, "What the hell do you think you're doing?"

"Oh, I know what I'm doing, all right," he laughed.

234

"And by the way, I'm Phillip Ashe. I'll call you for lunch tomorrow." And he turned around and walked back to the party, while she stared after him, feeling like a teenage ninny.

Well, that was the start of it. There were many lunches, and Phillip was becoming very insistent about getting her into bed. She couldn't possibly put him off any longer. That and Audrey's death making her aware of the importance of each day was the reason for this trip. As she explained to Phillip, she absolutely could not have an affair here in town. She refused to go to a motel, and her home was out of the question. Her maid knew all the other maids on the block, and it would be all over Beverly Hills before she finished douching. Also, Carol realized, it would never do to embarrass Herb. His practice was here, after all, and as her mother was fond of saying, "You don't shit where you eat!" Of course, not everyone had her kind of scruples about this sort of thing—look at Lisa Beckwith—but she was just too old-fashioned and considerate of Herb's feelings to be so blatantly indiscreet. She was, Carol reflected, really *very* considerate of Herb's feelings. Despite the fact that they had been married for almost seventeen years, despite the fact that he was not the world's greatest lover, despite the fact that he was only five-foot eight . . . despite all that, she had never in all the years of their marriage refused him his nuptial rights—except of course when she was sick or absolutely exhausted. However, and here she put her foot down, very early on she had made it quite clear to Herb that she would not, under any circumstances, do mornings.

She stood up, flicking off the movie-star lights, and lit another cigarette. She had begun to feel the effects of her diet pill; it always made her want to smoke. Anyway, Herb was very understanding about her rule of no sex in the morning—he never bothered her about it anymore—and, to be perfectly frank, she was absolutely right to have refused him morning work. His breath smelled in the morning, and they did, after all,

235

have two children, either of whom could simply walk into their bedroom at any time, since Herb stubbornly refused to lock the door at night. He said, "They might need us in the night, and they should be able to get to us if they have to." Well, that was really stupid, because if they screamed or something, Helen Keller would hear them, they had such piercing voices—even Robbie, who was almost fourteen and well into puberty.

Although she hadn't seen Robbie naked since he was seven, she was sure everything was as it should be down there. His voice was rapidly changing, and there were unmistakable indications that he should be using a deodorant. In fact, she had bought him a mild roll-on just last week and left it on his bathroom counter with a cute little note that said "Hint, hint." However, she thought in irritation, he certainly wasn't mature when it came to living with other people. He was sulky and uncommunicative, and often didn't answer her when she spoke to him, or indeed even acknowledge her presence half the time, except when he wanted her to drive him somewhere. He left his things all over the place, his new bike for one, and his room was an absolute sewer. It sometimes took Blanca half the morning just to straighten up his room and air it out. Thanks to slobby Robbie, Carol would often come home from her tennis lesson, aching for a shower, only to discover that Blanca hadn't yet gotten to the master bedroom and bath because Robbie had left such a mess! She made a mental note to tell Blanca to do the master suite first, before she tackled Robbie's room, and to work a little faster. Blanca was slowing up a bit, and Carol knew that if you didn't keep after them, they would definitely take advantage, even the best of them, no matter how much you paid them or how much clothing—most of it practically new—you gave them.

Stacey was not as much of a pig, although she had her days, but dealing with her was so unpleasant. And Herb was no help whatsoever. He simply told Carol to get off their backs, that they were acting perfectly normal for their respective stages of development. Easy

236

for *him* to say. The only time he ever reprimanded them was when they played their stereo too loud. Stacey was almost nine, and extremely pre-menstrual for one so young, private and uncommunicative. No matter how understanding Carol tried to be, the inescapable fact of the matter was that Stacey was a pain in the ass, and gave every promise of being homely. She was the image of Herb—and although he really had an interesting and intelligent face for a man, it was a disaster on a girl. Thank you, Stacey, I really needed that you take after your father. Naturally Herb believed that his little girl was the best thing since canned beer. After all, compared to what he looked at all day, Stacey was Miss America. Anyway, it wasn't Stacey's fault, although she might look better if she got that sullen look off her face, and Carol was hopeful that with the proper application of cosmetics, or if that didn't help, then a good plastic surgeon, Stacey could be fixed up adequately—at least she wouldn't be embarrassing.

Well, time would tell, and in the interim she would do her utmost to ensure that Stacey was the best-dressed child in fourth grade. Her clothes were really smashing and cost a fortune—some dresses were even specially made for her. The irony of the whole thing was that Stacey preferred Robbie's old jeans, and that Blanca received the bulk of Stacey's seldom-worn wardrobe. There were expensive Saks Fifth Avenue labels walking around the barrio or in some primitive village in Guatemala—and not one person with sufficient sophistication to appreciate a fine fabric. *C'est la vida.*

Blanca must have sent to Central America a good couple of hundred dollars' worth of clothes. Carol hoped she was properly grateful. She seemed to be—there were a lot of *gracias,* and she vacuumed the living room drapes without being told—but her understanding of English was so minimal, and Carol's ability in Spanish so rudimentary, that communication was restricted to the contents of "Helpful Phrases in Dealing with Your Spanish Maid" (a handbook sold by the thousands in Beverly Hills) and sign language. But it still was ex-

237

tremely difficult because Carol didn't have the linguistic facility to deal in nuances. It was one thing to be able to say, "Your salary is sixty-five dollars a week. You will receive more when you learn some English," and quite another to try to explain that "Lighter residence" and "Please no walk, floor still wet" did not constitute sufficient mastery of the language to merit the raise. However, after working for them for fourteen months, Blanca was earning seventy-five dollars a week. Not because her English was better—it wasn't, even though she claimed to have been a schoolteacher in Guatemala or El Salvador or wherever (and she *was* very light-skinned; white, in fact)—but because of a deal consummated with great delicacy and firmness on the part of Carol, and much wringing of hands and muttered *Madre de Dios* on the part of Blanca, and misplaced generosity and *stupidity* on the part of Herb, who, wandering into the kitchen for a beer during the negotiations, was moved to say, after noticing Blanca in tears, "For Christ sake, Carol, give her the fucking ten dollars already," and *that,* for some strange reason, Blanca seemed to understand.

Anyway, they settled on seventy-five a week if Blanca took only one day off, which she finally agreed to, albeit reluctantly, and that was that. Carol looked again at her watch: 9:45. "Where the hell is that stupid bitch? She should have been here a half hour ago," she said aloud, fuming, and walking nervously to the window. Of all days to return late, she would pick this one. They all seemed to have a sixth sense about how and when to create the greatest possible aggravation for their employers. Where *was* she? The only sign of activity was the Mexican gardener hosing down her neighbor's driveway.

She walked back to the vanity and lit another cigarette, suddenly struck by the realization of how very important a maid really was in her life—and in the lives of practically every woman she knew, except for Joan, who had fired hers, a typically ridiculous decision which reinforced Carol's estimation of her. Here she

238

was, looking forward to two weeks in Hawaii, and all the plans could be fucked up by, of all people, her maid. It was perfectly ridiculous. If they plotted a nuclear war, for Christ sake, it would have to be postponed if the maid didn't show. How had this situation developed? How had this ignorant peasant, this doer of dirty work, this idiot, become the most essential factor in determining whether or not she had a good day? It was really outrageous, and Carol knew that Blanca, that cunt, was somehow aware of it. It was as if Carol dealt the cards, made the rules, indeed even owned the deck—and Blanca held all the aces. How had it happened?

"Shit," Carol muttered, going to her night table where her personal phone and calendar book lay open to the seven days of the current week. From a flap on the corner she removed a card which had written on it in pink ink the names and phone numbers of all those persons who performed services necessary for the smooth functioning of her life—the plumber, the appliance repair man, Stacey's orthodontist, Ronay, whose number did not really have to be written down, she knew it by heart, Roto-Rooter, Saul's Auto Repair and Body Shop, Gourmet Heaven Home Delivery, her gynecologist (not Herb), the florist, Sam & Marty's Meatery—everyone but Blanca! Now what to do? She sat down on her bed and considered her situation, tapping the long nail of her index finger against her capped front teeth. She pondered for a moment and then rapidly turned the pages to look up Sharon's new number. It had been Sharon's maid, Anna, who had gotten Blanca for her in the first place.

Carol lifted the receiver of her white-and-gold custom-colored princess phone and carefully pushed the buttons with the ball of her finger. She did not want to chip her twelve-dollar manicure. She waited impatiently as the phone rang. She waited for seven agonizing rings before the phone was answered with an out-of-breath "Hello."

"Hello, Sharon? It's Carol."

"Carol, why are you calling me now? You know I have ten o'clock tennis. I was practically out the door. What?"

"I know, I'm sorry. Listen, Sharon, has Anna come in yet?"

"What do you want Anna for?"

"Well, Blanca hasn't shown up and I wanted to ask Anna about it. They share an apartment, don't they?"

"Carol, today is Monday. Anna is off on Sunday and Monday—and I have to leave too, it's ten to ten."

"All right. Look, Sharon, do you have Anna's number?"

"No, and I don't think they have a phone anyway. Are you all right? You sound hysterical. No, don't tell me now. I'll call you later. Good-bye."

After Sharon hung up, Carol sat motionless, the receiver still to her ear. After a few seconds, she slowly replaced the phone in its cradle and rose to her feet. She was going to have to call it off. There was no way of leaving without Blanca to look after the kids and prepare the meals, and if Blanca wasn't here by now, she probably wasn't coming at all. Phillip would kill her. He had canceled clients and meetings and hearings and God knows what else so that he could have these two weeks free. He had even told his wife he had business back East, and had probably had to buy her off somehow to keep her from going along with him. She had family in Connecticut, Phillip had once mentioned. "I'll bet she put up some stink about not going," Carol thought to herself. "He'll kill me. He'll absolutely kill me." She walked again to the window and, sliding the screen aside, poked her head out, looking both ways up and down the tree-lined street. Now even the Mexican gardener had gone. She drew back and slid the screen closed again.

"He'll be livid," she thought. But really, she told herself defensively, it was not her fault. How was she to know that Blanca would crap out? Phillip was a lawyer, and any lawyer knows that there are some events that absolutely cannot be foreseen. He would

240

simply have to understand, that's all. If he had any human decency at all, he'd simply have to realize that it was just one of those things, and completely out of her control. There was no way he could blame *her*. Wasn't she just as disappointed and upset as he would be when she told him? She glanced down once more at her wrist. Ten o'clock. She would have to call him. She started toward the phone, and then abruptly changed direction and went to her handbag on the vanity. She opened it and removed the mother-of-pearl box in which reposed her diaphragm. Walking back to her night table, she opened the drawer and slipped the box into its usual place under a pile of hankies. Carol did not use the pill. She was not the kind of person who voluntarily messed with possible blood clots.

"I have to unpack," she said out loud. "I have to call Phillip, unpack, get the note off the ice bucket, clean the kitchen, make the beds ... oh, shit!" Carol leaned against the brass bedpost and almost wept. Only the awareness of what two coats of mascara dripping down her cheeks would make her look like kept her in control. "It's all Blanca's fault," she fumed. "Why the hell should I have to sacrifice all my plans and drudge around the house because of her? Fucking bitch! She's supposed to make my life easier, not fuck it up. Well, I'm taking off ten bucks for this. How dare she not even *call?*"

By now Carol was pacing back and forth across the Flokati, smoking yet another cigarette, filled with hatred for Blanca and apprehension about calling Phillip. He had put down a big deposit on their hotel accommodations. Do they return deposits after last-minute cancellations? Oh, shit, it was 10:15, Phillip had probably left for her house already. Damn!

The soft chimes of the telephone broke into her angry mutterings. She ran to the phone, grabbing the receiver so fiercely that the phone almost fell off the night table.

"Hello?"

"Blanca? Where the hell are you?"

"Donde?"

"What? Listen, Blanca, you know I no comprende. Just get over here. What? *Mañana?* No *mañana*. Today! *Hoy!* Now! *Ahora*, Blanca. Why not? Sick? What do you mean, sick! Look, I don't care if you're dead, you understand, just get over here fast! What? *Vomitar?* You *vomitar?*"

Carol wearily sat down on the bed, fumbling for another cigarette, desperately trying to make sense of the garble of Spanish-English coming over the phone. Evidently Blanca was sick and couldn't come back until tomorrow. Shit! "Okay, okay, you come *mañana*, Blanca, you hear? Without fail! Look, do you comprendo? If no today, you come back *mañana*. Okay?"

Carol slammed the receiver down, cutting her off in mid-*mañana*. "Stupid bitch! Sick, ha! My ass she's sick!" For a brief moment, the awful thought that maybe Blanca knew about Hawaii flitted across her mind. No! How could she possibly know?

After a while Carol stood up, her face clear of anxiety. Audrey was being buried today, but *she* wasn't.

She suddenly felt strong and resolute and *decisive*. She pulled open the night-table drawer and grabbed her diaphragm box and replaced it in her handbag. She was Carol Lighter, the señora—why the hell should Blanca's malfunctions affect *her* life? Herb and the kids would just have to manage alone until tomorrow. They were not helpless babies. She flew to the window at the sound of a car pulling into her driveway, back to the mirror for a last check and, smiling, ran out of the bedroom, grabbing her handbag and loudly slamming the door behind her so that the mirrors vibrated.

Still smiling, she reached the entrance hall just as the doorbell rang.

24

Joan drove slowly, her blazing headlights identifying her as part of the convoy following the hearse carrying Audrey to her final resting place, where she would return to ashes and dust, where no phone lines connected, no black velvet capes were necessary, no punishment imposed for unpaid bills. The service at the chapel had been lengthy and difficult. Audrey would have fallen asleep, or more probably loudly proclaimed her boredom.

The casket had arrived sealed, for which Joan was grateful, although she was curious to see what Audrey was wearing, and the mourners were subdued. The rabbi spoke about the departed in a sorrowful, detached monotone, a speech that Joan suspected could have applied to anyone, and probably did, only necessitating a name change every time it was intoned. After his opening remarks, which acted on Joan like a Nembutal, he spoke of Audrey's family, her accomplishments, her unfulfilled promise. He spoke of her new endeavor and the success which would surely have been forthcoming had she not been taken so quickly, so unexpectedly, so tragically, with stardom so close and so attainable. Melvin's parents, who had never approved of or liked Audrey to begin with, feelings which had intensified through the years of her marriage to their son, had been the only ones who wept. Audrey's elderly parents had been unable to attend. They lay sedated at home, with their faces to the wall, wondering in agony why God had given them so many years and their daughter so comparatively few.

The chapel was crowded with Audrey's people. All her friends had turned out—not as many as she claimed to have had, but a respectable number nonetheless. Surreptitiously they eyed the casket that housed the remains of Audrey Miller. It sat there in front of the dais, too still to contain such as Audrey. Too somber and unmoving, too small, too modest for its occupant, who had been so noisy, so busy, so larger than life. Joan touched it in passing, nudged it, knocked on it . . . unconvinced that Audrey lay within.

Audrey had hated funerals and never attended them, no matter how dear the departed. Joan doubted that Audrey was at this one either. She would much prefer the local deli or even her bathtub. At least the casket was draped in black. It was one of Audrey's favorite colors. Audrey had always thought she looked smashing in black.

Joan studied the faces around her. Roberta Licht and her husband sat with Melvin and the children in the first row, along with Roger Fingerhut and Dick Bell. They sat quietly, all of them listening intently to the rabbi, eyes fixed on his face, sliding now and then to the casket and returning quickly to the speaker, and nodding here and there at an especially appropriate phrase. Dolores sat just behind them, with Milt, almost razor thin in her black dress and hat. There were others there whom Joan had never seen before. It looked like exam day for college entrance—all of them serious, nervous, impatient for the bell. Joan, too, was impatient to have the service end. She wanted to be out of the chapel with its gloomy air and sighing audience.

244

She wanted to get home and call Audrey to tell her about it, and what everyone wore and said. Joan had a handkerchief all ready in her hands, but never shed a tear.

When the service was finally over, Joan found that she had totally destroyed the embroidered edging of the handkerchief, thread by thread. After the long-awaited last "Amen," she and Eric and Nan expressed their condolences to the family. Mendy looked haggard, and Denise kept repeating "Thank you for coming." When she saw Joan, she asked her where Naomi was. Melvin appeared self-possessed. He was the star in the family now, but his eyes were bleak. He had always relied upon Audrey for the charming small talk, and Joan sensed that he was annoyed at her absence today.

Eric had a tight hold on her elbow, and she wondered why until she realized that without that supportive hand, she would have found it difficult to walk—her sense of direction had all but fled. She had attempted to head for the casket instead of the door, and despite Eric's painful grip she kept turning her body in an effort to get to it.

"I just want to touch her," Joan said to him. "I want to stand next to her before they put her in the hearse. Let go of me." But Eric wouldn't, and pulled her along.

"Do you agree with this, Nan?" Joan asked as Eric all but dragged her out. If Joan had to put a word to her condition, she would have said "drunk." Every time Eric said "Quit it, Joan," she felt like giggling. Even her thoughts seemed slurred.

Eric offered to drive to the cemetery, but Nan convinced him that it would be better if Joan did; it would keep her occupied. Joan looked bright-eyed from one to the other, enjoying their concern. It felt nice, she realized, to make people worry. She became aware of a marvelous insight into the behavior of her children. She had at last discovered why they did the upsetting and unsettling things they did. They did them specifically to make her worry. In their primitive wisdom, her children knew instinctively what Joan had just

245

flashed on. It felt good to have someone worry about you. It was powerful, it was heady, it proved people cared, it resulted in a tender and concerned outpouring of attention. Joan smiled at her husband and her friend. It wouldn't do to carry this too far. Tender attention could turn into angry frustration. She recalled how guilt and fear at her helplessness to cope with or amend her children's impossible behavior reduced her to furious, despairing shrieking.

Joan drove attentively, maintaining an even pressure on the accelerator, keeping the distance behind the car in front of her to exactly one-half car length. She hoped that the traffic lights would not suddenly change on her because she couldn't remember if the cars in a funeral cortege were permitted to go through red lights. She caught Nan's eye in her rear-view mirror and waved. Nan waved back and smiled. She, like Dolores, was wearing a hat, and Joan, conscious of her own bare head, pushed her hair back and wondered whether it had been unseemly of her to go hatless to a funeral service. She had owned only one hat in her entire life, and as far as she could remember, had never worn it. She supposed it was still around, boxed and moldering somewhere in her closet. She shuddered. Boxed and moldering. Audrey, who despite her sloppiness was obsessed with body odors and often bathed three times a day to avoid even the remotest possibility of offending herself, was now boxed and would soon be moldering.

Joan shuddered again, and Eric looked at her. "You all right?" he asked.

She nodded. "I was just thinking about the disgusting manner in which our dear departed become one again with nature. How unpleasant it is to have to rot in order to evolve into something useful. It's too bad that Jews don't permit embalming. Think about the six-thousand-year-old Egyptians we keep discovering, lying around and looking terrific, sleeping with treasures."

"I guess Jews don't think it's that important to be buried looking good. They'd rather spend and deduct
246

their treasures than sleep with them," said Eric.

"You never know," said Joan. "I have no doubt whatsoever that Audrey would have much preferred not being buried at all. If she'd had the choice, she'd have opted for being stuffed and mounted. But if there was no way to fix it, if it was that or being thrown into a trash masher with leftover salad, she would have picked being planted in full makeup, wearing her good rings. I hope she was. I hope she's lying there now in double mascara, blue eye shadow, and the reddest lipstick ever made...and perfumed and douched with Cupid's Quiver."

"What the hell is Cupid's Quiver?"

"A douche. It comes in a variety of scents—strawberry, vanilla, cinnamon..."

"Do you use that stuff?"

"Yeah. The pickled herring."

"So *that's* what it was."

"Eric, do you believe in reincarnation or life after death? Should we buy a plot?"

"Yes, yes, and not yet."

"I don't. I think once you're dead, that's it. You're finished. No transfers, no returns. We should begin thinking about buying a plot."

"Okay."

"Yeah? You're gonna buy one?"

"No. I'll think about it."

"Melvin seemed all right. Mendy looked awful."

"Hmmm."

"He's the one who will suffer most."

"What about Denise?"

"No. She'll be okay. She's a kitten. She'll attach herself to whoever pets her and feeds her."

"I hope so."

"I'll never speak to her again."

"Denise?"

"No, stupid. Audrey. I've talked to her ten times a day for five years, and now I'll never speak to her again."

"You never know."

"That's not funny, Eric."

"I know. I'm sorry, puss." He reached over, took one of her hands off the wheel and held and kissed it. He felt a great pity for his wife. She seemed to be sitting in a shock absorber, and he knew how greatly she would suffer when her protective armor was finally pierced.

Eric had always been amused and annoyed by Audrey. He had liked her, in the way one likes anything that makes one laugh and shake a head in wonder, but he was often angered at her ability to fire the sparks of Joan's discontent. He distrusted Audrey's motives, and often he had borne the brunt of her thrusts.

"I know a lot of big successful people, producers, writers, actors, bigger than Eric," Audrey would say to Joan. "And they all have plenty of time for their families. Why is *your* bargain never home? Don't tell me he's working. Even an elephant can't work twenty-four hours a day." And Joan would brood over that and attack him when he got home. Or Audrey would list all the chores she got Melvin to perform which Eric avoided or never was around for. "Now don't tell me he has no time. If he wanted to, *really* wanted to, he'd make time." Or, "He's never taken you to San Francisco? You're kidding! Even people from Watts get to go to San Francisco. Even my Aunt Minnie, who's a hundred and eight, gets to San Francisco."

Joan told Eric that Audrey meant well and wanted the best for her, but he wondered if that was indeed her intention. He felt that Audrey was jealous of their marriage, and was attempting to reduce it to the level of hers and all the others that were barely holding on, clinging to the frayed ropes of a swinging noose. He did not want Joan to be influenced by Audrey's criticism. What he did want was to have Joan remain happily appreciative of the good relationship they were so fortunate to have achieved.

But all in all, Eric had liked Audrey. He had never been taken in by her, but she was, for the most part, very supportive of Joan. Joan had needed the mirror which Audrey held up, in which she saw herself as bright, funny, unique and talented. With Audrey gone, would Joan's self-image also be gone? Who would lend Joan the sympathetic ear or furiously rip out the tongue of whichever villain had bad-mouthed or failed to appreciate Audrey Miller's friend, Joan Brenner?

He pressed her hand tightly, closing his eyes against the almost unbearable sadness he was feeling for his wife. Dealing with death, like death itself, is a lonely occupation. As in all the heights and depths of life, one is forced into an isolated and solitary struggle. He doubted that anyone could, as Audrey would have said, "fix it." Despite the fact that he would give whatever was demanded of him to hold Joan and shelter her and help her do battle with the merciless plunder of loss and bereavement, she was on her own now.

Joan herself was fully aware of the aloneness imposed by monumental events, even the joyous ones. When she was pregnant, she wanted nothing to do with natural childbirth classes. "I want to have that moment for myself," she had told Eric over her enormous belly. "I don't want anyone around telling me when and how to breathe, sponging the sweat from my brow or timing my contractions. I want to have that pain and that joy and that bittersweet good-bye and hello all by myself. I don't want to share that very first separation between my child and me with anyone, not even with you, whom I love better than my life . . . better than even hot fudge sundaes," she had added with a smile. "Do you understand that?" she had asked, her eyes almost pleading. "You're not hurt?"

"No," he had assured her, understanding completely. "No, my love. Aren't I a loner myself?"

Yet now, foreseeing his wife's impending agony and impotent to do more than weep for her, he uttered a silent prayer for mercy on behalf of this woman who was more dear to him than any living soul, even including his own. He clutched her hand until she retrieved it to make the turn into the cemetery and follow the winding road through this clean and quiet town of law-abiding and passive citizens, where the crime rate is nonexistent and the neighbors never complain.

They were directed into a parking space by a uniformed guard, and were happy to climb out and stretch aching muscles after the long, slow drive. The group of mourners, smaller now, spoke quietly among themselves and formed themselves into a line, which followed the hearse through the silent, tree-lined streets to the freshly dug grave into which, after ritual prayers for the dead, Audrey would soon be deposited.

Joan glanced up at the street sign and made a noise in her throat that was as much a laugh as a sob. The name of the street on which Audrey was destined to live out her death was called Broadway. "You've made it, bitch," Joan applauded silently. "You're on Broadway." She walked over to Dick Bell, who was standing with Roger and the Lichts. "Did you notice the name of the street?" she asked him.

"No. What is it?"

"Audrey finally got to Broadway."

He smiled. "That's wonderful," he said. "Too bad she's not around to appreciate her triumph."

"Oh, she appreciates it, all right," Joan said. "It's not everyone who gets her name on Broadway. She had to die to do it, but who else could have arranged a situation to work for her like our Audrey? If it were me, I would have ended up stuck for eternity on La Brea or Thirty-ninth Street or behind a weed. But leave it to Audrey. Broadway—how perfect." She smiled up at him, feeling an enormous pride in her amazing friend.

"Well," said Dick, "I hope she knows. She would have a good laugh." He reached into the pocket of his beautifully tailored beige suit and pulled out a gleaming white handkerchief. He wiped his suddenly overflowing eyes and blew his nose. Dick had been one of Audrey's people for twenty-five years. He knew all her secrets and all her deceits, and loved her anyway. He had suffered through a life of sickening ups and downs and realized that, for him, living had been reduced either to pain or the absence of it.

Dick had been an uncloseted homosexual even when it wasn't fashionable. His heart had been broken so often by pretty, pouting boys and cranky, disappointed men that even when mended it had become a seamed patchwork, a fragile eggshell of a heart. He'd seen it all, done it all, and had had it all done to him. He had treasured Audrey because she was the only person he knew who could still surprise him. He cried now, looking bleakly ahead to a life where he was doomed never again to see a rabbit pulled out of a hat or be flabbergasted into a shocked shout of laughter. "What are we going to do now?" he asked Joan, his voice breaking. "What are we going to do?"

"Oh, Dick," she said softly. "I guess we wait."

"For what?"

"For the light to change and the cars to stop and the walk sign to flash."

"Why?"

"So that we can get across and walk down a different street."

He nodded and kissed her cheek. "I hope my legs can make it," he said. "Nobody walks anymore."

Joan walked over to the yawning grave and looked down. The earth was yellowish and there were a few small rocks at the bottom. She pulled up a tuft of grass and tossed it in. The rabbi was now approaching, prayer book in hand. She looked over and saw Eric in conversation with Nan, Dolores and Milt. Melvin, his parents and the children were following the rabbi, coming toward her slowly. She turned quickly and almost ran back to her group, her shoes sinking into the ground, sucking her down.

"They're going to start soon," she said.

Eric took her hand and they turned toward the grave, standing quietly. Nan moved so close to Joan that their arms seemed to have grown together, and Joan imagined she could feel the blood flowing from Nan's arm into hers. Dolores stood directly behind her, her breath stirring Joan's hair. Milt had his hand on her shoulder and she leaned into him, as if she were

251

caught in a rainstorm and he was an open door. The rabbi cleared his throat and began to speak.

"To everything there is a season," he said softly, and Joan felt Nan stir. "And a time to every purpose under the heavens." Joan looked into Nan's face and saw that her eyes were wide open, riveted on the rabbi. She was breathing quickly, silently mouthing the words with him. "A time to be born and a time to die; a time to plant and a time to pluck up that which is planted . . . Joan looked at her curiously. She had no idea that Nan would be so affected. Dolores had begun to weep quietly. "A time to cast away stones, and a time to gather stones together," the rabbi went on. "A time to embrace and a time to refrain from embracing." Dolores took a ragged breath and put her hand on Milt's arm to steady herself. She too seemed transfixed. "A time to get, and a time to lose; a time to keep and a time to cast away . . ." Joan looked at the ground and at the people gathered in the small circle around the grave. She looked up and saw a cloud that resembled a giraffe. She felt giddy, and silly thoughts were skidding through her head. She began to parody the rabbi silently. "A time to get up and a time to eat lunch," she said to herself, "a time to get the kids to Hebrew school and a time to pick them up; a time to make roast beef and a time to buy fresh broccoli." She was annoyed with herself, worried that she would react inappropriately and start to laugh again. "Stop it," she commanded herself, and tried to think more spiritual thoughts.

The casket was now being placed on the two wide straps which lay across the grave. The rabbi and several of the men, including Melvin, Mendy and Roger Fingerhut, had begun to chant the ancient Kaddish. Slowly the four men holding the heavy woven straps released the pressure, and inch by inch the coffin was lowered into its space. Joan moved forward, her hand outstretched to touch the wooden box before it reached bottom, while its plain, rounded top was still visible. She had the irrational idea that in a minute the cover would fly open and Audrey would pop out laughing and yelling, "Gotcha! Thought I was finished, didn't you, you horses' asses!" Before she could take another step, Eric grabbed the hem of her jacket and pulled her back, her arm still outstretched. Slowly she lowered it, as the straps were pulled up and the first shovelful of earth was dropped onto the casket.

"Come on, Audrey," Joan said silently, trying to penetrate the wood with urgent thought waves. "Hurry up, before it's too late. The bastards are throwing dirt on your head." But the coffin lay still, no frantic rappings on the inside cover to indicate that the occupant was tired of lying around and wanted out.

Melvin was staring at the mound of earth that now covered the coffin, one hand cupping his chin, the index finger over his lip, the thumb pressing into his cheek. He seemed to be thinking great thoughts or stifling a scream. It was hard to tell which. Mendy lay against his father, weeping onto his chest, eyes tightly closed, embarrassed at being fifteen and crying in public. Denise stood with her grandparents, their arms around her, perhaps aware that never again would she be called "dreck" or search in vain for the milk money that her mother had forgotten to pack with her lunch. The little girl was dry-eyed, but her fingers under the ruffled navy blue jumper were nervously picking at the elastic of her underpants. Melvin's mother quietly removed the busy hands and straightened the Peter Pan collar of her granddaughter's white blouse.

As the last shovelful of earth was dumped onto the grave, the mourners seemed to sigh in unison. They glanced at one another and once more at the grave before they turned and headed toward their cars. Several had attempted to approach Melvin, but he had quickly gathered his family and started down the gentle slope to Broadway. Dick Bell stumbled as he turned, but steadied himself. He removed the yarmulke from his gray-blond baptized head and, folding it carefully, put it into his pocket. *"Ciao,"* he murmured to Joan as he passed her, and blew her a kiss. Roberta Licht nodded to her, then abruptly turned and walked back to the mound, on which she placed the small

253

bunch of daisies she had held throughout the service.

"I'm having a simply gorgeous bouquet of roses sent," Dick informed Joan. "Roses were her favorite flowers, you know."

Joan smiled and leaned against her husband. She felt weary and listless. She had bitten her lip at some point, and now flicked away a small drop of blood with her tongue. She tasted blood and lipstick and dust and found it pleasant. "Is my lip bleeding?" she asked Eric, who looked at it carefully and shook his head. "Well," Joan sighed, turning to face Nan, Dolores and Milt, "I guess that's that. A time to arrive and a time to split, a time for a burial and a time to get back to work."

Nan seemed deep in thought. At Joan's comment she blinked her eyes and glanced at her watch. "You're right about the time to get back to work," she said. "It's almost two."

Dolores removed a pebble from her shoe and straightened up. "I'm not going back to the office today," she said. "What I need is a big drink and a small lunch."

Milton offered to supply both, and invited the others to join them. "Thank you, my man," Eric said, "but I have to get a television show on the road. Let's head back, honey," he said to Joan, taking her hand.

"Eric," she said, gently disengaging her hand. "Would you mind if I stayed awhile?"

He looked at her sharply. "Why?" he asked. "There's nobody here. Everyone else is gone."

"Audrey's here," she said, "and I just want to be alone with her for a while. I can't go yet, I haven't said good-bye yet."

"We'll wait for you, if you like," said Dolores.

"No, it's okay, really . . . I'd rather be alone."

"How will you get home?" Eric asked. "I need the car."

"I'll drive you to the office in my car," Nan offered.

"I don't like leaving you here," Eric said, eyeing Joan concernedly. "Are you sure you want to do this?"

Joan nodded, already impatient for them to go.

254

"Well, all right," said Eric reluctantly. "But don't stay too long, and call me at the office when you get home."

"Don't worry, hon," Joan said gently. "I can't stay long anyway. I have to get the kids to Hebrew school."

Eric kissed her and held her for a moment, and then left to join the others, who were waiting for him on Broadway. When he reached the street he turned and waved, and Joan smiled and waved back. He turned once again when they reached the corner, and she waved him cheerfully on. She stood watching the four of them until they passed out of sight, and remained standing there until even the sound of their footsteps had faded away.

She became aware of the special stillness that an absence of human voices creates. Her senses seemed unusually sharp, and she found herself able to hear beetles clicking, bees buzzing, the birds on the tree-lined street chirping and beating their wings. A soft wind rustled the leaves and they rubbed against each other, making what Joan supposed was a velvety melody. She took a deep breath and inhaled the scent of mown grass and freshly turned earth. There wasn't a living soul around her. Even the cemetery workers had disappeared. From her position on the small treeless rise she could see another funeral procession winding around the curve of a distant road, its destination perhaps some other well-known street on the far side of the cemetery. The sun felt hot on her back. The only trees were those bordering the walks, leaving only mounds and headstones and floral remembrances to decorate the vast expanse of real estate under which the dead lay cool and comfortable, uncaring and un-affected by the baking California sun. Those sleeping shades needed no other, and of the many souls sur-rounding her, only Joan was perspiring.

She removed her jacket and spread it, lining side down, on the grass beside the bare mound of earth beneath which her friend Audrey reposed. She ar-ranged herself cross-legged upon it, and congratulated

255

herself for choosing to wear the one color that wouldn't show grass stains. She looked for a moment at the bunch of daisies Roberta had placed on the grave. "These are from Roberta Licht," she informed Audrey, and opening her large, bulky handbag, continued, "but I got you something you *really* like, bitch." From the cave of her bag she removed the jar of ice cubes, which was now cold water, and the two foil-wrapped turkey sandwiches.

"Here, rotten," she said, leaning over slightly and placing one of the sandwiches on the pile of earth before her, beside the daisies. The other she opened, and took a bite. "It's a turkey sandwich, your favorite," she said, chewing, almost expecting Audrey to reach out a hand and grab a center piece from the sandwich, as she had so often done at other lunches, much to Joan's disgust. "I like to eat from you," Audrey used to say, as though conferring an honor, while Joan would eye her mutilated meal. "I don't eat from anyone else, *ever,* so hold yourself."

"I hope water will do," Joan now apologized, indicating the jar of melted ice, "because I couldn't fit a wine cooler into my handbag. But this is good enough for you, putz."

"You have no class, cunt. You never did. Even warm wine is better than ice water. Don't you know *any*thing? And I'm not too crazy about your outfit. Where do you come to green?"

Joan sat back on her haunches. She heard Audrey clearly, as clearly as she did the birds or the leaves. No one who knew Audrey Miller could mistake that voice.

Even months later, Joan would remain incapable of completely denying to herself that her dead friend Audrey had spoken to her. She would maintain this despite knowing it was an impossibility, that it had to be a hallucination.

Now she sat back, regarding the grave. She didn't feel at all surprised to hear Audrey's voice. If Audrey could "fix" anything when she was alive, it only stood to reason that she could perform even greater miracles now that she was dead, when she obviously had superior connections.

"Well..." Joan said.

"Well what?"

"Well, if you don't like it, don't drink it. I'll drink it myself," and she took a long, cool, refreshing sip.

"Did you give a donation?" Audrey asked. "You said you would."

"Not yet. Did you save me a seat?"

"Naturally."

"A good one?"

"I only *get* good ones."

"So, how are you looking?"

"Better than you. I'm not crazy about green on you."

"I care a lot—anyway it's the darkest thing I own."

"Do you miss me?"

"I'll let you know."

"Do you love me, bitch?"

Joan remained silent. "Well, *do* you?"

Joan stared at the daisies and said nothing.

"You really are bad, you know that? Can't you even tell me *now?*"

Joan fidgeted and took a small bite of her sandwich.

"Well?"

"Well what?"

"Do you love me?"

"Yes," whispered Joan.

"Yes, *what?*"

"Yes, I do. I love you, Audrey."

A slight gust of wind blew bits of earth on Joan's sandwich. She brushed them off in annoyance, hiding the embarrassment at her admission behind an irritated exclamation. A blade of grass now lay on top of Audrey's foil-wrapped sandwich, stirred occasionally by the breeze, trapped in a silver crease. The daisy petals waved gently.

"I hope you're finally satisfied," Joan said, removing the grass from its trap. "And kindly stop asking personal questions that cause me pain. Do you remember when we fought over that?" She wound the grass

257

around her finger and waited for a reply. "Well," she said impatiently, "*do* you?" She sat very still, listening. "Audrey?" she asked tentatively—but all she heard was the buzz of a wasp thirstily circling the daisies. She rewrapped the uneaten half of her sandwich and replaced it in her bag.

"Stop playing games, Audrey. Come back." There was an edge of panic in her voice. "Where are you?" she screamed. "I told you I loved you. Why are you doing this to me?" She grabbed up a handful of dirt and flung it down, spattering the daisies and Audrey's turkey sandwich. Some of it blew back into Joan's face and stuck, glued to the tears now rolling down her cheeks. "Oh, Audrey, why did you leave me, why did you die? I wasn't...I'm not through with you yet. I can't—I just can't. You have a book to do...you still owe me money...Who's gonna get me diet pills? I said I loved you...Who will I play with and call 'cunt'? You're the only cunt I know." She smiled thinly through her tears and waited. Nothing. "Please, Audrey," she whispered. "I need you still."

She sat there, crying and waiting and ripping the petals off the daisies. Finally she dragged herself to her feet like a tired old woman and stood staring down at the grave. She bent and dug a small hole, and stood the daisies up in it. She packed earth around them to keep them erect. Then she uncapped the water bottle, took a drink, and poured the remainder around the flowers. She picked up Audrey's sandwich and moved it closer to the daisy tree. She straightened up again and regarded her handiwork. She stood there for a long time. Finally she picked up the empty water bottle and put it in her bag. She brushed off her jacket and hung it over her arm.

"I'm going now," she said. "I have to take my drecks to Hebrew school, so...good-bye. I'll see you at the unveiling. I'll tell Melvin to leave your date of birth off the headstone...I'll miss you. I don't like you, but I'll miss you...Good-bye." She began to walk away, then stopped and hurried back. "Remember, rotten egg, save me a seat, don't let anyone else sit there...please."

She started crying again. "I meant it, you know," she said shakily. "I love you. Good-bye, Audrey." And without looking back, her eyes blurred, her face streaked with tears and dirt, Joan hurried down Broadway to her car.

She didn't get lost on the freeway. When she walked into her house, she quickly washed her face, Visined her red eyes, and called Eric to tell him she was home.

"Are you all right?" he asked her.

"I have to get the kids," she answered.

"Joan, are you all right?"

"No," she replied. "I'm celebrating my first death. I have grave dirt under my nails. There's a hole in my insides as big as your nose. How can I be all right? My Audrey was buried today." She paused. "Eric?"

"I'm so sorry, my love."

"I'm sorry too. It's okay, Eric, because I have *you*."

"Don't ever doubt that."

She hung up and got into her car, picked up the kids and took them to Hebrew school. After dinner, Eric asked her if she needed him to stay home with her.

"No," she told him. "Go to work."

Joan went to bed at eleven-thirty after the news and fell asleep quickly. When she awoke the next morning, she remembered dreaming that she was swimming alone and naked in a cold blue mountain lake, doing a slow backstroke, gliding silently between the frogs and the water lilies, disturbing neither and leaving the surface of the water strangely still and unrippled.

25

After she dropped Eric off, Nan continued on toward her office, then changed her mind and made an illegal U-turn, which caused her heart to skip a beat and her eyes to dart nervously around in search of a lurking police car. Nan, who truly believed (and despised herself for it) that if a woman had sex with a man out of wedlock he would lose respect for her, also believed that if you broke the law, they'd surely get you in the neck. She had never smoked, couldn't stand the taste of liquor, and had refused to allow her ex-husband, Carl, to hook up even one illegal extension phone to the main line. She permitted her business manager to find loopholes and bend the law a bit in regard to her income tax deductions (she couldn't say the word "cheat" to herself), but spent sleepless nights and anxious days feeling the hot breath of the IRS on her back. Despite the fact that most of her friends were very hip and show biz and smoked and drank and sniffed and injected every substance known to man, she herself would rather her son grew up to be a faggot than smoke a joint, and wouldn't touch coke if her life depended on taking one sniff—unless, of course, it meant she would get Richard Brown. She would murder a kindly old monk or wash seven sticky kitchen floors on her hands and knees in a two-thousand-dollar beaded designer dress to get Richard Brown.

She pulled into her garage, closing the door behind her, guiltily edgy that her license number had been taken down when she made the illegal U-turn. She went to check the mailbox. As usual, Serena had forgotten to take in the mail, and also as usual, the box was packed. Nan hated the chore of sorting through the mail; putting the bills in one pile, the requests for speaking engagements in another, the demands from complete strangers for favors and money in a third, the hate mail sent by the crazies in a fourth, and the fan mail in yet another teetering stack. Now that Carl was not around to take care of this tedious chore, Nan was considering hiring a secretary to sort and answer her mail, and to drive Serena to the market and her kids to wherever they had to be taken.

She missed Carl at times like these. He had made living more convenient—dull and boring, but comfortable and infinitely easier. Yet she would gladly have taken a job in a post office and spent Thursdays in Safeway clutching coupons that said "Fifteen Cents Off" and driven eleven loudly misbehaving boys to a horror movie in Detroit, if it meant she would get Richard Brown. She dropped her armful of mail onto an already mail-laden table in the entry hall, and continued upstairs to her bedroom.

She began unbuttoning her blouse in preparation for a bath and shampoo. It seemed somehow vitally important to her to wash from her body all traces of death and the funeral. Nan rarely occupied her mind with thoughts of death and dying. She was not that kind of worrier, and was able to convince herself that, for her, Nan Blake, ceasing to exist did not apply. Unlike her friend Joan, who had an anxiety attack when one of her children got chapped lips, Nan was not a believer in random afflictions. She felt that unless she sinned grievously or perpetrated a nastiness on her fellow man, or failed to fast on Yom Kippur, God would not punish her. But she had knowingly broken a holy commandment. She had committed adultery with Richard Brown. The breakup of her sixteen-year-old marriage, the deteriorating quality of her work, the indifferent cruelty of many people whom she had considered to be her friends, the dreary pall of depression that clouded her once optimistic and confident outlook, the loneliness—all these and more were evidence of the retribution exacted by an outraged and unforgiving God. She, a married woman, had knowingly and nervously done it with Richard Brown, and had been unfortunate enough to do it while God was watching. It was obvious that atonement was demanded. She would have to erase the sin by marrying the man and sanctifying her adulterous act retroactively.

She wanted Richard Brown desperately, and because she had always (except for this one slip) been a good girl, today at Audrey Miller's funeral, God, in his infinite mercy, had given her the hook to hang the show on, the perfect line with which to end the overlong first act.

Nan finished undressing and turned on the water for her bath. She carefully measured out a capful and a half of bath oil and poured it in slowly under the spout of warm water filling the tub. She was seeing Richard that night and she wanted to come to him clean and uncontaminated by sadness and loss. Nan would never have gone to the funeral if it hadn't been for Joan. Joan had always been there when Nan needed her, and Nan wanted to be there now that Joan was needing. She had performed an unselfish and kind act with no motivation other than that of loving and caring, and she had been rewarded. She had gone there to help and had been helped in return.

Nan wondered if Joan were home yet. She thought about her staying behind at the cemetery. Come to think of it, Joan's reaction to Audrey's death had been unusual in that there was hardly any reaction at all.

There were moments of strangeness—indications of difficulties to come—but generally speaking, Joan seemed in control of herself. She always seemed to be in control of herself, Audrey's death aside. Joan exuded a basic sanity and an unconcern with the things that bothered most women in Beverly Hills. She cared, but not really, that she drove an old Ford in a new Mercedes world. It bothered her, but not really, that she was a cotton apron at a satin gown soiree. She deplored the fact that she was now fifteen pounds overweight, but not enough to suffer in order to conform to some designer's arbitrary conception of what the ideal female figure should be. Nan thought Joan was wonderful. She loved her. She wanted to be like her. But most of all, she wanted Richard Brown. Tonight she was going to get him. She had started the day with an ending. She would end the day with a beginning. She shut off the water and lowered herself into the scented and bubbled tub, pleased that she could still take pleasure in such a simple and (except for the bath oil, which was thirteen dollars an ounce) inexpensive activity.

She felt the weariness and disillusion slough off her soul. The funeral seemed now to have taken place in another time. Audrey had not been her friend—she had been a stranger who had indirectly and unintentionally done her a kindness. "I have always relied on the kindness of strangers," she said aloud. "Thank you, Blanche. Thank you, Tennessee. Thank you, Audrey."

"You call me, señora?" asked Serena, knocking on the door. "I'm hang up two blouses and I hear you. You want somethin'?"

"No, Serena," answered Nan. "Thank you." She leaned back and heard Serena picking up her clothes. She could almost see her eye them critically and surreptitiously sniff at the armpits of the dress before deciding either to put it on a hanger or toss it onto the dry cleaning pile. She heard the click of the door as Serena left the bedroom. Nan lifted up a leg and watched the water and bubbles glide down her calf, leaving a gleaming, oily sheen. She reached for the

263

Neutrogena and rubbed it slowly and thoroughly over her washcloth, until the purple velour was completely soaped and white. With one lazy hand she washed the other, then lathered her arms, her neck, her underarms. Sensuously, almost ritually, she soaped and rubbed and cleansed every inch of her body, sliding the soft cloth into and around every orifice.

When she was twelve years old Nan had begged to have her ears pierced. Her mother had been willing, but her father had refused permission. "Women," he said curtly, "have enough holes without adding two more." Nan had always felt that statement to be vaguely obscene and an uncomfortable indication of her father's sexuality. She didn't like body talk, and rarely referred to any area of the body which was covered by underwear. That had certainly been understandable when she was fat and unattractive, but even now, pared down and sleek, she remained self-conscious. She made love only in dark rooms and had never gone to bed in the nude. After her marriage, in the name of expediency and at Carl's impatient urging, she had switched from pajamas to nightgowns, a decision which discomfited her. The first time she ever slept with Richard, she was a nervous wreck. She had undressed fearfully and made sure her underpants were concealed beneath her pile of clothing on the bedroom chair. She was afraid he would look at and find fault with her body. She was afraid he would linger in dark private valleys. She was afraid he would laugh. It took her a long time before she allowed him to make love to her anywhere but beneath the sheltering sheets. She was a sometimes passionate woman who couldn't abide anyone's tongue in her mouth and who, even when greatly aroused, refused to kiss lips that had kissed her moist and hidden places.

At Audrey's funeral, when thoughts of death were unavoidably thrust upon her, it wasn't the fear of never again seeing her children that unnerved her, it was the realization that alien and unfamiliar eyes would view her nakedness, and that a stranger's careless hands would prepare and clothe her exposed body under a harsh, unforgiving light. A bit chilled, Nan turned on the hot water, making new bubbles bloom and reviving the now faint scent of the bath oil. She shut it off when the steam threatened to fog the bathroom mirror, and soaped her hair. Then she attached a spray contraption to the tap, rinsed her hair thoroughly and tested it for squeak. She shaved her already hairless legs and underarms, and reluctantly accepted the fact that her two-hour bath was over. She was pure, sterilized. If she were a surgeon, she could operate without gloves.

Wrapping a large soft purple towel around her, Nan stepped out of the tub. She began to blow-dry her thick, dark hair, so beautifully cut that it seemed to fall into place by itself. She still went to the hairdresser, but less often, for which she was very grateful. She worked long and hard and could ill afford to waste time under a hair dryer. It was infinitely more efficient to have a head she could manage on her own. She only wished she were able to do the same with her heart.

After one last blast of hot air, Nan shut off the dryer and dropped the towel on the floor (which Serena would later be irritated about picking up). She put on a soft, expensive dressing gown that belted at the waist. All formerly fat girls, she realized the day she bought the robe, take great pleasure in the purchase of any article of clothing that belts at the waist. All formerly fat girls are usually so thrilled to find that they even possess a waistline that it often takes them years to accept it as a natural condition. Nan had not had a waistline until she was in her thirties, and it was the only part of her body that she advertised. She owned thirty-seven belts of varying widths, and every one of her dresses was fitted at the waist. Joan was the only girl Nan knew who wore loose clothing even when she didn't have to. But Joan had never been fat. Even with her fifteen extra pounds, she looked the way Nan would once have given up her "A" in English to look.

"Missus," Serena said, knocking at the door. "Telephone for you, missus." Nan walked into the bedroom and was handed the phone by a put-upon, out-of-breath Serena who, she informed her employer, had to "run quick on the steps and make my heart go too fast, too fast—no good."

"Hello," Nan said, taking the phone and ignoring the complaint.

"Where the hell are you?" demanded Teddy. "Have you forgotten we have a show to put on and a script to get out? Am I supposed to do *everything* alone? Look, Nan, just say the word and I'll have your name removed from the crawl."

"Are you going to be sorry when I tell you where I was," she answered calmly.

"Where were you?"

"At a funeral."

Teddy paused for a moment. "Oh. Did someone die?"

"Can you think of another reason for a funeral?"

"Who died? I didn't see anything in the trades."

"Joan's friend, Audrey Miller."

"Well, that's a relief. I thought it was one of *us*. Let me tell you, Nan, I'm absolutely *exhausted*. Anyway, what were you doing watching an ordinary person get planted? The deceased was Joan's *amie,* not yours."

"I felt I should be with Joan."

"Was Eric there?"

"Of course."

"So what did she need *you* for?"

"Are you kidding? Eric's only her husband. I'm her *friend*."

"Was anybody there?"

"Lots of people."

"You know what I mean. Any names?"

"You're such a snob, Teddy."

"It's better than being humble, doll, believe me."

"How would *you* know?"

"Don't get nasty, angel, it's bad for the skin . . . Look, do you want to work tonight?"

"I can't, Teddy."

"Why not? Did your ex stick you with the brats? Leave them with your menial."

266

"I'm seeing Richard tonight."

"Oh. I see. Naturally that takes precedence over a twenty-five-thousand-dollar assignment."

"Dear Teddy, do stop worrying. I intend to wrap up Richard tonight."

"Goody. How do you intend to accomplish *that* little miracle? You haven't enough time for plastic surgery."

"I'm a *woman*, Teddy. I can do anything. If I am successful, I'll certainly help you all I can by giving you whatever expertise I possess on how to get a man ... No, no, don't thank me, it's my pleasure. I can't bear to see you lonely. It breaks my heart."

"Nan, you cunt, don't look now, but your tits are sagging."

"I love you too, Teddy, but I really must fly. See you in the morning."

"Nan, my poor darling, Richard is gay."

"Only in your dreams."

"Well, I tried. Have a marvelous coupling and good luck in your endeavors. *Ciao*, precious."

He hung up before Nan could reply. She enjoyed Teddy. She enjoyed sparring with him and looking at him. Teddy was very tall and very blond, with such long lashes, and a behind so delicious and tiny that it seemed to whisper "grab me" at everyone it passed. When he was on, he was fun to work with. He attracted people, big stars, and seemed to be one of those rare types who could cause things to happen, the way Uri Geller caused spoons to bend. But he was also very self-involved, with an ego as big as he wished his penis was, and could be insufferable. He seemed to be totally lacking in empathy or compassion, except for himself. Of the two of them, Nan felt herself to be the more talented and creative. She was an *author*. The only thing Teddy had done on his own was run over his neighbor's dog, and he got his houseboy, Bob, to take the blame for that by promising to import Bob's cousin from Japan. The cousin's name was unpronounceable to Teddy's Western tongue and hard on his ear, so he shortened it to Blum. After the animal was buried

267

(kindly paid for by Teddy on behalf of his careless house-boy), Bob had begun to neglect his household duties and stare out the window. On the rare occasions he looked at his employer, it was with baleful eyes.

"What the fuck is eating you? Or should I say who?" demanded Teddy, whose bed linen had not been changed for three weeks. Eyes lowered, more in resentment than respect, Bob muttered, "Where's Blum? You promised you would bring him over."

"Who on earth is Blum?"

"My cousin from Kyoto, for whom a dog died."

"Oh. But that was *months* ago."

"I took the blame."

"I said 'thank you,' didn't I?"

"If Blum doesn't come, I go."

"Suit yourself, dear lad, just make sure you change the sheets first."

And Bob, who in his Oriental wisdom recognized a superior being when he saw one, had not only changed the sheets but prepared a sumptuous dinner served only to aristocrats and those considering hara-kiri. It's amazing how lack of consideration and walking all over people breeds respect and subservience. Along with his cute ass, it was the only talent Teddy had that Nan envied.

"Serena," Nan called, walking into the hall.

"Si, señora?" asked Serena from the bottom of the stairs.

"Do you know where my red silk pants and blouse are? And the black belt?"

"You wanna wear thems?"

"I didn't ask just to make conversation, Serena."

"What?"

"Nothing. Do you know where they are?"

"Have you look in the closet?"

"Not yet."

"So look," said Serena, rolling her eyes to the ceiling.

Nan returned to her room and took the pants and blouse from the closet. Red for passion. She removed a pair of black sandals from one of many transparent plastic boxes stacked against the closet wall and stood them up beneath the red outfit. It struck her that Serena was getting testy. Teddy, who was the worst person in the world to work for, got nothing but respect from Bob, while she got only long-suffering looks from an ever-disgruntled Serena. Fortunately, Nan wasn't home that much. Unfortunately, neither was Serena. She had a long list of physical complaints, many of them caused, she managed to imply, by the wear and tear of her job. She spent more time in the doctor's office than she did in her chosen line of work, and the house never really looked right.

Nan was a very successful, well-known woman. People asked for her advice and her autograph. What was a person in her position doing poking through her drawers looking for a pair of pantyhose, suspecting with sinking heart that every pair she owned still lay unwashed in the hamper? Why should a woman earning over a hundred thousand dollars a year have a couch with dusty arms and a bathroom mirror with toothpaste splotches on it? Because she had a cranky housekeeper, that's why. Carl used to deal with Serena before the separation, but Nan found it difficult to give orders to a woman older than she—especially about housework, an occupation of which she was totally ignorant, in which she had no previous experience, nor wished to.

But Nan had always known what she wanted and generally managed to figure out a way to get it. Richard Brown had been the major exception in a life of very few frustrations, the strident NO in a chorus of harmonious yeses. At the funeral that morning, she had been a bit frightened by the unprofessionalism of death. Nan liked to plan ahead. She hated last-minute changes and was distressed at the sometimes amazing spontaneity of dying. She had been thinking this when the rabbi began to speak. She had been thinking that Richard Brown didn't go by the rules either, and for a gently bred, exquisitely mannered upper-class Catholic, who had been, as she, programmed from birth to conform,

269

this quirk was a glaring inconsistency. He too had fifties values so stamped on his psyche that the imprint was lousing up the seventies design in which he wished to cloak himself. On one occasion when they were lying in bed, Nan asked Richard why he had never married.

"How did you avoid it?" she asked, taking his arm and putting it around her.

"With great difficulty."

"Why are you so opposed to marriage?"

Richard removed his arm. "I'm not opposed to it, Nan. Allergic is more the word."

"Your brothers are all married. So are your sisters. I don't see any of them sneezing and popping Allerest."

Richard shrugged. "I'm an emotional hobo, Nan. I'm also Catholic, and marriage for me is a lifetime proposition. I couldn't inflict my roamantic—that's R-O-A-M-antic—tendencies on someone I loved."

"Are you able to love?"

"For a while. I don't sustain."

"Don't you want children?"

"I have fourteen nieces and nephews."

Nan put her head on Richard's shoulder. Her heart felt like lead. "But if someone drugged you and dragged you off and married you, would you honor your vows?"

Richard smiled. "Would I have a choice? It would kill my parents if I divorced."

Nan moved closer to him and put her hand on his chest. "Richard, when you were little, were you a good boy?"

"The best."

"You still are," said Nan, and kissed him.

This sharing of outdated attitudes was the important link between Richard and Nan. Basic guilt and parental introjections still echoed through their heads, and "Would Mommy be mad?" still determined their actions and instigated their rebellions. It was while the rabbi was speaking that Nan had at last hit upon the method of utilizing their shared hangups to capture Richard Brown. They were trapped by the old rules—therefore, she would use an old ploy to snare her wily and reluc-
270

tant prey. It was so very simple; perhaps that was the reason it had taken her so long.

Nan dressed and made up with infinite care. If her plan worked, she would have Richard. If it didn't, she'd have a fine mess and a part of her would die a little and she would be forced to "cast away the stones" and "pluck up that which is planted." But this was her last stand, and the risk was worth it. She would do what she had to. After the last dab of perfume was applied and the last hair in place and Nan at last was satisfied that she looked as good as she could look, she opened her jewelry box and removed an antique brooch that had belonged to her grandmother. She walked into the bathroom and lit the scented candle she kept on the marble counter of the sink. She opened the brooch and held the pin in the flame until the metal turned a blackish blue. She tested the tip with her finger and found it needle sharp. Then she opened the medicine cabinet and removed her diaphragm. With the sterilized pin, she carefully made eighteen small holes in the diaphragm—eighteen for the numerical equivalent of the Hebrew word *chai,* meaning "life." She inserted the device, washed her hands, blew out the candle, put the brooch carefully away and went downstairs to await the arrival of her future husband.

26

Joan was well aware of the fact that Audrey was dead. She had heard it from Melvin and spoken about it in a hushed, shocked voice with her friends. She had been to the cemetery and seen Audrey buried. But not until the phone didn't ring at eight-thirty on Tuesday morning did the realness of Audrey's death at last sneak through the cracks in her defenses and slice into her stomach like a bayonet. She stood staring at the telephone, willing it to ring, knowing finally that even if it did, it wouldn't be Audrey, and was suddenly gripped with a despair so chilling, so icy, that for a moment her breath caught. When she released it with an audible gasp, she was surprised not to see steamy vapor come whitely out of her mouth.

That call had been her alarm clock. It started her up, got her mind going and churned up her still sleepy reactions. By the time she had hung up, the gravel was swept from her eyes and her voice, her motor was running, the energies she would need for the day ahead had been released and tested and exercised by Audrey. Having successfully dealt with her outrageous friend, Joan knew she could cope with any challenges the day brought her.

Unless one of them was away, she had spoken to Audrey at eight-thirty almost every morning for five years. Only today, no fooling, Audrey Miller was dead and wouldn't call or receive her calls ever again. Joan had remembered the words, but now the awful music was getting to her, filling her with anguish so glacial and numbing that she turned the heat on under the kettle of water and held her hands above it in a vain effort to warm them. She stood, staring at the silent phone, until the kettle began heaving and whistling. She poured the spouting water into her cup, the dissolving coffee crystals sending the sharp, familiar aroma steaming up her nose. She shuffled to the table, slightly bent over, holding the hot cup in both hands, and lowered herself like an invalid into a chair. Her stomach hurt. The coffee flowed through her and bypassed completely the icy lump centered below her heart, that probably *was* her heart. She tried to read the paper, but found it an effort to turn the pages, so she simply sat there, looking at the blurring print and drinking until the cup was as empty and drained as she. Then for the first time in her life, Joan went back to her bedroom and got into bed, curling up in a fetal position under the covers, and tried unsuccessfully to sleep. She got up again and wandered through the day's routines, marketing, picking up and delivering the kids to and from their various activities, preparing meals. The only thing she didn't do was answer the telephone.

Once several years back, Joan had given up smoking. She had missed it hugely, the lighting up, the first pleasurable inhale, the cloud of smoke billowing from her mouth. She liked the feel of the cigarette between her fingers and on her lips. She liked the way she looked smoking it, and the feeling that smoking gave her. She loved lighting up during conversation, the rasp of the match or the click of the lighter, the pause between words as she sucked in the smoke. Apart from the craving, she found after giving up the habit that all the things she did while smoking were not fun without the cigarette—talking on the phone, drinking and

273

gabbing at a party, or just sitting down pooped and reaching for the pack. It took a long time to enjoy all those things again without the cigarette—and by that time she had gained twenty-five pounds, and began to smoke once more. It was the same now. It was no longer fun to speak on the phone if she couldn't speak with Audrey.

"Where were you all day?" Eric asked at dinner. "I called and called."

"Oh, you know," she replied. "In and out."

"I must have called when you were out then."

"I guess."

"How was your day?"

"The same."

"Are you all right?"

"I wish I had a dollar for every time you've asked me that lately."

"I wouldn't be asking if I weren't wondering."

"I know."

"Well, are you?"

"Not really."

"Audrey?"

Joan nodded, the tears filling her eyes. "Yes," she whispered. "I miss her so."

The children looked up from their plates. "You have other friends, Mom," said Jason.

"I know, Jason, but I miss Audrey."

"What was so great about Audrey?"

"She was my friend."

"But you have *other* friends."

"But they're not Audrey."

"You'll get over it."

"I know."

"So stop crying."

"Okay."

She cleared the table and sat down with Eric for a little wine before he left again for the office. "I can't answer the phone," she told him. "I just can't. It won't be her."

"That's all right. You'll get over it in time. Don't worry."

"You sound like Jason."

"I know. Death is a simple thing. I deal every day in words, and I've always found that simple words are the best for simple things. I know that for some feelings, the complicated feelings that arise from simple happenings, even clichés are better than involved reasoning. So Jason is right. The clichés are right. You *will* get over it. Time *does* heal. And please answer the phone. It might be important."

"I *can't* answer the phone. You see, I'm a simple person and I'm simply having a simple collapse. It's manifesting itself in a simple inability to answer the telephone. Would you rather I did a Nan or Dolores bit?"

"I would rather you simply cry and get over it."

"I'll try, but if you call me and I don't answer, you'll know I haven't succeeded."

"Joan, answer the telephone. I don't care about the door, but you *must* answer the phone. What if one of the kids calls from school?"

"What if?"

"It might be important."

"They won't call. I've told them not to call unless they've severed an artery."

"Let us give you a signal, at least. Two rings, hang up and call again."

"That's complicated already."

"We'll do it anyway."

"Tell them."

"I will."

"Okay." She paused. "I used to love talking on the phone."

"I remember."

"Now I hate it."

"You'll get over it."

"When?"

"Soon ... I hope. Joan, does your telephone thing extend to *making* calls?"

"Yes."

"Well, at least our phone bill will be reasonable."

"Which is more than *I* am, right?"

"To each her own, my love. If it makes you feel better not to use the telephone, don't use the telephone—unless we signal."

"How simple."

"Indeed. I love you. I wish I could help."

"I love you too—and I wish you could help."

"I have to leave. I should be home by eleven."

"Okay, honey."

"See you later. Feel better."

"I'll try."

But she couldn't seem to feel better. There were no signals and the phone remained unanswered. Eric, resigned, bought an answering machine and turned it on whenever he left the house. Joan, who now went out only to market and chauffeur her children around, would listen quietly to the messages that the machine efficiently recorded. Nan and Dolores called often, at first leaving inquiring messages, then worried ones, then angry and demanding ones, insisting that if their calls were not returned there would be dire consequences, and finally pleading ones: "Please, Joan, where are you?" "What's wrong?" "Can I help you?" She listened, feeling nothing, not even curious as to what was happening in the lives of the people she cared about so much.

The nothingness she had felt at the first shock of Audrey's death seemed to have expanded and dulled her senses, had enveloped her will and forced her to focus on the emptiness within, locking out every other sensation. She even stopped worrying about her children, and at night would fall asleep despite the fact that Eric was late coming home. She was living within herself, in the vacuum created by Audrey's absence, experiencing only a terrible, enervating sorrow. She would find herself crying at odd moments, tears that would cease quickly and leave her eyes raw and irritated as though they had been rubbed with sand. The children began giving her furtive looks and making angry demands. They ran through their entire stock of heretofore surefire irritations and annoyances,

276

taunting and fighting with each other. Things that would have normally sent Joan up a wall now left her unaffected, her eyes unseeing, her fingers twisting quietly in her lap. Naomi and the boys stopped making their beds and left their rooms even messier than ever, a feat that Joan had once thought impossible. But nothing worked. Even at the height of their obnoxiousness, Joan remained unaffected.

"Mommy," Naomi would whine, pleading for a smack, "I spilled milk on the rug in the den where you told me never to eat or drink."

"Okay," Joan would reply, and go to clean it up.

"Mom," Michael would bellow in her face, "your faggot son Jason just farted on my leg. I'm gonna kill him." And while Joan stared at this son, the other one would come bounding in, yelling, "He's a goddamn liar. He hit me and said 'fuck' on the telephone. Did you hear that? 'Fuck.' Michael said 'fuck' on the telephone . . . to a *girl!*"

To all of this Joan would merely say, "Leave me alone now. I'll take care of everything when I can. Maybe later. Now leave me alone." Eventually they did, following Eric's advice to be patient and wait it out. They reverted to their former ways. They made Herculean attempts to be the kind of children that Joan would once have swooned in pride over, the kind of children that she wistfully used to say "only *other* people have." But this behavior also went unremarked and uncomplimented. They subsided, bewildered and uncertain, anxious and clinging, touching their mother, staring into her face, sitting close to her, one hand resting on her unresisting and unmoving thigh.

After three weeks of not being able to reach Joan on the phone, Nan came over and rang her doorbell. Joan peered out at the driveway. She saw Nan's car parked there, and stood watching her friend and listening to her repeated and angry rings. "I know you're in, Joan," Nan called, "Your car is here. I'm just going to keep ringing until you let me in."

After five minutes of ringing, Nan began walking

277

around to the back, looking into the rooms through the sliding glass doors, trying to open them, finding them all locked.

"Joan?" she called. "Joan?"

But Joan had locked herself into one of the bathrooms, where she sat listening to Nan call her and feeling stupid. She wanted to let her in, but she had waited too long. She chafed at herself and the ridiculousness of being stuck in a bathroom, like a spiteful child, when she wanted to be out, talking to Nan. She had created a situation that was now too embarrassing and awkward to rectify. Finally Nan left, and Joan, sitting tensely on the edge of the bathtub, vowed never to be such an asshole again.

But a week later when Dolores dropped by, she repeated the scene exactly, sitting listlessly in the bathroom waiting and weeping at her inability to open the door and put an end to this foolishness. When Dolores gave up and left, Joan unlocked the bathroom door and paced through the house. She had succumbed to the self-indulgence of grief and found herself helpless, caught in its web. She wanted out and couldn't even lift her arms to push aside the sticky threads. She wondered if she needed a psychiatrist, and became frightened at the possibility that she did. Had one of her friends behaved the way she was behaving, Joan would have insisted on professional help.

Eric was very worried about her and the effect she was having on the children. It wasn't like Joan to be on an emotional binge this long. Her downs as well as her ups were usually short-lived. Mostly she was pretty even. He had known her reaction to Audrey's death would be monumental, but her inability to extricate herself from it, despite her obvious efforts, was frightening him. After two months of living with a zombie, he took her to Las Vegas for a weekend. She, who had always paled at the thought of flying and sat belted and pillowed, waiting for the fiery crash and crying over her orphaned children, stepped aboard the plane without a murmur. She even looked out the window during takeoff, and not once clutched in terror at his sleeve when the wheels of the plane made bumpy contact with the airstrip on landing.

The last time they had been to Vegas, Joan got into trouble in the casino of the MGM Grand Hotel. Eric had been called down to do an emergency operation on a faltering act, and Joan had been left on her own. "I won't be alone for long," she laughingly warned him. "You'll see, someone will want me."

"I don't doubt that for a moment. If there's anyone around here with good taste, they're without a doubt gonna want you. Just don't forget who you came with."

Eric went off to see his show, telling Joan he would page her later, and she went off to see "Hallelujah Hollywood," an amazingly sequined extravaganza. The line for tables was enormous, but Joan, feeling self-conscious and very important, was led past the roped-off line under the speculative glances of ordinary and patient Americans who had been waiting for hours and was immediately seated at one of the best tables and served a vodka and tonic. She felt like a star. She prayed she wouldn't knock over her drink.

The room was packed, and when a pleasant-looking man asked if he could share her table, she nodded regally. The show was gorgeous, as were the showgirls. Their faces and bodies were so perfect that Joan wondered if they were alive. She chatted with her table mate, who kept ordering drinks, and discovered that his name was Stan and that he was in the spice business.

"Are you married?" he asked her.

"Yes," she told him. "Are you?"

"I was. I'm divorced now," and as if a dam was open, his life story poured out. She watched the show and listened to Stan, who told her that he had met his wife in Ceylon while on a celery seed and cinnamon buying trip. Not once did he come on to her, not once did he seem to think that she was anything but a nice married lady whose husband was at one show while she was at another. Joan realized during a colorful animal act that

279

she would have enjoyed being taken for a Las Vegas hooker. She would have enjoyed having the opportunity to turn Stan down in righteous indignation. She would have enjoyed fending off his lustful advances. Instead, he asked her if she had any friends she could fix him up with. Irritated, she gave him Dolores' number and he told her that she was "wonderful company and a gracious lady. You remind me of my favorite cousin, Lois. She lives in Minneapolis—married to a doctor. You even look a little like her. Great person, Lois—one of God's good people. A real lady, you know? Not cheap like some of these bimbos you see around here," and he waved vaguely toward a laughing auburn-haired, spectacular "bimbo" whom Joan would have given her dishwasher to look like.

"Thank you," she said in disgust, knowing that even if she dyed her hair platinum, she'd still come off reminding someone of his favorite cousin. After the show he pulled out a pack of chips that made Joan's eyes bulge, and with no ulterior motive whatsoever, asked her if she wanted to gamble.

"Okay," she sighed. "I'm free until my husband pages me."

They walked through the crowded casino, looking for a spot at the jammed blackjack tables. Roulette wheels were humming, keno numbers flashing. Joan looked at the intent baccarat players sitting separated from the main casino at polished tables behind a barricade of velvet ropes. Everywhere were people, walking around, playing the tables, or just watching. The slot machines, Joan's favorite, were doing brisk business, the ringing of jackpot bells making heads turn and causing a momentary flurry.

Stan spotted an empty space at a nearby 21 table and they started toward it. "Hey, buddy," came a voice, and a man approached them. "How ya doin'?" he asked Stan. A short, crew-cut type with a turned-up nose, he looked appraisingly at Joan. They chatted for a bit, and then Crew Cut turned to her. "Are you from New York?" he asked.

Joan, whose New York accent was still unmistakable, looked at him. "No," she said sarcastically. "London." Stan laughed and patted her shoulder.

"Are you Jewish?" continued Crew Cut, unamused.

"Why do you ask?" she said, her Semitic genetic warning signals flashing.

"Because," he answered, "I have a joke for you."

"Not interested," she replied, and turned away.

Oblivious to her snub, he went on. "What's the difference between a Jew and a pizza?"

Joan tugged at Stan's arm. "Let's go," she said.

And as though she were paying strict attention, Crew Cut continued, "Well, I'll tell you. A pizza doesn't squeal when you put it in the oven."

Joan jerked around and stared at him, mouth agape, eyes wide open in shock. Slowly she turned to Stan. "That piece of filth is your *friend?*"

Stan shrugged his shoulders. "I hardly know him," he replied. "I just met him today on the golf course."

Joan turned back to annihilate her enemy, but he was gone. Without a word to Stan, she looked around at the crowds jammed into the casino. Slowly and deliberately she began walking from table to table, knowing that if she didn't confront the turd who had just insulted every Jew in the world, she could never live with herself again. The casino seemed to stretch on for miles. She took her glasses from her handbag and put them on. Twice she circled the entire place, and on the third time around she found him playing at a blackjack table in the center of the vast room.

"You disgusting worm," she said loudly, furiously jabbing her finger in his back. "You filthy excuse for a human being, turn around and look at me, you cowardly creep." Every head at the table turned, except his. She raised her voice and continued so loudly that even the dealer looked up. "I warn you, you miserable anti-Semitic piece of vomit, you stinking Nazi son of a bitch, you disgusting vermin that should have been aborted, you insult to decency—if you ever again make an anti-Semitic remark and I'm there when you do, I

281

swear on my children that I'll kick your obscene, unspeakably revolting face from here to eternity, but for now, you piece of shit, this will have to do," and she picked up her handbag and smashed him on the side of the head, noting in satisfaction that his ear was already reddening.

"And you," she said to the aghast blackjack players who were staring at her in shock, "should be ashamed to play at the same table with this vile abomination." And she turned and left, red-faced and breathing hard, and melted into the crowd. Immediately she became aware that she was being paged on the loudspeaker, and hurried through the milling people to the nightclub entrance where Eric was waiting.

"Where *were* you?" he demanded, annoyed. "I've been paging you for fifteen minutes."

"Avenging my people," she told him with a satisfied grin, and recounted the story.

He listened, then put his arm around her. "Can't take you anywhere," he said, smiling.

Joan was remembering that now as they entered their hotel. She remembered how she had rushed to the phone to call Audrey and tell her of the adventure. She remembered her pleasure when Audrey said, "That's the only good thing you've done since I met you, cunt. Only you should have hit him on the other side too, for me."

The next time, Joan promised her dead friend, the next time I encounter an anti-Semite, and I'm sure there *will* be a next time, I'll hit him twice, Audrey, once for you.

Audrey had loved Las Vegas and they had often planned to go there together, just the two of them, and wrap up the town. But they never had, and now they never would. All through the weekend Joan thought about Audrey. She knew that Eric had taken her there specifically to take her mind off her dead friend, but she couldn't help it. If Audrey Miller could be compared to any city in the world, it would be Las Vegas—not because she loved it best, but because they were so similar. Joan tried to relax and have a good time. She wanted to comfort Eric and assure him that she was all right. They saw two shows a night, made sweet, leisurely love, and slept late. Joan played the slots and won as much as she lost. If Eric hadn't remembered to call the children, who were with Nan's housekeeper, Joan would have forgotten all about them. But Vegas was hard. It reminded her so of Audrey, who intruded constantly.

"Even Audrey would have approved of this table," she said to Eric at the dinner show. Or, "Audrey would have loved the sauna. She could have sat in it all day, with her feet." When Joan lost twenty-two dollars in fifteen minutes at the quarter machines, she could almost hear Audrey say, "So what? I owe more than that to my milkman. Anyway, for what that dirty Eric does to you in the night, you should lose *fifty* dollars."

When it was time to leave for Los Angeles and they were boarding the plane, Eric was pleased to see Joan looking pale. "I think you're getting back to normal," he said. "You look terrified."

"As Audrey would say, 'I'm getting drippage from my low,'" Joan told him. "She was nervous about flying too. Whenever she was upset, Audrey got drippage in her low—even when she wasn't upset."

"Well, I hope the trip was a catharsis, that you got her out of your system."

"She'll never be out of my system, Eric."

"You know what I mean."

"I'm stuck with her. When she was alive I was stuck with her, and now that she's dead, I'm *still* stuck with her."

"You'll manage. Look at me. I'm stuck with *you,* and I live with it."

"Some stuck. As my friend Audrey would say, 'He should kiss your ass, that filthy animal dreck. All that rotten Eric does all day is fuck and make money.'"

"You're not the only one stuck with Audrey, puss. It seems to me I'm stuck with her too."

When they arrived home, the children were so glad

to see their parents that they kissed them even before asking "What did you bring me?"

Joan went into the bedroom to unpack. The phone rang, and she ignored it as she had been doing for over two months.

"Mommy," called Michael. "It's Nan."

"Tell her I'm busy, Michael."

"Come on, Mom," he said in annoyance. "You're supposed to be better by now. You tell her."

"Michael, *tell* her I'm busy!"

She was still unpacking when Naomi walked in, clutching the battery-powered plastic poker game they had brought her from Vegas.

"Hi, Mommy. Are you unpacking?"

"No. I'm milking a cow."

"Did you have a good time?"

"I tried to."

"Are you still sad about Audrey?"

"Yes."

"Well, I'm not."

"Okay."

"Can I play with Denise?"

"No."

"Is she still at her grandma's?"

"I don't know. I guess so."

"What's that?"

"Naomi, stop poking around in my suitcase. I can't milk the cow with you poking around."

"Why did Audrey die?"

"Because it was her time."

"Will you die?"

"Yes. Everything that lives has to die."

At Naomi's silence, Joan turned and looked at her daughter. Naomi was staring down at her poker game and twisting the handle. Her bottom lip was starting to tremble. Joan stopped unpacking and, putting a finger under her daughter's chin, lifted her face and kissed the tip of her nose.

"Don't worry, I'm not dying yet."

"How do you know?"

"Because it isn't my time."

"How do you know?"

"I just do."

"Audrey died."

"I'm not Audrey. She had a blood condition that caused her death. I don't have that condition."

"What if you die?"

"I'll save you a seat."

"In heaven?"

"Yes. Right next to me. But I'm not going to die. Not until I'm very old."

"Will I die?"

"Not until you're very old too."

"When you went to Las Vegas, Mommy, I thought you were dead."

Joan stood stock-still and looked at Naomi. Carefully she put down the pile of clothing she was holding and leaned toward her child. "My poor baby," she said, kissing her and lifting her onto her lap. "How scared you must have been."

Beginning to cry and unable to speak, Naomi nodded her head. Joan held her close and rocked her back and forth. When Eric entered the room he found them both on the bed, sitting and rocking and crying. Quietly he turned and left.

"Oh, Naomi," Joan sobbed into her daughter's hair. "I'm sorry, baby. I'm so very, very sorry."

Later that night when they were both in bed, Joan cried again, quietly, on Eric's shoulder. "I did a terrible thing to my children," she sobbed. "I made them suffer with me. It was my grief and I laid it on them. How selfish sadness makes us . . . how uncaring. I was miserable, so I had to make them miserable also. And you too," she added. "I had no right to do that. It was an unforgivable indulgence on my part."

"Stop feeling guilty. You couldn't help it. You did the best you could."

"It was as if I fell into a hole, Eric. And instead of climbing out, I just lay there and felt sorry for myself."

"You lost a friend, Joan. When that happens you

285

lose some of yourself also. It takes time to get it all back together."

"I know. I think I *am* starting to get myself together. You know how I know that?"

"How, my love?"

"I feel like calling someone on the phone. I want to know what's happened to everyone since I fell into the hole."

"Be my guest, Alice."

"It wasn't a Wonderland, Eric. Believe me."

"I know, puss."

"I have to let go of Audrey. I have to make her let go of me. I don't mean forget her ... I'll never forget her. She was a magic person, Eric. A very special person. There was no one quite like Audrey, and she made me feel that there was no one quite like me. What am I going to put into that space?"

"Why not leave it empty for now? You'll eventually find something or someone. Can I help you with any other empty spaces?" he asked, stroking her arm.

"Like what?"

"Like this," he said, showing her.

"What have you in mind?" she asked.

"Ooh," he said, kissing her gently. "I'll think of something."

27

Ever since turning down Milt's proposal, Dolores had walked through her days amazed at her daring. With Audrey gone and Joan incommunicado, she had been forced to arrive all alone at what had proved to be a decision. When Milt asked her to think about marrying him, she hadn't believed thinking was necessary, so eager was she to leap into marriage. It wasn't until the funeral that she realized that for her, marriage to Milt Gomberg would not be a beginning. It would merely be an end to her unhappy status quo. Knowing herself to be a coward, and wanting an easy way out of typing leases, she still was willing to end it all with Milt.

Watching the earth being heaped on Audrey's coffin, Dolores had realized that there was only one kind of legitimate ending—the kind that had happened to Audrey. She, Dolores, was alive. She didn't want to be buried that way. She wanted to love someone dearly, even more than she wanted to stop typing. To do that, one had to say "I quit," not "I do." She began to understand not so much what she wanted, as what she didn't want. She didn't want to settle, unless she was settling for love. She didn't want to be a person who was forever doomed to choose the lesser of two evils, she wanted to learn to accept herself as a person who deserved the best. Dolores had never really been happy and she was curious to discover what it was like. Audrey Miller had died in a minute. So could Dolores Levy, and she hadn't even lived yet.

Dolores, if she had to describe herself, would have said she was a feeling person rather than a thinking one. She had told that to Audrey once, and as usual, Audrey was Audrey. "Who do you want to be?" she had asked scornfully. "Einstein?" When she mentioned it to Joan, Joan, as usual, was Joan. "Well, kid," she had said cheerfully, "one outta two ain't bad."

Joan and Audrey, unlike her, never seemed to need any guidance. They didn't spend endless hours wondering whether to send their kids to camp or to summer school. Dolores once used up a month of her life debating between giving her girls piano lessons or guitar lessons. No wonder she was unable to think. Her head was clogged with indecision like a drain clogged with hair. Nothing could get through. Somehow Audrey's death and Joan's subsequent withdrawal had miraculously dissolved the blockage.

After the funeral she had sat across a table in a restaurant and looked at Milt Gomberg. The atmosphere of the burial was still upon her and the rabbi's words echoed in her ears: "A time to embrace, a time to refrain from embracing." She suddenly felt like a cartoon character with a light bulb over her head. From somewhere she became aware that it was not really his embrace she wanted. Not yet anyway. She knew before he spoke what his words would be.

"Dolores," he had said, reaching across the table and taking her hand. "Have you been thinking about what I said?"

"Yes."

"Is it too soon to ask if you've come to a decision?"

"No, Milton."

"Well," he said, after a short silence, "are you going to let me in on it?"

288

"Can I ask you something first?"

"Of course."

"If I needed money, would you lend it to me?"

"You know I would."

"If I wanted it to pay for a course in real estate, to be an agent, would you still lend it to me?"

"Yes. What are you getting at?"

"Wait. Would you do it even if I said I couldn't marry you now?"

"Dolores . . ."

"Would you?"

"Yes, of course."

"Thank you, Milton."

"How much do you need?"

"I don't know yet. I'll find out tomorrow."

The waitress arrived with their order and placed their plates before them. "Do you folks want some water?" she asked. Dolores laughed nervously as she nodded no and Milton nodded yes. They waited silently while the waitress filled their glasses. When she had left, Milton picked up his fork and wiped it off with the napkin. He examined it critically.

"Dolores, what do you mean by all that?"

"All what?"

"Don't be cute, Dolores."

"I'm sorry," she said softly. "What I meant was I want to learn how to be a real estate agent—so that I can support myself and my children."

"I see." He picked up a forkful of mashed potatoes and put it into his mouth. Carefully he sliced off the fat around his steak and pushed it to the side of his plate. Dolores looked down at her shrimp scampi. She took a sip of water.

"You know, I'm very surprised," Milton said, chewing his meat. "I never expected you to turn me down. I really thought you wanted to marry me. I really did."

"I *do* want to marry you, Milton—but for the right reasons, not for the wrong ones. I like you too much to do that."

"Can you kindly explain?"

Dolores leaned over her plate. No stranger to rejection, she was finding this so painful that her throat was closing.

"If I ever marry again . . . Milton, I can't get married simply because I want to get married. Not again. If I marry, it will have to be because I love someone so much that I smile every time I think of him—not because I hate my job, or because of the children, or because I'm terrified of dying alone. I want to love back the person who loves me. Oh God," she said, beginning to cry, "this is so hard for me." She picked up the napkin from her lap and with the corner wiped her eyes. She looked at Milton.

"Your scampi are getting cold," he said.

"I don't want to stop seeing you," she sobbed, "and I'm afraid to lose you."

"You won't lose me, Dolores. You're gonna be owing me money."

"You're not angry?"

"I'm a very patient man . . . and I don't want anyone to marry me for the wrong reasons either. You're some lady, Dolores."

"Thank you, Milton. Thank you," she whispered.

"Dolores, shut up already and eat."

The decision to refuse Milt Gomberg had startled her. Telling him about it had upset her. Where she found the courage and resolve to do it confounded her. She had never before been so proud of herself, and she became immersed, like a happy swimmer, in the warm waters of self-congratulation. She had finally done something right.

The next day, even before she called Joan, she registered for a course in real estate sales. Many of the agents in her office were making commissions of over fifty thousand a year, and Dolores, for the first time in many years, woke up in the morning feeling good. After several days of trying to reach Joan, she called Nan. She had always been shy with successful and achieving people. The contrast between herself and Nan made her very uncomfortable and tied her tongue. She admired strong and independent women. She would never be one—this she knew. She regretted greatly her lack of strength or luck or nerve or whatever it was that made some people succeed at everything and others only at staying afloat. She considered this lack in her makeup to be a genetic omission, and hoped that her children would be more generously endowed than she.

When Nan told her what had happened to Joan, she drove over during her lunch hour to visit. When Joan wouldn't answer the door, Dolores realized that she was more disappointed about not being able to tell her about real estate school and Milton than she was saddened by Joan's condition. Dolores ruefully admitted to herself that she was still Dolores, that nothing *really* changed, that even at this great turning point in her life the cloud above her head was still there—smaller and not as black, but with her nonetheless. She had finally been able to pull herself together a bit—how typical to have no one to tell it to. She pushed the doorbell one last time and then returned to her car. She would call Joan tomorrow and the next day and the next. Eventually Joan would answer. Two and a half months later, Joan finally did. But by then Dolores had gotten used to herself.

"Joan. It's good to talk to you. How are you?"

"Better, Dolores. How are you?"

"Also better. Can you meet me for lunch?"

"Not today. I can meet you tomorrow, though."

"I can't tomorrow. I have an appointment with my gynecologist."

"The annual peek and poke, eh? Who's your doctor?"

"Dr. Lighter." There was an awkward pause. "Isn't it funny? You and I haven't spoken for almost three months . . . and now that we finally are, there's nothing to say."

"It's like exercise, I suppose. You've got to keep it up."

"I'm going to real estate school at night."

"I know. Nan told me. I think it's wonderful."

"How does Nan know?"

"Milt told her."

"Milt?" Dolores asked in surprise. "How did he come to do that?"

Joan laughed. "Have *I* got news for *you!*" she sang.

"Wait a minute. Why did Milt call Nan?"

"To congratulate her."

"Did she write another book?"

"Nope."

"Come on, Joan. Please. What's going on? I saw Milt two days ago and he never said a word about Nan."

"That's because he didn't *know* two days ago. The invitations came yesterday."

"What invitations?"

"Guess who's getting married."

Dolores gasped. "Nan?"

"Yup."

"To whom?"

"To Richard Brown."

"That's wonderful."

"It's also necessary. She's a little knocked up."

Dolores laughed. "You've been out of circulation for almost three months and you know more than I do. When can we have lunch?"

"Friday?"

"Good. I'll call you Thursday night to discuss where. When you talk to Nan, give her a mazel tov from me."

"I will. Thanks for calling, Dolores."

For a moment Dolores felt a twinge of regret. She could have been getting married also. Those invitations might have been hers. She sighed and shrugged her shoulders. Maybe someday. She began to type quickly, engrossed in an unusual rental transaction. She went to school three nights a week and her exam was coming up soon. Dolores was forty-two years old and still trembled at the thought of a test the way she did when she was ten. But it was much better now. At ten, she also used to vomit.

"Shulman and Weiss Real Estate Brokers," she said, answering the phone.

"Hi, baby," said Milt. "Wanna go to a wedding?"

292

"More than anything."

"Okay, I'll pick you up in three weeks. In the meantime, what are you doing tonight?"

"School."

"Tomorrow?"

"Going to the gynecologist."

"Lucky guy. At night too?"

"No."

"I'll pick you up at eight sharp. Bye."

Dolores finished her typing. When her stomach rumbled, she picked up the pile of papers and tapped them against the top of her desk to align them. She glanced up at the clock. Lunch time. Her stomach was right. She reached for her handbag and took out her wallet. Her fortune consisted of thirty-eight dollars, enough for a down payment. Humming, she put on her jacket and left the office. Maybe she would be lucky and find a nice dress, green perhaps, for Nan's wedding. Milt liked her in green. He said it brought out the color of her eyes. Dolores thought about Milton liking her in green, and she smiled.

28

Joan held up the Bracelette and looked at it critically. It was padded and boned and about eighteen years old. It could have stood up alone. She had often encased herself in it in her single days, when she didn't need to—and now that she was fifteen pounds heavier and it had become a necessity, she probably couldn't get into it. The matron-of-honor dress she was wearing to Nan's wedding hung on her closet door, a long sweep of blue, low at the bosom and tight at the waist. A Bracelette dress if ever she saw one. Her shoes, dyed to match, lay in their box, ankle straps still buckled, promising to pinch after twenty minutes under the *chuppah*. Shoes nowadays, reflected Joan, were for mannequin feet unable to feel pain, for feet that never bore weight. For a small woman, Joan had huge feet. She was five foot two and wore a size-eight shoe. She had started married life with a six and a half, but with each pregnancy her feet had grown. After the boys were born she became a seven and a half, and now, since the birth of Naomi, an eight. Not that she needed excuses, but it was just one more reason for not having another baby. One more pregnancy and her shoes would be big enough to sail to Europe in . . . and her waist measurement the size of Liverpool.

Eric, who was six foot one and a half, wore a size-nine shoe. On cold mornings Joan borrowed his socks. She wondered idly if Nan's feet would grow along with her belly as hers had done. Leave it to Nannie, Joan marveled, to come up with a really creative solution to a really impossible situation. Well, she was a writer, after all. A very brave, determined, single-minded, persevering, fortunately fertile writer. And Richard was a crazy, guilty Catholic. Nan, in a spurt of genius, had realized that the only way to Richard's heart was through her stomach. Joan applauded her friend Nan and hoped the baby would be a girl.

Audrey would have loved it, because it was the sort of spectacular tactic she might have used. Except that Audrey would have lied about being pregnant. If her victim fell for it, *then* she'd remove her IUD. If he didn't, well, it would only be necessary to have hysterics, not an abortion. Nan was braver—but Joan was convinced that it was Dolores, timid, self-effacing, eternal underdog Dolores, who was the most courageous of all. She had been able to say "no" when "yes" was so tempting. No wonder she was thin.

Joan pressed the Bracelette to her body over her clothes to see whether the hooks touched in back. If there were one or two inches between hook and eye, then she would have to be Scarlett O'Hara, holding on to a bedpost while Mammy Eric broke his ass trying to hook her up and clucking sadly over what used to be an hourglass and was now a grandfather clock. More than two inches and she'd either have to hold her breath for six hours or get a larger size dress—and Joan was no more capable of doing the one than the other.

Nan was having a large formal wedding—long dress and veil and all. She and Richard were to be married by a priest and a rabbi who were obviously more liberal than devout. The priest was there to join them in matrimony for life and to satisfy Richard. The rabbi was there to soften the finality of forever and to satisfy Nan. He was also there to add this unspoken amendment: certainly for life, definitely, absolutely, without a doubt for life, unless of course something comes up and they get mad at each other.

Nan and Richard both were sticklers for doing the right thing—Richard more so. They both were very stubborn—Nan more so. Joan thought they couldn't be more wrong for each other. She also understood how that could be the basis for an enormous attraction. But she was worried. Nan was getting married because she wanted to. Richard was getting married because Nan wanted to. That was the basis for an enormous headache.

Joan had intended to give them a $250 State of Israel bond as a wedding gift. Now she wondered if a lifetime supply of Excedrin wouldn't be more appropriate.

Eric prophesied doom for the whole affair. He felt that the marriage would disintegrate after the birth of the child, and poor Richard would really be in for it then. When it was all over, he would be forced to add divorce to his already long list of mortal sins. If he managed to survive that one, Eric predicted that Hawaii would receive one more permanent resident.

Joan disagreed. "Nan will keep him in line, don't worry. Now that she's finally got him, she will allow nothing to alter the situation. Richard is in cement. He's caught between Nan and eternal damnation. Talk about choices."

"There are no choices. It all boils down to 'do you want a little spinach or a lot.'"

"Do you?"

"Want a little or a lot?"

"Yes."

"I don't want spinach at all."

"Then you mustn't pay attention to the question."

"Then I'll have to move to Mars."

"Or Montana."

"Why Montana?"

"A bomb will never fall on Montana."

Eric really wasn't concerned about weddings. He had just won an Emmy. Joan had been so delighted for him and so proud. All the winners had clutched their Emmys and glowingly thanked their wives in the acceptance speech. All but Eric. On one hand, Joan realized that she really hadn't contributed to his winning. On the other hand, she had wanted twenty million viewers to think she had.

"Boy," she said to him next day, "if Audrey were here, she'd have gotten you for that. Everybody thanked his wife but you."

"I'm sorry, puss. I just didn't think about it. Were you hurt?"

"I don't know," said Joan, and she really didn't.

"I'm sorry."

"Maybe you shouldn't be. Maybe all those guys who thanked their wives in full view of America went off after the show and fucked Miss Norway in private."

"Keep on looking at it that way."

"Do you know what gratified me most of all?"

"What? That I didn't fuck Miss Norway?"

"No. That everyone was delighted for you. That no one begrudged you the honor. That's very rare in this business. It's very rare to be a loved man."

"Maybe *you* should have thanked *me*."

"Uh-uh. Vice versa."

"I do thank you, my love. I thank you every day of my life."

Joan cried a little when he said that, because she knew it was true—and because she genuinely felt that it wasn't important whether America knew it. The only importance was that she, Joan Brenner, knew it. Audrey would have hooted, "Sure it's nice to hear something like that. But why couldn't the putz have given you a little credit? It wouldn't have killed him."

"It wasn't necessary," Joan would have answered.

"Neither is a ten-carat diamond. But it's nice."

"It's only for show—and it only becomes useful when you hock it."

"Bullshit. It's nice to look at on a rainy day when your roof leaks."

"Maybe. But it ain't gonna keep your house from flooding. I know what I mean to Eric. It doesn't matter if anyone else does. It doesn't matter what anyone else *thinks*. It doesn't matter, Audrey, what *you* think."

Joan had been having these internal dialogues for a long time. Ever since Audrey died. She couldn't stop herself. But after that one, they became less frequent. She couldn't exactly pinpoint when it happened, but she woke up one morning after that last conversation and just knew in her liver, in her intestines, that Joan Brenner was now valid on her own. She knew, with a confusing mixture of sadness and relief, that she would soon be asking Audrey to move out. Not yet, but soon. Joan hoped that Audrey would be nice about it and not put up a fuss. But one never knew about Audrey. And even if she did move, what kind of mess would she leave behind her—and what kind of empty echo?

Throwing the Bracelette on the bed, Joan ran to answer the phone.

"Are you sitting down?"

"Why, is there a hole in my pants?"

"Well, if you're not, do."

"Dolores?"

"Yes. Guess who called to ask me out."

"Paul Newman?"

"Shorter."

"Mickey Rooney?"

"No. Dr. Lighter."

"You're kidding!"

"He's separated from his wife and they're getting a divorce."

Joan lay back on her bed and put her feet on the Bracelette. She lit a cigarette gleefully and tried to control her intense curiosity.

"Tell me," she said excitedly. "Start from the beginning and tell me the whole story. What happened? Where's Carol? Why are they in splitsburg? Hurry!"

"I don't know," Dolores wailed. "I thought *you* would have heard something. I don't know Carol Lighter. You remember I had an appointment? Well, we talked and he asked me how I was doing—you know, the usual—

and then just now he called me up. I was," she said more softly, "a little embarrassed. After all I *am* his patient and he's a gynecologist, you know what I mean."

"Boy, Dolores, you must have sensational parts. Your place must look like heaven."

"Stop it," Dolores giggled.

"So what did he say? Come *on*."

"Nothing. He just told me he's filed for divorce and would I like to go out with him."

"Jesus. Look, I have to find out about this. I'm gonna call Sharon Silver. I'll call you back. Why didn't you ask him, dummy?"

"How could I ask him?"

"Okay, good-bye. I'll call you back—no, I'll see you at the wedding."

Almost ripping pages in her haste, Joan looked up Sharon's number and dialed it impatiently. She waited for Sharon to answer, sitting tensely on the bed and turning the padded cups of her Bracelette inside out, outside in.

"Hello, Sharon?" said Joan, tossing the garment aside and leaning back again. "This is Joan Brenner."

"Joan," said Sharon heartily. "How *are* you?"

"Fine. You too?"

"Uh-huh. What's new?"

"That's what I'm calling you about. What the hell is going on with the Lighters?"

"Oh, they're getting divorced."

"I *know* that. What happened? Come on, Sharon, *every*thing."

Sharon laughed. "Okay," she said. "When did your friend die? The end of May? Or June something?"

"June fourth. Saturday."

"Okay. Well, that sort of threw Carol. She wanted to do something with her life before it was too late— you know what I mean?"

"Yeah, go on."

"So that Monday, I guess on June sixth, she took off for Hawaii with Phillip Ashe and stayed there for two weeks."

"Jeez. She wanted to do something with her life, so she had a little affair. That's Carol all right. So?"

"So when she got home, Herb threw her out. I don't mean literally—he hit the ceiling and took an apartment on North Palm."

"Yeah, go on."

"Go on where? That's it. He filed for divorce."

"And Carol?"

"Well, Carol didn't even tell me about Phillip. I didn't know she'd gone until she sent me a postcard with a picture of the Kahala Hilton on it."

"Yeah, so what happened?"

"So . . . that's what happened. She thought she could get away with it and sweet-talk Herb into not minding, but she was wrong. As soon as she unpacked her bags, he grabbed them, threw his clothes in and left."

"Wow!" Joan paused to light a cigarette and found she was smiling. "I guess he's not the schmuck Carol thought he was."

"I guess not, and he's being very tough about the settlement."

"Good."

"Why good?"

"Look, Sharon, I know Carol's a good friend of yours, but the way I feel about her is no secret. My sympathies are all with Herb. As far as I'm concerned, she got exactly what she deserved."

"She got more than that. He's really rubbing her face in it. Do you know who he's dating?"

"I know he called my friend Dolores Levy."

"Do I know her?"

"How do *I* know? Who were *you* talking about? Who's he dating?"

"Blanca."

"Who the hell is Blanca?"

"Blanca is Blanca Flores. She used to be their maid."

"Herb Lighter is dating a *maid?*"

"Yup. And Carol is fit to be tied."

"I don't blame her. She's out a maid."

"That's only *part* of the reason. How would you feel

if your husband dumped you and started dating a Spanish maid?"

"As opposed to a French maid."

"As opposed to any maid."

"I suppose I would feel better if he left me for Sophia
Loren."

"Of course! This is like a smack in the face for Carol."

"How perfect. I love it, I just *love* it. I must tell
Audrey."

"What?"

"Nothing. So where is Carol now?"

"She's still in the house, but it's up for sale. *And*—
he's suing for custody of the kids."

Joan smiled with such satisfaction that she was almost ashamed. Who said there was no justice? When
she hung up the phone, her biggest regret was that she
couldn't call Audrey and tell her. Audrey would have
gotten such a kick out of it. Joan found it very difficult
to identify with a person like Carol Lighter. She knew
Carol was in pain, but it was a different sort of pain
from that which she, or most of her friends, would feel.
Early in their acquaintance, Carol had once informed
Joan that if she had to die, more than anything else
she wanted to die thin. For Joan, to whom even *living*
thin was not a top priority in her scale of values, Carol's
statement was inconceivable. And now, true to form,
Carol considered having an affair as doing something
meaningful and important with one's life. Even if Joan
had liked Carol Lighter, she couldn't have given her
the respect that she felt a friend of hers should receive.
Joan didn't really think she was vain, but she had ego
enough to believe that a person who didn't deserve to
be respected didn't deserve to be a friend of Joan Brenner's.

"Oh, Audrey, you stupid cunt," Joan said loudly to
the empty room. "Why didn't you have the sense to live
long enough to clap your hands over this business with
Carol? But wait a minute ... maybe *you* did this, bitch.
On the day you were buried, cunty Carol took off to
Hawaii with some character named Phillip Ashe. Were

301

you maybe offended that she didn't wait a day?"

Of course Joan knew that it wasn't Audrey. Audrey was dead and couldn't affect events anymore. But even now, more than four months after her death, Audrey was still affecting Joan. Would she *never* get rid of Audrey Miller? Loud and clear, Audrey's laugh echoed in Joan's ears. "Never, cunt. Not ever," laughed Audrey Miller, clapping her hands.

"Good," whispered Joan, "because you're welcome at any time. But just remember it's *my* space you're living in, rotten. Mine. And there will always be room for you—but not much. Someday, when I'm a big girl, I intend to move in myself."

That evening, before she and Eric left for the wedding, Joan phoned Scott Miller for the first time since Audrey's death. She apologized for not calling sooner and explained how emotionally incapable she had been of making the contact. He said he understood, and for the same reason had not called her. The children were adjusting as well as could be expected, he told her, and his sister from Portland, a widow with grown children, was living with them and caring for Mendy and Denise.

"I hope I'm not presuming, Melvin, but I was thinking about Audrey for a change, and I'd like to ask you a favor, for her and for me. Do you mind?"

"Of course not."

"Thank you, Melvin." She paused for a moment, collecting herself, because she suddenly felt teary. "Melvin, when you order a headstone for Audrey, please, please don't put the typical crap on it. Make it a nice one, maybe black marble or something, not too big, and no date of birth or death. Instead, smack in the middle you put a star, not a Jewish star, but one like the stars on Hollywood Boulevard, and right in the middle of the star you put her name—Audrey Miller—and nothing else. That's it. Am I very nervy to be saying this to you?"

For several moments Melvin did not speak, and Joan became very edgy. "Melvin?" she asked timidly. "Are you still there?"

302

"Yes," he said. "I'm still here. I think it's a wonderful idea and yes, you are nervy and you always were. Audrey would love that, a star like on Hollywood Boulevard. I'll have an identical one made. Thank you, Joan."

"Thank *you*, Melvin, and send my love to your kids."

"Send mine to your family."

"Melvin, will you keep in touch? Maybe?"

"Yes. Oh my God, yes."

"Bye Melvin. Thanks again."

She sat quietly trying not to cry and ruin her makeup. The Bracelette kept her almost rigidly erect, and even her mother would have approved of her posture.

"Why are you sitting there like that?" asked Eric. "The kids are already in the car."

After the wedding, which was really beautiful and had transported Joan back twenty years, she sat in bed waiting for Eric to get out of the bathroom and for the vivid red imprint of the Bracelette to fade from her body and stop itching. At last Eric emerged, his back still lightly beaded with drops of water. She told him of her conversation with Melvin, and he nodded his approval.

"But something else happened to me tonight. Something a little wonderful."

"The best is yet to come, puss," he said, sliding into bed and turning to face her. "But tell me first."

"No, never mind. I'll tell you second. I don't want to be pushy."

"You looked beautiful tonight. That dress was perfect for you."

She smiled delightedly. "Thank you. But I paid a pretty price for looking pretty-pretty." She lifted her nightgown and showed him her Bracelette marks.

"Why don't you throw that damn thing away? It's a torture device. Look at you."

They both looked up as Jason walked into the room. His face was screwed up and ashen. He appeared terrified. "Ma," he yelled, panicked. "I have to vomit."

"So why are you standing there?" Joan cried. "Get

303

into the bathroom."

He flew back to his bathroom and they heard the toilet lid slam up and Jason begin to retch.

Joan got out of bed and into her bathrobe. "It sounds like too much wedding," she said wearily. "Can I take a raincheck—or a vomit check?"

"Make your mind up, baby. I'm a busy man."

"You're gonna be busier if he missed the toilet. I don't deal in puky floors."

"Oh? And I do? Have you forgotten I'm an Emmy winner?"

"No. I've only forgotten the little bit of wonderful that happened to me tonight. All I seem to remember is that I'm a mother and my feet hurt and my body is welty and my son is barfing and my Emmy winner is gonna turn over and go to sleep as soon as I leave this room."

"You have an amazing memory."

"You're gonna get an amazing poke in the eye in a minute."

"Ma," Jason wailed from the bathroom.

"Mom," croaked Michael, "tell him to shut up. I can't sleep."

"Where the hell are my slippers?" Joan said crossly, getting down on her hands and knees and peering under the bed. "No way am I going to walk into that bathroom with bare feet."

She found her slippers and hurried to her son. Eric heard her cautiously open the bathroom door.

"Feeling better?" she asked.

"A little," said Jason weakly.

"Good boy. You didn't get anything on the floor."

Her tired, pale-faced child looked up at her and smiled wanly. He had flecks of vomit in the corners of his mouth. His eyes were glazed. From his bed, Eric heard the toilet flush. "Should I brush my teeth?" asked Jason.

"I would if I were you, and also wash your mouth."

"Will you stay with me?"

"I can't think of anything I'd rather do."

"I'll never eat six pieces of cake again."

"A wonderful decision."

Eric smiled and burrowed into his pillow. "That woman thinks everything is wonderful," he thought to himself, and he closed his eyes. Just before he drifted off, he felt Joan slide into bed. A faint whiff of vomit gently eased up his nose.

"Audrey wouldn't have gotten up if Mendy tossed his wedding cake," she muttered. "She would have made Melvin do it. But of course, Melvin isn't an Emmy winner."

"Melvin's good in vomit, or else he's a schmuck," mumbled Eric, half-asleep.

"Oh? And what are you?"

"Me? I'm wonderful," and in a moment he was sound asleep.

Joan lifted her head and looked over at her husband. His mouth was slightly open and he was snoring faintly. For a moment she stared into his mouth and at the tiny white slit of eyeball gleaming between his lashes. She smiled at him, and the words from a suddenly remembered song ran through her mind. "Somebody wonderful married me," she sang in her head. "So in that case you must be pretty wonderful yourself, cunt," a voice sang back. For a moment Joan thought it was Audrey's voice. But it wasn't. It was her own. Joan stretched and then pulled her legs up. She turned over and fitted her cold body to her husband's warm one. She placed her big icy feet against the heating pad of his back and felt him stir. She was very happy for Nan. A husband, even an Emmy-winning one, is a very good thing to have. Wonderful, in fact.

29

Nan Brown's baby, a little girl, was born at the end of March. Nan named her Alexis. Richard had wanted to call her Victoria, and Joan thought that Georgia would have been the sweetest choice of all. She threw an After Baby Is Born shower for Nan at the Beverly Hilton and invited the more than seventy-five women on Nan's list. Fifty-seven showed up for the luncheon and every one of the seventy-five brought or sent gifts.

Nan was very happy. Having a daughter had always been a favorite dream of hers. She put the infant on a diet immediately after birth and soon became the only mother in the world who was happy when her baby didn't gain. Richard had insisted on baptizing the child, especially when it dawned on him that Nan didn't intend to feed her much. He put Alexis in the hands of Serena, who adored her, and it was just as well because Nan was immediately back at work.

After the luncheon was over, Nan opened all the gifts, a process that took an hour and a half. Most of the gifts were pink and calculated to either keep Alexis warm and cute, or get her through college by seven. One woman gave the baby *The Joy of Sex,* and on the inside cover wrote "No one is ever too young or too old to read. Much love, Rachel Rabinowitz." Joan gave Alexis two shares of stock in the McDonald's Corporation, and immediately was sorry that she hadn't given her stock in Weight Watchers instead. Over brandy and dessert, Joan and Sharon Silver chatted about poor Carol Lighter, who had been forced to move to a mere six-room apartment south of Wilshire. Her ex-husband was much sought after by all the unattached women in town. He dated them all, including, still, Blanca Flores. Carol, Sharon told Joan, was in a very bad way. Her hair was still perfect, but she was gaining weight and getting lines around her eyes.

"Hello there," said a voice. "It *is* Sharon Silver, isn't it?"

Joan looked up. Once at a party a few years back, Joan had been speaking with Nan and a woman had insinuated herself between them and turned her back on Joan. This was she and, repeating history, she gave Joan a perfect view of her back by pulling a chair over and placing it between Joan's and Sharon's. But Audrey was no longer around to kick ass for Joan, and Joan was not about to "take no shit from nobody."

"Excuse me," she said, tapping the woman on the shoulder, "but did you by any chance happen to major in rudeness in college?"

The woman turned her head and looked over her shoulder at Joan. "Did you say something?" she asked, lifting her eyebrows.

"I'm glad your hearing is still good. Yes, I said something. Now kindly get your chair out from between me and my friend. In case your eyesight is poorer than your hearing, let me explain that Sharon and I were in the midst of a conversation before you pushed your way between us."

The woman quickly stood up and moved her chair.

"Well, *pardon me*," she said, and sitting down again next to Sharon, whispered loudly, "Who's your smart-ass friend?"

"Oh, I'm sorry," said Sharon. "Joan Brenner, meet Rachel Rabinowitz." The two women nodded at each other.

"How is Artie?" Rachel asked Sharon. "I haven't seen him in a good six months." For Artie, a good six months, Joan thought. She lit a cigarette. "Oh," said Rachel, "would you mind lending me a cigarette? I ran out."

Joan offered her pack. "Consider this a gift, not a loan," she said, deciding to smile.

Rachel looked at her over her lighter. "Have we met before? You look familiar. Are you ever over at Universal?" Joan shook her head. "Maybe at a party, then. Your name is Joan Brenner? What do you do?"

"I work at home," said Joan.

"Oh, are you a writer?"

"No. I'm a housewife." And Joan smiled broadly, because somehow saying "I'm a housewife" hadn't bothered her a bit.

"Don't you do anything else?" asked Rachel.

"Yes."

Rachel Rabinowitz smiled. "I thought so," she said. "What else do you do?"

"I drive the Hebrew school car pool on Tuesdays," Joan answered, and almost laughed out loud at the look on Rachel's face.

"Oh," said Rachel, after a pause. "How nice."

"Yes, I think so," Joan said, and for the first time she really did. She *really* did.

"And what do you do?" Joan asked.

"I'm in projects development out at Universal."

"Oh," said Joan. "Don't you do anything else?"

"Anything else?" Rachel asked in surprise.

"Yes. Is developing projects all you do?"

"Well ... yes," said Rachel Rabinowitz. "I'm married," she added lamely.

"Oh," said Joan. "How nice."

When the party was over, Joan and Nan and three busboys loaded the gifts into the back of Joan's station wagon. On the way to Nan's they chatted about the party. "Are you very friendly with Rachel Rabinowitz?" Joan asked.

"Not very. I see her occasionally when I'm out at Universal. Why?"

"No reason."

"Thank you, Joan. I loved my shower."

"My pleasure." They drove for a while in silence. Every time Joan turned a corner or stopped for a light, the boxes of gifts slid around the back of the car, thudding on the sides. Joan felt good. She took her eyes off the road for a moment to look at Nan.

"Nan, do you think there's any value in taking a writing course? Can a person *learn* to write? Isn't good writing more in the talent category?"

"Some of those courses are very valuable. Of course, the ability to write isn't in everyone, but anybody halfway intelligent can learn the craft. And writing is forty percent craft. Another forty percent is just sitting down and doing it. Only twenty percent is talent. If you catch on to the craft and apply the discipline, you're eighty percent a writer. And that's better than *ninety* percent of the writers in this town."

"*You* never took a course."

"No, but I was lucky enough to be able to learn on the job. Not everybody can get that kind of a break. Why? Are you enrolling for a writing course?"

"I was thinking about it."

"Then do it. You'd probably be terrific."

"I just might. Eric's always wanted me to write . . . and Audrey."

"Do *you* want to?"

"I think I'm a little bit ready for something, Nannie. Naomi is eight years old. I don't want to leave the house just yet . . . and writing is something you can do at home."

"It's a good idea."

"Yeah, I'll think about it."

"Stop thinking. Start doing."

"You'll help me?"

"I'll even be your agent." Nan smiled at her. "And you just passed my house," she said.

"I called UCLA," Joan told Eric when he came home.

"Called it what?"

"Very funny. They're sending me a brochure."

"Are college girls still wearing those?"

Joan looked pained. "Eric, I'm trying to tell you something, putzo. I'm going to take a writing course, but I don't know yet which one. Maybe play-writing."

"Good for you."

"No, good for *you*. When I become rich and famous, you'll be able to lie out on the patio like a gigolo."

Joan walked out onto the patio and looked up at the sky. There were no clouds, the sky was clear and the stars seemed to dart about imitating fireflies. Like a little girl, Joan wanted to make a wish. She had always been obsessed with wishes and as a child had spent considerable amounts of time figuring out one wish which would automatically assure the granting of all the others. Pauline Benani, whose every third sentence began with "I wish," once told Joan that if you are kind to beggars, then wishes come true. In that case, Joan had replied, all of us here in Beverly Hills are doomed to eternal frustration. The only begging that goes on around here is for the use of someone's tennis court. Pauline said she wished she had a tennis court and made sure to say it again in front of her husband, Maurice. Ground was broken behind the Benani mansion by the end of the month. No wonder there were no beggars in Beverly Hills. Pauline Benani obviously had been kind to them all.

Joan still fantasized about wishes miraculously coming true. She would imagine saving a child from some grave danger and later discovering that the child was the son of the richest man in the world. In deepest gratitude, the father would then ask Joan to name her heart's desire. Nothing material would be refused. That one was even a better wish than the being-locked-in-the-jewelry-department-of-Tiffany's wish. Even "choice" wishes were better than none. Would you rather be thin or be rich? Select one and you get it. Would you rather be smart or be lucky? The only trouble with choice wishes was that they were all so uncompromising. It was always one way or the other—always yes or no, always black or white. Not a loophole in the bunch.

Joan was absolutely sure that when her fairy godmother paid her a call, it would be with a choice wish up her wand. "What choices would give you the greatest difficulty, wishwise?" Joan had asked Nan once. Nan thought for a while. "Maybe," she said, "to have to choose between success and love, where a person could only have one or the other. What about you?" Joan closed her eyes. "I think," she said, pursing her lips, "that a real toughie for me would be a choice between multiple orgasm and linguini with clam sauce."

Audrey, of course, never needed to wish. Her blue fairy could read minds and loved to be ordered around. Joan remembered when Dolores was so diminished and her ego so starved that it took her a long time even to think of a wish, and when she finally did, she wished for a dinner date. Carol had wished her and Audrey dead. You can tell a lot about people by their wishes.

Now Joan stared up at the sky and picked out a fidgety star. She began to run down her roster of wishes. Long life and good health for her loved ones and herself, of course. That was number one. Someone, preferably one of her sons, to discover the cure for cancer was a nice one also. She quickly ran through the philanthropic wishes, the ones that proved she was a good person with compassion for her fellow man. Then she started on the personal ones. Joan always differentiated between prayers and wishes. With prayers a person had to be more selective, more cautious and, of

311

course, very polite. One was, after all, dealing with an awesome spirit, an unknown quantity. With a totally unimaginable deity who, if assigned human characteristics, might be described as impetuous, short-tempered and whimsical, it was the wise man who didn't ask for favors. For favors it was less risky to deal with stars.

She was startled by a rustling in the shrubbery and saw a small animal dash out from the bushes and dart back in again, so swiftly that she couldn't identify it. Strange night noises, creakings, hums, stirrings of all kinds of creatures that can only blink in the sunshine, surrounded her. She stared meaningfully at her star and threw a quick glance at the busy moon who, like a typical housewife, kept waxing and watching. But Joan found herself out of wishes. Wishless.

It dawned on her slowly that there really wasn't anything she wanted. She already had what she wanted. She felt calm and very peaceful. She supposed the word for it was *tranquil,* a feeling she had never experienced before. Nothing seemed to be nagging at her and she had no guilty secrets. She perceived that what she felt was "happy" and tried to trace it back, curious to discover who or what had uncapped the bottle and freed the genie. She stopped at, of all people, Rachel Rabinowitz. Joan hardly knew the woman, and what she did know she wasn't crazy about. But it was to Rachel Rabinowitz that she had told the truth and recognized it as such. Joan stood very still, her breathing so light that it wouldn't have stirred a feather. Something had happened. Something within her had loosened or tightened or come together or come undone. Whatever it was, something had altered, shifted a degree. The process had been sneaky and the alarms had been silent.

When Joan lived back East she had always been surprised when it snowed, but it wasn't the snow that surprised her. What surprised her was that it was already winter. During her first pregnancy she would

312

look down at her belly and wonder, not that it was so large and hard, but rather when it had suddenly become that way. And now this something had happened. Was it Audrey's death that triggered the change? Would it have happened anyway? Joan had never been tested by life. She had had no great tragedies. Except, perhaps, Audrey, and Audrey, after all, wasn't her mother or her sister or her child. She had never believed, though, that one learned much from dealing with despair. You don't have to drive a spike through your foot to understand pain. It does, however, point up the fact that feet can bleed, even big feet.

But tonight, finding herself not wishing for a thing in the world, she felt enormously relaxed, as though a tensely held breath had at last been released. Wishes were for people who couldn't remember their dreams, or perhaps for those who dream too little or too much. Joan liked wishing, but now, unlike before, she understood that there was a good chance her wishes would be granted. It was always that way, wasn't it? When you didn't care terribly about the job, you always get it. It's always the guy you want for a brother who asks you to the drive-in. Maybe, when one's wishes are not the mashed potatoes but only the gravy, they always come true. Who knows? Joan shrugged her shoulders. She looked at her star. "Get you next time," she said.

She turned around and, sliding open the screen door, stepped into the bedroom.

"Eric," she said quietly, "something happened."

"It's in the bookcase," he said.

"Something happened to me."

"What was it?"

"Wonderfulness." Eric looked questioningly at her. "Today at Nan's shower, I told some woman that worked at Universal that I'm a housewife. And when I said that, I didn't feel ashamed and my stomach didn't start dancing and I didn't have one ounce of guilt or unworthiness. Not one. It isn't that I never want an outside career. Not that at all—and I'm going to take

313

those courses, and if something comes of it, that'll be nice, and if nothing comes of it, it's still nice, because I am what I am whatever I am. You know what it is, Eric?" she asked, smiling. "I'm suddenly happy enough with myself. If I were a yoga person I'd probably think I'd found self-realization, and," she went on more rapidly, her eyes intent, "if I'm happy, if I'm at peace with myself, then I'm also so far ahead of the game that it doesn't matter what titles I go under. There's not one cunt at Universal who can touch me. I've become more than almost happy. I've become . . . happy enough. And I know it everywhere, not just in my head."

Joan paused and thought for a minute. "If Audrey were alive, she would have said, 'Happy? What's that? Enough? It's never enough.'" Joan paused. "I don't cry anymore when I think of Audrey . . . I smile now." And she smiled at Eric.

"I think you've finally accepted Audrey's death," he said, "and in the process, you've accepted yourself. You've filled in your own space."

She nodded. "I call that sort of nice, don't you?" she asked.

"No," said Eric. "I call that coming of age."

30

The unveiling of Audrey's headstone was scheduled for Sunday, June 4, exactly a year to the day since her death. Dolores and Milt were going away that weekend, and Nan, who had little enough free time as it was, planned to spend Sunday with Richard and the baby at home. Eric couldn't attend either, he had a taping to do. Joan was free on Sunday, June 4, but decided not to go. She simply didn't want to. It would be awkward seeing Melvin and the children, and she decided that rather than stand among the people and reawaken memories and feelings that she had so painfully tucked in and kissed good-night months ago, she and Eric would drive up on Saturday evening instead, to see the stone and visit the grave. Now she was standing where she had stood a year ago. Eric, waiting below, sat on one of the stone benches under the trees that lined Broadway. A short growth of grass, like stubble, had spread over the grave, making a neat green rectangle to match the others around it. Here and there were mounds of bare earth marking the resting places of the recently interred, soon no doubt, thanks to the climate and purveyors of perpetual care, to grow as green as Audrey's.

At the head of Audrey's grave stood the soon-to-be-revealed stone, covered now by a piece of cloth. Leaning over, Joan lifted a corner of the cloth and gazed at the marker. It was perfect. Exactly the way she had described it to Melvin. She let the cloth fall and looked up toward the sky, opening her eyes very wide so that the tears beginning to form wouldn't spill down her face. After a bit, she lowered her eyes once again and scanned the green surface of her friend's small patch of earth. If there had been twigs or leaves or dead flowers or cigarette butts—or even foil-wrapped turkey sandwiches scattered and resting among the blades of this grass that covered Audrey—there was left not a trace, all having been properly cleared away in preparation for the next day's unveiling.

Joan's eyes filled again, new tears growing like new grass and slipping down her cheeks. Her body began to shake and she bowed her head over her handbag, opened it with trembling fingers and removed one of Eric's handkerchiefs, specially brought for the occaion. She stood clutching the white square in her hands, and almost as an afterthought brought it up to her wet and contorted face. The sky was growing darker and the light was rapidly fading. The air was heavy and still as a lover's breath—tense, suspended, waiting for night. Already Joan could see the California fog beginning to drift in and she shivered, holding herself close and running one hand up and down the other arm.

Again she opened her bag, and took out the sandwich for Audrey. She squatted down and placed it exactly in the center of the green rectangle. Patting the grass gently and whispering so that the neighbors wouldn't overhear, Joan spoke to her friend. "Audrey," she said softly, "I brought you a corned beef this time." And as though Audrey were watching, she pointed to the sandwich. "Enjoy," she said. She straightened up slowly, wobbling a bit, and looked on the ground around her. Spotting a clean, small, almost round rock, she picked it up and held it tightly with both hands. Tilting her head, she wiped her eyes and cheek with her lifted shoulder, and then walked to the head of the grave, placing the rock on top of the tombstone.

"Audrey," she said, resting her hand on the new stone marker, "I might not be here again for a long time, or maybe even never... So, cunt, when you eat that sandwich, eat it slow."

Joan raised her hand in a farewell salute. Then she turned and ran awkwardly down the hill to where Eric was waiting. He stood up and put his arm around her. She looked back once more, and then, hand in his hand, walked quickly down Broadway to their car.

About the author:

Rhea Kohan lives in Beverly Hills with her husband and three children. Asked what positions she has held, she answers, "Wife, mother—presently and terminally employed." Within what she describes as her "Hawaiian modern house," she also writes television scripts and is at work on her second novel.